The Lucifer Network

ALSO BY GEOFFREY ARCHER

Sky Dancer
Shadow Hunter
Eagle Trap
Scorpion Trail
Java Spider
Fire Hawk

THE LUCIFER NETWORK

Geoffrey Archer

C

CENTURY · LONDON

Published by Century in 2001

1 3 5 7 9 10 8 6 4 2

First published in the United Kingdom in 2001 by Century
The Random House Group Limited
20 Vauxhall Bridge Road, London, SW1V 2SA

Random House Australia (Pty) Limited
20 Alfred Street, Milsons Point, Sydney,
New South Wales 2061, Australia

Random House New Zealand Limited
18 Poland Road, Glenfield
Auckland 10, New Zealand

Random House (Pty) Limited
Endulini, 5a Jubilee Road, Parktown 2193, South Africa

The Random House Group Limited Reg. No. 954009

www.randomhouse.co.uk

A CIP catalogue record for this book
is available from the British Library

Papers used by Random House are natural, recyclable products made from
wood grown in sustainable forests. The manufacturing processes conform to
the environmental regulations of the country of origin

ISBN 0 7126 84689 (hb)
ISBN 0 7126 69604 (tpb)

Typeset by Palimpsest Book Production Limited,
Polmont, Stirlingshire
Printed and bound in the UK by
Mackays of Chatham PLC, Chatham, Kent

This book is dedicated to the RN Submarine Service whose pivotal role in great dramas cannot always be revealed. The Service celebrates its centenary in 2001.

Acknowledgements

W HILE PREPARING THE factual backdrop against which this work of fiction is set, I was indebted to many people who were generous with their time in setting me straight. There isn't space to list them all and some of them spoke to me in confidence, but I would like to thank Glyn Ford MEP, *Searchlight* magazine and the EU Monitoring Centre on Racism and Xenophobia in Vienna for their insights into the extreme right wing in Europe. Officers from Scotland Yard's Racial and Violent Crimes Task Force were also most helpful.

Dr Wolfgang Preiser of the Department of Virology at Middlesex Hospital spent many patient hours explaining to me how viruses spread – any errors in this book are very much mine and not his.

The Royal Navy Submarine Service was also extremely generous with its time. I am particularly grateful to Commander Jeff Tall, Curator of the RN Submarine Museum at Gosport and to Lt.-Commander Mike Walliker, First Lieutenant of HMS *Turbulent*, whose captain and crew looked after me so warmly and so informatively when I was their guest on a submerged passage to the Mediterranean.

Finally I should acknowledge the colourful insight into the murky world of arms smuggling in Africa which was given to me by someone who will remain nameless. Subsequent to our conversations, he was tried for the murder of his girlfriend and sentenced to life imprisonment.

Zambia
Tuesday, 25 August 1998

T HE ENGLISHMAN SWITCHED off the engine of the hired car. The
emptiness of the parking area in front of the game lodge was broken
by a handful of four-wheel-drives. Beyond and above the lattice of trees
ringing this small country club a few miles outside Kitwe, the African
sky was purple with the start of a still night. Cicadas tickled themselves
in the trees. Under the bonnet of his rented Toyota something clinked as
it cooled.

The last time he'd been in Africa the job had been dirty and it was
dirty again. The same muck as before. 'Clearing up' London had called
it. 'You were in at the start, old son. Only proper you should be there at
the end.'

By rights it was a job for an in-house man, someone under diplomatic
cover, but they'd sent him because he was deniable. And because the matter
was personal – if the man he'd come to see were to talk and was believed,
it would be *his* head on the block as much as the Service's, *his* career
at an end.

The car window was open, the night air still warm but with a freshness
not there during the day. Sam Packer wanted a drink. Something large
and volatile. But he knew to restrain himself this evening. At the table
Jackman would order the house red, because that's what he always drank
here. Brain glue, he called the stuff that came in a deceptively plain bottle
from the Cape. A year ago Sam's headache had been memorable. This time
he would limit himself to a single glass. There was a deal to be struck. A man
to be got the better of. A man who was unprincipled and full of guile.

In his late thirties, Sam Packer had a strong, square face with a chiselled
chin whose determination was concealed by a close-trimmed beard. He
disliked facial hair but had grown it two years ago out of a need to
change his appearance. He had thick, dark hair and eyes that seemed

distant, yet recorded all they saw. He was a man women tended to take an interest in.

He watched a Range Rover pull up and four men get out. White men with the look of engineers − here for the copper mines, he guessed. With wives who tinkered with oil paints and did voluntary work at the local school. The group made its way in to the restaurant, bantering gently.

He knew that decades ago whites fell in love with this sultry continent, never wanting to leave it, but his own experience had been recent and the parts of it he'd seen had smelled of death. It was a place where he didn't want to be, particularly for a mission like this.

Headlamps swept round the car park, as a vehicle turned in from the Kitwe road. Packer slumped in the seat. Was this Jackman already, doing the same as him, coming twenty minutes early to check the place out? He felt crazily jumpy tonight. Too much was hanging on the outcome of this meeting. The halogen beams bounced round the potholed parking area and died close to him. He raised his eye-line above the door sill, enough to see out. It wasn't Jackman climbing out of the vehicle parked a few feet from his, but a young and beautiful Zambian couple. As they walked with the grace of gazelles towards the lodge, they entwined fondly. He felt a twinge of envy. He pushed open the car door and stood up.

Tall and straight-backed, he wore freshly pressed tan slacks and a blue cotton shirt. He stretched to shake out the stiffness from his shoulders − there'd been little sleep on last night's flight from London. The air smelled of some alien vegetation. Dust dry. It'd be December before the rains came, according to the hotel porter who'd carried his bags earlier that day. As he closed the car door and locked it, he listened to the rhythm of the tree crickets.

Pools of darkness surrounded the car park. He peered into them one by one, looking for shadows that moved. A year ago Jackman had told him the price for a contract killing in Zambia was fifty pounds. Sam touched the pocket of his trousers to check the wallet was there, then crunched over the gravel to the lodge, running a finger under the sweaty collar of his shirt to free it from his neck. Lights set high in the dark-leafed trees at one side of the building illuminated well-watered lawns and a few hardwood easy chairs and tables. But it was the mosquito hour and the guests were indoors. Instinctively Sam smacked a hand against a cheek, imagining some winged malaria-carrier braving the repellent he'd daubed on earlier.

The lodge was reed-thatched, as were the two small accommodation chalets that stood slightly apart from it. A private venture, Jackman had told him, a more restful haven than the hotels in town for visiting relatives of European mining specialists. And the restaurant served good steaks in reasonable privacy. The lodge was of timber, darkly varnished. On its walls, paintings of elephants, baboons and exotic birds glowed under their picture lights.

'I'm meeting Harry Jackman here,' Sam announced to the shirt-sleeved European who greeted him inside.

'May I ask your name sir?'

'Foster. Simon Foster.'

Today's name. And last year's. The one Jackman had known him by when they'd done the deal that was now causing the firm such pain. Twelve months had passed, almost to the day, a year that had proved, if proof were ever needed, that even the best of intentions could go sour.

'When he comes I'll tell him you're in the bar, sir.'

'Thank you.'

The restaurant was small, not more than a dozen tables, several set against wide windows overlooking a small lake. Beyond it, the western horizon glimmered deep violet, its colours mirrored in the water. The four men he'd seen emerging from the Range Rover were already seated, studying menus and gulping beers.

The almost empty bar was separated from the dining room by a Chinese lacquered screen and lit by flickering oil lamps. Packer glanced around pretending to be looking for a friend. Two couples sat at tables, white haired and with the even-tanned complexions of the well-heeled. He returned their smiles, then made for a cane armchair in the shadows at the far end. The barman followed him to his seat.

'*Mosi* please,' he asked, remembering the name of the local beer. The African retreated to prepare a tray.

Packer felt intensely uneasy. His tactics were bad. He aimed to wrong-foot the wily old gun-runner, yet their meeting was at a time and place Jackman himself had set. His home ground. There'd been no other way, of course. The Service wanted a solution fast and Jackman held all the cards. Short of silencing him with a bullet, there had to be a negotiation. A gentle probing to see what he wanted. So it had been the phone call from an untraceable number at the headquarters at Vauxhall Cross. 'We're upset, Harry. Just don't get it. Why are you doing this? We need to talk.' And now this dinner date where, if the man was truly bent on discrediting his own country's Intelligence Service, he might well have invited the press along to join them.

There was movement beyond the Chinese screen. Sam half covered his face. Instinct. Pure self-preservation. But it was only more dinner guests arriving.

Jackman could well arrive with a snapper, he realised. Some hack who'd flown out – maybe even on the same plane as Sam – to get the proof their story needed. Proof that the British government, through its intelligence arm, had involved itself in a coup in the small independent African state of Bodanga a year ago. A coup which had failed, leaving thousands dead, including the European staff of a refugee camp whose raped and machine-gunned bodies had been shown on a billion TV screens across the globe.

And it was Sam who'd paid Jackman to provide the guns for that coup. Paid him with a briefcase full of British taxpayers' sweat, handed over twelve months ago. The cash had bought a lot of guns. Hundreds of them. Hundreds of thousands of bullets.

After the débâcle he'd asked himself if it would have felt less dirty had the coup succeeded. A quick clean kill, a tyrant overthrown, victims in the dozens, not thousands. No violation of those sweet girls from Surrey and County Clare. Probably. The politicians would have crowed, assured of a place in history when the cabinet papers came out in thirty years. Consciences clear, instead of being burdened by guilt – and now by panic.

Two more elderly white couples entered the bar, greeting one of those already there. There was air kissing and many gentle embraces.

'My dears, it's been an age . . .' The flat accents of Europeans bred south of the equator.

No Jackman yet. No cameramen, thank God. Just these people. What were they? Tobacco farmers? Traders who killed with cancer instead of lead and never gave it a moment's thought?

The Service had been baffled by what Jackman was threatening. Why would a man who'd been the only real beneficiary of that deal to arm the coup plotters try to blow the lid off it? Why had he told a prominent British newspaper editor of MI6's complicity in the botched coup? And why *that* editor, Frank Hampson, a man whose links to the Intelligence Service had been common knowledge for years, a choice of mouthpiece that had led to the story being quickly blocked. Bad luck on Jackman's part, or deliberate? Telling a brown-noser because he *wanted* his intentions known by SIS? But what *did* he want, this man enriched by decades of illicit dealings?

Packer finished his beer. The chilled amber liquid had been pleasant, though watery. He rejected the barman's offer of another. He wanted the clearest of heads this evening.

The file on Jackman was thin – a few A4 sheets sketching suspected involvement in international intrigues and criminality, but little hard proof. The sort of bundle a graduate trainee would compile during induction at Vauxhall Cross. For more than twenty years Jackman had worked the rich vein of Africa's corruption, first gold and precious stones, then tapping the richer lode of arms. The Angolan war had bought him homes in Zambia, South Africa and Spain. Congo and the ANC had helped him

4

accrue property back in England under nominee names. There'd been money laundering and sanctions busting. Wisps of evidence. Not enough to convict, but possibly enough to frighten. It was Sam's only card, but hardly an ace.

The skin crawled on the back of his neck, telling him he was being watched. He turned his head slowly but couldn't see from where. A few minutes later the *maître d'* appeared in the bar.

'Mr Jackman asks if you will kindly join him in the restaurant, sir.'

'Does he? Right.'

Sam stood up without hurrying. He stepped past the Chinese screen, pausing in the entrance lobby to glance through the glass into the car park. A drab green Land Rover stood ostentatiously beneath one of the floodlights, its occupants dressed in army fatigues. Fear rippled through him, but he rebuked himself for it. This was friendly territory he was on, not some madhouse like Iraq.

Harry Jackman didn't rise from the table as Sam approached, instead he eyed him with an almost playful look. His bald head was red from the African sun. His eyebrows were smudges on a fleshy face, angled upwards into the middle of his brow, giving him the deceptive look of a clown. He wore a short-sleeved cotton shirt with a thin stripe. Small gold spectacles perched firmly on the bridge of his nose.

'I trust you've come alone,' he murmured as Packer sat, his accent vaguely north of Birmingham.

'You mean you're not sure?'

Jackman stifled a smirk. Of course he was sure.

'You on the other hand have brought some friends along,' Sam remarked, inclining his head towards the door.

'You noticed. I'm glad. You were meant to.'

'You pay them to look after you? Or they do it for love?'

Jackman chuckled. 'What do you think . . .' Behind the small, polished lenses his eyes lacked self-confidence. The look of a man used to peering over his shoulder. The armed men in the car park would be regular escorts, Sam surmised.

'Drink?' Jackman offered.

'That'd be nice.'

'I've ordered some Cape Red . . .'

'Fine.'

'Brain glue I call it.'

'I know. And a glass of water please.'

Jackman had only to raise his hand from the table for the waiter to be at his elbow.

'Some water for my guest, Emanuel.'

'Tell you what,' said Sam, glancing up. 'Mind if we change tables? There's a terrible draught here.'

The waiter looked to Jackman for guidance. The stony consternation on the gun-runner's face was enough to harden Sam's suspicion of a microphone beneath the mahogany.

Jackman chuckled again. 'Why not,' he beamed. 'Anywhere you like. You choose.'

The *maitre d'* was summoned to reseat them. When they were alone again, Jackman glowered at him. 'Happy now?'

'Stiff neck. From the flight,' Sam explained.

Jackman settled back like a Buddha, nodding knowingly.

'Please yourself. They look after me pretty well here.' He said it with the smugness of a man for whom being served by others was important. 'I can remember them building this place,' he added, reminding Sam how long he'd been around in these parts. 'The bloke whose idea it was had done well from emeralds and wanted to put down roots. He'd gone native for a while, stupid bugger. Had an African lady-friend he was talking of marrying. Didn't happen, as it turned out. Went for a Norwegian instead. The wife of one of his first clients when he opened the lodge to tourists. Classic long legs, although the blonde hair was from a bottle. Only discovered that when she dropped her drawers.' He chortled, his laugh rattling unhealthily in his chest.

'He still runs it?'

'No. Sold out five years ago. Moved back to Europe with his Scandi woman. Switzerland, I think.'

The waiter was back with the wine, a jug of water and two menus.

'Steaks are always good,' Jackman advised.

Sam chose a T-bone. A CD of Miriam Makeba played in the background. They were a reasonable distance from the next table and wouldn't be overheard here.

'Good flight out?' They were fencing. Waiting to see who would be first to raise the issue they'd come here to discuss.

'A 747 to Lusaka then a hop up to the Copperbelt on a turbo-prop.'

'I trust HMG sends its representatives first class.'

'Limousines at each end and a personal porter.'

'I mean, I wouldn't want to think that the man I'm being asked to deal with only merits being stuffed in the back of a jumbo with the families and the blacks.' He said it with venom, as if such status issues really mattered to him.

Packer's patience gave way. 'Fuck the flight, Harry.' He forced his mouth into a smile for the benefit of anyone watching. 'What are you up to?'

Jackman drew back.

'Testing the water.'

'Meaning?'

'That I've had enough of this continent, Simon. I want to go home. And I want to be sure I'm treated right when I get there.'

'You've a funny way of going about it.'

'Think so?' The eyebrows shot up again, the eyes beneath them twinkling. '*You're* here, aren't you? The string-pullers have sent their boy.'

Sam bristled. 'Those string-pullers, Harry, you've upset them. Writing outrageous letters to the papers isn't wise.'

'One paper.'

'Whatever. Wasn't wise at all. You ought to be careful.'

'*Me* need to be careful? I think you'll find the boot's on the other foot, chum.'

The waiter returned to reset the cutlery for what they'd ordered. He was joined by a waitress with a basket of bread, a slender woman with braided hair, clad in a low-cut African dress. Her skin had the burnished glow of roasted coffee and her teeth dazzled as she smiled. She leaned forward and her breasts quivered with a life of their own. Then she withdrew and a third server came with soup.

When they'd all gone Harry Jackman passed a hand over his shiny dome.

'Fancied that one, did you?'

'She was very beautiful.'

'A lot of them are. And a lot of ex-pats develop a taste, of course.'

'Not you? How many years have you been here?'

'Twenty-five, give or take. But no. They're different, you see, African women. The smell. The shape of their mouths and their arses. To me it'd be like shagging a sheep. Not that I've anything against sheep. Or Africans. They've got their place in nature's blueprint and we've got ours.'

'Apartheid.'

'Exactly. The idea was right. It's the way the Afrikaners handled it that was wrong.'

'And because apartheid's dead you want to go home?'

'Not that simple. Although you know as well as I do what's happening here. This is no place any more for a white man wanting an easy life. Blighty, old boy. That's where my roots are.'

Roots, thought Sam as he spooned tomato soup into his mouth. As twisted as the rest of Jackman's law-dodging life. The file in London had shown a blank when it came to the man's parentage. The first note of the young Harry's existence had been at one week old when found in the doorway of a pub.

'So let me get this straight, Harry.' Sam edged his voice with sarcasm.

'You want to settle back in the UK. And you want to be sure officialdom is nice to you when you get there. So what's the first thing you do? You offer a story to the papers that'll blow a hole in the government's claims to have an ethical foreign policy. You're off your trolley.'

'I need to be sure, Simon.'

'Of what, for Christ's sake?'

'Of being allowed to live the rest of my life in peace. I'm pushing fifty. Fifteen years older than you?' He overestimated by a handful of years. 'I can afford to retire. To do a bit of this and a bit of that, just for the fun of it. Not for the money. I've got enough.'

'I'm sure you have.' Thousands of dead Africans had seen to that. 'But you're still confusing me, Harry. How does writing a letter to a newspaper claiming the British government was involved in a bungled African coup get you safe passage home?'

Jackman's eyes became deadly serious.

'Come on. Don't play the virgin with me. A warning shot, that's all it was. I knew damn well that good-ole-boy Hampson wouldn't go into print about Bodanga without the say-so of C or whatever you call him these days.'

'Meaning?'

Jackman hissed with exasperation. 'That I just wanted to show you what I *could* do if I was so minded.'

'Oh. Is *that* what it was about?' Sam mocked, trying to get Jackman on the back foot. 'You've miscalculated, old son. The people you're dealing with don't take kindly to threats.'

'Don't be daft. They need my co-operation as much as I need theirs. The world's a dangerous place. You scratch my back . . .'

Sam gave up on his soup which tasted unpleasantly of the can it came from, and pushed the plate away.

'So, spell it out to me, Harry. What exactly is it you want?'

'Immunity from any sort of prosecution.'

Sam lifted his eyebrows.

'Come on,' Jackman insisted. 'It's a small return for the services I've done for my country.'

It was true there'd been other small jobs for SIS before last year's arms deal. Smuggling people across borders and providing untraceable funds to political groups that the government of the day was embarrassed to be associated with.

'What sort of prosecutions did you have in mind?' Sam inquired sceptically.

Jackman's gaze became a tunnel with no light at its end. He wiped his mouth with a napkin.

'Can't imagine,' he murmured with a contrived mysteriousness. 'But there's people out there who'll dream something up. You boyos have found me useful over the years, but I don't kid myself you're my friends.'

'So. Let me get this right,' Sam persisted, spreading his fingers across the edge of the table. 'You want HMG to promise that you'll never be prosecuted, whatever crimes you've committed. Is that it?'

Jackman swallowed. 'Yes, essentially.' He paused for a moment. 'Odd word *crime*, don't you think? The definition of it seems to depend on who's carried it out.'

Sam folded his arms. Time for some home truths. 'They'll never buy it, Harry. Not a blanket immunity. You'll need to be specific. Have to spell it out in black and white.'

The gun-runner's shoulders sagged as if the wind had been knocked from him. He shook his head. 'No can do.'

The soup plates were cleared away and the steaks set before them.

'Best beef in southern Africa . . .' said Jackman listlessly. The words sounded like a mantra he'd grown rather tired of.

'You'll miss it,' Sam goaded. 'We're all getting brain disease from the stuff back home.'

The gun-runner fired a glance towards the door. Sam recognised the look and empathised with it. Fear of enemies closing in.

'Expecting someone?'

Jackman grimaced. 'Look. I *do* want to go home, Simon. Back to England. Don't make it hard for me.'

'What makes you think you'll be safer there?'

'I'll blend in easier . . . Surrounded by people my own colour.'

'You're out of touch. Times have changed.'

'Not out in Suffolk they haven't.'

Sam remembered the file again. An ex-wife and a daughter living in Ipswich.

Jackman's eyebrows arched in despair. 'I've *got* to get home, Simon. Too many enemies here. That's why I'm prepared to play rough to be left in peace.'

Packer watched him begin picking at his food. He was puzzled. There was something fundamentally odd about Jackman's fear of legal retribution. Before coming out here his controller had told him there was nothing pending. No warrants waiting to be served. No misdemeanours under investigation. So long as he kept his mouth shut the ex-pat could return home and merge with the background as much as he wanted. But Jackman clearly thought otherwise, a paranoia that was perfectly understandable after so many years of bending rules to suit his own pocket. But Packer sensed there was something specific Jackman was concerned about. Some deed in his recent past which he expected to backfire.

If so, his mission was changing. No longer merely a matter of agreeing terms for Jackman's silence, but a need to discover what the bugger had been up to. Success would require more subtlety than he'd used so far. He decided to sidetrack. To soften up the ground.

'Why Africa, Harry? What got you started here? Twenty-five years ago, you said.'

Jackman's eyes melted with self-satisfaction. His mouth puckered, like a bully's given an unexpected excuse to brag. 'You really want to know?' Sam nodded. Jackman took a gulp of wine. 'Dust. That's what got me started.'

'Dust?'

Jackman grinned. 'I was a chemist by training when I came out. First job was managing a lab at a copper mine. Boring as hell. I had two Kaffirs who did all the real work. Then one day a black came to me who'd been given the job of cleaning the whole place up. Copper production sites get littered with all sorts of junk. This Af had found some drums of powder and didn't know whether it was safe to dump them. Didn't know what was in 'em, you see.' Jackman's eyes twinkled at the memory of it. 'So what did I do? I did a little test in the lab after my two assistants had gone home. Found out the powder was condensates from the smelter chimneys. Packed with cobalt and nickel. Worth a fortune to somebody with the hardware for extracting it. So, I told the Af the drums weren't worth anything but because they contained toxic minerals, they couldn't be taken for dumping. Then I got in touch with a feller I knew in South Africa . . .'

'And the rest is history,' Sam interrupted. 'A life of crime was under way.'

'Crime? Come on, my friend! Out here that's not crime, it's business.'

'But a business which has now turned sour, you're saying.'

Jackman sighed. 'It's become harder. A lot harder. Too many people wanting a cut.'

For a while they ate without speaking. The beef was as good as Jackman had promised. Sam noticed an increase in frequency of the glances towards the door.

'Somebody after you, Harry?' There'd be plenty of candidates.

Jackman feigned a look of wounded innocence.

'Who is it?'

'I don't know.'

Sam clicked his tongue. 'Come on, old son. If we're to get anywhere, you've got to be straighter with me than that.'

'No, I mean it.' Behind the oval lenses Jackman's eyes were like gob-stoppers. 'I really don't know, Simon.'

'Explain.'

Jackman hesitated again. 'Things . . . things have been going on.'

'Such as?'

'People dying.'

'It happens.'

'Unnaturally, I mean.'

'Friends of yours?'

'Yeah.' Jackman's expression became pained, as if he were really putting himself out. He glanced down at his hands and began picking at his cuticles with a thumbnail. 'Look. There *is* something in particular – you know, that I want immunity from.' Sam smiled inwardly. Progress. 'The death I'm talking about was to do with that.' He looked up again, his eyes wanting sympathy. 'It's a deal I wish I'd never got involved with, to be honest. And it's something you boys really ought to know about.'

'Perhaps we do already. Tell me.'

'I'd like to. And I will. But only after I have it in writing that I'm being granted immunity.' He bunched his fists and rested them on the table.

Packer let out a long sigh. For a moment he'd thought a breakthrough was in sight. 'You know what you have to do, Harry. In black and white up front, so they know what's involved.'

The sweaty red brow crinkled with concern. 'You're asking me to put my head on the block. I can't do that.' He glanced towards the door again then leaned forward. 'Look . . . That bloke who died was a partner of mine in Jo'burg. Involved in the deal I'm talking about.'

'Tell me about it.'

Jackman leaned even closer, his voice less than a whisper. 'They'd sawn his effing head off, Simon.' The fear in the eyes looked convincing. Jackman thought he was next. 'For God's sake let's settle things with HMG, so I can tell you about it.'

'*If* they can be settled . . .'

'Oh they will be, Simon,' Jackman bristled, winding back, angry at being played with. 'You see, there's other letters ready to be sent. To the media and to people I'm close to. A whole bunch. All sealed up. Envelopes addressed. Left with someone I trust in case something happens to me.' He thumped a fist on the table. 'And next time they won't go to one of your bloody lapdogs.'

They finished their food in silence, heads down like weary bulls. When he'd done, Jackman puffed out his cheeks.

'You know, I'm beginning to think they've sent the wrong man.'

'Why's that?'

'I need to talk with someone who'll take me seriously.'

'Oh I'm taking you *very* seriously Harry. Be in no doubt about that. But you haven't understood what's possible and what isn't as far as HMG is concerned.'

Jackman seemed not to hear. He hovered like an angler pondering how much bait to lay down before the fish could be hooked.

'This deal I'm talking about . . .' He was whispering again. 'I'll tell you this much. It involved the shipment of something pretty nasty. And I think it was heading for the Islamics.'

The mention of the 'I' word triggered alarm bells for Sam. It was less than three weeks since the car bombings of the US Embassies in Kenya and Tanzania.

'What do you mean *think*?'

'Because I don't know for sure.'

'What sort of nasty stuff? Weapons? Biological? Nuclear?'

Jackman shook his head. He'd achieved his aim. Didn't need to say more. The man was like a streetwalker, flashing her interesting bits then hiding them again.

'You say you want to move back to England,' Sam growled. 'Why not Venezuela or Monaco? Someplace where they won't give a shit what you've done in the past.'

'Personal reasons.'

'You're not telling me you want to get back with your wife?' Sam prodded.

'Which one? I've had three. And no, I'm not planning anything like that. Just take it that I want to return to my own country.'

Sam told himself to cool it. Letting the man rile him wasn't going to help. 'Tell me about your ex-wife and daughter. The ones in Ipswich.'

'Your file's out of date. It's Woodbridge. I bought them a place by the river a couple of years back. The estate where they'd been living was going downhill. Anyway, what about them?'

'You've kept in touch?'

'Stayed friends with all my exes. And Julie – my daughter – she's just great. You married? Kids?'

'No.'

'I was twenty-one when I met Maeve. Shacked up with her because it was the thing to do in 1970. A nurse. Irish, but with the morals of a Dane. Birth pills in her handbag instead of a rosary. But careless with it. She got pregnant. I agreed to marry her, stupid kid that I was. She was wrong for me. Too placid. And, you know, when it came to the business, the sex stuff – it was something she felt she had to do because everyone else was. Not because she got any pleasure out of it. You know the sort.'

Happily for Sam he didn't.

'So I left her after a couple of years,' Jackman continued, 'and came out here. Went back from time to time. Not very often.' He paused. 'Little Julie never knew who I was when she was tiny.'

'Do they know what you do for a living?'

Jackman squirmed slightly. 'No. It isn't always wise being truthful in relationships, don't you find?'

Sam ignored his question. 'So you started off selling black market chemicals. How did you get into guns?'

'Somebody asked me if I could get them some. One of Mandela's boys.'

'And . . . ?'

'And I discovered how easy it was. AK47s could be prised from the Zambian army like peas from a pod. This country's packed with people wanting to earn a dishonest penny.'

'And it never concerned you what the guns might be used for?'

Jackman raised a cynical eyebrow. 'Don't come the naïve kid with me, Simon. I was filling a hole in the market. If it hadn't been me, it'd have been someone else.'

The old excuse. They all used it.

'And this other deal. The one you'll only tell us about if you get immunity – was that *filling a hole* too?'

Jackman fixed him with a steady eye. He selected a toothpick from the holder in the middle of the table and removed some beef fibres from between two molars.

'It was supplying somebody with something that was damned hard to get,' he said enigmatically. 'Something they wanted very bad.' Then he leaned forward. 'I'll tell you something else. The shipping arrangements were real high security. Never done anything quite like it before. The warehouse I fixed up – it was like *Ali Baba,* Simon. Like bloody Ali Baba.'

An odd image, thought Sam. 'Meaning?'

'Meaning that you and I have to do a deal, Simon.' The eyes were playing with him again. 'So I can tell you about it.'

Sam felt his patience going. He had a sudden urge to deprive Jackman of sleep and food for a few days.

'For God's sake, let's do a deal, man,' Jackman pleaded melodramatically. 'For the sake of the civilised world, if not for you and me.'

Packer narrowed his eyes. What sort of line was he being spun? Fact, fiction – did Jackman even know the difference?

'Look,' he snapped. 'The bottom line is this. You simply cannot expect the British government to give you immunity from prosecution without knowing what crimes you're talking about. Suppose some African nation were to charge you with genocide. There's no way HMG would protect you from that.'

Jackman pulled himself up straight. He twisted his head to one side and studied Sam out of the corner of his eye as if seeing whether a different perspective would show him the way forward.

'Have another drink,' he suggested unoriginally. 'Something a little stronger? They've got good single malts here.'

Sam would willingly have seen off most of a bottle.

'No.'

Jackman clasped his hands. 'Okay. Let's get back to basics. HMG needs my silence. I need a *laissez-passer* from HMG. There's two people who can sort this out. You and me.'

'I've been trying my best, Harry.'

Jackman nodded. For a delirious moment Sam thought he was about to concede something meaningful.

'We *can* reach a compromise, you know,' Jackman assured him. 'I mean it *is* why you've come here, Simon. To do a deal.'

'It's your move, Harry. It really is.'

Jackman pushed the spectacles up his nose and stroked his chin. The cockiness had gone from his eyes, replaced by an expression Sam couldn't quite define.

'Well . . . if you won't have a night-cap here, what about one back at my place,' Jackman suggested. 'The house rattles a bit. My last girlfriend left me a couple of months ago. Went back to the Cape.'

Loneliness. That's what his eyes were showing, Sam realised. Jackman was lonely. Giving up on Africa because Africa had given up on him. He'd found a chink in the man's armour. Big enough to stick a screwdriver in for now. Soon it'd be a chisel, then a whole DIY workbench.

'All right. I'll have a quick one with you,' Sam conceded.

Jackman called for the bill and paid it. They made small talk about the upcoming Springboks' tour and England's chances for the coming season. Then they walked out to the car park. Seeing Jackman appear, the army officer in the Land Rover shook his soldiers awake.

'You'll follow me in your car?' Jackman checked.

'Be right behind you.'

Sam kept half an eye on Jackman as they each moved to their own vehicle. He heard the Land Rover engine rattle into life, then as he unlocked the door of the Toyota the Zambian officer crossed to Jackman's Mercedes to talk to him. The two men's palms touched. Payoff time.

The Mercedes was first onto the road back to Kitwe, followed by the army patrol, a nearly full moon turning the palm trees by the gate into ghostly sentries. Out on the road the three vehicles settled into a steady run towards the outskirts of town. Sam's spirits had lifted. He felt absurdly confident all of a sudden. A few more hours and Jackman would be eating from the palm of his hand.

Five minutes into the journey, the Land Rover's brake lights flickered and the vehicle lurched over to the side of the road. Sam overtook, expecting it to fall in behind like a tail gunner, but when he looked in the mirror the lights had been doused. His antennae twitched.

When the tail lights of Jackman's Mercedes also disappeared he began to feel distinctly uneasy, but then they reappeared as he rounded a bend. He accelerated to close the gap. Suddenly, further ahead, there were other lights in the road. A red lamp being swung. A road block. Army or police. The Merc's brake lights blazed and Sam also touched the pedal, telling himself there was no need for alarm. Random traffic checks were normal on Zambian roads. Part of the government's anti-crime programme. The fact that the men involved used them to extort 'fines' from guiltless car drivers was just an inconvenient fact of life. He fingered his wallet for a suitable note.

As the two vehicles approached the checkpoint in tandem, Sam braked harder. Suddenly a man in fatigues sprinted forward, shouting at him to stop short of the other car and to switch off his lights. An icy chill came over him – the soldier wore a black cloth hood with holes for eyes and mouth. This was no ordinary road block.

Jackman's car had stopped twenty yards in front of his. A spotlamp on the roof of an army truck lit up its pale cream paint. Sam's window was half open. The soldier who'd stopped him rested his rifle barrel on the top of the glass. A strong body odour wafted in, leavened by eucalyptus from the roadside trees.

His unease growing by the second, Sam watched Jackman being dragged from his car, a gun at his chest. The old expat still seemed unconcerned, extracting a wad of banknotes from a hip pocket. Sam told himself they'd be okay. A robbery on a larger scale than usual perhaps, but if they stayed cool and let the men have what they wanted . . .

Then a shot rang out, echoing through the trees like the sound of splitting timber. Jackman buckled and fell.

'Shit . . .' Sam grabbed at the door handle to open it, but felt the cold of the gun press against his temple.

A second shot had Sam thinking his own brains had been blasted. But it was Jackman again. Spread-eagled on the tarmac, a vivid red bubbled from his chest. Then the spotlight turned on Sam, blinding him.

His throat tightened. He couldn't speak or breathe. Any moment now they'd do the same to him. There'd been times before when he'd faced death, and he knew there was no way to manage it. No way to control that cringing feel as you waited for the hit.

Two more shots, each sending shocks through his body, but not touching him. He heard air hiss from a tyre. There was a shout of impatience and the lorry started up. Two engines revving, the truck and the Mercedes. The light shining in his eyes wobbled and went out. Then with a crash of gears the two vehicles accelerated away.

Silence again. And darkness. Just the eucalyptus smell. Overpowering. Like a stench. Sam clicked his headlamps back on, banged open the door and ran forward.

'Harry . . .' he breathed, crouching over him. Jackman lay in a thickening pool of blood. No response. The striped cotton had two small holes in the middle of the chest, but Jackman's life was leaking from the craters in his back.

The ashen face twitched suddenly. 'Simon . . .' More of a breath than a voice.

Packer leaned forward.

'Yes. Help's coming.'

'Merc . . .' Jackman croaked.

'The car?' Why worry about a motor at a time like this?

'No,' Jackman hissed, suddenly finding the strength to pull Sam closer. 'Mercury. Red mercury . . .' Sam felt a chill shoot through him. 'S'what I didn't tell you. That deal . . .'

'The stuff you shipped to the Islamics was red mercury?'

'Julie . . .' The hand that had been hooked into Sam's shirt fell away. 'Ask Julie 'bout it. She knows . . .'

Then the breath left him. Quite suddenly. Like a tap being turned. Sam felt for a pulse in the neck, but there was nothing. Not a flicker.

'God . . .'

Try mouth to mouth? Get the life back into him? Then blood oozed from the lips and it sank in that Harry Jackman was utterly dead.

Stunned, Sam sat back on his haunches.

Red mercury. The one-time holy grail for terrorists bent on making nuclear bombs. Except the bloody stuff didn't exist.

'Harry . . .' He patted the man's face. Pointless. Harry Jackman *would* be going home, but in a box.

Red mercury. Fucking nonsense.

'Damn you, Harry.' A night of riddles from the man, right up to the end.

He looked up, shooting glances up and down the road. Engines approaching from each direction. A car from the Kitwe road stopped first. As its headlamps picked out the bloodied corpse, a woman screamed at her husband to drive on. Then the vehicle from out of town pulled up behind Sam's car. From the engine rattle he knew it was the Land Rover – Jackman's 'protection' that had conveniently given up on them half a mile back.

Before he could turn his head, Sam felt hard metal press into the bone behind his ear.

'Mistah Foster! You under ahrrest!'

2

THE METALLIC BLUE car that emerged from the underground garage of SIS headquarters was driven by a dark-haired woman in her late thirties called Denise Corby. She wore a slate-grey jacket and skirt. Beside her sat a fair-haired man, who was her immediate superior. As the security gates slid shut behind the Vectra, it turned right and blended with the traffic heading north over Vauxhall Bridge. The morning was dull, the sky overcast.

'I spoke to Julie Jackman last night,' the woman announced in a mellow, matter-of-fact voice that was almost low enough to be a man's. 'She can see us at noon.'

'Good.' Her boss, Duncan Waddell, spoke with a Belfast accent. A small figure, he sat rigidly upright to maximise his height. 'You know, when the FCO consular department rang the ex-wife on Wednesday, she expressed no surprise whatsoever at the manner of Jackman's demise. Says something, don't you think?'

'Says she didn't care any more. I should hope not. It was twenty-six years ago that he dumped her and the child.' Denise Corby was a big-boned woman who'd probably looked middle-aged since childhood.

'Where exactly does the daughter work?' Waddell queried.

'In the virology department of the St Michael's Hospital Group. It's one of the top labs in the country, so I'm told.'

'How did she sound?'

'Oh, shaken up still. Naturally. And anxious about why we wanted to talk to her.'

'What reason did you give?'

'Bland as hell. Told her there were a couple of legal ends to tie up.'

'If she's anything like her father, you'll need to watch her. Devious to a fault, that man was. The world's a better place without him.'

Waddell's close-cropped hair gave him an austere, unforgiving appearance. He wore a light grey suit and his manner suggested an acute awareness of his own importance. He rested his elbow on the open window and glanced to his right where a shaft of sunlight had caught the roof of the Tate Gallery just visible beyond the bridge parapet. There was a Jackson Pollock exhibition on. Not his cup of tea.

'What d'you know about Sam Packer?' he asked.

'Not a lot.' Denise Corby pursed her lips. 'Except . . . didn't he have a spot of trouble with Ukrainian mobsters a couple of years back?'

'He did. He's still on a hit list.'

'And wasn't it linked to a certain piece of in-house scandal that we don't talk about?'

'It certainly was. An adulterous relationship with another field officer. She also worked eastern Europe.'

Suddenly Denise Corby stamped on the brakes. An elderly woman in green and brown had drifted onto a zebra crossing. 'Sorry. Didn't see her.'

'Won't live long if she makes a habit of that,' Waddell commented, bracing himself against the dashboard.

'She sort of blended into the background.'

'Probably works for us,' Waddell quipped.

Corby let a smile flicker as they waited for the ancient pedestrian to get safely across.

'A long-running affair, was it?' she asked.

'Sam's? Yes. Went on for years. The husband hadn't a clue until the very end.'

'And he was one of ours too, I seem to remember.'

'Indeed. The whole thing was highly incestuous. And I have to say the quality of the deception applied by all the parties involved did great credit to their tradecraft.'

Corby smiled politely. 'Pity about the quality of the judgement.'

'Aye. That's the bit we don't like to think about. Anyway, apart from that little hiccup, Sam's been a good field man for us, which is all you need to know. Ex naval intelligence, he did fine work in Eastern Europe in the early nineties, then switched to the Middle East beat three years ago. His cover job was in trade fairs.'

'So how come he was working in Africa?'

'Well, his legend got well and truly blown in Baghdad. Then, when the Odessa mafiya wrote a contract on him, we had to lose him somewhere.'

'And where better than the dark continent.'

'Precisely.'

Denise Corby drove expertly, heading up through Chelsea until they hit the Cromwell Road. The morning rush hour was over, but traffic flowed thickly in both directions.

'You'll have to direct me when we get closer,' she warned. 'Hounslow is not a part of the metropolis I make a point of frequenting.'

A couple of miles later Waddell told her to turn left off the A4. 'Flightpath-blighted housing and dreary industrial estates,' he growled distastefully. 'But there's a nice little firm here that provides Sam with cover. The characters who run it are ex-SAS sergeants. Dave and Ron – Davron International Trading they call themselves.'

'How sweet. Tell me, how did you prise Sam from the clutches of the Zambian police?'

'Loud diplomatic noises and a few well-placed banknotes. The High Commission in Lusaka has a slush fund that saves an awful lot of paper-work.'

'And the investigation into the shooting?'

'Not getting very far.' He made it sound both to be expected and perfectly satisfactory. 'They've failed to identify the army unit that carried out the killing, and judging by their past record on such robberies they never will.'

Ten minutes later the car turned into a trading estate full of buildings trimmed with brightly coloured corrugated plastic.

'Block C6. Bottom of the row, then left,' Waddell directed.

The unit they stopped outside had three Audis in the car park, all with personalised plates.

Sam Packer had arrived at the Davron International offices ten minutes earlier, dressed in the light grey suit, pale blue shirt and striped tie that he'd travelled in on the night flight from Lusaka. He'd dumped his bag in a corner of the dusty, little-used, first-floor office that was his operating base and logged onto the Internet to check the main newspaper archives both in London and southern Africa for reports on Jackman's murder. Specifically he wanted to see if connections had been made with red mercury. There were none. Before leaving Lusaka the station officer at the High Commission had shown him short articles in the local *Post* and *Times*. Both papers had dismissed the murder as robbery with violence – the police line – but Sam was certain they were wrong. Jackman had been targeted. Targeted for the simplest reason of all. Someone had wanted him dead.

Compared with the torture chamber he'd experienced in Baghdad two years earlier, the police cell he'd been confined to in Kitwe had been luxurious. In Iraq, he'd thought his end had come. This time he'd felt certain of release within hours. After recovering from the shock of seeing a man die in front of him he'd picked his way back through their conversation, searching for clues to his killer.

He was well aware that the world would, generally speaking, be quite content with Harry Jackman's passing. From what he could gather, Her Majesty's Secret Intelligence Service was over the moon. But for him the murder had been a disappointment as well as a shock. He'd begun to believe that he *could* silence the man through negotiation. Believed too that in the process he would glean valuable intelligence about Islamic terrorism.

Sam had not met Denise Corby before. Her appointment to Counter-Proliferation was recent. When she walked into his first floor office, towering above their diminutive boss, the skin-stripping stare of her dark brown eyes warned him that she was a career-hungry perfectionist, intolerant of human weakness, a woman it would be unwise to cross. He was big on first impressions.

'Welcome back, Sam.' Waddell made the introductions and they shook hands. 'You okay?' he asked.

'Fine.' Admitting to being shaken up by seeing people's innards being blown out wasn't the done thing for employees of the firm.

Waddell staked a territorial claim on Sam's black leather recliner. He pointed to a couple of stacking chairs by the far wall, wiggling a finger to indicate they should grab them.

'We've read your report, Sam,' he began stiffly, 'and the Lusaka station's still doing follow-ups of course, but the whole thing's pretty opaque. We've no idea why Jackman was shot, but so far we favour the robbery theory.' He leaned back in the chair, rocking it on its springs. 'And to be perfectly frank, we don't give a shit,' he added predictably. 'He's much less trouble to us dead.'

'Unless those letters about Bodanga that he talked about start turning up in newspaper offices,' Sam reminded him.

'We're working on that,' Waddell told him. 'Shouldn't be hard to discredit him, particularly since he's not around to defend himself. Anyway that was probably a bluff, Sam. The man was mostly piss and wind.'

'Whatever. He'd have been a lot more useful to us if still alive.'

'This red mercury crap, you mean?'

'Sure. We'd have found out what the hell it was about, rather than having to guess.'

'Red mercury simply doesn't exist, Sam,' Denise Corby told him firmly.

'I'm well aware that's the perceived wisdom,' Sam responded. 'It's just that for some reason Harry Jackman seemed to think otherwise . . .'

'Playing games,' Waddell muttered. 'A false hare for us to waste time on.'

'He was in shock,' Sam protested. 'You don't make up things like that when you know you're about to die.'

'Remind him, Denise,' said Waddell dismissively. 'Tell Sam about the red mercury scam.'

'It began with glasnost at the end of the eighties.'

'That much I remember,' Sam nodded.

'Word came out of Russia about this amazing new chemical compound which could make neutron bombs more lethal, or worse still, dramatically reduce the size of an H bomb. The media had visions of terrorists armed with thermonuclear footballs – particularly after certain perfectly reputable scientists, British and American, came back from a visit to Russia fully convinced of red mercury's existence. They wrote it up in the scientific press.'

'But you're saying the Russians made it all up? The stuff didn't exist?'

'Or if it did, it certainly didn't have the capability they claimed for it. But that didn't matter, because in 1992 a Russian entrepreneur persuaded the Kremlin that overseas interest in red mercury was so strong they could all make a fortune from it. Export licences were granted – up to ten tonnes a year at a price of $350,000 a kilo. If you do the maths, that gives an earnings potential of over three billion dollars.'

'But if the product didn't exist,' Sam queried, 'how could they make any money?'

'From gullibility. Some customers were ready to pay up front without even seeing the stuff, let alone testing it. Foreign banks gave huge credits to the Russian exporters on the promise of whacking interest payments. The cash of course was used to finance a whole raft of other highly profitable business activities nothing to do with red mercury, most of them criminal. The banks didn't care. Their paperwork said the loans were for a legitimate export business, and they got their money back with a hefty profit.'

'And the people trying to buy the stuff?'

'Lots of long faces,' she answered. 'Iraq tried for it. South Africa and Israel. Even Nigeria.'

'Jackman told me about some business partner of his in Jo'burg having his head severed,' Sam reminded them. 'There *was* a South African connection, you said?'

'Indeed,' said Waddell pushing the chair further back and resting his feet on Sam's desk. His brown shoes were immaculately clean. 'A series of odd and rather grisly murders in the early 1990s supposedly linked with attempts to buy or manufacture red mercury. All sorts of villains were suggested, including Mossad.'

'But the man Jackman talked of – that was more recent.'

'Three months ago – at the beginning of June. A dodgy trader, rather like Harry himself. Name of Van Damm. At first the South African media did speculate it was another red mercury killing, but the police found a simpler motive. The victim spent his spare time and ill-gotten gains on young, black rent boys.'

'I see.'

Sam's mind clicked back to Tuesday night. All the double talk, the teasing hints that might or might not have been important.

'Jackman was playing games with you, Sam,' Waddell declared dismissively.

'With his dying breath?'

'Delirium perhaps,' suggested Corby in a burst of generosity. 'Or maybe you misheard him.'

'He was lucid,' Sam answered flatly. 'Red mercury. That's what he said. That and "Julie knows about it". Quite deliberate and clear. Said he'd shipped a load of it somewhere and was worried it had ended up with Islamic fundamentalists. And now he was regretting it. Conscience troubling him.'

'*Conscience*!' Waddell exploded. 'Since when did that bugger have a conscience?'

'It's just an impression I got, Duncan. I never did pass GCSE mind-reading.'

'Sketch him for me,' said Corby briskly. 'A gullible type?'

'Gullible isn't right. But a conspiracy theorist, yes.'

'People who still believe in red mercury usually are.'

'Don't dismiss him as a nutter,' Sam warned. 'Harry Jackman was scared about what he'd got mixed up in. He was paying for protection. Had the appearance of a man who thought he was going to be topped.'

Waddell swung his legs down to the floor again. 'And you reckon his death was not unconnected with this deal he was supposedly so worried about.'

'Possibly.'

'Robbery sounds a more likely scenario to me,' Waddell insisted.

'The staging was too elaborate. The soldiers he'd hired to look after him had pulled off the road for a piss just before the road block. Coincidence? I don't think so. And if it *was* just robbery why didn't they do me over too?'

'You were in a Toyota. Jackman's car was a Merc.'

'An old one.'

'Well, whatever.' Waddell shrugged and put his hands on the table as if about to rise. 'I have to take my leave of you. There's a minister needs briefing, heading out from Heathrow for talks on Kosovo. The Foreign Office should have sent a car for me. There's only one way forward on this Jackman case, and that's if his girl Julie really does know something about his fantasies. You two go and find out.' He levered himself to his feet. 'But I tell you, unless she opens doors, this particular red mercury trail is heading for the bin like all the others.'

Waddell strutted towards the door and left them to it. Sam could see from Corby's face that she shared her boss's scepticism.

'I really have got better things to do than this, but let's get it over with,' she said, picking up her bag and slipping its long strap onto her shoulder.

'What's the arrangement?' Sam asked.

'Noon,' she replied. 'You and me at the place where she works, off Tottenham Court Road.'

'Any idea what sort of state she's in?' He hated interviews with the newly bereaved.

'Sounded okay on the phone. Suspicious more than anything else.'

The Central Virology Laboratory, St Michael's Hospital
11.50 hrs

Julie Jackman sat on a stool by the bench in the laboratory, her rubber-gloved hands working a measured-dose pipette to fill a grid of tiny test tubes for an immunoassay. A white lab coat covered her normal clothes – blue jeans and a grey T-shirt. She had a pretty, heart-shaped face with wispy brown hair, some strands of which fell forward to the corner of her mouth. From time to time she brushed them away with the back of her wrist. From behind the oval lenses of small, silver-framed spectacles, her pale, grey-green eyes concentrated hard. One mistake and the whole test procedure would need to be started again.

She was finding it difficult to work, with her father's death preying on her mind. It hadn't truly sunk in that she wouldn't see him again. The fact that the funeral was happening that very morning in a place half a world away seemed quite unreal. Her mother had suggested asking for a delay so she could travel to Zambia to attend it, but she'd decided not to go. She knew next to nothing of his life in Africa. In a strange land surrounded by strangers. Questions would be asked which she wouldn't want to answer. And she was afraid. Superstitiously scared that whatever evil had struck him down might seek her out too.

Her relationship with her father had always been more shade than light. She'd come to think of him as a serial deserter. The first time, when she was two years old, she'd been unaware of what was going on, but the act of abandonment had repeated each time he returned to the house in Ipswich for a visit. Her mother used to say 'this is your father,' like he was a complete stranger. Then he would start acting the part, showering her with gifts and affection until sure he'd secured her adoration again. Then he would leave. Suddenly. Without a 'goodbye' or a 'see you soon'. And each time those flights in the night had broken her heart.

And now he'd gone for good. It had been a hell of a jolt when her

24

mother had rung to tell her. She'd been shocked at the news. Shocked too to discover she wasn't able to cry about it.

She looked up at the wall clock. The Foreign Office people would be here any minute. She dreaded talking to them, yet at the same time wanted to hear what they had to say, hoping for some explanation, some reason for what had happened. To make it real.

She put down the pipette. The test was almost prepared, but her mind was wandering and she feared making a mess of the final set of insertions. In the next bay sat a fellow scientific officer. He was the sort of earnest, reliable type her mother would have loved her to settle with, but his efforts to arouse her interest in him during the past few months had been fruitless.

'George . . .' She removed her glasses and ducked her head to one side to see through a gap in the shelving separating the bays. 'Would you do me a favour?'

'What is it?'

'Just say yes.'

'All right then, yes.'

'There's only the antigen to be added to these samples. Do it for me, would you? I'm running out of time.'

'Time?' he asked tetchily.

'I've got people coming in to see me any minute. To do with my dad.' She'd already told the lab staff about her father's murder.

'Oh, sure.' He was suddenly sympathetic. 'You run along. I'll look after everything. When the results are through I'll put the printout on your desk.'

'God, I'll be back long before it goes into the analyser, George,' she assured him, peeling off her rubber gloves and slipping them into the yellow bin for contaminated waste. She stood up and thrust her hands deep into her lab coat pockets. 'It's just Foreign Office officials. Don't suppose it'll take long. They're probably after some of his back tax.'

'Want me to sit in with you?'

'Thanks, but no.'

She crossed to the hooks by the door and hung up the coat. Outside in the corridor she walked the five paces to the small office she shared with George and a woman called Janet. For now the office was empty. She sat at her computer terminal, logged in and checked for e-mail. There were a couple of messages to do with a correspondence with a virologist in Memphis, but nothing interesting. She logged off again then put her head in her hands, massaging her forehead. The conversation she was about to have concerned something far more sinister than tax, she suspected. From the little she'd known about her father's business life, she'd guessed that most of it had been on the wrong side of the law.

It had been sweaty in the lab because the air conditioning was on the blink. She decided to freshen up. She grabbed her backpack from the floor beside her desk and hurried past the labs to the washrooms. Inside she found the department's receptionist Ailsa Mackinley checking her eye make-up and hair. She had long, dark, spiralling curls which required maintenance in front of a mirror at least once an hour.

'I told you about these people coming to see me?' Julie checked, concerned that Ailsa mightn't be back at her desk before they arrived.

'You did, Jul. A Ms Corby, you said. Twelve o'clock. Where will you be?'

'At my desk.' For the first time she began to think of the mechanics of the visit. It would be hopeless receiving them in her office if George and Janet wanted to be in there too. 'God, Ailsa! Where can I talk to them that's private?'

'The professor's away for the day. You could use his room. I'm sure he wouldn't mind. He's so amenable.'

'Great idea. Thanks, Ailsa. You're certain he's not coming back?'

'He's in Birmingham. Rang from there ten minutes ago.'

'Perfect.'

'What's it all about, Jul?'

Julie ducked the answer by feigning an urgent need for the loo and diving into one of the cubicles. Then, when she heard the door bang with Ailsa's departure, she re-emerged and splashed water onto her face in a vain attempt to get rid of the shadows under her eyes. She'd hardly slept the last two nights. She dried her skin, ran a comb through her hair, then replaced her spectacles. Straightening her grey T-shirt and tucking the hem more tightly into her jeans, she returned to her office and began tidying papers. The professor ran a clean desk policy, which she, like the others in her office, tended to ignore.

Then the phone rang. Her visitors were here.

Sam had been dreading this meeting. There were no right words to say to the daughter of someone you'd watched being shot to death. The first thing he noticed as she walked towards them was that she was pretty. Shiny hair, wide cheekbones and a small mouth. None of her father's clown-faced looks.

'Miss Jackman?' The Vauxhall Cross woman held out her hand. 'Denise Corby from the Foreign Office.'

Sam let his companion take the lead. This was a head office show.

'And my colleague here,' she went on, turning to Sam, 'is a businessman. I asked him to come along with me because he was actually with your father when he died. They'd just had dinner together.'

'Oh!'

For the first time Julie felt she was about to cry. She searched the man's visage for some sign of his having been there – shock, sorrow, or just plain distress. But all she saw was a pleasant face despite the beard – which looked wrong on him – and a pair of kindly eyes.

'We're so sorry,' Corby whispered. 'You must have been terribly shocked.'

'Not quite sunk in,' she said.

'Of course not.'

They stood there in the entrance lobby, not moving, each waiting for the other to take the next step.

'Is there some place we can talk in private?' Corby prompted.

'Yes. Yes of course. I'm sorry.' Julie led them through the first set of swing doors. 'My boss, Professor Norton, he's away. We can use his office . . .' She ushered them into it. Apart from the virginally clean desk there was a small boardroom table with six chairs.

'What do you work on here, Miss Jackman?' Sam asked in an effort to normalise things. He closed the door behind them.

'HIV mostly. The hospitals in the group have four wards for AIDS patients.'

'Interesting work,' Denise Corby commented.

'Yes. It is.' As she lowered herself into a chair, Julie removed her spectacles and placed them on the table, an automatic action, done without thinking whenever a male registered on her personal radar. She felt drawn to this man, as if the fact that he'd been with her father in the last moments of his life had made him a part of hers.

'I'm sorry . . .' she said, looking at Sam's now slightly out-of-focus face. 'I didn't catch your name.'

'I'd rather keep my name out of it, if you don't mind,' he told her. 'I deal in a lot of confidential projects. Wouldn't be helpful if my competitors knew I'd been talking to your father.'

Julie felt rebuffed. Suddenly she wanted this business over with as quickly as possible.

'Would you tell me what happened exactly? It was at a road block, wasn't it? Soldiers?'

'Yes. Men in uniform, anyway. And wearing masks. Your father and I were driving back to his place for a night-cap. In two cars. He was in front. Suddenly a red light was waved in the road. We both braked. There were soldiers all around us. One of them stopped me short of where your father pulled up. The soldiers grabbed him from his car. I thought they wanted to search him for money, but instead they shot him. There was a gun at my head, so there was nothing I could do. I'm . . . I'm sorry.'

Julie shivered at his matter-of-fact description.

'But *why* did they kill him?' she asked, her voice breaking.

'That's what we're trying to find out,' Denise Corby told her, reaching across the table to comfort her.

Julie shuddered at the gesture and withdrew her own hand quickly.

'The police think it was robbery,' Sam told her. 'The soldiers took his car.'

'Which hasn't been found,' Corby added. 'There's always a market for Mercedes Benzes.'

Julie wiped her eyes. To die for a car was so horrible. 'Was it quick?' she whispered.

'I don't think he suffered,' Sam assured her. 'And you – your name – was the last thing that crossed his lips before he died.'

Suddenly the dam broke. The tears she'd been unable to weep since learning of the murder coursed down her cheeks. Her body shook uncontrollably. She buried her face in her hands. Denise Corby offered a tissue from a new pack in her bag, which Julie took gratefully. It was nearly a minute before she could speak again.

'It's just such a waste,' she said. 'I mean I never really knew what he thought about . . .' She was going to say 'me', but stopped herself in time. 'About *anything* . . .'

'I understand.' Denise Corby pulled a large notebook from her handbag. 'Would it be all right if I ask you some questions now?'

Julie nodded. 'Of course.'

Corby straightened her back and cleared her throat. 'First, if you don't mind, I'd like to know a little bit more about your relationship with your father.'

Sam raised his eyebrows, surprised by Corby's indirect approach. As far as he was concerned there was only one question that needed asking.

Julie recoiled. The big notebook. The inquisitorial stare. Suddenly this was an interrogation. 'How d'you mean?'

'Well, with him living in Africa and you in England, you can't have seen each other very often,' Corby continued.

'No. We didn't.' That much was obvious.

'You were pretty young when your parents' marriage broke up.'

'I was two.'

'So you would hardly have known him when you were small. How often did you actually see him?'

Julie wondered why this could possibly matter. 'I don't know. Once a year, perhaps.'

'You must have resented his abandoning you and your mother,' Corby suggested, in a ham-fisted attempt at being sympathetic.

Julie bristled. 'That's hardly any of your business.'

Sam wondered if departmental budget cuts had eaten into interview training for SIS desk officers.

'It's just that your father gave my colleague here the impression that you and he were really close,' Corby explained, steaming on regardless. 'I wondered if that's the way *you* saw it, that's all.'

Close? How could one be truly close to someone who was hardly ever there when you needed them? Julie squared her shoulders and directed her response at Sam.

'What *exactly* did dad say about me when he was dying?'

'He said he thought you were great,' Sam soothed, finessing the truth. 'I think he loved you very much.'

The tears came back. Julie turned away. 'Well . . .' she sniffed. She didn't want to talk about it, yet in a sense she did. 'People show their love in different ways, I suppose. His was mostly with a chequebook.'

Denise Corby hunched forward. 'Meaning?'

'Oh, I don't know,' she floundered, wishing she hadn't got into this. 'Meaning that I may not have seen him very often, but he did pay for me to go to a nice school. He funded me through university and . . . and he bailed me out when I was having personal problems.' The last part spilled out before she'd thought to stop herself.

'Personal problems?' Corby prodded. 'Would that have been to do with your becoming a single mother?'

Julie jerked bolt upright. 'You know about Liam?'

'It's on the file.'

Sam raised his eyes to the ceiling.

For the first time Julie began to wonder exactly who these people were. A chilly finger ran down her back, as if some unseen presence was warning her to take care. She was recalling a late night conversation with her father on his last visit home. Talk of his having got involved with MI6, saying they were people he didn't trust. He'd been rambling and she'd paid no heed to his words. But she vaguely remembered mention of letters he'd written about MI6, to be posted if something happened to him.

'How old would Liam be now?' Corby asked, softening her tone.

'Seven.'

'And your father helped with the boy. Financially?'

Again Julie wondered why it mattered. She hesitated, thought carefully, then told herself that she really had nothing to hide when it came to her son.

'Liam was a kind of catalyst for our family,' she explained. 'In a way, his birth brought my father back into my life. The bloke I'd been having a relationship with had dumped me, you see. In the same way that Dad had dumped my mother twenty years earlier.'

'History repeating itself,' Corby noted.

'That's what he felt. That he'd passed his own bad judgement about relationships on to me. There was more contact after that – letters, phone calls. And there'd been almost none before.'

'And in recent years?' Corby pressed. 'The letters continued? He was still writing you cheques?'

Julie bristled. 'Look, I earn my own living, right?' She snatched the spectacles from the table and put them back on. 'What *is* the point of all this?'

'I'm simply trying to establish how close you two were,' Corby pleaded. 'In order to judge how much you'd have known about his business activities.'

'Nothing,' Julie insisted. 'He never talked to me about his work.'

Denise Corby glanced at Sam as if to say *I told you so*. He took it as a cue to intervene.

'Julie . . . That evening I spent with your father, he had something on his mind.' Sam spoke gently. If she knew anything it would need to be coaxed from her. 'He hinted at it during dinner. Some business transaction he'd done that was troubling him. After he was shot he started telling me about it, but didn't get far. He was fading fast. But the very last thing he said was that *you* knew about it.'

'*What?*' Julie shivered, sensing that finger down her spine again. 'What was I supposed to know about?'

'Something to do with *red mercury*,' Corby interjected.

'What the hell's that?'

Sam sensed the girl's bafflement was genuine.

'Your father never talked to you about it?' Corby pressed.

'Never.'

'And he hasn't written to you about it recently?' Sam asked. 'He told me he'd prepared letters to be posted in the event of something happening to him. They haven't come your way?'

Julie frowned. 'Certainly not. Nothing like that at all.'

Sam sat back, arms folded, suddenly fearing he'd got it wrong.

'What *is* red mercury?' Julie asked, looking from one face to the other.

By the time Denise Corby finished explaining, Julie had understood precisely why these people had come hotfoot to see her.

'I can assure you I know nothing about it,' she repeated, looking hard at Sam.

He found her certainty puzzling. Jackman had been so definite that 'Julie knew'. All at once it dawned on him. The gun-runner must have meant she *would* know very soon. Because after he'd died a letter would be in the post to her. Posted from where? From Zambia might take an age. But if it was from London then it could have already arrived.

'Had the postman been before you left home this morning?' he asked.

Julie shook her head. 'He comes mid-morning.'

'You see I think your father *had* written to you about red mercury,' Sam suggested. 'Very recently. One of those letters that were to be sent after his death.'

'I doubt it. I told you. He never wrote about business,' Julie insisted.

Denise Corby cleared her throat. 'Nonetheless we'd better go back home with you in case it arrived this morning,' she announced, retaking control. 'You share a flat or live alone?'

'It's just a room,' Julie protested. 'In a grotty part of Acton. You can't seriously want to go there.'

Corby nodded.

'Just to see if the postman's brought anything? I can ring you this evening after work.'

'Please, Miss Jackman. It's in the national interest that you co-operate.'

National interest. Julie shivered. She felt certain by now that these people were to do with intelligence. 'I'll . . . I'll have to see if the lab can spare me,' she whispered, standing up.

'Do it now, please. We'll wait by the main door until you've got it sorted.'

Out in the corridor she hurried along to her own office. In reality she was playing for time. There'd be no problem about getting away for a couple of hours. What concerned her was the *real* reason these people had come. It had suddenly occurred to her that red mercury could be a red *herring*.

Her father had been drunk when he'd ranted about the untrustworthiness of MI6 a few months ago, and at the time she'd dismissed it as paranoia. But supposing it wasn't? What if her father had been on the point of exposing some of their dirty tricks when he died? What if *they'd* killed him? To silence him . . .

'Oh God . . .' Her mind was running away with itself.

Suppose a letter *had* arrived that morning? Her father relying on her to expose the dirt he'd been stopped from revealing.

She hovered by the door to her office, torn as to where her duty lay. The law-abiding half of her character told her she should assist these agents of the government. But the stronger half said that somehow she had to make damned sure they didn't get their hands on anything her father might have sent her.

3

D ENISE CORBY DROVE the Vectra west through the lunchtime traffic with Sam beside her in the front and their reluctant passenger in the back. Sam felt his neck prickling. The girl was no fool and he realised she was suspicious of them. She was different from what he'd imagined. He'd expected a creature with Harry Jackman's deviousness, yet he felt she'd been open with them so far. He cautioned himself not to judge her too kindly, however. He was attracted to her. Her compact sensuality and the flashes of feistiness she'd displayed in response to Denise's left-footed questioning had stirred up his hormones. And the tears. He was a sucker for tears.

Denise Corby drove for forty minutes before being directed from the back seat into a particularly dreary west London street.

'Beggars can't be choosers,' Julie apologised. 'Anywhere decent in London is prohibitively expensive, especially when you've a child to support. Liam doesn't like it when I buy his clothes at Oxfam.'

'The trainers are the worst, aren't they?' Denise replied. 'I've two kids of my own. Where do I stop?'

'Here on the right. The house with the broken washing machine out the front. The landlord's been promising to shift it for months.'

Julie's heart hammered as the Vectra pulled up. She had no idea how she was going to handle things if there *was* a letter from her father. She pushed open the car door and hurried towards the house, hoping to get in ahead of them and work some sleight of hand. The Yale lock played up however, and by the time she opened the front door the other two were beside her.

The hall was carpeted in blue cord and on a small, oak table the morning's mail had been laid out neatly by one of the other residents. Julie blocked their view until she was sure there was nothing for her.

'What did I tell you?' she said, shoulders sagging with relief. 'You've had a wasted journey.'

'Which is your flat?' Denise Corby asked, disregarding her remark.

Julie indicated a door at the far end of the hall.

'We'd like to see it.'

'I'd rather not. The place is a tip. I wasn't expecting visitors.'

'We're not fussy.'

'Well *I* am. Look. You wanted to know if there was a letter. There isn't. If there's one tomorrow or the day after, I'll ring you. Okay?'

'We'd like to see your flat please.' Denise Corby squared up to her like a rugby player.

Julie responded by jamming her hands onto her hips. 'Why?'

'To see if there's a letter from your father,' Corby snapped.

'Please, Julie,' Sam intervened, fearing the women were about to come to blows. 'It won't take long.'

Julie gave in – because it was the man who'd asked her, and she liked him. Liked him better than the Corby woman, anyway. And when men whom she liked asked her to do something, she tended to comply.

The bedsit was long and narrow, two small ground floor rooms knocked together. At one end was the sleeping space with a double bed and rumpled sheets. Julie walked over to it and jerked the duvet up to the pillows to tidy it. Beside the bed stood a wardrobe and a chest of drawers in bargain-basement pine. A panelled-off section in the corner contained a shower and toilet. At the other end of the room was a sitting area with a grey-covered sofa in a window bay facing the street. Halfway along stood a small dining table draped with a plastic cloth. Next to it a tiny kitchen alcove, its draining board stacked with unwashed plates.

Julie stood with her back to the cooker, pushed her spectacles onto the bridge of her nose, then folded her arms.

'As I told you, I just sleep here,' she repeated, trying to excuse the mess. 'It's dirt cheap. My money goes on Liam.'

'You see your little boy every weekend?' Corby asked, with what passed for maternal interest.

'Yes. And during the week if there's a problem.' Julie told herself to control her anger. She had nothing to hide. She opened a cupboard to see what she could offer in the way of a drink. Nothing. She'd forgotten to shop.

'I'm afraid I'm out of coffee,' she mumbled.

'That doesn't matter. We'll just do a quick search.'

'There isn't a letter,' she told them.

'Then it won't take long, will it?'

Sam considered that for someone who a few hours ago had been dismissing Harry Jackman's red mercury as 'delirium', Denise Corby was taking her investigating role remarkably seriously. It was a power thing with her, he decided.

'You know you've no right to invade my privacy like this,' Julie protested.

'I could get a warrant very quickly . . .' Corby told her.

Sam winced. It was a lie. A magistrate would probably refuse.

'God!' Julie's mouth set in a thin angry line. 'And people think we live in a free country . . .'

'It's because people make threats to that freedom that we have to act high-handedly at times,' Corby stated primly.

Julie pictured her in court, sitting in a judge's seat with a silly wig on.

'Then get it over with,' she snapped. 'And quickly, because my work is important both to me and to the people in the lab, and I want to get back to it.'

'Of course. We'll be as quick as we can.'

'Sorry about this,' Sam mumbled as he followed Denise Corby towards the sleeping end of the room.

When the woman started fingering the bedclothes, Julie felt sick. She watched her pillow and mattress being checked, then saw the hands feeling through the sheets and the duvet. *God!* What did they think she was up to?

Sam opened the top drawer of the chest.

'Hang on a minute,' Julie scowled. 'I thought you said you were a businessman?'

'That's right.' Sam smiled uncomfortably. He'd moved without thinking.

'Then how come you're involving yourself in all this police-state activity?'

'Just trying to hurry things along,' he rejoined sheepishly. 'I realise how unpleasant this must be for you.'

Julie wanted to believe him. To feel that *someone* here was on her side. But when he began his search of the chest by putting his hands in amongst her underwear she angrily turned her head away. The two were a pair. As bad as each other.

Sam hesitated. The girl was right to be incensed at what they were doing, but it was a job and he couldn't afford sympathy. He pushed aside tights, pants and bras to see if they concealed anything.

They did. An opened packet of fruit-flavoured condoms.

He glanced towards the girl again, just as she spun back to face him. Her glare warned him that passing comment on his little discovery wouldn't be wise. He moved quickly on to the next level – pullovers and T-shirts – idly wondering whether she had a regular lover or if the prophylactics were for chance encounters.

The bottom drawer was empty. He closed it and turned his attention to the wardrobe. A couple of pairs of trousers dangled next to a skimpy black dress. The clothes smelled of cigar smoke. On the floor were some trainers

34

and a Chinese lacquer box. He took it out and set it down on top of the chest. When he opened the lid music tinkled. Swan Lake.

Suddenly Julie propelled herself towards him. 'That's private,' she snapped. She grabbed the box from him and banged the lid down. The music stopped.

'We'll need to see inside,' he told her apologetically.

'*We*,' she mimicked. 'Some *businessman*.'

'Please don't be difficult.'

'I said it's private,' she repeated. This whole process was beginning to feel like rape.

'Tell you what,' he suggested gently, 'why don't *you* take the stuff out while I watch? It's a nice box, by the way.'

'No it's not,' she retorted. 'It's cheap tat. But my dad gave it to me for my twelfth birthday . . .'

'Then I can understand why it matters so much to you.'

Julie had been given it full of emeralds, but she wasn't going to tell *them* that. The stones weren't worth anything. Chippings from the mines her father had said, but to her they'd been jewels worthy of a princess. Today they were in a muslin bag at her mum's house for Liam to play with.

'Please,' Sam pressed. 'It's important.'

After a few more moments she relented. Despite her certainty by now that he worked for the same organisation as the Corby woman, he had a totally different way about him. It was his eyes. There was a hazel softness about them that made her think of old cardigans.

As she opened the lid, the music tinkled again, imperfectly. Some of the notes were broken through excessive use. She took out the photographs and old letters that were faded with age, then replaced them in the box one by one as if dealing cards. One of the envelopes looked thicker than the others.

'May I?' He reached in to take it.

'That letter's years old.'

She was right. The Zambian postmark said 1989.

'From your father?'

'Yes. He sent it to me when I went to college. He wrote to say how proud he was.'

Sam checked it cursorily then dropped the letter back in the box. 'What did you study?'

'Biology.'

'Of course. Hence your work.'

The last items were snapshots which she replaced in rapid succession, as if wanting to gloss over the years they represented.

'Who's that?' Sam pointed to a picture of a young man with long dark hair and a leather jacket.

'Liam's father,' she told him curtly. 'Brendan.'

'Not still around?'

'No.'

'There's someone else?' he asked idly. 'Some other bloke?'

'Mind your own business.'

Sam watched her close the box. As she bent down to replace it on the floor of the wardrobe, her shoulder-length hair fell forward to reveal a neck as slender as a child's. Creamy white skin with soft, cirrus cloud tufts at the nape. He was in love.

He looked up to find Denise glaring, as if she'd caught him doing something disgusting behind the bike sheds. She marched over to them, questioning Julie about whether her father had been in the habit of leaving papers at her mother's place.

'For safekeeping. Legal documents. That sort of thing.'

'Never seen any. At the bank, maybe. He had an account at Barclays in Ipswich.'

'But there might be letters at the house in Woodbridge, even if you've never seen them?'

'It's possible,' Julie wavered, dreading going through a repeat performance of this.

'We'd like you to accompany us there,' Corby announced. 'To Woodbridge.'

'What, *now*?' Julie turned to Sam, hoping to play him off against the woman, but he averted his eyes. 'I'll need to ring the lab,' she stated testily. 'I don't have a phone here, but there's a callbox on the corner.'

'You can ring from the car, if you like,' Sam told her, pleased to be having her company for a little longer. 'I'll lend you my mobile.'

Julie rubbed her temples. 'Hang on a minute. It's the weekend coming up. I'll be staying on at Woodbridge, which means packing a bag.'

'Five minutes long enough for you?' Denise offered.

'I suppose.'

'We'll wait outside in the car.'

As they emerged from the house, a black teenager was pushing a buggy along the cracked pavement with a grizzling child in it. She didn't look up. Denise unlocked the Vectra and they sat inside.

'Better get their mail intercepted from tomorrow,' she fretted. 'But what a waste of time. There is no red mercury, Sam.'

He didn't reply. There *was* a point to it all. Because whatever Harry Jackman had been trading in, it had put him in fear of his life.

4

IT WAS JUST before midnight when Sam paid off the cab a few hundred yards from his rented flat overlooking the river at Brentford. He never let a taxi drive him right up to the door. These days he was super-conscious of security after having to move from his old home down the river because of the keen interest shown in him by a hit squad. The vehicle swung in a U-turn back towards central London where Denise Corby had dropped him twenty-five minutes earlier. As the head office woman had predicted, the visit to Woodbridge had proved a waste of time.

The house where Harry Jackman's first wife lived was in a recently converted sailmaker's loft on the Deben estuary, an upmarket development with most of the apartments owned by weekenders. They'd found no letters there relating to red mercury, a pair of words as meaningless to Julie's mother as they'd been to Julie herself.

The Jackman home had been modest in size, three bedrooms, a decent living room, a playroom and a kitchen. Seven-year-old Liam had had an attractive, curly-haired wildness about him. He'd flung himself at his mother as soon as she opened the front door and refused to leave her in peace until she settled on the sofa and read him a story. Sam had liked the way Julie had been with the boy. They'd shared a sense of belonging. Of being integral to each other's life. Sam had felt pangs of jealousy watching them. They had something he didn't.

Mrs Maeve Jackman had the same wide cheekbones as her daughter. With the docility of a woman well used to having her life messed about, she'd shown them around her home, letting them delve into anything they wanted. She'd behaved with a patent honesty which neither Sam nor Denise Corby had been inclined to doubt. If Harry Jackman had written them a letter explaining red mercury, then it was still in the post.

There'd been rain in the last few hours and the Brentford air smelled of it. He could see the vaulted roof of the apartment block where he lived, towering over a pub at a bend in the road. He pulled the phone from his pocket and dialled the number of his flat. The answerphone voice that cut in was not his. Security had prepared the tape for him, rapper style, complete with funky music. Sam pressed four numbers in quick succession and the tape stopped. He heard a hum and then a digitised voice telling him the intruder alarm had detected no motion in the flat since the day he left it nearly a week ago. He put the phone away, walked on briskly and let himself into the building.

The plane from Lusaka had been full last night and he'd found it hard to sleep. By now he was dog tired. He dumped his suitcase on the floor of his bedroom, deciding to wait until the morning before unpacking it.

A drink was what he needed most urgently. He opened the cocktail cabinet that was an integral part of the rented flat's furnishings, scowling as it struck up a tune. One day when he found the time, he would work out how to kill it. He poured himself a good measure of whisky and water, then took the tumbler to the picture window overlooking the river. The apartment block was just upstream from Kew Bridge. Directly below it, cormorants nested. Beyond the far bank lay the botanical gardens. The residence had been designed for the smart and the well-heeled and he felt out of place in it. He'd moved here two months ago because of its security arrangements – electronic gates and security guards. For the past couple of years there'd been many changes of address for him as he'd kept ahead of those intent on killing him. He tossed back the whisky and poured himself another. Two shots would be enough to put him to sleep.

He switched on Sky News, just to make sure the world hadn't come to an end while he'd been chasing phantoms in Suffolk. A tedious piece about some spat in the House of Commons was followed by a report on Kosovo. He sat down to watch. The newscaster revealed new UN figures estimating that 300,000 Kosovars had been driven from their homes by the Serbs' summer offensive and had taken refuge in the mountains. The video showed wide-eyed children and weeping grannies. He pitied them. There'd be no quick solution to their problems.

The report turned its focus to one ethnic Albanian family that had decided to seek a better life outside their homeland. Sky would be following their progress, the reporter declared, as they searched for asylum in western Europe. Sam winced. Good TV, pulling at the heartstrings, but he hated the kind of journalism that flipped the minds of politicians, driving them to react with emotion rather than sense.

The phone rang, startling him. He looked at his watch. It was well after midnight. He wasn't used to calls this late, not since the days of Chrissie, when she would ring in the middle of the night to say she'd escaped from her husband again and wanted to share his bed for a couple of hours. He switched off the TV and snatched up the receiver.

'Yes?'

'Sorry about the late hour.' Sam recognised the Ulster growl of his controller. 'But I understand from our mutual friend that you've only just got back.' The diligent Denise Corby had reported in already.

'What's up?' He could tell from the background noise that Waddell was in his car.

'We need to talk.'

'In the morning?'

'No. Right now. You know where.'

'Well, yes.' They had a rota of locations for short-notice meetings. 'You sure it can't wait?' Stupid question.

'Absolutely. See you there in five.'

'If you say so.'

Sam crossed the wood-block floor to the window again, wondering. He guessed that some new mission must have come up. A flight back to Africa first thing in the morning, with Jackman's red mercury being left to the Vauxhall Cross pen-pushers to follow up – if they bothered.

Outside, the night sky was clear. A half-moon cast a silvery reflection on the water. The aircraft which at peak times filed past every ninety seconds on their way into Heathrow had stopped for a few hours to let those on the flight path sleep. Sam finished his whisky and patted his trouser pocket for his keys. He switched on the TV again, pushing the button for channel O, the security camera concealed outside his front door. It showed the landing to be empty.

He took the lift to the underground garage, and unlocked his Mondeo estate. His inclination was for older, more characterful machines, but the 1984 Mercedes which he'd owned for many years had had to be sold, along with his share in a 31-foot Moody sloop and several other trappings of his former life. All in the interests of preventing the Odessa mafiya picking up his trail.

At the garage exit gate he swiped a security card and the pole lifted. The Kew Gardens car park which was this week's meeting place was a couple of minutes away, just the other side of the river. The traffic over Kew Bridge was light but fast moving. He stuck himself in the right-hand lane with his indicator going, praying that the nocturnal boy racers who touched sixty over the bridge would spot him in time before running into his boot. If the cops breathalysed him it would be he who got the blame.

He turned onto Kew Green past the beautifully preserved Georgian houses, then hooked right into the lane running parallel to the river which ended in a large parking area for visitors to the Gardens. Packed during the day in the summer, there were just two cars there now. Lovers or dog-walkers, he decided. He drove to the far end, turned the headlamps towards the river and switched off.

In less than a minute another car swept in, its lights blazing in the Mondeo's mirrors as it pulled up behind. It was a warm night. When Waddell slid silently onto the passenger seat of the Mondeo, he was dressed in a white T-shirt and blue jeans. Sam stared in bemusement. He'd seldom seen his controller without a tie.

'What's this? Come here to cruise?'

'Fuck off. I was at a barbecue at my sister's place.'

'Nice for you.'

'Would have been if I hadn't been hit by a call from Washington just as I was leaving the office.'

'Red mercury?'

'No way,' he scoffed. 'No. A different matter altogether.'

Sam waited for him to continue, but he didn't.

'You're going to tell me?'

Slowly Waddell turned sideways in the seat, his head backed against the window. 'You're not going to like this, Sam. It's to do with your father.'

'My *father*? But he died when I was eleven. Brain tumour.'

'I know. Trevor Patrick Packer,' Waddell intoned. '1931–1971. At the time of his death he was a chief petty officer in the Royal Navy submarine service. On HMS *Retribution*.'

'A Polaris missile boat,' Sam interjected, baffled as to what this was about.

'The starboard crew, whatever that means.'

'They had two crews on the bombers,' Sam explained uneasily. 'Took it in turns to man the boat. That way they could maximise the time the hardware was at sea. So what?'

Waddell paused momentarily.

'The Americans think your old man passed secrets to the Russians.'

Sam gaped into the gloom, thinking he must have misheard.

'Bollocks.'

For a moment he suspected Waddell was laughing at him. That this was some sort of practical joke.

'You're not serious?'

'The Yanks are.'

'Then they need their brains examined. Where's this crap come from?'

'From the Russians, Sam,' Waddell told him. 'Or rather from one particular ex-GRU officer who's just been given an American passport. The quid pro quo was a file full of intelligence on what the Sovs knew about British and American naval operations in the seventies and eighties.

I tell you, over in the States they're having heart failure. Two retired US admirals were arrested yesterday.'

'Jesus.' Sam felt poleaxed. 'But this is crap, Duncan. Utter crap. My old man was as proud as punch of the submarines he served on. He would never have betrayed his country, or his mates.'

Waddell didn't comment. They both knew that when it came to spying, appearances and reality could be very different.

'What does Five say about this?' Sam demanded.

'Too early. They've only just been briefed,' Waddell told him. 'What do *you* say, more's the point?'

'I've told you. It's rubbish.'

'Did you ever wonder about him?'

'Don't be daft. I was a kid. What eleven-year-old suspects his father of spying?'

'You don't remember odd visitors at home? Men with funny accents coming round for tea and walking away with brown envelopes?'

'Do me a favour, Duncan. This is a joke. Isn't it?'

'The funny accents, yes. But for the rest, it's deadly serious. We need to get to the bottom of it.'

'You're talking twenty-seven years ago,' Sam protested. 'Were there any suspicions at the time?'

'None at all.'

'Well, there you are.'

'Och, all that does is suggest the buggers got away with it.'

'Or that it never bloody happened.'

'The Russians had your dad's name on file, Sam. You think they plucked it out of thin air?'

Sam turned to stare through the windscreen. The moon was to their left, its soft light picking out a shape moving along the towpath, a couple, clinging so closely together that they made a single outline.

'So what's being done about this nonsense?' Sam blustered.

'The Security Service are going to start trawling tomorrow. Tracking down people who worked alongside your father.'

'Fucking madness,' Sam hissed.

'Whatever . . . It needs clearing up.' Waddell tapped a hand on the dashboard. 'For the *Service's* sake.'

Sam sensed some threatening edge to Waddell's voice. 'What are you talking about, Duncan?'

'You're his son. And the firm employs you.'

'So?'

'It makes certain people in the firm's upper layers a little uncomfortable, that's all.'

'Because some nutcase has accused my father of being a traitor? For Christ's sake, that doesn't make me one.'

Waddell shifted in his seat.

'On the top floor they think in headlines, Sam. Negative stories that could hit the newspapers. If it leaked out about your father, and the press started asking what his son does for a living . . .'

'Why should it leak out?'

'Our American cousins. Anything to distract attention from the scandal within their own Navy.' He tapped his fingers together. 'Any of your family know how you earn your crust?'

'My sister has some idea,' Sam croaked. 'Nothing specific.'

'Well stick some tape across her mouth and take her phone away . . .'

'You're getting hysterical, Duncan.'

'No I'm not. This could go horribly wrong. And it could happen fast. I want you to sniff around. Go back to the time when you were ten or eleven and see what you can find there. With a bit of luck we can strangle the whole thing at birth. Your mother, she's still alive?'

'Died five years ago. There's nothing left of that time, Duncan,' Sam sighed, 'except what's in my head.'

'Nevertheless, go and look. See your sister and shut her up. Make some excuse to contact your parents' old friends. Give me a ring in a couple of days to let me know how you're getting on.'

'And Harry Jackman's so-called red mercury?'

'It's going nowhere. The man lived a fantasy life half the time. If anything does come up, Denise can sort it.' He reached for the door release. 'I'm going home now. It's been a long day.'

'Back to the barbecue?'

'Oh sure. Ashes to ashes.' Waddell fumbled for the handle, conscious of a bad choice of words. 'Don't take it hard about your father. Life's full of surprises and they can't all be nice ones.' He got out. 'Ring me,' he said before clicking the door shut.

Sam heard Waddell's car start up. The headlamps dazzled again and then swung away. For several minutes he stayed where he was, sinking lower into the seat.

It wasn't true. It simply couldn't be. His father was no traitor. And if the firm was hoping to avoid trouble, they were looking the wrong bloody way. Harry Jackman was the man to watch out for, the one who'd bring sleepless nights to the top floor of Vauxhall Cross.

5

London
Saturday, 08.10 hrs

O N THE OTHER side of the capital from where Sam Packer had his flat,
stood a cluster of 1960s apartment blocks whose occupants were on
far more modest incomes than those with a view over the river at Kew.

On the twelfth floor of one of them, a tower that had never lived up
to its name of Windsor Court, a computer screen flickered in the corner
of the small, plain living room. The man hunched in front of it checking
his e-mail had short hair and a face dominated by a broad, putty-soft nose.
He shot a nervous glance at the time icon, needing to be out of the flat
before his girlfriend returned from her hospital night shift. Fifteen minutes
to go. The last of his four anonymous mailboxes reported empty. There was
no message from 'Peter' calling off the job. Half of him had been hoping
for one.

Rob Petrie logged off, shut down the PC and stood up. He had a broad
chest and narrow hips, which gave him a top-heavy look. Normally a neat
dresser obsessed with looking clean and spruce, today he wore old jeans and
a T-shirt bought at a charity shop to help him pass unnoticed in a crowd.
He was tense. Very tense. A tension that bordered on fear.

He knew he had to eat something if his brain was to keep alert. At
the breakfast bar in the tiny kitchen he filled a bowl with cornflakes, but
halfway through eating he gave up. Butterflies. He checked his watch. 8.15.
Sandra would appear at half-past on the dot, her blue uniform crumpled and
stained, smelling of the geriatrics she spent her nights watching over. He'd
told her it would be kinder to gas the old crapbags. Five minutes and he
needed to be out of here. She might be early, although she never was.

He shoved the bowl under the tap and left it to drain, then banged open
the door to the toilet – his second session of the morning. Nerves.

At twenty-two minutes past he was out of the front door and onto the
open landing. As he walked along it, he glanced down at the grass and

43

concrete a hundred feet below where children would be playing before long. For most people in the block, Saturday morning meant a lie-in, so when he reached the end of the passageway the lift came quickly and was empty.

Eighty households in Windsor Court, all nursing secrets behind their draughty aluminium-framed windows. Some with children, some just couples, few of them married. It wasn't a place Petrie would have chosen to live, but the loss of his job in the City eighteen months ago had left him no choice. Sandra was the breadwinner now. £16,000 a year, she earned, a tenth of what he'd made before the Jews he'd worked for had booted him out. She claimed not to mind being the provider, saying they'd managed to stick together in the good times, so they could do it in the bad. But *he* had a problem with it. Failure to find another City job had wrecked his confidence – in all aspects of his life. Sandra was suggesting Viagra.

Amongst the occupants of the block were a few Afro-Caribbean families and a handful of Asians, but most of the residents were white. He stepped from the lift and walked briskly across the open yard. Few people about, which was a relief. On the far side was a row of lockups where he kept his car, a twelve-year-old Escort. The garage door swung up on its weights. He checked that the Tesco bag was still on the back seat, together with the baseball cap and dark glasses. He'd prepared the gear last night after Sandra had gone to work.

He started up and drove into the daylight, then got out and closed the door, telling himself that if he left the garage open some nigger would come and piss in it. He headed west, keeping carefully to the speed limits. The last thing he needed today was for a dutiful plod to feed his number into the Police National Computer. His path cut across London – Angel, Euston, Baker Street, then out past Hangar Lane onto the A4. At the Polish War Memorial by Northolt airport he turned left, cutting through into the heart of Southall.

His skin began to prickle. Every face here was Asian. Men with turbans, women swirling in synthetic silks. He could smell the curry spices through the car's ventilation system. Another country in everything but name, a part of England which the criminals in government had allowed to turn foreign. It angered him, seeing the state of the place, which did him good, giving him the bottle for what he had to do next.

He drove the Escort into a parking area behind the High Street, tugged the baseball cap down on his head and jammed the dark glasses onto his face. On this day in history, his leader had told him in the e-mail he'd received a week ago, all across Europe, people would be standing up for their heritage. This was the day when the fight back started, the moment when the streets would begin to be reclaimed by those they belonged to.

He got out, locked the doors, then, with the Tesco bag dangling from his right fist, he set off towards the street market.

Brentford
09.25 hrs

It had been another bad night for Sam Packer. Instead of sleeping, his restless mind had relived the day twenty-seven years ago when his father died. It had been early July 1971. Looking forward to the summer holidays, he'd come home from school to find his dad on the living room floor, grey and gaunt, mouth agape, eyes glassy and still. Then the district nurse had appeared. Fat, professional fingers closing the lids on the face that looked so different from the chirpy grinner in the black-and-white wedding snap that was framed in silver and anchored to the tiled mantelpiece in their Fareham living room. A uniformed sailor with his self-conscious bride.

Sam had managed to switch off those memories eventually and had dozed a little in the early hours, a light sleep quickly broken by an early Jumbo at 4.35. He'd got up soon after seven, pummelled his brain under the power jets in the gold-tapped shower cubicle, dressed in pale cotton trousers and a polo shirt, then breakfasted on fruit and scrambled eggs at the smoked-glass table in the marble-floored living room. The glitz of the place – he hated it. It wasn't his style.

When his father died he'd felt abandoned, left to the mercies of a bitter mother and an elder sister who despised boys – a sister whose attitude to him had changed little over the years and whom he now had to visit. He'd rung her a few minutes ago to say he was going to be in the area and might drop in. Dead casual. No hint of why, on the basis that an enemy unprepared was easier to overcome.

He packed an overnight bag, because he wasn't sure where this delving into the past would lead him, and was on the point of setting off for Hampshire when the phone rang.

''Lo?' he grunted.

'Oh good. You're back.' A woman's voice, strong and jolly, which he recognised immediately.

'Steph! How are you doing?'

Stephanie Watson. A detective chief inspector with Special Branch, a woman who'd become as close to him as any female could expect to get, short of getting physically intimate.

'I'm doing well, thanks,' she told him cheerily. 'Ringing to ask if you fancied a game of tennis? Gerry's away for a few days and I'm feeling frisky.' Gerry was the new man she'd hitched up with a couple of months ago.

'Oh, Steph! Under normal circumstances I'd take huge pleasure in knocking you around the court, but unfortunately I can't. Something's come up.'

'Something to your taste? In a skirt?'

'Sadly not. Family problems.'

'Oh. Sorry.'

'Don't be. It's probably nothing. But I need to make sure.'

'Sounds intriguing.' She was canny enough not to press for details.

'But later in the week perhaps?' Sam checked. 'Or maybe a lunch?'

'You're joking! Don't get time for a sandwich these days. But I could face a curry one evening. Midweek, say?'

'You mean Gerry'll give you time off?'

'I told you. He's away.' The flatness in her voice made him wonder for a moment if 'away' meant her new man had walked out on her.

'A curry would be great,' he told her. 'Give you a ring in a couple of days?'

'I'll look forward to it. Might even challenge you to a vindaloo.'

'No chance,' he growled. 'You know my preferences. A flaming arsehole cramps my style with the boys.'

Stephanie laughed. 'You're so disgusting, you could be a copper. See you later in the week.'

'Bye.'

He knew that in many ways Stephanie was precisely the sort of woman he ought to pick as a partner. She was clever, witty and level-headed. Their minds sparred beautifully, but they'd never clicked physically. For a woman she was on the stocky side and he liked them more girlish. Gerry, her new man and an Armed Response Team officer, was the right size for her. Six foot two with the build of a bouncer.

Sam grabbed his mobile phone and his wallet. He went through the routine of monitoring the security camera, then let himself out of the flat. Down in the underground garage he noticed some of the light bulbs had failed, casting dark shadows amongst the line-up of German-made cars. He made a mental note to get the caretaker to fix them, then drove up the ramp and over Kew Bridge, heading for the M3 motorway.

He had no clear plan for the day, apart from the need to visit his sister. Beryl, married to a naval scientist and well settled in an estate outside Portsmouth, was the custodian of all their father's paperwork. It would be an uncomfortable meeting, the first since their mother's funeral five years ago.

The traffic was heavy heading for the coast, families making the most of one of the few sunny weekends of that bleak, wet summer. He turned off the motorway and took the Meon valley road through the Hampshire countryside, passing rain-flattened wheat fields and the lush green parks of old mansions.

His father had been serving on a diesel boat in the year of his birth, a Porpoise class submarine based in Gosport. Away at sea for months at a time, he'd missed his son's coming into the world, an absence his wife had never forgiven him for.

Fareham where they'd lived was an overspill town for Portsmouth. Sam found his way easily at first, driving through the housing estates as if on autopilot. But when he entered his old road it all looked different. The houses had been upgraded with B&Q doors and coach-lamp porch lights. To identify his old home he had to check the house numbers. It was odd seeing it again. Everything looked smaller than he'd remembered. Staring up at the window of his one-time bedroom, he shivered as he remembered the chill there'd been in that house when his father wasn't there.

He wasn't sure what he'd expected to find. Today's residents of the estate were not from his time. They all looked so young. Not much more than teenagers but with small children snapping at their heels. His own mother, one of the last of her generation to move, had left ten years ago for her sister's in Southsea. There was nothing to see here, and what there was, he didn't want to look at.

He switched on again and drove down the road, then took the A32 north for a few miles before turning onto the high down that overlooked Portsmouth. His sister's husband worked in a windswept Admiralty research centre perched on the ridge. Sam had met him a few times. The quiet type. Beryl liked her men docile.

Four years older than Sam, Beryl lived with Jim and their two girls in a modern house of dark brick. He found his way to their village and through the estate, passing homes with tricycles and speedboats in their drives. Outside number 12 Magnolia Close a teenager's bike lay on the lawn and a trug full of weeds blocked the path. The front door was open. Sam switched off and got out. As he stepped over the basket a figure emerged from the house wearing gardening gloves.

'Well, bless my soul!'

Thinning fair hair brushed back, metal-framed glasses and a long thin nose, Beryl's husband was shorter than Sam. He wore old cords and a blue check shirt.

'Hello, Jim.'

'Nice to see you, Sam.' Jim Butterworth pulled off a glove and reached out his hand. His voice had a touch of Hampshire about it. 'What a surprise!'

'Beryl didn't mention I rang?'

'No. Must've slipped her mind,' Jim said charitably.

'Well, I was in the area so I thought I'd try my luck. High time and all that . . .'

'Absolutely. How are you?'

'Fine. Just fine. And you?'

'Oh, you know. Rubbing along. Come on in.'

Sam's sister emerged from the hall. She'd put on weight but it had done little to soften the pinched, disapproving expression she'd inherited from her mother. She wore green shorts, revealing pasty legs that had lost their once decent shape.

'Well . . .' she grunted. 'So there you are.'

They made no attempt to embrace and went into the kitchen. The children were summoned to say hello to this uncle they'd seldom seen. Two girls, aged twelve and fourteen, both quite pretty, studied him with idle curiosity.

'Still no wife in tow?' Beryl enquired, peering theatrically towards the door. 'You *would* have invited us to the wedding . . .'

'I imagine I might have done. No. I'm not married.'

Sam didn't want them probing into his life. He'd come here for one reason only.

'So . . . to what do we owe this pleasure?' Beryl asked, perching her hands on her ample hips. She had the same wiry hair as Sam, but it had been cut short in a style like a teacosy.

'As I said, I was just in the area,' Sam explained uncomfortably. He couldn't broach the subject in front of the girls.

'Oh no you weren't.' She turned to the sink to fill a kettle. 'Dropping in isn't your style. You're after something. I take it you'd like some coffee now you're here?'

'That'd be nice. Thanks.'

The girls took it as their cue to go back to whatever they were doing. Sam gave them a smile.

'So? How's things?' Beryl asked when she'd plugged in the kettle.

'Not bad. Not bad.'

'Your work still all hush-hush?' She tried to make it sound inconsequential, but he knew that she was rather in awe of what he did.

'That's right.'

'Travel a lot, do you?' Jim chipped in.

'Now and then.'

'Nice for you.'

Beryl put custard creams on the kitchen table and they all sat round it. There was silence for a few moments.

'Come on Sam. Spit it out,' Beryl told him. They watched him expectantly.

'It's to do with our father.'

Beryl blanched. 'Our *father?* But he's been dead nearly thirty years.'

Sam stood up and crossed to the kitchen door, checking that the girls weren't in earshot. Then he closed it.

'Something odd's come up,' he told them, sitting down again and keeping his voice low. 'Bit of a bombshell. And it's highly confidential. Not the sort of thing to be talked about with children or friends.'

'Sam! Don't be so mysterious. What's happened?'

'Well . . . the Russians are claiming he spied for them.'

Jim and Beryl's mouths sagged and their eyes became saucers. Neither of them spoke.

'A former Soviet military intelligence officer who's defected to the United States has handed over a list of people they recruited back in the 1970s,' Sam explained. 'And Dad's name was on it.'

Beryl covered her mouth. Jim was the first to speak.

'Lordy . . .'

'No,' Beryl reasoned, shaking her head. 'That can't be right.'

'That's what I said,' Sam told her. 'It's a mistake. Has to be.'

'Whatever our father was, he wasn't a spy,' she went on heavily. 'He lived for the Navy. Put it above everything else. Particularly his own damned family,' she stressed, her voice rising in pitch. 'He went to sea, came home, patted his beloved little boy on the head, ignored his wife and daughter, bedded a handful of women he wasn't married to, then went to sea again.'

Sam closed his eyes at this familiar litany of complaint. 'You've only got our mother's word for the other women,' he told her defensively.

'And when did she ever lie?'

Sam groaned inwardly. His conversations with Beryl always went this way.

'Well . . . whatever he did in his spare time, he wasn't a spy and I intend to prove it,' he told her, determined not to be sidetracked.

'Quite right too,' said Jim, his brow furrowing. 'But how?'

'I don't know yet.'

Beryl's complexion was turning a blotchy red and her eyes had become dark dots of anger. 'I simply don't believe it,' she hissed.

'No. Nor do I,' said Sam.

'No!' she squealed. 'You, Sam, you! That's what I don't believe. I do not understand how you can sit there and say we only have mother's word for his womanising.'

Jim rolled his eyes and passed a hand across his face.

'You're missing the point Beryl,' Sam soothed.

'Oh no I'm not. The man was a lecher. And after all these years you're still defending him. *That's* the point.'

'*Lecher* is a bit over the top, Beryl. Anyway the charge is spying. And at this particular moment nothing else matters.'

'Oh yes it does. The trouble with you is that you're just like him,' she countered. 'One woman in your life has never been enough for you, has it?'

'Bee . . .' Jim's pained expression said he'd heard far too many of these outbursts.

'Look, forget about women,' Sam growled. 'I came here to warn you.' He wanted to be gone from here. 'The press may get on to you. If they do, say nothing about my work, understand? If anyone wants to know what it is I do, say it's import-export.'

'We understand, Sam,' Jim assured him. 'Don't worry. We know the rules.'

Sam took in a deep breath. 'There is one other reason I came here.'

'Ah. I knew it,' Beryl snorted.

'You've got some things of his. A tin box with old passports, service documents, driving licences and so on.'

'Went years ago,' Beryl snapped, her face scarlet.

Her husband turned to her. 'Isn't it in the . . . ?'

'I said it's gone,' she yelled. 'Chucked out. Mother kept it under her bed when she moved in with her sister. God knows why she hung on to it when she hated him so much.'

'And after she died all those oddments came to you,' Sam reminded her. 'When did you throw them out, Beryl?' He was losing patience.

'I really don't remember,' she said vapidly. 'We have clear-outs from time to time. Most *families* do.'

She stressed the word to emphasise the abnormality of his single state.

'That box was all that was left of him,' Sam snapped.

Jim half stood. 'You know, I do have a feeling that . . .'

Beryl cut him off with a slicing movement of her arm, but her husband persisted.

'I am pretty sure that tin box is in the loft,' he declared.

'Well *you* must have put it there,' Beryl charged. 'Because *I* certainly didn't.'

'Quite possibly,' Jim mumbled.

Her pinprick eyes fixed Sam with loathing. 'You are so disgustingly like him, you know. Particularly with that beard which doesn't suit you *at* all. How long have you had that . . . that dreadful fuzz?'

'A couple of years.' Odd how he'd forgotten that his father had been bearded once. He'd been clean shaven in the wedding photo.

'And this is typical, of course,' Beryl added, her voice rising to a yell. 'Your turning up like this. It's only because you want something. Not to see us. Not because you're interested in how your nieces are doing. *Exactly* like Dad. He really was a prize shit, you know.'

Her husband sighed. 'Leave it out, Bee, for God's sake.'

Sam held back, startled by his sister's virulence. She was displaying signs of mental instability. Upstairs he heard a door slam and guessed it was the children shutting out a noise they'd come to hate.

As tears filled her eyes, Jim put an arm round her shoulders and rocked her gently, grimacing an apology to Sam. 'Bee . . .' he cooed.

'Oh, give him his damned tin box for heaven's sake and then he can go,' Beryl gulped.

Jim stood up and beckoned Sam to follow him upstairs. On the upper landing he opened an airing cupboard and brought out a boat-hook which he used to pull down a ladder concealed above the hatch to the loft.

'Shan't be a mo,' he said, handing Sam the hook. 'Hold this, would you?'

He shinned up the ladder and reached up to the rafters, fumbling for a light switch. Then he hoisted himself into the roof space, emerging half a minute later with a black metal deed box. He turned it over to show the initials on the lid. T.P.P. – Trevor Patrick Packer.

Sam took it from him. There was a key in the lock, but it wouldn't turn.

'I'll drench that in WD40,' Jim told him, gingerly descending. He patted his hands to shake off the dust, then pushed the sliding ladder back into the cavity. 'It's in the garage.'

Sam followed him downstairs. Glancing into the kitchen, he saw the door to the back garden was open.

'This way,' said Jim, leading him out through the front. He eased up the garage door weights and rummaged on a tool shelf next to the small, green Rover parked there. He took the box from Sam and squirted oil into the keyhole until the mechanism freed up.

'There you are,' he said, handing it back.

Sam opened the lid to check it was the material he'd remembered.

'Thanks, Jim.'

His sister's husband took his arm and hurried him back to the Mondeo.

'Best you don't hang around,' he mumbled. 'She's been having treatment, you know.'

'I didn't. What for?'

'Psycho-stuff. You know, counselling and so on. That sort of thing.'

'Really. What brought this on?'

Jim shrugged and let out a sigh. 'Dunno. Something to do with your father.'

'But what?'

Jim pressed more firmly on his arm and urged him towards the car. 'God knows! It's made her think all men have a bit of the beast in them. Fertilising females wherever they can find them. Even me!' he added, laughing at himself. 'I mean, who'd be interested in Jim Butterworth apart from your sister Beryl?'

They'd reached the car. Jim opened the door for him, then held out his hand.

'Bye, Sam.'

'Thanks for your help, Jim.'

Beryl's husband turned back to the house, stooping to pick up the trug of weeds. 'Cheerio,' he called, head down, avoiding Sam's look.

Sam watched him go inside and close the door. Then he got into the car and drove slowly away.

A mile or so outside the village he found a lay-by and stopped. For several minutes he watched a combine harvester working the neighbouring wheat field, finding its steady, relentless progress soothing.

He shook his head like a dog. Had his father really been the sexual predator Beryl described? Or just a man with an eye for a skirt living in a household of frigid females?

He didn't know. And that was the trouble. He knew so little about the man whose genes he carried. Had no idea whether he'd had it in his soul to be a lecher or a spy.

The deed box was on the seat beside him. He opened its lid. On top was his father's naval service record. Signed up in 1949, died in service 1971. A list of the vessels he'd served on. A record of one man's working life. Of his pride. Ending up with HMS *Retribution*, based at Faslane.

He delved deeper into the box and found a diary. The date on the cover was 1942. Sam frowned. His father had been eleven years old then. He opened it and discovered it belonged to his grandfather, also a submariner. He skim-read some paragraphs. Descriptions of being bored for long periods on wartime patrol. Nicknames of shipmates – Bunny. Tiger. Chips and Taff. Two years later, he remembered, the boat had been depth-charged and his grandfather consigned to the fishes.

Submarines and the men who lived and died on them. They'd been in his father's blood. It wasn't credible he could have betrayed them.

Sam sifted through the rest. He looked at the photos in two expired passports. The same determined chin as himself, the same thoughtful eyes. Then, lying loose in a corner of the box, something that surprised him.

Two tickets for the ferry from Wemyss Bay to Rothesay on the Isle of Bute. Date stamped the 21st of May 1971, six weeks before his father died. Who had his companion been? Certainly not his wife. Sam's mother had told him time and again that she'd never been north of the border. Said it with pride in her voice, as if the very act of going to the place where her husband's submarine was based would be succumbing to his will.

Two tickets which his father had wanted to keep for the memories they bore – memories of a year when Russian military intelligence added his name to its list of foreign agents.

Were they significant? It was the only lead he had.

He checked the time. Just turning midday. He switched on the car radio to catch the news, wanting to know if word about his father had leaked. The headlines came. All about a nail bomb explosion in Southall. Sixteen people seriously injured, one elderly Sikh dead from heart failure.

'Bastards!' he hissed. He hated terrorists.

All the main right-wing groups were infiltrated, Steph had told him. They could hardly fart without Special Branch knowing. So it was probably a loner. Hard to catch. He listened through the rest of the news, but there was no mention of a spy scandal.

He looked again at the Scottish ferry tickets, then pulled a road atlas from the pocket in the door and located Bute in the Firth of Clyde. The Wemyss Bay ferry terminal was on the Ayrshire coast about an hour west of Glasgow. Driving to Scotland would take the rest of the day, he realised. It'd make more sense to fly. He began to calculate how soon he could get there. Then his phone rang.

'Hello.'

'Simon Foster?'

He tensed. He'd only used that name in his dealings with Harry Jackman. The voice was a woman's which he didn't recognise.

'Who is this?'

'Julie. Julie Jackman.' Her voice was strangely hoarse. Nervous, he guessed.

'Oh. Hello.'

'You're surprised to be hearing from me?'

'I am rather. Where did you get this number from?'

'You'll never believe this, but it was totally by accident. When you lent me your phone yesterday, I was pressing buttons trying to turn it off when the number of the phone came up on the display. And it just so happens I have a very good memory for numbers.'

Sam didn't believe in accidents like that. He'd slipped up. A security lapse.

'Okay,' he said suspiciously. 'So, what can I do for you?'

'It's what I can do for you, really. There's been a letter. I thought you'd want to know.'

'A letter? From your father?' He felt an adrenalin rush.

'Yes. It arrived here in Woodbridge this morning. And it talks about red mercury.'

'Does it now . . .' He struggled to contain his excitement. 'Have you contacted Denise Corby?'

'No.'

'I think you should.'

'Look. That woman got right up my nose yesterday. She came on like the Gestapo. I don't mind showing the letter to you – and please drop the pretence that you two don't work together.'

'Never met her before yesterday,' he replied with total honesty.

'Whatever . . . I won't have Denise Corby anywhere near me again.'

Sam knew the headquarters woman would blow a fuse if he acted on his own. And if he took up Julie's invitation, the investigation into his father's past would have to go on hold. But he was intensely keen to read that letter. And – it would mean getting another eyeful of Julie Jackman again, which he wouldn't object to at all.

'Where are you?' he asked.

'Woodbridge.'

'Could you bring the letter to London?'

'No. I promised to take Liam to the beach this afternoon.'

'This letter could be very important, Julie.'

'Liam's important too.'

He glanced at the dashboard clock. Twelve-fifteen. 'Very well. I could be with you by four.'

'Make it after six, could you? I won't be back until then.'

He recoiled. The nation's intelligence machinery was being put on hold so a seven-year-old could build a sand castle.

'All right,' he agreed reluctantly. 'Six o'clock it is.'

'You on your own, right?'

'Me on my own. Oh, one more question. Did the letter talk about anything else?'

Like a bungled coup in Bodanga.

'No-o . . .' she answered hesitantly. 'Not really. Just red mercury.'

He felt relieved. 'See you at six, then.'

Sam clicked the phone back into its holder. The call had unsettled him. Even if he accepted her unlikely explanation about how she knew his number, there was something else.

Despite his insistence on anonymity yesterday, the damned girl knew his cover name.

6

It was five minutes before six when he pulled up outside the converted sail loft by the river in Woodbridge. Shafts of sunlight broke through buttresses of cloud, giving a mellow tone to the building's dark red bricks and grey slate roof. Two S-Reg Range Rovers and an open-top BMW stood like trophies on the pea-shingle drive. The weekenders were in residence.

He tapped on the brass knocker for the ground floor flat at the left-hand end of the building. When Maeve Jackman opened the door, he felt awkward suddenly, like a spotty-faced youth on a first date.

'Didn't expect to see *you* again so soon,' she said in wary greeting. 'She's not back yet, but you can come in.'

'Thank you, Mrs Jackman.'

'Maeve. Do call me Maeve.' She wore pale cotton slacks, a grey sweatshirt printed with the slogan GIVE THE NURSES THEIR DUE and spoke with a soft southern Irish accent. 'They're still at the beach, but shouldn't be long. Would you like a cup of tea?' She looked him up and down as if trying to decide his tastes. 'Or there's some of Liam's pop. No beer, I'm afraid.'

'Tea would be fine.' The weird feeling of being nineteen again lingered – 'Mum' checking him over while the girl fixed her hair.

The ground floor was an open-plan living area. There was a corner for toys, a tidy kitchen with a woodblock worktop and a wide, stainless steel hood over the stove.

'You have a nice home,' Sam commented.

'Oh yes. Can't complain. Swankier than the last place, although I miss the neighbours. There's no one here to talk to most of the time.'

'Harry bought this place for you?'

'That's right. My ex-husband was a bastard in some ways, Simon' – That use of his cover name again sent a *frisson* through him – 'but Harry looked after us in his own way. Julie and I can live here as long as we want, but when we're dead it all goes to Liam. A good investment, Harry said. And I'm sure he was right. Money was the one aspect of human relationships that he understood.'

'I can believe that.'

Much of the far wall of the open-plan was glass. A sliding patio door opened onto a lawn which extended to the water's edge. Sam crossed the hardwood floor to take in the view.

'The grounds are communal,' Maeve Jackman told him, standing beside him. 'We pay a service charge, then somebody comes and cuts the grass. Did it myself at the last place.'

The estuary glowed a golden olive green in the early evening light. Further downstream a fleet of dinghies was making slow progress upriver.

'It is a lovely spot,' Maeve Jackman chattered, 'although I'm not really one for the boats. Don't mind looking at them, just so long as I don't have to step into one of the things.'

She returned to the kitchen area, leaning against the work surface with her arms spread, as if defending her territory. Her expression, when Sam turned to face her, was wary again. Her body which had probably once been as trim as her daughter's had lost its shape. As the kettle began to sing behind her, he noticed that the Mr Blobby wall clock above her head showed five minutes after six. Julie's tardiness was beginning to jar.

'Harry's letter, Maeve,' he asked briskly, 'I don't suppose you have it to hand?'

'No I don't,' she answered firmly. 'Julie has it somewhere safe. She wanted to show it to you herself. She won't be long.'

The kettle clicked. Maeve Jackman turned to make the tea and Sam settled on the flower-patterned sofa. The room was light and airy. The books on the shelves were few and mostly with bright covers, suggesting they were for the boy. A colour photo of Liam in a brown card frame, taken in a mass session at school, stood on top of the TV.

'Good picture of the lad,' Sam commented as the boy's grandmother set a tea tray down on the coffee table, then sat in an armchair opposite him.

'It's nice, isn't it? He's a bit of a handful, but we do our best for him, despite there being no man around.' She poured from a silver pot into bone china cups. 'Fortunately he's in a home where there's two women who are well used to that situation.'

'Liam's father . . . ?'

'Brendan. He was a useless so-and-so.' Her brow wrinkled contemptuously. 'Long gone. And changed his name a few times since, I shouldn't wonder. Sugar?'

'No thanks.'

'A bad lot, that man was. The worst sort of Irishman, and that's saying something. Believe me. I come from the country myself so I know.'

'He doesn't send Julie any money for Liam?'

'That's a joke! He was gone the day after she told him she was going to have his baby. Not a word since.'

'That must have shaken her up.'

'It wasn't a good time for her, Simon, that's for sure.' She watched him sip at the tea. 'Are you married?'

'No. No woman'll have me, I'm afraid.'

She laughed politely. 'That I don't believe. But you'll have your reasons, no doubt.'

Sam looked at his watch. Ten past six.

'Don't fret. She'll not be long now because Liam'll be desperate for his tea. And anyway, you mustn't begrudge Julie her relaxation. Life hasn't done her too many favours, you know.'

'I'm sure you're right.' He reined in his impatience. It was true that a few more minutes wouldn't matter.

Maeve Jackman leaned forward and lowered her voice, despite there just being the two of them there. 'Between you and me, she's never had a man that didn't let her down. Doesn't stand up to them, that's the trouble. Tries too hard, you know what I mean? To my mind it's all because of Harry running off when she was a baby, though she won't admit it. Always makes out she didn't care that much about her daddy, but whenever he made one of his little visits to us, she was all over him. If he'd told her he wanted to step on her, she'd have lain on the floor and let him do it.'

Sam nodded. He could imagine her as a child, constantly seeking her father's approval. 'So Harry's death must have . . .'

'. . . upset her a lot more than she's saying, yes. To be honest with you, she should have gone to the funeral. But she said she'd only go if I did, and there was no chance of that. Somebody had to stay and look after Liam. And anyway, I had no feeling for the man any more.'

'No, I don't suppose you did,' Sam murmured.

'You know, Julie really has had more than her fair share of life's rough face, Simon. She got in with a bad lot at college. Drinking and clubs and all that. And then there was drugs. That's when she started going with Brendan. He was a disc jockey. Good-looking feller, but he had no thought for anybody but himself. By the time the baby came and she dropped out of college she was pretty near bottom. She'd not been in touch with home for months. I didn't even know she was pregnant. She just turned up one day, grey as a ghost, with this three-week-old scrap in her arms, and the two of them suffering withdrawal symptoms.'

'Withdrawal symptoms?' Sam raised his eyebrows.

'Julie was addicted to heroin.'

'Really? I'd never have guessed.'

'She's clean now, thank God. It took her a while. And Harry played his part, I'll give him that. When he heard the state she was in with a newborn baby, he was back here on the first plane. Blamed himself for never being there when she needed him.'

'So he stayed for a while?'

'Oh no. Said his business didn't allow it. But he phoned a lot. And he fixed a clinic for her − to get her off the drugs. Eventually he persuaded her back to college to complete her degree.'

'While you looked after Liam.'

'While I looked after Liam,' she confirmed. 'Had to give up my own job to do it.' She looked embarrassed suddenly. 'Och, you poor man. You came here to read some crazy letter and you get a life history rammed down your throat.'

He was about to tell her it didn't matter when he heard tyres on the gravel at the front.

'That'll be them now. They went in my Clio,' she explained. 'Julie doesn't have a car of her own.'

A few moments later Sam heard a key in the lock. He stood up. The boy stumbled in, rubbing his eyes.

'Fell asleep,' Julie mouthed to her mother as she gathered her grandson into her arms.

'What'll it be, Liam?' the older woman asked. 'Fish fingers, I suppose.'

The sleepy boy dumped his head on her shoulder, then stuck a thumb in his mouth.

Julie turned to Sam. She still had her glasses on from the driving, but took them off and held them in her hand. There were tight lines of tension round her eyes. 'I'm sorry if you've been waiting,' she told him.

'That's all right.' She looked sun-baked and wholesome and he could forgive her anything.

'I'll get you the letter.'

Sam stared longingly at her lean limbs as she climbed the open staircase to the floor above. She wore blue shorts and a white sleeveless vest that clung to her breasts. Her shoulders were red from the sun. She reappeared a few seconds later with an envelope.

'If you want to read it in peace, there's a bench in the garden,' she told him, sliding the patio door fully open. She was eyeing him with reserve, as if trying to form a judgement of him.

'You said it arrived this morning?' Sam asked as they crossed the lawn to where it sloped to the water.

'That's right. It shook me when I picked it off the mat and saw the writing.'

'Why would it have come here instead of to Acton?'

'He chopped and changed. Anything he wanted to be sure I got he sent to Woodbridge, for some reason. He knew I was here at the weekends.'

The seat was under a willow tree. She sat close beside him, as if not trusting him to be alone with the letter. Solemnly she handed the envelope to him and he extracted the contents.

Harry Jackman's handwriting had a slight backward slope. 'There's no date,' Sam commented, inhaling the orange-blossom smell of her sun cream with the intensity of a solvent sniffer. She sat close enough for him to feel the warmth of her body.

'No. There's nothing to say when it was written.' She hugged her arms to her chest and clamped a hand over her mouth, staring downriver to where the racing dinghies were being hauled from the water.

Sam began to read.

'If you ever get this letter it'll be because I'm dead, my dearest. Don't grieve for me long. We all got to go some time.'

He glanced at Julie, wondering how it must have felt for her to read those words. In the next sentence Jackman explained he was leaving the letter with a trusted friend to be mailed if anything happened to him. Sam checked the envelope. The postmark was Kitwe.

'Any idea who this friend was?' he asked, turning to her again.

'Not a clue.' She pushed her hair back, revealing a perfectly shaped ear with a small mole behind the lobe. Her slender neck was white where the hair had covered it, but reddened by the sun where it plunged below the T-shirt collar. He was in love again.

He regained his concentration and read on.

'I've done lots in my life that I'm none too proud of, my sweet. Forgive me. But if I hadn't done it someone else would have. If African tribes are going to kill, they're going to kill. The press always blame the "merchants of death" for selling them guns, but it's nonsense. If the Afs didn't have guns it'd be pangas. Look at Rwanda. All those split heads.'

Julie had her hand clamped over her mouth again, as if by doing so she could hold everything together. She felt perilously close to disintegrating. Pressure was being put on her from the grave which she was finding hard to handle. She knew the letter by heart. Knew the words of this one, and of the other which she'd received that morning, a more personal letter hidden for now under the floor mat in the boot of her mother's car.

Conscious of her tension, but unaware of the reasons for it, Sam read on.

'But there is one trade I did that troubles me. It happened a year ago. One of

the other fellows involved has been murdered. I'm scared I may be next. I wasn't a big player, just a shipper for the cargo, but the deal was a bad one. I'm telling you my sweet, because someone needs to know about it. I intend to tell the British intelligence people, but only if they agree to leave me in peace when I come back to England. If you get this letter, you'd best show it to the police. They'll pass it on to the appropriate place.

Did you ever hear of red mercury? It was supposed to be a chemical the Russians invented for making miniature nuclear bombs. Some people say it doesn't exist, but I think it does.'

His pulse quickening, Sam turned the page over.

'It started in the summer of 1997 when I was contacted by a Russian trader who operated out of Vienna. He wanted me to import something into Zambia under diplomatic seals. I had good contacts with Zambian officials, so I could arrange for there to be no police or customs. The Russian told me to find a secure warehouse in Kitwe to store the cargo for a few days before it was collected by a man I knew called Van Damm, who traded for a big chemicals company in Jo'burg. I asked him what the cargo was, explaining that I wouldn't touch Class A drugs. Because of you, my darling. What you went through.'

Sam glanced at her smooth skin, imagining her arms once scarred by needles. Julie guessed where he'd reached in the letter. She met his look.

'It's history,' she said flatly.

'I know,' Sam answered. 'Your mother told me.'

Julie hissed. 'She's got a mouth like a runaway train, that woman . . .'

'The Russian told me it was red mercury from a Siberian laboratory. People had been trying to get hold of the stuff for years, so I was pretty excited by the deal. And there was big money in it. The cargo was to be delivered to a Zambian embassy compound in Moscow in late July, then boxed up with the diplomatic seals and flown first to Vienna and on to Kitwe. I had everything arranged, the aircraft booked, the Zambians paid off, and I went to Vienna to finalise the plans and meet the Russian trader, Vladimir Kovalenko . . .'

Sam sat bolt upright. Kovalenko's name was uncomfortably familiar to him. The man was a major player.

'. . . an impressive fellow, whose connections in Moscow went right to the very top.'

He knew that to be true. It was Kremlin links that had allowed Kovalenko's bent business empire to flourish. Sam read on, his attention now riveted.

'When I got to Vienna, Vladimir told me there'd been a change of plan. The red mercury wasn't going to South Africa after all but to somewhere else. The shipping arrangements had to be extended. Once in Kitwe the boxes were to be put onto another plane, still under diplomatic seals, and flown to Italy. I told him it made things very complicated for me. Van Damm might think I'd stolen the cargo, but

Kovalenko said I had no choice. You see he knew about you, my love. Where you lived. Everything. Said that if I didn't co-operate I would never see you alive again.'

'Christ,' Sam breathed, suddenly understanding Julie's nervousness. But it puzzled him. *How* could Kovalenko know about her?

'Dad was a bigmouth at times,' she whispered, answering his unasked question. 'He used to tell people about this daughter of his he was so *proud* of.' She said it self-effacingly.

'This Kovalenko – you met him?'

'No.' She was emphatic.

'He's never been in contact with you?'

Julie shook her head. 'There's one more page,' she prompted, as if wanting to change the subject.

Sam read on.

'*I fixed it. Five containers, each weighing about ten kilos, were flown from Russia to Zambia and then to Rome, all under diplomatic cover.*'

Fifty kilos. Enough red mercury for a whole arsenal of nuclear bombs – if the stuff had ever existed.

'He never talked to you in person about any of this?' Sam checked.

'Never.'

The letter was nearing the end.

'*Last week I heard that Van Damm was dead . . .*'

Last week . . . Killed three months ago, Denise Corby had said. Now they had a date for the letter.

'*My guess is the Israelis were expecting to get some of the red mercury from the South Africans and thought that Van Damm had double-crossed them. Probably suspected he'd slipped the cargo to the Islamics. That's what worries me, Julie. If those ragheads get hold of nuclear weapons, they'll cause mayhem. And also, with Van Damm gone, I could be next for an Israeli bullet. If you get this letter it'll be because I'm already dead. And if I'm gone it'll either be because of the red mercury or because my negotiations with the spooks backfired.*'

Sam's spine prickled at the realisation that Jackman had anticipated that MI6 might take him out rather than negotiate with him. If Julie believed that, then the letter was a ticking bomb. He swallowed hard. 'Any idea what that last bit means?' he asked, playing the innocent.

'I thought *you* might,' she responded curtly.

'No idea at all.'

'You're still pretending you're not a spook, then?'

He gave her the blankest of looks. There were rules to follow and he wasn't going to break them.

'From the little I know about spooks, as you call them,' he explained patiently, 'they'll never under any circumstances admit what they do. That's why it's called the *Secret* Service. Understand? So, for the record, I'm a trader who's had contact with MI6. Like your father was, Julie. Except I'm an honest one.'

'An *honest trader* . . .' Men were such skilled liars. 'That's like saying a red-hot iceberg.'

He smiled, admiring her choice of words.

The final paragraph of the letter was more personal than what had gone before. A dead man's farewell to his daughter. Regrets for not being the father she deserved, an awkward 'goodbye' and a signature.

'I'm sorry,' he murmured. 'Must have been a terrible shock to get this.'

Julie bit her lip. It was the other letter, the one she wasn't telling him about, that had shocked her more. She turned her head towards the house, from where strangulated noises were coming – Liam watching a TV cartoon while he had his tea. She couldn't help liking this man. And she really wanted to believe in him. But if what her father had written in the other letter was true . . .

'So . . . Was your journey worth it?' she asked with a shyly curious glance. 'Does it make any sense, what he wrote?'

'Well . . .' Sam hedged, sticking to his line, 'from what the experts at the Foreign Office say, whatever material your father shipped out of Russia, it wasn't red mercury, because the stuff doesn't exist. They'll want to study this letter in detail.' He got to his feet. 'Okay if I take it with me?'

'Of course. The experts you're talking about being Denise Corby, I imagine.'

'Yes. Amongst others.'

Julie got up too and stood closer to him than she'd intended, her unspectacled eyes making him appear further away from her than he actually was. Sam noticed specks of sand in her hair. He had to stop himself from brushing them off.

'Mind telling me why you've taken such a strong dislike to Denise?' he asked.

Julie hesitated for a moment. 'Let's just say I'm homophobic.'

Sam recoiled in surprise. 'She's got two children.'

'Fine. But the impression she gives other women is that her preference is for her own sex.' Julie began walking towards the house. 'And I have an aversion to dykes. You did ask,' she added, fearing she'd been too direct.

'Yes. I did. Oh, just a moment.' He put a hand on her arm to stop her going into the house. He'd suddenly remembered Jackman's odd description of his mysterious cargo when they'd dined at the country club. 'You may think I'm mad to ask this, but did your father ever tell you the story of Ali Baba?'

'And the forty thieves? Probably. He used to read things to me when he came on his visits. I don't remember. Why?'

'Just something he said to me that evening I saw him. You remember what the story is about?'

'Not really. I have a mental picture of big jars full of treasure. Then the thieves hide in them – or is it the people trying to catch the thieves?'

'That's right.' He'd forgotten about the jars. 'One or the other.'

'We could ask Liam,' she offered.

Sam shrugged. 'It's not important.'

Inside the open-plan living area, Liam sat totally engrossed in his TV programme. Sam said goodbye to Julie's mother and thanked her for the tea.

'It was a pleasure meeting you again,' she smiled. 'Safe journey back now, Simon.'

Simon. He still had to discover how they knew that name. He'd half expected to find that Jackman had referred to him in the letter, but he hadn't.

Julie walked with him to the door of his car, moving slowly as if in no hurry for him to leave. When he turned to face her, she had that odd look in her eyes again as if still trying to fathom him.

'Maybe we could meet again some time,' he suggested. The words slipped out before he could stop them. Brain on dick-drive.

Her panicky reaction surprised him. She started to blush.

'For a chat over a drink, perhaps,' he added, digging himself in deeper. 'I'd like to know you better.'

'I don't know . . .' She stared at him in alarm.

'Well, maybe in a week or so, when things have settled down.' He felt like a downhill skier unable to stop.

'You see, I'm not sure that . . .'

'No, of course not. I'm sorry. Shouldn't have suggested it.' He unlocked the car. Then to cover his embarrassment he ploughed on with the question he'd intended to ask. 'Tell me something.'

'What?'

'How did you know my name?'

He watched the blood that had flushed her cheeks drain away again. She stared past him, avoiding his eyes.

'I don't know. Denise Corby must have told me,' she stumbled. 'I suppose. Yesterday. While you were upstairs with my mother, searching the bedrooms.' She said the last part cuttingly, reminding him of the outrage she'd felt at their intrusion. But her eyes lacked the sharpness of her voice. They were the eyes of a one-time junkie, he reminded himself. Of someone who knew how to lie.

He gave her a watery smile then got into the car and wound down the window.

'Bye, Julie. Thanks for the letter.'

As he drove off, he saw in the mirror that she was still watching him.

Trembling, Julie turned back to the house. She found her mother standing just inside the door with her arms folded.

'You should have said yes,' she told her.

'To what?' Julie demanded, angry that her mother had been listening.

'When he asked you for a drink. The feller's lovely, Julie. And he's interested. I could see from the way he looked at you.'

'Mother . . .' Julie scolded.

'*And* he's not married. He told me so.'

'Look, keep out of it! D'you hear? You don't understand.'

She stormed out into the drive again. She'd left the beach things in the car. And the other envelope.

A quarter of a mile down the road towards Ipswich, Sam stopped in a lay-by. For a couple of minutes he sat there with the engine off, feeling the car rock as the weekend traffic swished past. He was irritated with himself for trying to get personal with her.

But what mattered more was the fact that she'd lied about how she'd learned his name. He was certain Denise would never have been so careless. He picked up his mobile and dialled her home number.

The headquarters woman answered a little breathlessly. There were children shouting in the background.

'Be quiet, Fiona!' she yelled off-mike. 'Sorry, Sam. What is it?'

She listened frostily as he told her about Julie's phone call to him asking him to visit her on his own.

'I don't approve, Sam,' she told him gratingly, in a voice that said she thought he probably had his own reasons for wanting to see the girl alone. 'Anyway, what did the wretched letter say?'

He told her. When he'd finished there was silence at the other end as if she were still evaluating it.

'Kovalenko of course is a serious player,' she stated eventually.

'I know.'

'I'll need to see the letter.'

'I'll scan it when I get home and e-mail it to you.'

'Fine. But we'll want the original by Monday for Forensic to check over.'

'I'll get a messenger to collect it. Oh, and Denise – one other thing . . .'

'What?'

'Julie knew my cover name. Simon Foster. Yesterday you didn't by any chance . . . ?'

'No, Sam. I certainly did not.'

A couple of minutes later, back on the road to London, he switched on the radio. The lead story on the 7 p.m. news was still the Southall nail bomb – one more victim dead, this time from shrapnel wounds. A statement from the PM condemned the attack and there was a footnote to the story – reports of simultaneous anti-immigrant violence in France and Germany. Unnamed 'experts' were speculating about a co-ordinated racist campaign. He switched off, making a mental note to pick Stephanie's brains about the case when they met for their curry later in the week.

As he drove on, he realised there *was* only one way Julie could have learned the name Simon Foster. From her father. And if not in the letter which he had in his pocket, then in another.

In a missive that for some reason Julie was keeping to herself.

7

Sunday

B Y THE TIME Sam Packer got up the next morning, he'd resigned himself
to putting the Jackman case on the back burner again. Last night after
returning home, he'd reported to Duncan Waddell about the visit to his
sister and to Woodbridge, and been told firmly to leave all red mercury
matters to headquarters from now on. It was the bad publicity that could
flow from his *father's* activities which concerned the firm's hierarchy more.
Waddell had approved his plan to visit Scotland and Sam had decided on an
early flight this morning, although his hopes of the ferry ticket clue leading
him anywhere were slim.

Rain beat against the windows. The forecast for the north was similar.
The sun that had reddened Julie Jackman's delectable shoulders yesterday
afternoon had been no more than an interlude in an otherwise hellish
summer.

He dressed in dark cotton trousers and a sweatshirt and prepared breakfast,
his mind wandering back to that open-plan living room in Woodbridge. He
kept imagining a freshly showered Julie and her scrubbed-faced son digging
spoons into cereal bowls. It worried him sometimes, his hankering for the
domesticity of cornflake ads.

He took his tray of fruit, toast and coffee into the living room, glancing
at the bookcase and the small wooden crest of HMS *Retribution* which his
father had given him a few months before he died. Apart from memories
and the tin document box, it was the only memento of the man that he
possessed.

When he'd finished eating he phoned British Airways for the times of
shuttles to Glasgow, discovering that with a mid-morning flight he could
make it onto an early afternoon ferry to Rothesay. He tidied away his
breakfast things and repacked the bag from yesterday, adding warm and
waterproof clothes. He was on the point of calling a taxi when the
phone rang.

'Hello?'

'Morning, Sam.' It was Duncan Waddell. 'Change of plan. We need to meet.'

'What, now? I've got my kilt on. Even had porridge for breakfast.'

'Scotland's going to have to wait. See you in one hour, okay? To do some brain scouring on the Jackman file.'

'You told me I was off the case.'

'That was yesterday.'

'So what's new?'

'The cousins have taken an interest. I had Washington on the line late last night.'

Their rendezvous venue this time was on the Thames embankment just upriver from Hammersmith Bridge. Both carrying umbrellas, they met by the flood wall and turned to look at the converted barges moored alongside.

'So, surprise me,' Sam began. 'The CIA's decided red mercury exists after all.'

'No way,' Waddell snapped. He wore sludge green cords and a navy pullover. 'But Jackman's dates match with something on their files.'

'What d'you mean?'

Waddell turned his back on the river to check no one was within earshot.

'I mean the disappearance of five atomic demolition munitions that were being broken up in Tomsk as part of the arms treaty process.'

'Shit!'

Waddell nodded frenetically as if the seriousness of what he was saying could not be overemphasised. They began to walk along the paved footpath.

'As you know, those things are small enough to be carried on a soldier's back,' he stressed. 'Designed for Spetznaz infiltrators to use against NATO installations prior to an invasion of western Europe. They pack about ten kilotons of explosive power.'

'Handy for terrorists,' Sam commented.

'Exactly. Security at the dismantling site was a joke – you know the form. The bombs had been reduced to their component parts, but whoever took them got a full set of pieces for five devices. Putting them together again would need skills, but skills that can be bought on the open market these days.'

'When did the FSB latch on?'

'To give them credit, the Russians began an investigation quite quickly. They followed a trail as far as Moscow, but there it died.'

'When did all this happen?'

'A year ago. And that's the key point. The Americans say the dates fit perfectly with the shipment that Harry Jackman thought contained red mercury.'

'A shipment he feared was destined for some Islamic group,' Sam reminded him. He was quietly pleased that Waddell's early dismissal of the business had proved an ill-judgement.

'Which is why we're having this conversation,' Waddell rejoined. 'There must've been *something* Jackman said to you on Tuesday evening pointing to who they were. Something you've overlooked.'

Sam shook his head. He'd been through that conversation a million times. 'I got the impression Harry didn't know who the buyer was.'

'That could have been bluff.'

'Of course.'

The rain had stopped and they furled their umbrellas. They were approaching a pub from which several young men were emerging to enjoy their drinks under the brightening sky. Sam was about to suggest a pint when Waddell indicated they should retrace their steps.

'We've been following up wherever we can,' he told him. 'The Italians have checked their customs logs for last summer. They confirm a flight from Kitwe with a cargo under diplomatic seals.'

'But no information about who collected it.'

'Other than it was staff from the Zambian diplomatic mission. Where it went after that they have no way of finding out.'

'Do the Israelis know anything?'

'Harry Jackman was on their files, of course – every intelligence service in the whole damned world seems to have heard of him – but they laughed when I mentioned red mercury. Now they know what could really be at stake they're wetting themselves.'

'A Hamas team armed with atom bombs would not be funny . . .'

'Too right. Although after what happened to their embassies in Africa, the Americans are convinced it's Osama bin Laden who's after the gear.'

'We need to get to the source of all this,' Sam stated. 'Vladimir Kovalenko.'

Waddell sighed. 'Of course we bloody do. But he disappeared from our screens several months ago. You met him once, I think.'

'*Met* is too strong a word. I got within twenty feet of him. A small, wiry man. It was at a St Petersburg trade fair back in '93 or '94. He made a lightning visit there. Wasn't the sort to linger anywhere for long.'

'D'you have any contacts who might know where he is?'

'Can't think of any.'

'Well, mull it over.' He stopped and turned on Sam as if the whole Jackman affair was his fault. 'You're disappointing me. You know that?'

'I've told you before,' Sam responded. 'Mind-reading's not my thing. Where was Kovalenko last time you heard?'

'Israel. The Russians issued a warrant for his arrest – for the illegal sale of state assets. Pressed Israel's Shin Beth internal security people to snatch him, but he was tipped off in good time and did a bunk from Tel Aviv. Hasn't been seen since.'

'Maybe a bullet's found him,' Sam suggested.

'If only . . . Enough people have tried. A year ago three of his bodyguards got taken out in a drive-by shooting.'

'Or else he's enjoying himself in the sun somewhere, waiting for Moscow to invite him home to run the economy.'

They paused by the river wall again to watch a half-empty pleasure boat steam past on its way up to Hampton Court. Waddell pursed his lips.

'I'd really hoped you might remember something, Sam. Chew it over some more, will you? Give me a call later.'

'From the Highlands and Islands.'

'Actually, I'd rather you remained in London today. The CIA may want to talk to you.'

'I can't tell them any more than I've already told you.'

'I know. But they've asked.' He leaned his elbows on the wall as a flight of geese cackled their way to a landing on the water. 'There's another little matter I need to raise with you,' he murmured.

'Yes?'

'This Julie Jackman girl . . .' Waddell eyed him puritanically. 'What are you up to, exactly?'

'Eh?'

'Denise Corby was spitting blood over your interviewing the woman on your own. Even suggested you had a personal motive.'

'Crap!' Sam exploded. 'If you must know, Miss Jackman thinks Denise is a dyke. That's why she asked *me* to pick up the letter.'

'Homosexuals in the Intelligence Service? Heaven forfend.' Waddell clicked his tongue and averted his eyes in mock horror. Then his face darkened. 'One question I do want an answer to. And this is serious. How come Miss Jackman knew how to contact you?'

Sam grimaced. 'I let her use my mobile. She got the number off the screen.'

'Well get the damned thing changed.'

'I will.'

'In fact you'd better start changing numbers more frequently.'

'Why's that?'

'Because we've heard your Ukrainian friends have sent a hit man to London.'

'Bloody hell.'

'They have as much forgiveness in their black little souls as a hive full of Iranian ayatollahs. And they're not beyond using phone intercepts to track down their victims.'

Austria
A lake south of Vienna

Eight hundred miles south-east of London, the Austrian sun had a warmth to it that was forecast to become uncomfortably hot later in the day. Families from Vienna had left the city early to get their sunbathing in before lunch. In the parking area by a small freshwater lake, the tailgate of an elderly Volvo estate stood open. From the inside of the car, a tall blond Swede by the name of Anders Klason extracted a bright blue cool-box and a couple of folding chairs. His evenly tanned bare chest bore a scattering of golden hairs. He closed the door again, locked up and carted the gear across the scorched grass to the edge of the water where his dark-haired wife Nina had spread a rug on the ground. Their two pale-skinned children aged five and seven stomped around impatiently while their mother tried to smear them with a high-protection waterproof sun cream. Nina was German. She wore a long, cool skirt and a shirt with baggy sleeves down to her wrists. To her, sunshine wasn't a pleasure but a danger to health. A cancer risk. But she'd long since abandoned trying to make her husband protect himself from it.

'The boat, the boat, the boat!' the children chanted, jumping up and down.

'Yes, but it's about time you learned to pump it up yourselves,' their father told them, setting down the cool-box and opening the bag containing the small plastic dinghy. He wore a tight pair of denim shorts and Reef sandals. The hairs on his legs gleamed like a translucent second skin as he foot-pumped the dinghy to life.

'Don't go far out,' their mother called as their son and daughter carried it to the water. It was a good lake for children. The sandy beach shelved gently and the water never got deeper than a couple of metres.

Klason stretched out on the towel.

'Don't worry, I'll watch them,' Nina told him dutifully. He was working twelve-hour days, six of them each week. Sunday was his only break and as far as she was concerned he was entitled to seek relaxation in whatever way he wanted. So long as it was with her and the children.

'I told you about the conference in Brussels next Wednesday?' he asked, eyes closed against the glare of the sun.

'No. You're going?'

'Yes. A 6.30 flight in the morning. Back late on Friday.'

'Oh. That's really convenient for you,' she snapped.

'What d'you mean?' He raised himself on one elbow.

'Don't pretend you've forgotten.'

'What?'

'My mother.'

'Oh.' He smacked a hand against his forehead. 'Wednesday and Thursday. She's coming to stay, yes?'

Nina looked away. 'You always do this.'

'I don't.' But on reflection he knew she was right. 'I forgot, Nina. I've been so busy . . .'

'When won't you be . . .'

Anders knew that his wife had begun to resent his work. When they'd first met he was a human rights lecturer at the university in Stockholm and she an exchange student on the postgraduate course he was teaching. She'd hoped for a pleasant, unstressed life with him in the Swedish capital, never imagining he would end up as head of the EU's new racial equality centre in Vienna, with an absurdly small staff and a ludicrously heavy workload.

'It'll be better in a few months,' he told her. 'We're still settling in.'

They spoke in a mixture of German and Swedish, each resorting to their own language when things got tense.

'*Grüss Gott.*'

Nina spun round. The voice had come from behind her. The accent was local.

'*Grüss Gott,*' she answered.

A couple in their thirties, dressed in jeans and sports shirts, had stopped by their 'camp' and were pointing towards the lake.

'Are those your children?' the man asked. He had a pointed face, like a terrier's.

Nina looked. The altercation with her husband had made her take her eye off them.

'Anders. They're too far out,' she whispered.

'They're okay.'

'Anders, please.'

'Oh, all right.' He levered himself up and ambled to the water's edge, muttering about wanting a swim anyway.

The Austrian couple crouched down by the Klasons' towels.

'You can't be too careful,' the woman said. She had dark hair that was untidily curly.

Nina Klason didn't like these busybodies. There was something hard about their faces. She'd seen many people like this in Austria and could imagine that it had been the same types lining the streets to greet Hitler's arrival back in 1938.

'Oh, look over there,' the woman said, pointing to the far side of the small lake. 'Somebody fishing.'

'So it is,' said Nina, uninterestedly following the line of the woman's hand. The lake was narrowest at this point, where the beach was.

'He won't catch anything there.'

'No?'

'Not with all the children splashing about. Better to go out in a boat into the middle.'

'I suppose so.' Nina couldn't care less. She had her eye on her husband whose easy crawl strokes had taken him quickly to where the children were.

'He's saved them now,' the woman told her. The couple stood up again.

'I don't actually think they were in any danger,' Nina insisted. 'But thank you anyway.' *Why* was she thanking these people for interfering? Embarrassment. That was all.

'Auf wiedersehen.' The couple began to walk away.

'Auf wiedersehen.'

Five minutes passed before Anders was back by her side. She'd watched his effortless swimming up and down the shore with a degree of envy. She herself had a fear of water.

'It's so warm, the lake,' he told her, picking up his towel to dry himself.

'So it should be. We've had over thirty degrees all week.'

She watched him drape the towel over his shoulders and work it from side to side.

'Ouch!' Suddenly Anders froze in mid motion, arching his back.

'What is it? Cramp?'

'No. Something cut into me.' He flicked the towel from his shoulders.

'Let me see. You're bleeding,' Nina gasped.

Anders felt it, a warm trickle down his back like a bead of sweat.

'How on earth . . . Is it bad?'

'No. Just a small cut. I'll put a plaster on it in a minute.' She found a clean tissue in her bag and pressed it against the tiny gash to stop the flow.

Anders reached down for the towel which he'd dropped. 'Must have picked up a piece of broken glass.' He examined it gingerly, not wanting to cut himself again.

'Be careful.'

'I am.' The fragment wasn't hard to find. A smear of blood pointed the way. 'It's a little splinter,' he told her. 'Caught in the loops of the fabric.'

'Can I see?' He showed her. 'How strange. I washed this last night.'

'I'd better look on the grass to see if there's any more.' He crouched down, lightly touching the ground.

'Be careful,' Nina warned, fixing the sticking plaster on his shoulder blade. 'I don't have too many of these.'

'Nothing here,' he said, standing up again.

Then the same thought occurred to them simultaneously. They turned towards the car park. The couple who'd warned them about their children were driving off in an old VW Golf.

'Odd,' said Klason.

'Very,' said his wife.

London

It was late afternoon before Sam got a call from Waddell clearing him to carry on with his postponed trip to Scotland. Annoyed about his wasted day, he was on the point of checking out the flights again when he discovered the battery indicator of his mobile was close to zero. He was about to place it on its charger, deciding to catch the first flight in the morning, when the handset rang.

'Hell!' He punched the receive button. 'Hello?'

'Mr Foster? Simon . . . It's Julie.'

His first reaction was pleasure. Then he checked himself. 'Look, you really shouldn't be calling me,' he said sternly. 'Denise Corby has to be your point of contact, whether you like her or not. They're civil servants, these people. They get upset if you don't follow protocol.'

'Yes, but that's . . . that's not why I'm ringing.' Her voice sounded a little husky. He wondered if she'd been crying. 'I'm not ringing about the letter.'

'Oh.'

'It's just . . . Well, you said we might meet again.'

'Yes . . .' He paced quickly to the window, as if the brief burst of exercise would help him think straight. Professionally he knew he should keep his distance from her after Waddell's cautionary words, but all he could think of was the addictive fragrance of her orange-blossom sun cream.

'This evening. Is it possible?' she asked.

Taken aback, he groped for a response. 'This *evening*? That's not so easy . . .'

'I really do need to talk to you, Simon. I . . . I'm in a bit of a state.' She sounded it, her voice high and strained.

'Well I can understand that. It's all been a terrible shock.'

'Yes. It has. And since you were the last person to speak to him, Simon, I just thought . . .' He heard a sniff at the other end. '. . . thought that if you could only talk to me about it, about how he was that evening, it might help.'

'Yes. Of course. Of course . . . The thing is, I was going away this evening,' he hedged.

There was silence at the other end as if the line had cut. His handset bleeped a low-battery warning.

'Julie?'

'I'm sorry, I shouldn't have rung,' she sniffed.

'No. Look. It's all right.' What the hell. If all she wanted was a shoulder to cry on . . . 'I can see you. But this phone's about to die, so where and when? You're ringing from Acton?'

'No. Woodbridge. I'm about to catch a train,' she said, her voice brightening. 'Could we make it eight o'clock?'

'Where? At your flat?' he suggested, optimistically.

'No. There's an Italian café in the Chiswick High Road. Corner of Turnham Green Terrace? D'you know that area?'

'A little.' It was five minutes away. 'At eight, you said?'

'Yes.'

'All right, then.'

'Thanks Simo—'

The battery died before she could finish. He replaced the phone on the charger then returned to the window. Down below him, the tide was out, exposing stony banks on each side of the river.

He told himself that it *was* okay to see her. He was off the case now, so it wasn't business any more. Nothing to stop them getting acquainted personally if that's what they both wanted. No rush. He would play it by ear.

Then for some reason he thought of Steph. She wouldn't have minced her words if she knew what he was planning.

'You're thinking with your dick, Sam. It'll end in tears.'

★　★　★

At fifteen minutes to eight, showered and in clean clothes, he took the lift to the garage.

He drove eastwards under the M4 flyover and down the Chiswick High Road. Traffic was heavy. The sky was purpling with dusk and the rain had stopped again. Restaurants and pizza houses were doing a good trade. He saw the café Julie had mentioned and drove past it, catching a glimpse of a lone figure at a table. A couple of others were also occupied. He turned right into a side street and parked, then walked back, pausing for a few moments in a bus shelter opposite the café to make sure it *was* her and that she was alone. He waited for a lorry to pass then crossed the road.

Julie wore a grey rollneck pullover which accentuated her slenderness. Sam noted her lack of spectacles and that she'd tarted herself up with a bit of eye make-up. She screwed up her eyes as he approached, checking it was him. When she saw that it was, she became flustered. He liked her shyness.

He sat down opposite her. 'Hello.'

'I . . . I wasn't sure you would come,' she whispered, with a tight, rubber-band smile.

'Well . . . damsel in distress and all that.'

She looked down at her hands, then surprised him by grimacing.

'A little nervous,' she murmured. 'I . . . I don't really know what I'm doing here . . .' She seemed to be waiting for him to take control.

He felt a compelling desire to touch her, to break through the invisible barrier separating them. He was considering how to do it without seeming too presumptuous, when he became vaguely conscious of chairs being scraped back and some of the other occupants of the café getting to their feet. Julie lifted her head again, but this time it wasn't him she was looking at. Someone had taken up a position immediately behind his chair.

'Mr Foster?' The voice was male.

Sam's insides dissolved. As he turned to see who it was, a flashgun went off in his face.

'Fuck . . .'

'*Daily Chronicle*, Mr Foster. We'd like to ask you a few questions about the death of Harry Jackman.'

Sam glared at Julie. There was an expression on her face that he'd seen once before. On a woman attending a bullfight. A knowledge that although she'd paid to see a killing, she wasn't sure she could stomach it.

He still wanted to touch that lovely neck of Julie's, but this time with both hands and to squeeze them together with all his strength.

Some men die early, he found himself thinking. People like Harry Jackman went quickly in a hail of bullets. But others – men who were really, really, unbelievably stupid – did it slowly and painfully, in an act of professional suicide.

8

S AM CRANED ROUND to see how many of them had ambushed him.
'You work for MI6, Mr Foster.' The reporter spoke with a well-bred accent and stood close to the back of the chair to make it hard for Sam to stand up.

'I most certainly do not,' he fumed. 'Who on earth told you that?'

'Harry Jackman, actually,' the reporter yapped. The camera continued to flash. 'In a letter posted to my paper after his death. He also described how you paid him $250,000 of British taxpayers' money to supply arms to the rebels in Bodanga.'

All there. Everything. Harry Jackman's revenge had been total. The chasm opened beneath his feet.

'Pretty appalling piece of ethical foreign policy, don't you think, Mr Foster? How many was it who died under the guns that the British government paid for? Two and a half thousand. Most of them women and children.'

Sam shook his head. 'Got your wires crossed, sonny. No idea what you're talking about.' It amazed him how calm he sounded. 'I've done business with Harry Jackman, yes. But I don't deal in arms. And I don't work for the Intelligence Service. Now if you'll excuse me . . .' He shoved the chair back against the reporter's stomach.

The journalist winced but stood his ground.

'Did you kill Harry Jackman, Mr Foster?'

The skin crept on the back of his neck. He shot a glance at Julie. Was *that* what she believed? The thought that she had so misjudged him cut deeper than the betrayal itself.

'I most certainly did not.'

'You were there.'

'Tragically, yes. He was shot by a man in Zambian army uniform. You can check that with the Zambian police. There was nothing I could do to save him.' He stared fixedly at the girl, his face as expressionless as he could make it. 'And I came here this evening because in a misguided moment I felt sorry for his daughter.' Her instant embarrassment gave him a jot of satisfaction.

He swung his elbow back into the reporter's stomach and stood up.

'So sorry, old chap. Have to go. Do try to get your facts straight. Okay?'

He barged his way to the door, counting the opposition again. Four – two scribblers and two snappers, one dressed in leathers. The other photographer blocked his path.

'Excuse me.' Sam brought his knee up.

'Oof! Bastard!'

Outside on the street, Sam sucked in air and marched. A bus drove past. Throwing himself under it seemed an attractive option. He couldn't go back to the car. They'd trace him from it.

The winded cameraman caught up and did that perilous backwards walk which photographers do, snapping wildly. Sam put a hand over his face, with half an eye on the road, praying for a taxi.

'The public has a right to know, Mr Foster . . .'

'They also have the right not to be hounded by the likes of you.'

Suddenly Sam saw what he'd been looking for and dived towards the kerb, his arm reaching out into the road. The taxi tucked into the side and stopped. As he wrenched open the door Sam heard a motorbike start up.

'135 Clapham Common South Side,' he ordered. The reporter tried to get in too. 'Do you mind?' Sam pushed him back with his foot and slammed the door. He noted the journo scribble down the address he'd just shouted out then leaned forward to the sliding glass. 'Just drive, chum!'

'Clapham Common, you said?'

'Never mind that. Just get me away from these reptiles.'

The driver jerked in the gear and accelerated away, stealing glances in his mirror to see if he'd got some celeb in the back.

'I had that Nicole Kidman in my cab the other week,' he announced stoically.

They make it up, Sam decided. He twisted round. The motorbike was catching up, the photographer with the leathers astride it.

'Can you lose that bike?'

The driver looked in his mirror.

'Naah. No chance, mate. Sorry. They've got two wheels, see? Go anywhere I can and more.'

'Then take me to a tube station.' Sam racked his brains. 'Acton Town. You know it?'

'Course I bloody do,' the driver bitched, annoyed his fare would be smaller than he'd anticipated.

The bike was right behind. If it came to hide-and-seek in a train station it'd be him and the photographer. One on one. Odds he was used to.

In four minutes they were at Acton Town tube. The meter showed £3.20, but Sam thrust a fiver through the gap.

'Keep it.'

'Thanks very much, guv. Hopes you wins.'

Sam sprinted into the station. An inspector held out his hand for a ticket. Sam held up his membership card to a south coast yacht club.

'Police. Special Branch,' he snapped, running straight past. 'Stop that guy in the leathers, okay?'

'Hang on a min—'

Sam knew this station. There were two main platforms and several staircases. He clattered down the first, praying a train would be waiting. But the tracks were empty.

He sprinted along the platform, using billboards as a screen. At the far end he risked a look back. No sign of his pursuer. He'd been forced to buy a ticket. Sam reached the stairs at the far end and climbed. The landing above was deserted.

He waited, chest pounding. God, what a mess. What a stupid, fucking mess. How the hell had he fallen for Julie's 'please help me' act? In the distance, he heard the snick of wheels on track as a train approached. Heading west.

The snapper would expect Sam to get on the first train that came in, right? So, he would wait for the second . . . And pray a little.

As the westbound tube came in he heard the hum of an eastbound train sliding into the platform below him. He thanked God for this undeserved blessing, then started down the steps, pausing near the bottom out of sight of those on the platform, waiting for the bleeper warning of the train doors closing. When it came he darted across and squeezed through.

A handful of occupants in the carriage. Backpackers from a late flight into Heathrow and some Asian manual workers heading into town for a night shift. Through the glass he saw that the westbound tube had pulled out already. As his own train accelerated, he spotted the photographer on the other platform glaring at him. He resisted the temptation to wave.

The next stop was Hammersmith and he got out, willingly coughing up the £10 fine for travelling without a ticket. A row of phones lined one side of the station lobby. He punched in a number.

It rang out. Went on ringing. He'd dialled on instinct, needing a clear head to talk to, someone to get sympathy from before the big guns opened up on him. And she wasn't there.

'Hello!' An angry voice suddenly, out of breath.

'Steph?'

'Sam?'

'Yes.'

'God! You don't half choose your moment. I was in the bathroom.'

'Got to see you, Steph. Now.'

'Too late for a curry, mate. I've eaten already. Cooked myself a nice little stir fry. Should've rung earlier.'

'That's not it. Got to talk, Steph. I'm in deep, deep doo-doo.'

She heard his anguish. 'What's happened?'

Sam glanced over his shoulder. There were people in earshot. 'Can't talk here. Can I come round?' Steph's flat was in Shepherd's Bush, a short bus ride away.

'Umm . . .' He could hear the cogs turning and knew what it was about. She'd told him that Gerry was the jealous type and had made her promise not to let other men come to the flat. Despite his suspicions yesterday they were clearly still an item. 'Problem with that,' she declared. 'Better to meet in a pub.'

'So long as it's got a quiet corner where nobody'll see me cry.'

'Christ! You are in a state.'

'I've fucked up, Steph. Fucked up really badly.'

'Where are you?'

'Hammersmith.'

'Okay.' She thought for a moment. 'There's a place called the Green Dragon halfway up the road that'd bring you to Shepherd's Bush. If we both start walking now we should meet there in about ten minutes. Okay?'

'Okay. And Steph . . .'

'What?'

'I think you're wonderful.'

It was nearer twenty minutes before she joined him at the pub. He'd taken his pint to a table, which if not in a corner was at least reasonably secluded. Stephanie offered him her cheek to kiss, then he went to the bar to get her a gin-and-tonic. She had broad shoulders and a bright, attractive face. She wore black trousers and a dark blue sleeveless fleece over a white cotton shirt. Her straight, brown, collar-length hair was still damp from the hurried shower she'd had before coming out.

When he returned to the table he let out a long sigh. 'You're looking at an idiot, Steph.'

'Yeah, but I've always known that. A lovable idiot, though.' She grabbed his hand and squeezed it. 'Are you going to tell me what's happened or do I have to guess?'

'I walked into an ambush. Straight in there like a rookie.'

She made a point of looking him up and down. 'No bullet holes.'

'Flashguns, not rifles,' he told her.

'Oh Lord. Don't tell me. The bait for this ambush had boobs like a Barbie doll and legs up to her armpits.'

Sam grimaced, embarrassed at being so predictable. Steph inclined her head sympathetically.

'I think you'd better start from the beginning if you want me to do a counselling job.'

Sam told her everything, almost. Steph was one of the few people in the world he felt he could really trust.

'About five foot four, this Julie woman? Quite petite?' she asked when he'd finished.

He looked away, detecting a touch of jealousy. He'd always suspected Steph's interest in him was not as platonic as his in her.

'I mean I'm not blaming you,' she went on, unable to resist the gibe. 'A feller who's as bad at relationships as you are needs to take his chances whenever they come along.'

'Thanks, Steph. That's just what I needed.' He downed the remains of his pint. 'What the hell do I do, that's the question?'

'Do your lords and masters know about it yet?'

'No. It only happened an hour ago.'

'Well tell 'em fast before they find out from somebody else,' she scolded. 'God almighty, Sam, you're behaving like a ten-year-old.'

'I reckon I've got twenty-four hours. They're bound to get the lawyers in before publishing anything this sensitive, which'll make it too late for tomorrow's papers.'

'But the sooner you get Duncan Waddell involved, the better your chance of surviving the mess,' she insisted.

'You're right, of course. I'm just putting off the evil moment.' He looked down at his empty glass.

'S'pose you want me to buy you a whisky to chase that pint down.' She got to her feet.

'Well it *is* your round . . . And if you can see a sandwich in that cabinet that hasn't curled into a ball, I wouldn't mind it.'

'I'll tell 'em to fill it with chicken vindaloo,' she muttered, making for the bar.

When she brought it back, it turned out to be tuna mayonnaise. She watched in silence for a minute or two as he ate it.

'I suppose you could try a transplant,' she said after a while.

81

'What are you talking about?'

'The part of your brain that you use for assessing women. I mean I assume the brain *is* involved at some stage in the process.'

'Steph . . .' he warned.

'I mean, this creature – a quick flash of thigh and a "please help me I'm so unhappy" and you're putty in her hands. And that Chrissie . . . How many years was she pulling the wool over your eyes?'

'Steph, I can do without this.' He glared across the bar which was crowded with a young clientele. All looking so carefree. So *together*, damn them.

'I think you'd better go and ring the Belfast bully-boy,' Steph told him, forcing a cheer-up smile.

He reached for her hand and squeezed it. 'Thanks for listening, Steph. You're the best. You know that?'

'Go on with you. What are friends for?'

They finished their drinks, got up and walked out into the street.

'Criminals keeping you busy?' Sam asked as they stood on the pavement, delaying the moment of parting.

'Up to my neck in fascists,' she told him.

'The Southall bomber . . .'

'The local station's handling the scene of crime, but Special Branch is trying to establish if there's something wider going on here. There were other incidents on the continent at the same time. Neo-Nazis torched an immigrant hostel in Leipzig – three dead – and in Toulon some Le Pen supporters smashed up shops belonging to Algerians.'

'I know. I heard it on the news.'

'Any connection between the incidents is only speculation so far. We've no intelligence on it.' She kissed him affectionately on the mouth. 'Now be a good boy and go tell Daddy about the mess you've made.'

He gave her a bear hug.

'You know the worst thing about it?'

'What?'

'The bloody woman thinks I arranged for her dad to be killed.'

She looked at him aghast. 'You mean you *didn't*?'

He raised an eyebrow, turned and walked back towards Hammersmith, keeping an eye out for a taxi.

Thirty minutes later, he'd broken the bad news to an apoplectic Waddell, collected his car from the side street in Chiswick and returned to his flat. Once inside, he closed the front door and leaned hard against it as if it was his last defence against a vengeful world.

One part of him hated Julie Jackman for tricking him, wanting to string her up. But another part was more offended than hurt, distressed that she'd believed her father's paranoid ramblings rather than his own word.

Half of him sought revenge for what she'd done, the other simply wanted to set her straight. To make her recognise that he wasn't an assassin.

But he needed more from her than that, because the wound she'd inflicted on him affected his pride.

He wanted her to desire him. With the same blundering blindness that had driven him onto the rocks this evening.

9

Brussels
Monday, 11.00 hrs

THE EUROPEAN COMMISSIONER for Social Affairs was a woman of boundless energy, an elegant and sophisticated Parisian in her mid-fifties whose paramours had included some of the most senior politicians in France. Her left-of-centre credentials dated back to the barricades in the Paris Latin Quarter in the hot, neo-revolutionary summer of 1968.

Dressed in a crisp, beige suit with a skirt ending just above the knee, she walked the short distance from the metro station to the Brussels headquarters of the Commission. She was entitled to an official car to bring her from her home, but on most occasions she spurned it, preferring to feel the press of ordinary people about her for a few short minutes before plunging into the rarefied world of Euro politics.

This was to be a busy week for Blanche Duvalier. On Wednesday she was to chair a two-day conference on race relations, a subject close to her heart but one of the hardest to deal with. Improving attitudes to the minorities in their midst required more than brave words. Race hate was a sickness endemic to the human species which she'd campaigned against for most of her adult life. Most of today and tomorrow would be spent in preparation for the conference. Much effort would be needed to prevent it degenerating into pointless polemic.

The entrance to the Commission building was set back from the road under a huge porch which gave shelter from the elements for the official cars as they dropped their passengers at the rotating glass doors. A few more seconds and she would be there.

Walking towards her along the pavement was a woman in her forties with wild brown hair in desperate need of a combing. For a moment Blanche Duvalier thought it was one of the journalists from the diplomatic press corps and began to think of a quote. Then she realised that she didn't know the woman at all. The creature looked an oddity. Face flushed, eyes wide and staring as if driven by some inner demon, her clothes clashed horribly. She was encumbered by shopping bags, the control of which she seemed about to lose as she detached a hand from them to wave it in Blanche's direction. Did she know this woman after all, Duvalier wondered? The Commissioner glanced behind her and quickly realised her mistake. The wave had been directed at the driver of a car which had illegally halted at the kerb a little way behind her. The passenger door swung open.

The woman was only a couple of metres in front of her now, eyes locked on the car, when she began to stumble, tripping over heels far too narrow for speed. Too late to take avoiding action, Blanche Duvalier braced herself for the impact. The woman tumbled against her, making no attempt to prevent a collision, her armful of possessions cascading forward. Duvalier felt a sharp prick as the corner of one of the bags jabbed into her just below her left breast.

'Merde!'

As the woman grappled for control of her shopping, Duvalier felt a second scratch at her flesh.

'Eh alors!'

'Sorry. So sorry.' The woman spoke in English. She regained her balance and hurried on towards the open door of the waiting car.

Instinctively Blanche Duvalier rubbed at the place where she'd been hurt. Her fingers touched moisture and she gasped. She looked down and saw blood on her cream silk blouse and a tiny rip in the fabric.

'Merde!' she said again, spinning round, ready to confront the ludicrous woman who'd caused the accident, but the car was already easing its way into the traffic.

She looked down at herself again. It was the tiniest of cuts, but the blouse was ruined. Fortunately she kept a spare in the office in case of lunchtime accidents. The blood was continuing to ooze. She took a handkerchief from her handbag, slipped it between the buttons to press against the nick in her skin, then carried on into the Commission building, trying to regain her composure.

She stepped into the elevator and found it occupied by Piers Hyams, her English first secretary.

'Madame, good day to you,' he began before noticing that all was not well. 'Something wrong? What happened to you?'

'Some stupid woman crashed into me on the pavement outside. Had something sharp in one of her bags.' She withdrew the bloodstained handkerchief.

'Oh good heavens! Do you need a doctor?'

Blanche Duvalier gave him a withering look. 'Really, Piers! Do I look as if I'm about to faint?'

The young Englishman smiled weakly.

'But really,' she continued scathingly. 'There are some people who simply shouldn't be allowed out on the streets.'

Piers Hyams fixed his eyes on the illuminated floor counter above the doors.

'Madame,' he murmured drily, 'as Commissioner with responsibility for the elimination of intolerance, let's hope the media haven't bugged this lift.'

London

Sam Packer caught a mid-morning shuttle from Heathrow, glad to be escaping from the recriminations his controller had hurled at him first thing. Depending on what the *Chronicle* published, his employment with the Intelligence Service was now in jeopardy. For much of the flight north he despairingly tried to work out what an ex-spy could put down on his CV.

The flight landed at Glasgow airport at 2.15 and he carried his rucksack straight to the car hire desks to pick up the vehicle he'd reserved. It was a blustery day in Scotland, dark grey boulders of cloud charging across a pallid blue sky. As he stepped out of the terminal the wind hit him, blowing through his brain like a purgative.

The motorway led westwards along the white-flecked Clyde. The tide was low, the green and red channel markers rising out of the river bed like giant salt cellars. On the far bank a shaft of sunlight caught the russet stone of Dumbarton castle atop its rock. At Greenock the road cut inland before emerging on the blustery west coast. A couple of yachts beating the choppy, grey waters between Ayrshire and the Cowal Peninsula had their mainsails reefed hard.

Sam tried to envisage his father coming here twenty-seven years ago but couldn't. Couldn't because his memory of the man had no bones to it. All he had was a naïve eleven-year-old's fantasy of a father's life – heroics beneath the waves, interspersed by short periods at home as head of the family and Sam's temporary ally in a house dominated by women. A figure who bore no relation to the sex pest and spy that others now talked of. Grudgingly he'd accepted that his sister's impressions of the man would have been more sharply formed than his own. She'd been fifteen already when their father died. Foreboding gnawed at him. This investigation looked set to destroy an icon, the only one he'd ever had.

The road wound through trees and suddenly he was at Wemyss Bay where the ferries left for Bute. To the right stood the terminus, a low building with half-timbered gables, a red tiled roof and a clock tower with a sandstone base. As Sam swung the car into the assembly area, a youth in a yellow waterproof came over, leaning into the wind.

'You for Rothesay?' He hurled the words against the gusts.

'Yes.'

The marshal pointed to the line of cars at the top of the ramp. Beyond it, the ferry waited, a craft like a large trawler, with funnels each side of the car deck and an 'A' frame bridging it.

'Sails in twenty minutes. Tickets in the station.'

'Thanks.'

Sam parked behind the last car in the row then struggled into the dark blue waterproof he'd brought with him. Inside the terminus, pale green Edwardian ironwork supported a glass roof above a circular concourse. Beyond it the platforms curved towards Glasgow, from where scores of thousands had flocked during the annual holidays in the inter-war years. A wide, covered ramp swept down from the concourse to the quay, its glazed grandeur more suited to a transatlantic liner journey than a boat trip to the isles.

Would *they* have come here by train twenty-seven years ago, his father and whoever he'd been with? Sam stood by the buffers, looking along the rusty track, picturing a bearded, smiling figure loping towards him, a guilty grin on his face and his arm round some woman who wasn't his wife. It *had* to have been a woman, he'd decided. Why else would he have hung on to the tickets?

He turned and made for the booking office.

The car deck was less than half full when they closed the ramp and slipped the warps. Sam climbed to the upper deck to watch the mainland shore slip away, standing in the shelter of the bridge as other passengers scurried to the saloon to escape the wind. Despite the chop of the sea there was no swell and the ferry cut a smooth track across the water to Bute. A lone yacht braved the gusts with its storm jib up and a small triangle of main.

Five minutes later, when a squall hit the bridge wings, he took the stairs down to the saloon where the small rectangular windows were obscured by salt spray. Teenage boys prodded desultorily at electronic games machines in a corner. From an open serving hatch he bought a cup of tea and a cheese roll and took it to an empty seat. A couple with young children came inside, shivering, all bravely dressed in shorts. It took character to holiday in Scotland in a summer like the one they'd had this year.

As Sam sipped his tea, his mind relived the nightmare of yesterday evening. Half of him still wanted Julie Jackman's blood, the other being consumed with shame at his own stupidity. He wondered if Waddell was getting anywhere stifling the *Chronicle*.

He checked his watch. They would be approaching Rothesay shortly. The sun was out again, so he drained his cup and returned to the deck, reaching the railings as the ferry rounded a headland. A line of buoys led into the bay and to the island's only town. Neat brownstone houses stood back from the water, separated from the rocky shore by bright green lawns. A couple of minutes later a loudspeaker announcement summoned drivers to their cars.

From behind the wheel, Sam watched the side ramp drop and the family in shorts amble down it onto the quayside. For now the sun shone strongly, warming the children's legs. He drove ashore, passing a small basin filled with yachts and fishing boats. At the promenade he turned right and found a place to park, trying to decide what to do, trying to guess what his father would have done twenty-seven years ago. If it had been *him* here with a girlfriend, he'd have checked straight into a boarding house and spent the afternoon in bed.

Amongst the shops along the front stood a small tourist information office. He went inside, not sure what he was looking for. There was nobody in attendance but an array of brochures on the shelves. He browsed one cursorily.

'Can I help you at all?'

Sam looked up. A stocky, middle-aged woman had emerged from a small back office.

'I was on the phone,' she told him. 'Didn't see you come in.'

'No matter.' He hesitated, doubting she would be able to do anything for him. 'I suppose it's historical information I'm after, really.'

'Oh well, then it's the castle and the museum you'll be wanting,' she told him helpfully. 'And we've some magnificent Victorian toilets down by the ferry terminal. Maybe you've seen them already. The restoration's been done brilliantly.'

'That's not quite what I had in mind.'

'Oh?' She cocked her head like a blackbird listening for a worm.

'I'm trying to retrace the steps of a couple who came over on the ferry twenty-seven years ago for a day or two's break. D'you have any idea what they might have done with their time?'

The woman's brows arched like hoops. 'Och, what sort of question is that? What are you? A private detective?'

'No. A relative.'

'Well, now . . . A couple, you said? I suppose it would depend on their inclinations.' She smiled coquettishly. 'You know, a lot of visitors simply used to hang around the town looking at the boats during the day. There's the promenade outside this very door, the putting green opposite, and in the olden times there was a tram taking people to the beaches.'

'And where would they have stayed?'

'There's no end of hotels and guest houses, mostly along the front. You've got the brochure in your hands. If they were keen on walking or riding, they'd have found somewhere out in the wilds. There's a section on that.'

The door to the street opened. A man poked his head round and asked about caravan sites.

'Come on in,' the woman told him. 'I'll soon sort you out.' She turned back to Sam. 'But you know, to be honest, a lot of the time people simply walked up and down the promenade eating ice creams and looking at the view. Life was less complicated twenty-seven years ago. A holiday meant doing *nothing*.' She looked at him out of the corner of her eye, still trying to guess what it was he was really after. 'I'm not being much help, am I?'

'Oh, you are,' he assured her. 'To be honest I don't really know what it is I'm looking for.'

'I'll tell you something,' she said, seeing the chance of a sales pitch, 'if this couple of yours were people looking for a wee bit of peace and quiet just to find themselves, there's no better place to come than Bute. And that's still true today.'

Sam thanked her for her wisdom and left her to deal with the caravanner's more routine enquiry. He crossed the road towards the promenade gardens, which were ablaze with dahlias. A signpost pointed to the Victorian toilets. He saw the family in shorts emerging from the grim-looking block, the parents smiling and the children bored.

Was he wrong to think his father had been here with a woman? Might the second ferry ticket have been for his Soviet intelligence contact – a quiet outing to discuss the terms under which his father would spy for the Kremlin? Sam shivered. The whole idea of betrayal still wasn't conceivable to him.

He began to stroll along the front, passing a prettily painted pavilion housing a cinema and a café. Wind-blown palms and neatly trimmed shrubs surrounded a green-baize putting green being manicured by a man with a mower. Out across the water, shafts of sun dappled the foam-flecked sea and daubed gold onto the purple mountains to the north.

Queuing at a white-painted kiosk for a round with the putters was an Asian family, the women's saris exploding with vivid colour, the men in white shirts and dark trousers. Grandparents, adults and grandchildren, about a dozen in all, they carried their clubs and balls to the green, chattering and laughing as if at some country club at Simla.

Suddenly they were confronted by a photographer, a down-at-heel creature in grey, whose trouser bottoms spread like bells over his dusty shoes and whose jacket pockets ballooned with films and order pads. Aged sixty at least, his bald scalp was covered by a thin flap of greasy hair, which miraculously or because of glue lay undisturbed by the blustery breeze. The man launched into his spiel, pointing to an old plate camera standing on a heavy tripod at the edge of the green. Intrigued at being snapped by an apparatus they thought had died with the Raj, the Indian family marshalled themselves into a pose. After much business with a black cloth, the photographer took three shots, then got them to spell out their family name on his pad.

'Any time after ten tomorrow morning.'

He gave them a ticket. Laughing, the family got on with their game as the old man re-primed his equipment. All of a sudden Sam realised the significance of what he'd been watching.

'Good season?' he asked, walking up to the photographer.

'Terrible. Te-rrible.' The man spoke with funereal sorrow, instantly sizing Sam up as a non-customer with whom he could speak freely. 'It's video that's done it. Killed the trade stone dead.' He glanced round to see they weren't being overheard. 'That's why I dug out the old plate camera – to inject a little novelty into the process.'

'Clever idea. Been taking pictures long?'

The old man raised his chin and narrowed his eyes. 'Therrty-two years. Chairman of the Chamber of Commerce three times. Oh yes . . .' He looked set to launch into his life history.

'Always pictures of tourists?' Sam asked, cutting him short.

'Och no. Not only the visitors. *Anything*. Anything anybody wants captured in a photograph, I'll do it for them. Weddings, christenings, twenty-firsts . . . Even did a *berrth* for someone once.'

'You must've taken thousands of pictures over the years . . .'

'Oh aye. Mind you, it'd take me the rest of my life to count them.' He dug a hand into one of the voluminous jacket pockets and came out with a pack of cigarettes. 'And if I go on using these things, that life may not be so very long.' He chuckled, a sound like chains being dragged over gravel, then offered the packet to Sam, who shook his head.

'Could you do it?' Sam asked.

'Do what? Count up the pictures ah've taken?' The photographer eyed Sam as if he were a mental defective.

'What I meant was, do you have a record of them?' Sam explained. 'Names, dates, that sort of thing.'

The man scoffed. 'More than that, laddie. I have the negs. Every last one.'

For one short moment Sam felt as if a hand had gripped his shoulder and given it an affectionate squeeze. A touch he'd not felt since he was eleven years old.

'Thirty-two years' worth?' he whispered.

'Absolutely. It's an archive, ye see. Worth a lot of money. My cameras have recorded the passing of history. Fer instance – this is a wee example – in my possession I have an unbeatable record of fashion trends in the west of Scotland over the past thirty years.'

Sam raised an eyebrow.

'Och yes. Clothes, hair styles. All the fashions have come to us here in Bute. On the backs of the visitors, y'see. I've offered it to Scottish TV. They showed a lot of interest. Sent a wee lassie over to take a look. They're still thinking about it, mind.'

'And you've got all your pictures indexed?' Sam hardly dared believe what he was hearing.

'Oh aye. I live in a big hoose. No wife or family to clutter it up. I have three rooms full of filing cabinets.'

'So if I gave you a date from twenty-seven years ago, you could produce the pictures you took that day?'

The man's eyes began to calculate.

'I shouldn't be surprised,' he answered. 'It'd take a bit of time, mind. And of course . . . it'd need to be worth my while.'

'Of course.'

'I'm expecting four figures from Scottish TV,' he added cannily.

Sam made a clucking noise to show how impressed he was by the wealth the dowdy old man was sitting on. 'Can I put you to the test?' he suggested.

'How d'you mean?'

'Oh, I don't know.' He screwed up his face as if changing his mind. 'No. It's a waste of time. It's too unlikely.'

'What is?'

'It's only a personal thing. Nothing of any great significance. To do with my family.'

'Go on. You've got me interested now.'

'Well . . . On the twenty-first of May 1971 my mother and father came here on a day trip – or maybe it was to stay a night or two, I don't know. My dad was a submariner just back from a patrol, so I guess they were after some time on their own without us kids getting in the way. Then, a few days later, when they were driving back home to Portsmouth they had a car crash. Both of them killed. Instantly.'

'Och that's terrible.' The man looked genuinely shocked. 'You'd have been a wee bairn.'

'Eleven. With a sister of fifteen. Yes it was tough for us. We were brought up by grandparents after that.' Sam bit his lip, worried he was over-egging it. 'Now, I've no idea, but I suppose it's possible you took their photograph when they were here.'

'Aye. It certainly is.' The old photographer drew heavily on his cigarette and blew the smoke out of the side of his mouth.

'Care to have a look for me?' Sam asked.

The man's eyes narrowed again. 'It's the time it takes is the problem,' he wheedled.

'Packer was the name,' Sam told him. 'Trevor Packer.'

'There's always so many other things to do . . .'

'How about a tenner as a search fee?'

The lips pursed round the cigarette. 'Och, I don't know. It could take me a wee while. I couldn't be putting my finger on it straight away.'

'Tell you what. Twenty quid for the search, if you can do it today,' Sam pressed. It was mid-afternoon already. 'And I'll up it to fifty if you find a neg with his name on and do me a print.'

'Done.' The photographer slammed his hand into Sam's and shook it firmly. 'Craigie's the name. Tom Craigie.' He pulled out an order pad. 'It'll make a change, doing something like this. Give me that date again? You're sure of it, are you?'

'Best check the days immediately after as well. As I said, they might have stayed a while.' Sam wrote the date down for him, together with the name.

'Guid.' Craigie stuffed the pad back into his pocket, the corner of which had been torn and stitched. He handed Sam his business card. 'Now if you'd care to put the twenty pounds in my hand right this minute, I'll call it a day here and get on with your commission.'

Sam extracted a note from his wallet. 'Okay if I ring you in a couple of hours?'

'Make it around seven o'clock.' The photographer capped his lens, hoisted the tripod onto his shoulder and set off with a rolling, arthritic gait.

Sam watched him go, suspecting he was wasting his money. No sensible sailor playing away from home would have risked having his picture taken with a girlfriend.

He decided to find a bed for the night and drove along the front until he hit a small hotel which looked cleaner than most and had a vacancy sign in the window. A rosy-cheeked couple in their thirties ran it. Sam paid in advance and the husband showed him to a pleasant room with a view of the sea.

'Which newspaper would you like in the morning?'

Sam shuddered.

'Do you get any of the English ones?' he asked cautiously.

'*Times* or *Chronicle*?'

He hesitated.

'I'd better have both, please.'

'No problem. Breakfast's from 7.30 to 9.30. And if you're wanting to be late out this evening the second key on that key-ring opens the front door.'

Sam thanked the man. When he'd gone, he glanced into the small, clean bathroom, finding it generously supplied with shampoos and soaps. There was even a disposable razor in a cellophane wrapper.

He sat on the candlewick bedspread, fantasising that it might have been here in this very room that his father and his companion had stayed. Would they have kept a register from 1971? He kicked himself. It was nonsense to expect anything like that. Probably nonsense for him to have come here in the first place.

He suddenly felt desperately tired. His normal sleep pattern had been shot to pieces in the past few days. His life was in limbo. Waiting. Waiting for old Craigie to do his stuff. And waiting for a clutch of London scandal-mongers to wield their axe on him. Powerless to influence any of it. He felt increasingly bitter towards Julie Jackman. Whether or not the newspaper had cajoled her into springing the trap for him, it had been her decision. Her action that would wreck his career.

He felt an overwhelming need to shut it out for a few hours. There was a small TV in the corner which he switched on and tuned to Sky News. Then he took his shoes off and lay back on the bed. The stories about a missing child in Essex and the love lives of footballers washed over him like Mogadon. He let his eyelids droop, but the headlines on the half-hour prodded him awake again. Some little known white-supremacy group had posted an Internet message claiming responsibility for the Southall bomb. The police were treating it with caution, the newscaster said, and asking for more witnesses to come forward.

Sam was on the point of turning the television off again, but the report that followed stopped him. It was from the Balkans, a follow-up on the Albanian Kosovar family seeking asylum in Europe. Sam leaned on one elbow, watching angry scenes at a port in Italy as the family – one small part of a boatload of refugees – was confronted by protesters demanding they be sent back where they came from. Only after police fired teargas at the demonstrators were the refugees able to land.

When the report concluded, Sam switched off. The bedside radio had an alarm clock. He set it for 7 p.m. and lay back.

London

In his East End flat, Rob Petrie had also been watching Sky News. He'd turned the channel on the moment he was sure Sandra had fallen asleep after her night shift. From tomorrow she would be off duty for a couple of days, which would force him to be more circumspect.

When he'd first seen the TV images of what he'd done in Southall, the sight of the blood had shocked him, but only in the way that any mortal would be affected. Not because it had anything to do with him. Two Sikhs dead – they were just numbers. Statistics on the TV. Not *people*. He felt nothing for them. The link between his execution of the attack and its consequences was missing. It hadn't surprised him not to feel anything for his victims. After all, what he'd done was a clinically planned act of war. He'd read enough about the military in World War II and the Gulf to know how easy it was for men to kill without guilt.

Two days had passed since the attack. With the investigators showing every sign of cluelessness, his natural fear of being discovered had started to evaporate. He felt a deep satisfaction at what he'd done, and pride. He'd put himself up there. Voted for what he believed in. Stuck a finger up the bum of multi-ethnicity, and shown the whole wide world there were people out here who wouldn't stand for the multiracism being forced on the European population by its compliant, Zionist-backed politicians. He'd even got his erections back.

The Sky News report on the Albanian Kosovars poised to flood into Europe had done much to reinforce his belief in the need for urgent action. Already the streets of Europe's capitals were dogged by dark-skinned, shaven-headed beggars with baggy trousers and beads of eyes that could spot a wallet through several layers of clothing. The politicians wouldn't stop that tide of gypsies becoming a flood. None of them had the guts to say that European culture must be preserved for the Europeans, a people whose blood had been mongrelised quite enough over the centuries and mustn't be mongrelised any more. So it was down to the likes of him, individuals prepared to use cunning and courage to achieve their ends.

He could never have acted on his own. He had neither the fighting materials nor the vision. It had taken a man with the power to reach out and influence the far corners of Europe to stir him into action. A leader who appeared well practised in the skills of subterfuge and non-conventional warfare. A man whose identity would remain a secret, even from his closest lieutenants.

It didn't matter to Petrie not knowing who his leader was. He knew him by his ideals, by his impressive organisation and by his words. The World Wide Web had brought them together, an article posted on one of the American white-power sites. On a guest page six months ago they'd published a treatise on the future of Europe, written by a man with the pseudonym of 'Freeman'. His words had made perfect sense to Petrie, a clarion call declaration that encompassed his own beliefs. Caucasian Europeans needed to unite against the enemies from outside. Against the dark races and the Muslims. But Europeans were not all one people. Germans were German, French were French and the English English. The homogenisation of Europe being engineered by Brussels needed resisting too. There were two enemies to be faced. The greater, polluting one from beyond Europe's outer boundaries, and the enemy within, the woolly liberals and leftie idealists determined to make Europeans all the same.

There'd been an e-mail address for 'Freeman', to which Petrie had written, saying how much he agreed with his policies. A correspondence had ensued using PGP encryption and involving frequent changes of e-mail postboxes. Freeman's responses had contained questions, probing Petrie's own philosophy and his commitment. Eventually, three months ago, a request had come for some token demonstration of his readiness to act. A simple task, the daubing on a wall of two words – Lucifer Network – at a time and a place prescribed for him. Done in the middle of the night in an area where graffiti was part of the normal landscape, it had gone unnoticed by the local populace. But during the act itself, Petrie had sensed he was being watched, checked over by the man who had now become his general.

Then, a month ago, he'd been alerted to the imminence of the first Europe-wide action by the Network. A blow for racial purity by volunteers like himself, men without police records who'd never been involved in the infiltrated right wing. He'd been asked to choose three targets for nail bombs which the Lucifer Network would supply. He'd acknowledged himself ready, then been given a time and place to collect the explosives. He never saw who it was who'd left the package behind the garden wall of a terraced house ten minutes' walk from his flat.

Petrie left the TV on but turned down the sound. He got up from the two-seater, brown leather sofa – one of the few quality possessions he'd retained from his former life – and stepped into the narrow hall, listening for sounds from the bedroom. Nothing. Just shouting from next door – a single mother who'd got too fond of the bottle, arguing with her troublesome teenage son. Sandra always slept through it.

Once she started putting up zeds it would take an earthquake to wake her.

Petrie returned to the lounge. One thing *was* troubling him. He hadn't had an e-mail from his leader yet. 'Peter' – 'Freeman' had changed his code name when they went onto a war footing – had warned him not to expect any instant reaction to the first of his three missions, but he'd hoped for something by now. Three times a day he'd been logging on to check his e-mail. Four hours ago was the last connection.

The computer was on a wheeled unit in the corner of the living room farthest from the window. A slide-out tray beneath the monitor held the keyboard. Shelves below were for the printer and the PC case. Above it, fixed to the wall, was a cupboard made of MDF and painted black, its double doors secured with a Yale lock. Hovering by the door for a moment to ensure there was no sound of Sandra stirring, he took the bunch of keys from the clip on his belt and opened this holy of holies. The doors swung back. Neo-Nazi books and magazines were stacked neatly on each side. From a pile of CDs at the back he selected a Skrewdriver album, slipped the disc into the drive on the PC, then carefully closed and relocked his trophy box. Sandra had never seen inside it.

He sat in front of the screen and clamped on a fat pair of earphones. He got the player going, then with his squat head moving to the beat he dialled his ISP. His login was 'Anthony Harden', using the initials of the only man in recent history to attempt to rid Europe of its racial interlopers. He had mail. He smiled. The message was from 'Peter Stone'. A different surname every time, but a common theme. Stone, Steel, Fist, Blood.

> *Congratulations!*
> *As you saw, the effort on Saturday was across Europe. The Lucifer Network is well established thanks to you and the other comrades. Now we must prepare for the next stage. Further action is needed this weekend!*

He felt a somersaulting in his stomach at the thought of striking again so soon.

> *Again your efforts will be matched in many parts of the continent. Together we will win! The struggle for the European ideal goes from strength to strength!*

Always the exclamation marks! Always the sense of urgency.

Petrie liked seeing his own words and ideas in print in the messages he'd exchanged with Peter. Liked trawling through the professionally produced right-wing websites, feeling he belonged to a brotherhood growing in strength and influence. Loved the feeling he was in the vanguard of the Revolution.

Please confirm you have selected a target and will act next Saturday.

Selected? Not quite. The racial group yes, the location no. The reconnaissance was yet to be done. The materials were in his garage: plastic explosive, detonators, timers and nails – and a booklet of bomb-making instructions as simple to follow as a manual from IKEA.

United we shall not fail!

He clicked on the 'new message' button and began to type. 'Yes. All will be ready. The revolution goes on.'

Rothesay, Isle of Bute

When Sam awoke he could smell onions frying. The hotel didn't do evening meals so he assumed it was the couple who ran it preparing their own supper.

He got up and put his shoes back on, then made the call to the photographer. No reply.

'Damn.'

Four hours almost to the minute since he'd handed over the £20 note on the putting green. He rechecked the number on the business card and rang it again. Still nothing. He grabbed hold of the map of Rothesay that he'd picked up from the tourist office and spread it on the bed to locate the street where Tom Craigie had his shop. Then he locked the room and went downstairs. As he passed through reception he noticed a familiar set of legs by the counter. The family in shorts were checking in.

Outside, the wind had dropped. A huge patch of blue dominated the sky from which the sun had recently disappeared behind hills to the west of the town. Sam found Craigie's photo 'studio' easily. Next to the local paper office, it was little more than a booth. And it was locked.

He cursed. Failure hovered over him like a cloud of Highland midges. He cupped a hand against the window to see if there was a light on in the back, but the place was in darkness. Then he heard footsteps behind him and a gravelly clearing of the throat.

'Och, now there you are.'

'Mr Craigie! I thought you'd run off with my money!'

'Och yes! So much of it, I was nearly tempted.'

Sam made way for him to get at the door with his keys. He noticed an old manila folder under the photographer's arm and his spirits lifted.

'You've had success?'

'Emmm . . . I don't know. I have some contact prints for you to look at but my confidence isn't high. That year's files were all out of order for some reason. And a lot of the negs were missing their index cards. It's why I came down to the shop – to see if I'd got them here for some reason. Come on inside.'

He switched on lights and led Sam through a raised flap in the counter at the back. Shelves in the tiny shop were decorated with examples of Craigie's work. The premises had the sour smell of stale chemicals.

'You can sit in the studio.' He pointed into a minute space with black walls and a rail with three different colours of curtain. Room enough for two chairs and a tripod – and something which to Sam seemed oddly out of place. A computer and scanner on a corner table.

'Don't tell me you're into digital photography as well as the plate camera,' Sam commented.

'Not yet. But the Island of Bute has a website and I top it up with new pictures from time to time. The webmaster's in Glasgow, so I scan the shots into the computer and send them by e-mail.'

'Amazing,' Sam mouthed, unable to reconcile the new technology with such a down-at-heel character.

'Och, well you have to keep up wi' the times. Now if you'd cast your eye over the prints in the folder, I'll start going through the shelves in the darkroom.'

The snaps were 6 × 6 centimetres, some crystal sharp, others fading. Fat people, thin people, but none that looked anything like his father.

'Any luck?' Craigie shouted from the darkroom.

'Unfortunately not.' The ferry ticket trail was leading him nowhere.

'Och, I'm sorry. Looks like I'm going to be letting you down.'

'It was always a long shot.' Foolish to have set so much store by Craigie's archive.

The phone trilled in his pocket, its sound startling him.

'Hello?'

'Where exactly are you?' asked Duncan Waddell.

'Rothesay.'

'Is that anywhere near Helensburgh?'

'About a couple of hours. Why?'

'An appointment's been made for you there at noon tomorrow. The man's name is Ted Salmon. Mean anything to you?'

'No. Should it?'

'According to the Submariners Association he was a good pal of your father's. They were on the same crew on HMS *Retribution*. Our security friends across the river came up with it, but say they haven't the time to go and talk to him. Chasing communist agents who may or may not have been active twenty-seven years ago doesn't seem high on their list of priorities.'

'You amaze me . . . Give me the address.'

Waddell did. Then he cleared his throat and the voice dropped half an octave.

'And I have some bad news for you.' Sam's heart sank. 'Do they get the *Chronicle* up where you are?'

'Unfortunately, yes.'

'Then you'll need to wear a balaclava tomorrow. The lawyers have failed to get an injunction. The first editions are already on their way north and you're on the front page. Little Miss Jackman's stuffed you good and proper, Sam. Stuffed you as tight as a Christmas turkey.'

IO

Scotland
Tuesday

S OME TIME AROUND three in the morning a foghorn started moaning, its mournful tone making Sam think of death row. He put in the foam earplugs which he always carried when travelling and tried to sleep. At 6.30 he abandoned the attempt and got up to make tea from the tray in the room. At seven he looked outside the door for the papers. When they weren't there he took a shower.

Fifteen minutes later, when he was putting his trousers on, there came the dreaded plop from the corridor. He waited until the footsteps had receded, then stepped out.

Although he knew what to expect, it shook him to see his own face staring back at him. It was as bad as it could possibly have been. Nothing fudged about the picture, his grizzled visage on the right of the frame, a straight-on shot looking guilty as hell. To the left, the woman who'd set him up, her expression taut with the uncertainty of what she'd unleashed.

The caption was simple but explicit – *Ms Julie Jackman, virologist daughter of the murdered gun-runner, with alleged MI6 officer 'Simon Foster'*. The article itself filled the bottom right quadrant of the front page under the headline DEATH OF A GUN-RUNNER. DID WHITEHALL PULL THE TRIGGER?

'Jesus . . .'

As his eyes flicked through the text his anger grew. They were as good as accusing him of murder, of setting up the killing of Harry Jackman on the orders of the government.

'Bollocks . . .'

He shook his head in dismay. That picture would be stared at over breakfast tables the length and breadth of the country. Businessmen he'd chatted up in bars abroad would study it on the train to work and start remembering the confidences they'd let slip. His neighbours in Brentford would gossip like hens.

'God damn you, Julie Jackman.'

He combed the text in more detail. Harry Jackman's letter to the *Chronicle* had been thorough. The guns, the money and the identification of Simon Foster as the rep from MI6, all there. A direct quote from the dutiful daughter was the cream on the cake – a statement that ever since the Bodanga coup's embarrassing failure her father had lived in fear of being silenced by British intelligence, and by Simon Foster in particular. She'd nailed him to the cross. Any lingering sympathy he had for her, any readiness to forgive had evaporated. He wanted her dead.

He conceded that there was a token attempt at balance in the article – the reporter had damned Jackman's unsavoury career, describing him as unscrupulous and amoral. Also a quote from Zambia's police chief about Jackman being murdered by robbers and a 'nothing to say' from the Foreign Office. But the denials wouldn't help. The mud had been thrown.

Sam stared at his image on the page. The beard had been grown two years ago as a flimsy shield against the Voroninskaya mafiya. Now it must go again in an even feebler effort at protection, this time against his fellow countrymen.

He quickly checked that the *Times*'s early edition hadn't picked up on the story, then dumped the newspapers on the bed and stepped into the bathroom. He filled the basin with hot water, removed the complimentary razor from its cellophane, lathered his face with hand soap and began to scrape at his jaw. It gave him pleasure to be removing a part of his persona that he'd never liked.

Ten minutes later he had two small cuts underneath a chin that looked startlingly white. Not bad for someone so out of practice. Deciding to be on his way, he packed quickly, took the shortbread biscuits from the tea-maker tray and pushed them into a side pocket of his rucksack, then left the room. As he passed the dining room the smell of bacon tempted him, but he strode out into the street, unlocking the car and throwing his bag onto the back seat.

He sat there for a moment, gripping the wheel and staring out towards the still choppy waters of the firth. One way or another the woman who'd dumped him in this mess was going to have to be taught the error of her ways.

London

When she began her journey to work on the tube, Julie found herself sitting opposite a man reading the *Daily Chronicle*. To see her own face staring across the gangway brought home what she'd done. Whichever way she turned, she imagined people ogling her. The paper's front page had been shown on the morning TV news. She put her glasses on and hid behind a book, holding it high to conceal her face.

Halfway through her journey she felt a hand touch her knee and nearly jumped out of her skin. She lowered the book to see a grubby-faced child waving a plastic cup at her. Towering above the girl, clothed like a Russian doll, stood her fat-faced, olive-skinned mother holding a card on which some sad story of suffering had been written in broken English. Julie shook her head and raised her book again. She was fed up with Balkan beggars. The other day she'd watched one step from a train onto the platform and pull a mobile phone from the folds of her clothes.

Her feelings about her appearance in the newspaper were confused. She'd had to admit to a sneaky sense of exhilaration. For the first time in her life she knew her father would have been proud of her. She'd taken a big, public stand on his behalf. But there was a price. She'd thrust herself into the public gaze and she wasn't suited for it. And it disturbed her how hard the paper had gone on the insinuation that Simon Foster had had a direct hand in her father's murder. She still found it difficult to believe that a man she'd rather liked could be a murderer.

She'd considered not going in to work today, but decided she had to face things. When with deep trepidation she passed through the doors of the department, Ailsa Mackinley was the first to confront her, rising awestruck from behind the reception desk.

'Jul! Brilliant!' she beamed. 'You're famous!'

'I hope not,' Julie answered, making straight for her office. 'That certainly wasn't my intention.'

'Well I'm with you all the way,' Ailsa assured her, hanging on to her arm. 'People like that shouldn't be allowed to get away with it.'

'Oh Ailsa,' Julie moaned. 'It's not that simple.'

'I'll bet.' She gripped Julie's arm more firmly and blocked her path. '*He* wants to talk to you.' She pulled a long face.

'The professor?' Julie's heart turned a somersault.

'Asked me to tell you as soon as you got in. Said you should see him before you did anything else.'

'Hell.'

'Don't let him bully you. Stick up for yourself.'

'Oh sure. Don't fuss, Ailsa.'

Inside her office her two colleagues were already at their desks. Janet smiled awkwardly, then looked away. George, her unsuccessful admirer, took it upon himself to voice what the two of them had just been saying to each other.

'We wondered whether this was your idea or someone else's?' he asked without any preamble.

'What d'you mean?'

'This accusation about spies and dirty tricks. Hardly your style, we'd have thought. Someone pressure you?'

He's being patronising, thought Julie. The little woman unable to take big decisions for herself.

'It was my choice,' she answered sharply. But yes, she had been pressured. By a man now dead. 'And I don't want to talk about it. I . . . I'm not in the habit of discussing my personal life with the people I work with.'

'But you're quite ready to discuss it with the rest of the nation,' George snorted. He turned back to his computer and began downloading a screensaver from the Internet.

Julie put her bag on the floor and sat down, blinking back tears and forcing herself to ignore what had just been said and to think about the day ahead. There were some test results to be studied. God knew how she would be able to concentrate. She picked up the phone and dialled the professor's number.

'Norton.' He had a soft voice.

'Professor, good morning.'

'Ah, Julie . . .'

'You wanted a word, I believe.'

'Yes. Would now be convenient?'

'Absolutely.'

'Good. Come on in, then.'

She stepped out into the corridor and walked to the room where she'd first crossed paths with Simon Foster four days earlier.

'Come and sit down.' The professor, a tall, thin man, of the old school as far as women were concerned, rose to his feet, his lined face a picture of discomfort.

'This business with the newspapers.'

'I'm sorry. I should have told you in advance,' Julie mumbled.

'Yes. I'd have welcomed knowing it was coming, rather than reading it over breakfast.' He sat down as she sat. 'Now look. As far as I'm concerned this is your private affair. I have no wish to know anything about it. I have no views on the likely truth of the allegations you've made, nor on the rights and wrongs of getting mixed up with the papers like this.' But he did have, Julie realised. Strong views. And they weren't supportive. 'My sole worry,' Norton continued, 'is that this institution might in some way be tarnished by it.'

'Tarnished? I don't see . . .'

'No, I'm sure you don't. If you did, you'd have discussed it with me beforehand.' He clasped his hands on the meticulously tidy desk. 'The point is this. What you've launched yourself into comes under the heading of scandal. And scandal tends to stick to anything mentioned in the same breath. I was relieved to see that the St Michael's Hospital Group and this department were not named anywhere in this morning's article . . .'

'No. They weren't,' Julie interrupted defiantly.

'. . . but there will doubtless be many more. Both in the *Chronicle* and in other parts of the media. Presumably the journalists you talked to know where you work?'

'I don't think I ever said . . .' She racked her brains, trying to remember.

'Well it doesn't matter whether you did or not. The job description "virologist" will be enough. A quick search of the websites and they'll find your name on our department's. I expect we'll be inundated with calls in the coming hours.'

Julie sank back into her chair. It hadn't occurred to her there'd be follow-ups.

Norton pulled himself up straight. 'I've instructed Ailsa to say you're not here today.'

'But there'll be legitimate calls for me, there always are,' she responded, startled.

'Others can deal with those. For now I'd prefer your absence to be fact rather than fiction.'

'What d'you mean?'

'That you stay away from the lab until this blows over.'

Julie gaped. 'But I've got loads to do. What are you saying? You're suspending me from duty?'

'Oh no. Call it compassionate leave. I just don't want us to be involved in any way.' He stood up again to show her the interview was over. 'Why don't you give me a call in a couple of days and we'll see how things look?'

She hated being railroaded. 'But . . .'

'Best not to hang around,' Norton interrupted, opening his office door as she stood up. 'And best slip out through the goods bay at the back. In case there are camera crews.'

Julie turned to leave, saying nothing. A great lump blocked her throat. Back in her own room George was on his own. He watched Julie pick up her bag and head for the door.

'Anything I can do?'

'No. I'm taking a few days off.'

'And if anyone rings?'

'Better say you've never heard of me.'

The deliveries entrance was in a mews which joined the main street twenty metres from the front entrance. A quick glance revealed no media types anywhere. She headed for the underground station, uncertain where to go. The *Chronicle* people knew about her room in Acton. In the clubby world of journalism others would soon know it too. She'd do better in Woodbridge, she decided. At least Liam would be glad to see her.

Suddenly a hand grabbed her elbow, making her jump.

'Excuse me, Miss Jackman.' A male voice close by her ear.

She turned. A man and a woman stood each side of her, boxing her in. Media, she decided.

'I'm sorry,' she began, heart thudding. 'I've got nothing more to . . .'

'We're police officers, Miss Jackman.' The man flashed an ID. 'You're to come to Paddington Green for a chat.'

'Why?'

'We're investigating your father's involvement in the illegal transportation of strategic materials,' the woman told her.

'But I've already told the intelligence people I know nothing about his business dealings.'

'Except when the newspapers ask you about it, eh, Miss Jackman?' The male officer's manner was unpleasantly aggressive.

'Come on, Julie,' the woman pressed. 'There's some important people waiting to speak to you.'

'Do I have a choice?' Julie was scared. This was a whole new ball game.

'Not really,' the man told her. 'I'm entitled to arrest you on suspicion of concealing information relevant to a breach of the nuclear non-proliferation treaty.'

'This is outrageous . . .' Julie mouthed.

'Our car's round the next corner,' the woman told her as she took Julie's arm. 'I really would advise you to co-operate. It'll save so much time.'

'They're on their way,' said Detective Chief Inspector Stephanie Watson as she entered the interview room where the SIS woman was waiting. 'Be about fifteen minutes.'

'Excellent.' Denise Corby crossed and uncrossed her legs. She wore black stockings beneath a dark grey skirt. 'Thanks for setting this up so rapidly.'

'Not at all. I needed a break from the Southall business,' said Steph. 'White nationalists aren't my favourite sort of people.'

The arrangement to bring in Julie Jackman for further questioning had been made little more than an hour ago. The call to Special Branch from Vauxhall Cross had found a depleted team on the sixteenth floor at Scotland

Yard because of summer leave taking, but they'd agreed to spare Steph for the morning. Which had pleased her, since she had a personal interest in the case.

'What exactly have you got on this girl?' she asked, sitting down on the opposite side of the interview table.

Corby held out a plastic folder. 'Something highly significant. Proof that she lied about her involvement with her father's business activities.'

'May I see?' Steph took it.

'When I talked to her on Friday,' Corby continued, 'she denied all knowledge of her father's scams. And she repeated those denials on Saturday when the letter turned up. The so-called red mercury – and Vienna? It was all in the fax I sent you.'

'I read it. Go on.'

'Well, the inquiries we've been making in Austria tell a different story.' She pointed to the folder.

Steph ran her eye over the pages and handed them back. 'I get the drift. But what's the UK angle? There has to be one if you're involving the Met.'

'Conspiracy. We suspect that the material her father shipped out of Russia could have been nuclear weapon components. If we can get her to admit discussing the smuggling of them with him when he was last in England, then we've grounds for a prosecution.'

'Possibly. Conspiracy's hard to get past a jury,' Steph cautioned. She'd have liked to see Julie Jackman banged up for life after what she'd done to Sam, but there were rules to be followed. 'We'll give it a whirl.'

'Good. You're happy for me to lead?'

'Makes sense.' Steph stood up again. 'I'll see if they can get us some coffee. Like some?'

'Wouldn't say no.'

Julie recognised the Paddington police station as the one they took terrorists to. She'd seen it on TV. Her nerves began to fray as they led her into an interview room. When she saw who was there she groaned inwardly.

'Thank you for coming in, Miss Jackman.'

'Wasn't given much of a choice,' she answered stonily. She'd hoped never to see Denise Corby again.

The narrow room had a plain table in the middle with a tape-recording panel at one end. The other woman there looked almost as butch as Denise Corby, she decided, and was staring at her with a curiosity too intense to be merely professional. Two bull dykes ready to work her over.

'My colleague here represents the Metropolitan Police,' Corby began. 'No need for you to know her name,' she added sourly.

The door opened and a uniformed policewoman entered with a tray of coffee, this small act of hospitality belying the hostility that crackled in the air.

'We thought we'd talk informally at first,' Corby began. 'If we reach a point where the Chief Inspector thinks you need to be cautioned, then we'll switch the recorder on. Understood?'

Julie found it hard not to be cowed by them. 'Would you mind explaining why you've got me here?'

'Because we don't think you've been truthful with us.'

'That's nonsense. I have.'

'Really? That letter your father wrote – you claimed it was the first time you'd ever heard of red mercury and also said you'd never been involved in your father's business activities.'

'Correct.'

'We think that's a lie, Miss Jackman. We have evidence that says otherwise.' Denise Corby coughed behind her hand. 'It suggests you may even have been his accomplice.'

'*What?*'

Julie shivered. Her father's warnings about the deviousness of the intelligence people were coming true. They were going to frame her.

'July 1997. Your father was in Vienna setting up the shipping arrangements for the so-called red mercury. He said so in his letter.'

'Yes,' Julie whispered. She felt her neck begin to glow.

'A criminal business deal which you claimed to know nothing about.'

'That's right,' she croaked.

'Which is odd, because you were there in Vienna too. Weren't you, Miss Jackman?'

Julie opened her mouth, but no words came. She shook her head in dismay.

Denise Corby opened the folder and produced a sheet of fax paper.

'According to the register of the Intercontinental Hotel, on three consecutive nights that month you had room 115 and your father room 120.'

Julie felt the ground opening up. An innocent happening was to be twisted and used against her. The establishment's revenge for what she'd said to the *Chronicle*.

'But you don't understand,' she protested feebly. 'Yes, I was in Vienna at that time. But under my own auspices. It was pure coincidence my father was there too.'

'Coincidence?' Corby mocked.

'What auspices?' Stephanie asked, deciding to take a hand. Still unsure what to make of the girl, she had a suspicion she was telling the truth.

'An international conference on HIV. My boss, Professor Norton was one of the speakers. And a few days before I went, my father happened to ring, saying he had to be there at the same time. For business – but the point is, I have no idea *what* business.'

'You can't expect us to believe that,' Corby insisted. 'Same hotel. Rooms on the same floor. You knew exactly what he was doing there.'

'I did not. We co-ordinated our plans, of course we did. We wanted to see each other.'

'How much time did you spend together?' Steph asked.

'Just one evening. On the other nights there were conference events.' She noted Corby's disbelieving glance towards the policewoman.

'Tell us about that evening,' the Vauxhall Cross woman continued. 'Was your father alone?'

'No. He had his latest woman with him. South African, I think. Quite nice. Most of them were, his wives and girlfriends. I never understood why none of them lasted.'

'Know her name?'

Julie frowned, trying to recall it.

'Linda, I think.'

'Where did you meet them?' Steph asked.

'In the hotel bar. They were sitting with three or four others. All men. My father introduced me. The men just nodded, then carried on with their conversation. In whispers mostly. I didn't speak to them at all.'

Stephanie's uncertainty deepened. Any man with a normal set of tackle would have made a pitch for a pretty girl like Julie. Sam had.

'And your father was involved in their conversation?'

'Most of the time, yes.'

'What was it about?'

'I didn't hear. I was talking to Linda. She and I got on really well. I'd not met her before.'

'You spent the whole evening there?'

'We stayed in the bar for a while, then the three of us went to the restaurant and had dinner.'

'You, your father and Linda,' Corby checked.

'Yes.'

'What about the men your father was with? They didn't join you?'

'No.'

'Later?'

'No.'

'Tell me about them.'

'For heaven's sake,' Julie complained, 'I hardly looked at them.'

'Nationalities?'

'God knows. It was a year ago.'

'But they weren't English . . .'

Julie frowned, trying to think why she'd always assumed they were foreign. 'I believe not.'

'Was one of them Russian?'

'Could have been. I really don't remember.'

'Names? Does Vladimir Kovalenko ring a bell?'

The name in the letter. She shook her head. Only one man had registered with her that evening, and that was long after she'd bade her father goodnight.

'What about the Arab?'

She shook her head again. 'I don't remember any Arabs.' She was surprised at how calm she was sounding now.

For several seconds, maybe as much as half a minute, they just looked at her, digesting what she'd told them.

'You're quite sure your father never told you the specifics of why he was in Vienna?' Steph queried again.

'Certain.'

Denise Corby leaned forward across the table. For a moment Julie feared a re-run of the hand-holding trick.

'You do understand what sort of deals your father did, Miss Jackman?' Corby asked, hush-voiced.

'I always assumed they weren't a hundred per cent straight,' she replied.

'Not a hundred per cent,' Corby mocked. 'His whole world was a web of lies, Miss Jackman.'

'He wasn't a saint,' Julie answered defensively, aware that a change of direction was under way.

'His speciality was avoiding customs controls – that's a serious criminal offence. He paid bribes to officials – also a crime. His career in Africa began with the theft of precious minerals that didn't belong to him, which he sold for personal gain. A fraud in anybody's language. Need I go on, Miss Jackman?'

'I'm not sure what point you're . . .'

'Simply wanting to make sure you understand that of all the considerable wealth he amassed in recent years I doubt whether one penny was earned honestly. He lived by lies and deception.'

'That's as may be, but whatever my father did, I'm different,' Julie insisted, riled by the implication that she was dishonest too. 'Everything I've got, I've worked for.'

'The simple point I'm trying to make,' Denise Corby persisted, 'is that your father was one of the most untrustworthy men you could ever hope to meet.'

'Maybe, but *I'm* not a liar.'

'Oh really? What about that extraordinary load of tosh in the *Daily Chronicle* this morning? Where did that come from?'

Julie looked down at her hands. 'There was a second letter from my father,' she admitted softly.

'We gathered that. What did it say?'

Julie swallowed. Her throat was as dry as a bone. Reluctantly she told them. 'It said that if he were to die suddenly, then Simon Foster of MI6 would probably be to blame.'

Denise Corby sighed with exasperation. 'And you believed him? Despite knowing what a liar he was?'

Julie turned her face away. She felt wretched and looked towards the door, anywhere to avoid them seeing into her soul. There *was* no factual justification for doing what she'd done. She'd known it all along. She'd co-operated with the press to impress her father. To make the wretched man love her, wherever he was now.

'Did he give you money when you saw him in Vienna?' Corby asked, going for the kill.

Startled, Julie nodded. 'A little. It made him feel good to be generous.'

'How much?'

'A few hundred.'

'Pounds?'

'Yes.'

'More like a thousand?'

'Possibly.'

'He gave you money whenever he saw you?'

'Not every time, but usually. It was his way of making up for not being around when I was a child.'

'And with you working in a health service laboratory, you wouldn't be paid much . . .'

'Not a lot,' she agreed.

'So getting cash from your dad was something you came to rely on,' Corby suggested.

'Look I don't know what you're getting at, but the money was to help support Liam,' Julie floundered. She looked up at the ceiling, a single lamp burning in the middle of it, protected by a metal grille.

'But you were grateful for the cash. Probably felt you owed him something for his generosity. Felt that one way to repay him was by giving voice to his lies and fantasies through the media.'

'I don't know that they're lies,' Julie whispered, wretchedly.

'Well you should do, Miss Jackman,' Corby said harshly. 'One final question. What did you and he talk about when he was last back in England? Smuggling nuclear weapons?'

'Of course not. We spoke about him wanting to come home. Life in Africa was beginning to frighten him.'

Corby let her eyebrows float up in an exaggerated expression of derision.

'*Really?* And what was he scared of, pray?'

'Of being robbed, mostly,' Julie answered, not realising the hole she was digging. 'He said whites were being killed for the cash in their pockets and for their cars . . .'

They let her words hang in the air, waiting for it to sink in.

Death by robbery. Not by conspiracy. Not through the agency of one Simon Foster. Julie felt as small as a flea.

'I think I'd like to go now,' she whispered, staring down at her hands.

'And hang yourself, I shouldn't be surprised,' Corby snapped. 'You do realise that your slanderous allegations have destroyed the livelihood of a perfectly decent businessman?'

'He's not a businessman,' Julie retorted. 'He's one of you lot.'

Denise Corby folded her arms and raised a sceptical eyebrow.

Steph could see that the girl was on the verge of breaking down and took pity on her. 'The officers who brought you in can take you back to the West End, if you like,' she offered gently.

'I . . . I'd rather walk,' Julie sniffed.

'As you wish.'

As she stood up, Denise Corby thrust a business card at her. 'In case you've lost the last one I gave you. If you remember anything else about Vienna, do yourself a favour and give me a ring.'

Julie nodded. When she reached the door she half turned.

'Would you do something for me, Ms Corby?'

'I'll try.'

'Tell Simon Foster I'm sorry.'

She left the room.

'That'll be a huge comfort,' Corby spluttered when she'd gone.

'A silly *little* girl,' Steph declared, her comment tainted with personal venom. 'And quite out of her depth.'

'But with the power to inflict enormous damage,' Corby added, getting to her feet. 'Thanks for your support, Chief Inspector. At this point in time it seems we don't have a case.'

'No, but congratulations. I don't think she'll be talking to the papers any more.'

Denise Corby smiled.

'Probably not. Unfortunately the harm is already done.'

Steph itched to ask about Sam's fate but didn't dare. Her friendship with him was private and she wanted to keep it that way. 'Would you like me to run Julie's story past Professor Norton, just to see it stands up?' she checked.

'Yes, please. It'd be mad not to.' Denise Corby held out her hand. 'Now I think I'd better get out of your hair and leave you to concentrate on nailing the Southall bomber.'

Stephanie grimaced. 'We're painfully short of leads there. Nothing from the usual neo-Nazi sources. Hoping like crazy that there's something on the surveillance videos. Sharp eyes and a bit of luck is what we'll need if we're to catch this little runt before he strikes again.'

'Hope you get your break. And if you do, pass the luck our way. We've got a man on our books who could do with some.'

11

Scotland

S AM HEADED UP the Glasgow road, fortified by a bacon sandwich consumed on the ferry back to the mainland. There was a little under an hour to go before his appointment with Ted Salmon, the man who'd served on HMS *Retribution* with his father. This morning his priority was to try to prove the innocence of a long-dead sailor. In the days to come, it was his own name he would have to clear.

He turned left onto the Erskine suspension bridge that arched across the Clyde, driving like an automaton. He wanted to complete his business in Scotland and get back to London to fight his corner with his bosses. Waddell had been unavailable when he'd rung from the ferry and had yet to respond to the message he'd left. The distancing process had already begun, it seemed.

On the north bank of the Clyde, the road wound west through Dumbarton, following the line of the Firth. After a few miles a sign proclaimed the outskirts of Helensburgh, 'Birthplace of John Logie Baird, the inventor of television'. The town was at the mouth of the Gare Loch down which HMS *Retribution* used to pass on her way to the Atlantic from Faslane. To the right of the road, soulless, grey estates erupted like fungus from the hillside, built cheaply to house the workforce needed when the Navy located its new nuclear deterrent in Scotland thirty years ago.

Beyond these purpose-built slums lay the old Victorian town, an elegant resort of wide streets and weathered stone, whose sea front was dominated by a funfair, a swimming pool and a car park. Sam pulled in. He would need directions to find the address where Ted Salmon lived.

He got out and crossed the promenade to the shops opposite. Amongst them was a café. The decoration inside was eclectic: Edwardian brass, sixties kilims on the walls, and in a corner beneath garish computer game posters, two PCs with a board attached saying 'Internet connection £2.50 per half hour.'

'Get much call for that here?' Sam asked the shaven-headed young man behind the counter. He had a small gold ring through one nostril of his bulbous nose.

'Weekends mostly. Students out from Glasgow. What can I get you?'

'A cup of tea, please.'

'Assam, Darjeeling or Earl Grey?'

'PG Tips if you have it.'

Without batting an eyelid the man produced a box from beneath the counter.

Sam took his mug to a table by the window and looked out towards the sea. He watched the sky darken and let a shower pass before finishing his drink and asking the café owner for directions.

Back in his car, he headed away from the sea, into a grid of streets lined by grassy verges and hawthorn trees. Bungalows gave way to comfortable mansions which became grander as the road climbed the hill. He turned right into a side street and found Ted Salmon's home easily, a grey stone cottage in a pretty garden, separated from its neighbours by high laurel hedges.

When he rang the bell, it chimed somewhere far back in the recesses of the house. The front door was metal-framed with dappled glass. Through it he heard the sound of someone tidying things in the kitchen. He waited, but when no one came he pressed the bell again. It took a third attempt before he saw movement behind the glass and the door was opened.

'Yes?'

Sad, grey eyes were set in a lined face crowned with untidy white hair. The man was fiddling with a hearing aid, trying to settle it in his ear.

'Ted Salmon?' Sam asked.

'Why, yes.' The eyes widened as if recognising someone from the past. 'You must be Trevor Packer's boy.'

'That's right. The name's Sam.'

'Bless us! You're the spitting image.'

Salmon was a small man who spoke with a south of England accent that could have been Devon.

'Come on in. Last time I saw you was at your father's funeral. You were in short trousers.'

'Well, yes. I suppose I would have been.'

'Not much fun, funerals, are they?' They were standing squeezed together in the small hall, Salmon peering intently up at his visitor.

'One of the worst days of my life,' Sam confirmed.

'Cremated my wife last week.' Ted Salmon said it matter-of-factly, but couldn't disguise the downturn at the corners of his mouth.

'I'm so sorry,' said Sam. 'This isn't the best time to call, then.'

'That's all right. It's nice to have company. Come on in to the front room.' He led the way. 'I'm afraid I've reached the stage of life where too many of the people I've known have gone. Shouldn't complain, I s'pose. Lucky to have known them. And meself, I've had a good life.' He turned to face Sam, extending his hands in an awkward gesture of welcome. 'Can I make you a cup of tea? I was just about to have one.'

'Well . . . that'd be great. Thanks.'

'NATO standard?'

'Without sugar, thanks.'

Salmon urged him to take a seat then disappeared to the kitchen. The sitting room felt curiously unlived-in. Lace antimacassars on the chair backs, a glass-fronted cupboard full of plaques from the ships the former CPO had served in and a collection of family photos in silver frames.

'Was it sudden with your wife, Mr Salmon?' Sam asked sympathetically. He'd stood up as the old man re-entered the room with a tray and two mugs.

'Kidney disease. Been shaky for years. Two weeks ago she never woke up one morning. Good way to go, I suppose.'

'How are you managing?'

'Oh not so bad. I've got a son and a daughter who live nearby. And I keep myself busy with the garden.'

'I could see that. It's immaculate.'

'Tidy, certainly. You learn to be as a submariner.' His brow furrowed as he tried to recall something. 'You had a sister, didn't you?'

'That's right. She's married with two daughters.'

'And your mum?'

'Died five years ago.'

'Did she really?' His eyes widened as if wondering whether everyone he'd ever known would be dead before him.

'I wanted to ask you about my father, Mr Salmon,' Sam began, not wanting to stay longer than he had to.

'So they said on the phone.'

'How well did you know him?'

'Pretty well, pretty well. We'd done a lot of postings together. The first was on HMS *Andrew*. Remember her?'

'My father probably mentioned the name, but I've forgotten.'

'Last submarine in the Royal Navy to have a deck gun. And the first to snort her way across the Atlantic – submerged all the way. That was back in '53. Your dad and I were on board for that one. She was a famous boat, the *Andrew*.'

'And you served together again on *Retribution*.'

'And on a couple of other boats in between. What're you after? Researching his life story?'

'Sort of. Things have been happening that made me realise I never really knew him.'

Salmon shrugged. 'Not surprising. You was only eleven when he died.'

'I knew him as a dad, but not as a man, you could say.' Sam let his words sink in. 'Can I be blunt?'

'Course you can. Blunt as you like. Not easy to shock a Navy man.'

Sam took a deep breath. 'I'm trying to find out whether my father betrayed his country, Mr Salmon.'

The old sailor spilt his tea on his trousers. 'Blimey!' He put the mug down and took a handkerchief from his pocket to mop himself up. 'That's a question and a half. What's brought this on?'

'An allegation's been made that he passed secret material to the Russians while he served on HMS *Retribution*.'

Salmon gaped in astonishment.

'Never! I can't believe that. We was all in it together. Trev wouldn't have put his mates' lives at risk. Who's been telling you this nonsense?'

'The Russians.'

Salmon was flabbergasted. 'The Russians say he spied for them?'

'Yes.'

The old man puffed out his cheeks. 'I'm stunned. Don't know what to say. If it's true, then I never had a clue. But I can't believe it.'

'How much did you know about his life outside the submarine service?' Sam asked.

'Oh . . . some,' he replied warily. 'You know. You chat a bit when you're away on patrol.'

'Did he seem short of money?'

'No more than the rest of us.'

'Did he talk to you about his girlfriends?'

Salmon lifted one eyebrow. Then he puffed out his cheeks. 'Oh you knows about that, does you?'

'My mother used to slag him off for womanising.'

Salmon gave a wry smile. 'He was the sort of bloke we all used to envy. Know what I mean?'

'Not entirely.'

Salmon looked uncomfortable. 'Don't think I should be saying this. Sort of speaking ill of the dead, like. And you being his son and all.'

'Please be frank, Mr Salmon. Totally frank. There's a very big issue at play here and I need to know the truth about him.'

Salmon blinked. 'Yes, well . . . What I meant by us envying him was that he was the type who could spot a woman in a crowd of strangers, point her

116

out to his mates and tell 'em he was going to have her.' He looked up to check Sam was coping with his bluntness.

'Go on.'

'Well, sure enough he always did have her. I felt sorry for your ma, of course,' he added quickly. 'She put up with a lot.'

'So she always said.'

Salmon's eyes twinkled suddenly. 'I'll tell you a story, Sam. Now this is really telling tales out of school, but if you're after the whole works . . .'

'Yes.'

'When we was on *Retribution* your dad made a point of never telling your mum when he expected to be home. I mean the patrol dates were secret anyway, but the point was that Trev wanted a week ashore with some girl or other before he went home to his marital duties, if you know what I mean. Well, one patrol, which had been a particularly arduous one, the Jimmy – the First Lieutenant – he sent off a signal when we was approaching home waters asking that all the wives be told we'd be coming alongside in a couple of days' time. Thought it'd be nice for the blokes to have their loved ones standing on the shore waving as they came in, see? Well . . . When your dad hears about it he goes potty. Threatens to nut the Jimmy. For two days he's wetting hisself in case his local popsie gets wind of the boat coming in and turns up to welcome him too. Turned out all right in the end, mind, because your mum was such a hard case she wouldn't dream of trekking up to Scotland to see the boat in.'

'And the girlfriend was there?'

'Don't remember. I had my own fish to fry, if you know what I mean.' At the thought of his recent loss, the sparkle faded from his eyes.

'D'you remember the name of my father's girl?'

Salmon sucked his teeth. 'There was a few of them over the years, you know. Some of them was . . .' He wrinkled his nose. 'Well . . . pretty rough, to be honest with you. Wasn't always too choosy, your dad.'

Sam swallowed. Another slash to the canvas of his icon. 'Remember *any* names?'

Salmon looked blank, then slowly shook his head. 'It's nearly thirty years,' he murmured. Then he looked up again. 'That spying business – you serious about that?'

'Yes, unfortunately. The GRU had his name on their books.'

Salmon pushed fingers through his crown of white hair and whistled. 'You think you know someone and then all of a sudden . . .' He shook his head in dismay.

This was getting nowhere. In the meantime Sam's own fate was being chewed over down in London, without any input from him.

'Were there any other mates of his who knew him better than you?' Sam asked, desperate not to leave Scotland empty-handed.

'Possibly. Possibly. But I can't think of one. And a couple of them are dead anyway.'

'Tell me something else,' Sam asked. 'What sort of secrets would my father have had access to?'

Salmon pursed his lips. 'Well, to be honest, most of the chiefs on board wouldn't have had a lot to tell the Russkies. I was on tactical systems and I certainly didn't. The secret stuff was all inside the boxes. But your dad now, he was chief signaller. Knew the codes, the signals routines. All the arrangements as to how we'd get our instructions if it came to nuclear war and we had to fire the missiles.'

'The perfect man for the Russians to target,' said Sam sombrely.

'Well, yes.'

'But you never had a clue?'

'Not a one. On board, your dad was straight down the middle. No side to him. One of us.'

Sam decided he would get nothing more from Salmon. 'Well, thanks for your time,' he said, putting down the mug and getting to his feet.

'Off so soon?' Salmon sounded disappointed.

'Other people to see,' Sam lied.

'Of course.' Salmon pushed himself upright using the arms of the chair. 'Nice to have met you anyway.'

When the old man was steady on his feet Sam shook his hand. 'Could I ask one last favour?'

'Of course.'

'Not to speak about this to anyone. Official secrets and all that.'

'Understood. My lips are sealed.'

At the door they shook hands again. As Sam drove off, he saw Salmon watching from the step.

He drove despondently back to the sea front and parked overlooking the water in order to think. Nothing from Rothesay and now nothing from Salmon. He was at the end of the line. And without evidence to the contrary, the record looked set to stand. His father had made a habit of cheating on his wife, so it was possible he'd cheated on his mates as well.

'Hell!' He banged his fist on the wheel.

He looked at his watch. A quarter to one. The airport was half an hour away and Waddell's silence was needling him. He needed to be back down in the capital, hammering on doors for a hearing.

He restarted the engine and engaged first gear. Then as he swung the car towards the promenade, the phone rang. He snatched it up, stamping on the clutch and the brake, hoping the little Ulsterman was deigning to speak to him at last.

'Yes?'

'Mr Packer?'

Sam didn't recognise the voice. He envisaged a press man having been given his number by Julie Jackman.

'Who is this?'

'It's Craigie here. The photographer in Rothesay.'

'Mr Craigie! Hello.' He pulled sharply on the handbrake and turned the engine off. The old photographer had promised to keep searching his files and had taken his mobile number just in case. 'Something's come up?'

'Well I'm still not too hopeful, but there's three more negs I've come across which could be from the dates you gave me.'

Sam felt a sudden surge of hope.

'If you'd care to pop into the shop I could show you the contacts. Then if it's still no, at least you'll be sure I never took your parents' photo.'

'Trouble is I'm not on Bute any more,' Sam hedged, quickly calculating how long it would take to return to Rothesay, then rejecting the notion. London was where he needed to be next.

'Och, now that's a pity. Well I'll keep them aside for when you next come back.'

'Thanks. But I've no idea when that'll be.'

'Or I could post them if you give me your address.'

After the spread in the morning paper, he didn't *have* a usable address any more.

'No,' he answered, searching for a way. Suddenly he realised that he was staring at it. Opposite where he'd stopped the car was the café from earlier.

'Mr Craigie . . .'

'Aye?'

'I've an idea.'

Ten minutes later and £2.50 poorer, he was staring at a PC screen, watching the e-mail download. The attachment contained three 6 × 6 cm prints, scanned in together on a single page. As the bottom one of the three revealed itself, his breath froze. His father's grinning visage inched its way onto the screen. And he was with a woman.

It felt like being blasted through a time warp to see him there. Sam was in short trousers again, re-experiencing his childhood's worst fear – that one day his dad would go away to sea and never return. He could even smell the unfiltered Virginia his father used to smoke. In the picture, the man was hugging his girl like a trophy. A very young woman with peroxide hair.

Sam saved the photos to a disc provided by the café owner then reopened the file in a photo-handling program. He excised the pictures that didn't interest him and enlarged the one that remained.

His father had been clean shaven on that day back in 1971, closer to the image in the wedding photograph than to Beryl's memory of him. More the way Sam recalled: steady, soft eyes with a twinkle of mischief – and sheepishness. He'd never thought to wonder why he looked that way. Now he knew the reason.

The fluffy-haired girl seemed to be in her early twenties. A pretty thing with a smile as wide as the Clyde, a grin which said that being with his father on that island was like winning the pools.

Sam printed the picture twice, then shut down the computer.

'All in order?' the young man with the nose ring asked.

'All in order,' Sam replied.

Back in the car he phoned the Bute photographer again.

'Thanks for all your efforts, Mr Craigie. I got the pictures okay, but unfortunately none of them were of my parents.' If the spying story leaked out, the last thing he wanted was to see that snap in the papers.

'Och, I'm sorry to hear that. Well we tried. Can't do more than that.'

'Quite right. Good luck to you, Mr Craigie.'

'And to you, Mr 'em . . . *Foster* . . .' The line clicked dead.

'Oh shit!' Sam gulped. Craigie had seen the *Chronicle*. He smelled more trouble coming.

He started the engine and drove off. Within a couple of minutes he was pulling up outside Ted Salmon's cottage again. This time the front door opened at the first ring.

'Forgotten something?' the old man asked uneasily.

'No. But a photograph has come into my hands. I wanted to show it to you.'

'Better come in then.'

When they'd moved to the sitting room, Sam presented him with the computer printout.

'Where's this popped up from all of a sudden?'

'It was taken in Rothesay twenty-seven years ago.'

The old submariner reached for a spectacle case on the table beside his chair and slipped on bifocals with heavy, square frames.

'Bless us! Look at that. Large as life and twice as ugly, that's your dad all right.'

'Yes, but the woman?'

He held the photo closer.

'Well I'm buggered! That was . . .' He snapped his fingers. 'Wassername. Oh! It's on the tip of my tongue. She was a lassie who was er . . .' He glanced up apologetically. 'Well, *in business*, is what she was, to be honest. Looked after the needs of a number of the lads before your dad came along. She was looked on as being a bit special, you know. Not your average totty.'

'And her name?'

Salmon favoured the photo towards the window to catch the light. He shook his head. 'It's gone. Memory's not what it was. Where was this taken did you say?'

'On the Isle of Bute. May the 21st, 1971.'

The old man screwed up his face.

'Wasn't that the year Trevor died?'

'Two months later, in July,' Sam reminded him.

Salmon pursed and unpursed his lips. Then he closed his eyes and rubbed his forehead. 'Something's coming back. I don't know if I'm remembering this right, but I've a feeling he told me it was more than just physical with this one. I think he might even have fallen in love with her. Or thought he had.' He looked up. 'She was quite young, by the look of her. Your dad liked them young, I remember.'

'But you can't remember this girl's name?'

The old man closed his eyes. 'This is stupid. She was from here. Helensburgh. Used to see her around the town from time to time.'

'What, recently?'

'Oh yes.'

Sam's hopes shot up. 'Think hard. What was her name?'

'She married a butcher.' The old man's eyes brightened at the recollection. 'Coggan's the shop was called.' He snapped his fingers again. 'Jo Coggan!'

'That's her name?'

'Yes! Marriage didn't last long. Jo Macdonald she was, originally.'

'You're certain?'

'Totally. How come I forgot that? Jo Macdonald. Your father called her his little Josephine.'

'Brilliant,' Sam smiled. 'Any idea where she lives in Helensburgh?'

'No. None.' He stared at the photograph again, enmeshed in the memories it had unleashed. 'Tell you somebody who might know, though, and that's the minister. I've seen her going into the kirk from time to time.' He looked up suddenly, his eyes widening. 'You're not going to tell me *she* was mixed up in this spying thing? With the Russians? Sort of Mata Hari?'

'Highly unlikely. But she might remember something.'

Salmon fidgeted a little. 'If you find her will you do me a favour and not mention it was me that put the finger on her?'

'Of course. Not a word.'

'It's a small town, see.'

'I understand.'

'Try the manse. The minister's been here for over ten years. A decent sort, even for a Presbyterian. And this is probably a good time of day to catch him.'

The manse was on the eastern edge of the town close to the Defence Ministry's Churchill housing estate. Brown paint peeled from its huge sash windows. The dark-suited minister had just returned from a funeral and was in sombre mood. Keeping Sam standing in the porch, he received the request for information about a parishioner with a degree of suspicion.

'Might I ask why you're seeking to speak with Mrs Coggan?' he demanded. His steel-framed spectacles gave him a cold, ascetic look.

'My father was in the Navy. A submariner.' Sam's explanation seemed to intensify the reverend's doubts. 'He died when I was young, and I'm trying to piece his life together. I've just learned that he used to know Mrs Coggan when she was Jo Macdonald.'

The clergyman grunted. 'You'd better come into the study.' He led Sam into an oak-panelled room lined with bookshelves. In one corner stood an old roll-top desk, in the other, an exercise bike. 'Do sit down.'

'Thank you.'

The minister clasped his hands together. 'Can I ask what exactly it is you want with Mrs Coggan today?'

'My father's life had many sides to it,' Sam began, treading cautiously. 'And some of them I've only just recently learned about.'

'One of those being Jo,' said the minister knowingly.

'Exactly.'

'Was it a shock?'

'Not exactly. My father had a reputation for putting himself about. It was a cause of family friction.'

'I can imagine.'

'Still is. I'm trying to ease it by finding out the truth.'

'I see. Well I don't know if Jo will be able to speak to you. She's out of it a lot of the time.'

'Out of it? I don't quite understand.'

The minister cleared his throat. 'Didn't you know? She's terminally ill.'

'I had no idea.' He had a sudden fear that he would be too late and she'd be gone already.

'Yes. I don't think it'll be long now before the Lord takes her. She's on morphine a lot of the time. It's cancer. She's already lasted longer than expected.'

'I see. Which hospital is she in?'

'It's a hospice. Here in Helensburgh.' He clasped his hands. 'How did you hear about her?'

Sam showed him the photograph and explained where it had been taken. The reverend took it in both hands, studying it with fascination.

'She was a pretty wee thing in those days and no mistake. No wonder she was in such demand.' They exchanged glances to show that they understood one another. 'But she's paying a heavy price for the sins of her early life. I hope the Lord will be merciful in the next. You'd need to be gentle with her. She's very frail.'

'I shall be.'

The minister's eyes became thoughtful. 'It might be best if I come with you.'

'I'm sure I can find the place,' Sam told him, not wanting a witness to the conversation he hoped to have. 'If you just tell me the address . . .'

'Actually it's next door.' The clergyman stood up. 'But I will come with you, because I want to make sure she's prepared to see you.'

Jo Coggan, née Macdonald, lay propped on pillows in a small, ground floor room whose windows overlooked a large garden that was dark with the foliage of rhododendrons. Her head was without hair, her skin a bloodless cream. No way to tell her age, but Sam calculated she was about fifty. As he walked towards the bed she lifted a frail hand. Her eyes were small brown pools of pain which widened in astonishment as he drew nearer.

The minister had forewarned her of her visitor's identity and as Sam approached, he backed towards the door. 'Leave you to it,' he whispered.

'Thanks,' Sam murmured, shaking his hand.

'You're so like him.' Jo Coggan's voice was cracked and feeble, her Scots accent broader than Sam had expected. 'It's incre-dible.'

'You're okay then, Jo?' a nurse called from the door.

'Yes, Jen. I'm okay.'

'Press the bell if you need anything.'

'I will.'

The nurse left them.

For a while his father's one-time girlfriend lay looking up at him as if all her energy had been drained by the few words she'd uttered. Then her lips began to move, shaping her thoughts so they could come out as sounds.

'So you're Sam.'

He sat on the chair beside the bed. There was nothing about this woman that he could recognise from the photograph.

'How did you find out about me?' she asked hoarsely.

He showed her the picture and her eyes filled with tears. 'Och, I lost that wee snap years ago! Where on errth did you get it from?'

Sam explained about the ferry tickets he'd found in his father's deed box and the chance meeting with the Rothesay photographer. She looked down at the picture, biting her lip.

'We were in love, y'know. Terribly in love. It broke m'heart when he passed away.' Then she looked questioningly at him. 'But this was all so long ago.'

'I know. It's why I've come. To learn about my father. And about you.'

She looked afraid suddenly, as if the past was a place she wanted kept hidden. She pressed a tissue to her eyes before settling back on the pillows, engulfed by weariness. 'I get so tired,' she gasped, turning her face away. Her neck glistened with perspiration.

'Yes. I'm very sorry. I'll try not to tax you too much.'

'You were eleven years old, when he died,' she whispered.

'That's right.' He wondered where to begin. 'Did he ever talk to you about . . .'

'About you? Oh yes. All the time. You were the apple o' his eye. Couldn't do no wrong. He always told me you'd go into the Navy one day, but as an officer. Because you were clever and because he'd made sure you got a better edication than he had.' She turned her face towards him. 'Did you?'

'I did.'

'Submarines too?'

'No. Intelligence Branch.'

He watched for her reaction. When it came it shook him, because it confirmed his fears. There was shock, then despair. Finally a dreadful weariness passed across her face. She turned her head away and closed her eyes.

'*Intelligence* . . .'

'Yes.'

'So you know . . .'

'A Russian defector told us.'

She nodded and a tear squeezed between her lids. For a full half-minute they stayed silent, her tortured features a mirror of the agony inside his own head.

'I've waited twenty-seven years,' she whispered eventually. 'Twenty-seven years waiting for someone to come.' She opened her eyes and dabbed them with a fresh tissue extracted from the sleeve of her bed jacket. 'But I never dreamt for one moment it would be his own son.'

Sam leaned forward. 'Please. Will you tell me about it?'

She tugged at the bed sheet as if to cover herself more.

'How much do you know about me?' she whispered.

He decided to be blunt. 'I've been told that you worked as a prostitute and had several clients who were sailors.'

'*Several*. Och, you make it sound like I was big time. There might have been a dozen at the most.' She spoke without any sign of shame and took in a deep breath to sustain herself. 'But yes. I earned a little money from business. Life here was dull in them days. I had a mother to look after who'd gone senile. Having men pay me for doing what I liked doing anyway seemed a harmless way to earn some cash. But I was only an amateur at it. Months would go by without a single client.' The effort of speaking was exhausting her. She lay back with her eyes closed. 'Just get me breath,' she croaked.

'Of course.'

When she opened her eyes again, she forced them wide. The whites were yellow and brown veined.

'I gave it all up for ye da, y'know,' she said, looking at him intently. 'After I'd been going with him a while, I gave it up. Cos I loved him, you see. Loved him to bits.'

Her mouth puckered suddenly, whether from physical pain or a mental hurt, Sam couldn't tell. But he knew he had to press on, to discover the extent of his father's betrayal. 'These sailors you . . . you took in, you knew from the start that they had access to military secrets?'

'Och, I didn't know anything of the kind,' she protested. 'To me they were just men who'd been shut away in the dark for too long. They were all decent fellers. I made sure o' that because I turned away the rough ones. I wasn't that desperate for the cash.'

'And many of them were married, of course.' He'd sounded unintentionally reproachful.

'Och, you're no a prude, are you?' she snapped. 'Telling me I was a wicked woman taking your father away from your mither? Let me tell you something. In his heart your father left that woman long before he met me.' She began to pant for breath again. Sam gave her time to recover.

'Tell me about him, Jo,' he probed, more gently this time. 'Tell me how he came to be spying for the Russians. Was it blackmail?'

She nodded. There was the look of a cornered animal about her. 'They sought him out because he was the wireless operator,' she whispered. 'Followed him around, in secret like, until they knew more about his life than he did himself.'

She adjusted her position in the bed, then reached feebly for the glass on the bedside table. Sam picked it up and held it for her while she drank.

'Thank you.'

She breathed heavily for a few moments, summoning strength and gathering her thoughts.

'It started the Christmas before Trev died. I had a foreigner come to me for business. I'd just about given the work up because of your da, but I was in bad need of money that day. He spoke good English, this feller, but with an accent. Said he worked at the naval base and had heard of me through friends.' She paused, as if to think through what she was going to say next. 'But when I let him into the house it wasn't sex he wanted. He was after Trevor. Showed me pictures he'd got of the two of us together on the bed. Somehow he'd hidden a camera in the room – we never found out how.' Her eyes widened, as if still astonished at his ingenuity. 'And he knew about you and your sister. Said he'd make sure the pictures got to you two kids as well as to your mother. He was ruthless. Said if Trevor didn't give him what he wanted, the pictures would be in the post the next time he went away to sea.'

Sam frowned. 'The man didn't approach my father direct? He did it through you?'

'Aye. I don't know why.'

'Did the man give you his name?'

'Johann. Like Johann Sebastian Bach, he said.'

'And this was a Russian?'

'No. German. From the east. Working for all the peoples of free Europe, he said.' She flicked up her eyes at the absurdity of it. 'According to Johann, the Russians had been having trouble with MI5 and were using him because he could move around the country more easily than they could.'

'I see.' Sam remembered a spate of tit-for-tat spy expulsions at around that time. 'And my father agreed to provide information?' he asked, resigned to the worst. 'So that my mother wouldn't learn about your affair?'

Suddenly tears streamed down her face. She picked up the hem of the bed sheet and pressed it to her eyes. 'It was because of *you*,' she sobbed. 'Not because of *her*. He didn't care if your *mother* found out about us. She couldn't think any worse of him than she did already. But he knew that you idolised him. And he couldn't cope with the idea of seeing your crushed little face after you'd had an eyeful of those pictures o' us together.'

He shook his head, dismayed that he himself could have been the ultimate reason for his father's agreement to commit treason. 'And he gave Johann some Navy secrets . . .'

'No! No he never,' she protested. 'You mustn't think that.'

'I don't understand.'

'Nothing that mattered, anyway.' She dried her eyes, her wan face totally washed out. 'He gave Johann old signal codes – that's what he told me. Information that looked right but which was already out of date.'

'The Russians would have seen through that,' Sam told her.

'Oh aye. They did. The next time Trevor returned from a patrol Johann made the threats all over again.'

'And?'

'Your father played for time. Keeping them at bay until he worked out what to do.'

'Which was what?'

'He didn't have to do nothing in the end. The headaches started and they found the brain tumour. Johann backed off when he realised Trevor was going to die.'

'You mean that was it? Out-of-date signal codes was all he ever passed to them?'

'Absolutely.'

Sam felt absurdly relieved. 'You're quite sure about that?'

'It's what Trevor told me. And he never did hide anything from me.'

'And what about Johann? Did he just fade away?'

'Aye. But he was kind to me. *Keep your chin up*, he said. Sounded odd the way he said it, like he'd read the words in a book. And then when Trevor died, he sent me money to buy a wreath for the funeral.'

'You were there?' Sam asked, astonished.

'Och no! I couldn't be. But I sent the flowers.'

He remembered the scent outside the crematorium, made heavy by the heat of summer.

As the woman recovered her breath Sam sat back and pondered. Through the wide window he saw a uniformed nurse helping a stick-thin man in a dressing gown inspect the flower beds.

'The German, Johann, you never knew his proper name?' he checked.

'No. But . . .' She put a hand on his arm, looking at him uncertainly for several seconds as if trying to think through the consequences of what she was about to tell him. 'But there was something strange as happened a couple of years ago. I got a letter. Written by someone saying he was a friend of Johann.'

'Really?'

'He said that now the cold war was over, Johann wanted to say sorry for the pain he'd caused.'

'Extraordinary . . .' Compassion wasn't exactly commonplace in the spying business.

'The letter asked me to write back and say how I was.'

'And did you?'

'No. I didn't want to be reminded.'

Sam saw her flinch as some internal spasm took control.

'Sometimes it shoots through me like a sliver of glass,' she whispered.

'D'you want me to call someone?'

'No. I'm not allowed the injections too often. They'll be round when it's time.' She closed her eyes and sank into the pillows, her mouth half open. 'It'll pass in a wee while.'

Sam knew he should let her be now, but there was more he wanted to know. For his own sake.

'Will you tell me about my father? Why were you attracted to him more than the other sailors?'

Slowly her mouth formed into a smile which, if it hadn't been contorted with the pain, might have been mischievous.

'He was awful good in the sack,' she whispered. 'The best there ever was.'

'That was it?'

'Och no. But that was the start of it. He was just lovely. Kind. Funny.'

'My mother and sister saw him in a rather different light,' Sam murmured.

'Your mother? Och, what d'you expect from a woman who tells her man there'll be no more sex?'

'She said that?'

'It's what your father told me. He said that after giving berrth to you she wouldn't let him near her.'

'No wonder he had a wandering eye.'

'And hands.' She managed a laugh. 'He was dead sensual, you know.' She put her hand to her mouth. 'Och I shouldna be saying such things to his son . . .'

'Say whatever you like,' he told her. 'Did he . . . did he ever talk about my sister?'

'Oh aye.' Another spasm gripped her. Sam handed her the glass again. She swallowed some water, then breathed heavily and evenly to control the discomfort. 'He was dead upset when Beryl took against him too.' Her voice came out as a whisper. Sam could see she was fading. 'Said your ma worked hard on her, poisoning her mind against him.' She picked up the Rothesay photo again and managed a smile. 'It was three days we had together in Bute. The longest we ever had alone. Three of the happiest days o' my life.'

The door clicked open and the nurse came in.

'You'll be tiring her out, Mr Packer. I need to give her some medication.'

Jo Coggan grabbed his hand. 'Don't go just yet. I've talked too much. I want to hear about you.'

'Would you wait outside while I do the injection,' the nurse asked firmly.

'Of course.' He stood up. 'I'll be back in a minute, Jo.'

Outside in the corridor he leaned against the white wall and sucked in air. Mysteries had been unlocked. He understood now about Beryl. And he'd learned that although his father had been a rogue, he had probably not been a traitor. The icon was torn, but not destroyed.

'You can go back in now, Mr Packer,' the nurse told him, holding open the door. 'But not for long because she'll be asleep soon.'

'I understand.'

Already Jo Coggan was having trouble keeping her eyes open.

'You,' she whispered. 'Tell me about you.'

'I will. In a moment. But I have one more question.'

'Questions, questions . . .'

'The man who wrote to you from abroad with the message from Johann. Do you remember his name?'

'No. But . . .' She turned her head towards the side of the room where a dark brown wardrobe stood. 'In there.'

'I don't understand.'

'On the floor. A small green case.'

He opened the cupboard door. A few clothes hung from the rail. Below, next to a pair of trainers was a vanity bag.

'This one?' He held it up.

She nodded. He placed it on the bed and she indicated he should open it. When he lifted the lid she reached in and brought out a bundle of letters held together with an elastic band.

'From your da, mostly,' she croaked, sleep rapidly overtaking her. 'But there's one in there with a foreign stamp.'

Sam flicked through the letters, recognising his father's immature hand. He dearly wanted to read them but knew it would be a mistake to do so. Eventually he found the envelope she'd meant. Franked in Vienna. From it he extracted a single sheet of white notepaper.

As he read the address at the head of the page, a shiver ran down his spine. It was startlingly familiar. He turned the letter over to be sure. The signature was neat and forward-leaning. The name – Günther Hoffmann.

Sam shook his head in amazement. This was extraordinary. The letter had been written by a former Stasi officer whom he'd helped debrief several years ago.

He felt a hand on his arm. The woman was almost asleep, but she knew he was about to go.

'Will ye come an' see me again?' she whispered.

'I will,' he promised, staring disbelievingly at the page.

Her lips quivered as she summoned up her failing strength.

'We were to be married, you know, your da and me. I'd have been your step-mummy, Sammy. Would you have liked that, d'you think?'

She fell asleep before he could think of a reply.

12

London

FROM THE POLICE station in Paddington Julie had returned to Acton to collect a bag before heading for Woodbridge. She'd found photographers outside her flat. Before they could spot her she'd fled back to the underground and thrown herself onto the first train. She had a desperate need to be away from people – from everybody. At Hammersmith she'd left the tube and walked over the bridge to the south bank of the river, finding a bench amongst the horse chestnut trees.

An hour later she was still sitting there, watching a rowing club eight carry their razor-shell craft down to the water. Strongly built boys and girls with nice accents. Normal teenagers at the end of the summer hols. She imagined secure, two-parent homes with siblings and dogs, and she envied them. On the bank opposite, people in suits stood outside pubs, enjoying an extended lunch break in one of the few bursts of good weather they'd had that summer. Her spectacles were smudged. She took them off, polished them with a soft cloth from her bag, then watched a police launch purr past, heading upriver.

She knew that if she didn't talk to someone about the mess she'd got herself into she would probably explode. It wasn't just the Simon Foster business. Her personal relationships had always been a mess. For the past year she'd been having an affair with a man much older than herself which was going nowhere. The man, who was married, was kind and generous and seemed happy for their arrangement to continue indefinitely, but she knew it couldn't. She didn't love him. Never had. The relationship had been fun, jet-setting, and trouble-free. It had taken her out of herself. But its very easiness was stopping her looking for the soul mate she'd always hoped to meet.

Her mother was too judgmental to talk to in situations like this. And anyway Julie hadn't told her about the affair. Most of her friends were too preoccupied with their own problems to be interested in hers, but there was one she could talk to – a girl she'd met at university – not through her studies, but through the shared misfortune of having unplanned children. They'd met at the ante-natal clinic, both grossly pregnant by men who'd abandoned them. Rosemary Smith had given birth on the same day as Julie and the traumas of single-motherhood had forged a bond between them which had lasted.

Soon after their confinements, their paths had separated, Julie returning home to her mum and Rosie getting lucky with a man. A westernised Iranian postgrad studying textile technology had fallen in love with her and her darkly beautiful child and insisted she should marry him. She'd abandoned her degree course and become a housewife. Her husband now traded in oriental carpets and they lived in some affluence in north London. Rosie was a kind and constant friend, but above all she was a listener.

Julie got up from the bench and walked back towards the bridge to look for a telephone box.

Rosemary's apartment in St John's Wood was paved in marble and dotted with gilded *objets* and classical bronze statuettes. Julie didn't know whether it was good taste or bad. All she was certain of was that Rosie's life was very different from her own.

'How's Liam?' Rosemary asked within seconds of her welcoming embrace. 'Gosh! New glasses?' she commented, not waiting for a reply.

'He's fine and yes they are,' Julie answered. 'Got to keep up with the fashion.'

She was led through into what her friend called the 'family room', a spacious extension of the kitchen where the furnishings were more child-friendly. The two younger ones were there, being given their tea by a dumpy Filipina.

'Andrew will be back in a minute,' Rosemary told her. 'He'll be thrilled to see you, Julie. Absolutely thrilled. That's if the football practice hasn't *totally* worn him out. I think it's ridiculous making them do so many things when they're that young, but the head insists it does them no harm and the school's academic results are *fanta-astic.*' She whispered the last word as if afraid the whole world would discover how successful the place was at getting their pupils into the best public schools.

Andrew. Such an unsuitable name for a child with dark Arab looks. The father who'd vanished had been an overseas student from Kuwait.

'Cup of tea? It's *so* good to see you again.'

'That would be wonderful. And it's great to see you too.' Julie decided her friend had put on weight since they'd last met, but refrained from commenting on it.

Rosemary plugged in the kettle. She was dark haired and had a nose that most Englishmen would consider indelicately large. She wore a voluminous purple patterned dress that was probably made of silk.

'How sweet of you to ring,' she said, pouring water into a silver teapot. 'Only the other day I saw a little boy in the supermarket who reminded me so much of your Liam. I've been wanting to get in touch for ages, but you're so high-powered and busy these days.'

Typical, thought Julie. Blaming *her* for her own failure to communicate. 'Busy, yes. High-powered? Hardly.'

Rosemary gave a knowing smile as if 'modesty' was Julie's middle name. 'Well . . . I'm so glad you rang. How's things?'

Julie looked about her to see if there was a newspaper in evidence. 'You don't take the *Chronicle*, do you?' It would be easier if Rosemary had seen the story already.

'No. Mehdi reads the *FT*. I don't have time for papers. Get my news from the TV.' Suddenly her eyes lit up and she clamped a hand to her mouth. 'Don't tell me! I've missed it. There was an announcement. You're getting married!'

Julie shook her head. 'Sorry to disappoint you.'

'Oh, no. *I'm* sorry. Always saying the wrong thing . . .' One of the little girls came over to complain about her sister. Rosemary picked the child up and cuddled her. 'What about your Austrian millionaire?'

'Sort of still happening,' Julie told her. 'But I'm not sure I want it to. Could we . . . ?'

The doorbell rang before she could suggest they went somewhere more private to talk.

'That'll be Andrew.' Rosemary put her daughter down and headed for the hall. 'We have a rota for the school run. My day off, but it's still bedlam at this time of day.' Just before the door she stopped and turned. 'Once I've got him settled, you and I will go into the drawing room and put a "do not disturb" sign on the door.' She winked conspiratorially.

Julie crouched down to talk to the two girls. They were nice children, relaxed and open with adults. 'Have you been to my house before?' one of them asked.

'Yes, but the last time I came you'd gone to bed already.'

When Andrew was wheeled in he solemnly shook hands with Julie, his dark eyes anything but thrilled to see her. He was dog-tired, his mind full of the day just passed. Dressed in the smart, private school blazer and grey shorts which set him apart from her own son, a smudge of earth on his forehead showed he was a boy like any other. The Filipina took charge of him.

Rosemary touched Julie on the arm and beckoned.

The large living room had a huge Persian rug on the floor and a window bay that had been extended and glazed like a conservatory. Yuccas and flowering plants decorated it. They sat on softly upholstered cane chairs and put their teacups on a small glass table.

'So why *did* you ask if I read the *Chronicle*?' Rosemary asked, burning with curiosity. Julie bent down and extracted the cutting from her handbag.

'Because of this.'

Rosemary took it from her. As she read it, her jaw dropped. 'Oh Julie, how awful for you! And God . . . your father! I had no idea. I'm so sorry.' She leaned forward and put her hand on Julie's knee. 'It must have been a dreadful shock.'

'It was. But what d'you think?'

Rosemary frowned. 'About . . . ?'

'The article. Was I mad to get involved in defending him? You know what a crook he was.'

'Yes but he was your dad. You loved him.'

Julie had always envied Rosemary's uncomplicated perspective on relationships, but on this occasion it wasn't enough. 'You're not answering my question, Rosie.'

'Aren't I? I can't really say any more than that.'

'Why not? You must have a view.'

'Don't be silly!' she scolded. 'I don't *have* views. Except on things to do with children. But I can see that *you* think you were mad to get involved. It's written all over your face.'

'Well . . . half of me does.'

'And the other half . . .'

'Suspects that MI6 *did* kill my father.'

Rosemary let a nervous hand flutter up to her mouth. This was territory well beyond anywhere she wanted to go. 'Well if you really think that, why *not* tell the papers about it?'

'Because of the man involved,' Julie breathed, looking down at her hands.

Rosemary's brown eyes widened. She looked at the picture more closely. 'This man . . . ?'

'Yes. He's probably going to lose his job because of me.'

'But if he . . .' The hand floated up to the mouth again. 'If he killed your father . . .'

'That's just the problem, Rosie. I mean, I'm sure he works for them, but I don't really think he could have done it. Not him personally. He's too nice.'

'Too nice,' Rosemary whispered, her eyes widening further. 'Julie! You're not saying what I think you're saying?'

'I don't know *what* I'm saying, Rosie. Except that I'm in a dreadful mess over it.' She felt tearful all of a sudden and turned her face to the window.

Rosemary leaned forward again and squeezed her friend's hand. At times she'd envied Julie her degree, her career and her exotic parentage, but just now she was extremely glad to be a mere wife and mother.

'Have you talked to Max about it?'

'God no,' Julie spluttered. 'With Max I talk about European politics – which I know nothing about – fashion, food and the best ski resorts. Occasionally we discuss virology, since that's the subject that brought us together, but most of the time our chat is simply a polite prelude to the real reason for his wanting to see me.'

Rosemary tittered, glad to be back on ground she understood. 'But you sound so bitter,' she frowned. 'Last time we spoke you were perfectly happy with the relationship.'

'I was,' Julie confirmed. 'It gave a bit of glamour to my life. It was a break from Liam and from routine, a chance to travel a little. And Max always paid for everything – air fares, a separate hotel room – for the sake of *my* reputation he said, although of course it was for *his*. Meals. Concerts. Ski passes . . .'

'A true sugar daddy.'

'Yes.' Julie allowed herself a little smile. 'But actually he's not bad in bed either.' The two women giggled.

'So, you got yourself a *sexy* fifty-year-old millionaire!' ·

'Sexy . . .' Julie pondered the word. 'That might be over-egging it. He's a good physical fit, but . . . well, he doesn't have much imagination.'

'Oh dear. A *stolid* fifty-year-old. Winds up the cuckoo clock, then lights out. Tell me, does he keep his socks on in bed?'

They giggled again sillily. Julie was terribly glad she'd come. Laughter had been in short supply in the past few days.

'Oh Rosie, I don't know what I'm doing.' She was in need of explaining things to herself as much as to her friend. 'It was the sort of relationship I thought I could do with. Pleasure without involvement. I mean, whenever I *do* get involved with someone it goes horribly wrong.'

Rosemary's eyes harboured thoughts which she wasn't revealing.

'What?' Julie demanded.

'Oh . . . no. It's none of my business . . .'

'I'm making it your business. What did you want to say?'

Rosemary's mouth puckered as if she were sucking a lemon. 'It's just that I've always felt the reason your relationships go wrong is that you try too hard and give in too much. Tell me to shut up.'

'No. Go on.'

'You see, you're such a lovely person, with a wonderful personality, yet when you fall for a man you suppress it all. You become a mouse. His plaything. It's almost as if you're frightened of letting yourself be yourself in case you put him off.'

Julie stared at her hands. Her mother had said the same. She knew it to be true but could do nothing about it. Whenever she fell in love with a man, she was ready to be his slave.

Beyond the kitchen door a child began wailing, then they heard the raised voice of the Filipina trying to calm things. Instinctively Rosemary stood up, but checked herself and sat down again, realising that the 'child' in front of her was in greater need of help than her daughter.

'You should try to be yourself more,' Rosemary added, always reluctant to give advice.

'I've tried. But it's how I am, Rosie. It's the way I'm made.'

Rosemary took a deep breath, about to say it was because Julie had spent her entire life trying to win her father's approval, but she reached for the silver teapot instead.

'More?'

'Please.'

Rosemary spilled a little on the tray and dabbed it up with a linen napkin.

'But returning to the subject of Max,' she continued. 'The relationship's begun to lose its charm, is that what you're saying?'

Julie nodded, her misery written on her face.

'So, have you decided to stop seeing him?'

Julie sighed. 'I think I should. He's asked me to go to Vienna this weekend. The ticket's booked. I just have to pick it up. But I'm not sure about *anything* at the moment.'

'No. Because you're in a bit of a state, poor love.' She picked up the newspaper cutting and re-read it.

'God!' Julie hissed. 'Why can't I ever get things right?'

'Oh you do, dearest Julie. Lots of things.'

'As long as it's not to do with men. I always fall for the wrong ones.'

Rosemary looked up and cocked her head on one side. 'Did I just miss something there, darling?'

Julie reddened slightly. 'I just keep thinking about him, that's all.'

Rosemary waved the press cutting at her. 'You don't mean this one? You're not seriously telling me you've *fallen* for the man you've exposed to the papers?'

Julie pressed her lips together and shrugged.

'Oh *dear*.'

'Yes. Oh dear, Rosie. I can't seem to get him out of my head. It's those pheromones or whatever they're called.'

Rosemary gawped at her, lost for words.

'Sometimes I think I'm a sackful of chemicals rather than a human being. Hit me with the right whiff and I turn from a decisive, professional female into a broody duck.'

'Now you're being daft.' Rosemary tugged at a tuft of her hair, twisting it round her finger. 'I think I've lost the thread of all this somewhere,' she cautioned. The truth was she was beginning to suspect her friend might be having some sort of breakdown. 'Go back a few pages and explain how this divinely complicated infatuation of yours came about?'

Julie told her about her father's death in Africa, the letters and the mysterious shipment he'd referred to as red mercury. Then she described how the *Chronicle* people had cajoled her into entrapping Simon Foster. She talked about the backlash from the laboratory after the newspaper piece came out and the grilling she'd been given by the police that morning.

'You poor, poor thing,' said Rosemary when she'd finished. 'If it had been me going through all that I'd have just burst into tears and found a hole in the ground to hide in.'

'No you wouldn't. Anyway, you'd never have got yourself into such a mess in the first place.' Talking it through had left Julie more undecided than ever. She leaned forward and grabbed her friend's hands. 'Oh Rosie . . . what should I do? Please tell me what I should do.'

Rosemary pulled her old friend into her arms and gave her a huge hug.

'I don't know. But whatever you do, be careful.'

Sam was met on the air jetty at Heathrow by a fidgety man called Bennett from SIS security who wore fawn trousers and a navy blue pullover. He led him down a staircase onto the tarmac and into a waiting car.

'We're taking you out the back way, just in case,' Bennett explained as he drove off. 'The media have rumbled your flat already. Been staking it out since lunchtime. Nice neighbours you've got. At least three of them phoned the papers.'

'They'd sell their own mothers if the price was right,' Sam grumbled.

'Anybody give you trouble in Scotland?'

'Not exactly. Although there's one bloke in Rothesay who knows more than he should.'

'Give me a name and address and I'll have him taken out for you.'

Sam smiled grimly at the joke. He settled back in the passenger seat as they sped through the security barrier and onto the loop road that led to the exit tunnel. His controller had called him shortly before he boarded the flight from Glasgow. They were to meet later in the afternoon.

Bennett glanced at him as he drove onto the motorway. 'That clean chin helps,' he commented. 'Might be wise to lighten the hair though, and start wearing spectacles. We can arrange all that this afternoon.'

Sam cringed at the thought of another identity change. 'I'd rather leave it a day or two. I'll be going abroad as soon as I've fixed a flight.'

During his wait for the shuttle from Glasgow he'd reflected on his conversation with Jo Macdonald, and been left dissatisfied. He'd begun to question whether a young prostitute could really have known whether the information his father passed on was sensitive or not and decided he needed to hear it from the horse's mouth. The 'horse' being Günther Hoffmann.

He'd made a phone call from Glasgow airport to an old friend in the German equivalent of MI6, the BND. Fifteen minutes later he'd been called back with confirmation that Hoffmann was currently at his Karl-Marx Hof apartment in Vienna and, judging by recent form, was unlikely to be going anywhere.

But before heading for the Austrian capital, there were two pressing issues to sort out. The first was to find out where he stood with his employers, and the second was to procure a change of clothes. The latter could prove difficult. If the media were outside his apartment, returning there to get them would be impossible.

'So where are you taking me?' he asked Bennett.

'We've found you a room in Ealing for now. In what they call a private hotel.'

'Sounds like a knocking shop.'

'No such luck. It's full of refugees. Half of them Ukrainian.'

'*Ukrainians!*' Sam jumped. 'Have you read my file?'

'Course I have. Don't worry. You'll be in good company. These people are dodging the mafiya too.'

'I don't think much of your sense of humour.'

'It's only for a few days – until the grownups decide what to do with you.'

'What about my stuff?'

'All done. One of my girls went to your place last night. There's a couple of suitcases waiting for you in Ealing.'

'Efficient of you.'

The Arcadia Private Hotel was in a side street off the Uxbridge Road. A dozen rooms, the rent for eleven of them paid by the local authority. Bennett showed him upstairs and handed him the key. The room was little wider than a corridor. There was a single divan with his cases on it and a cracked sink in the corner.

'I'll be leaving you now, sir.' Bennett stood by the door with a silly smirk on his face.

'S'pose you're after a tip.'

'Never know your luck. Here.' He handed Sam a card. 'Give me a ring when you want your hair done. My bloke who "does" is as gay as a glee club, but he's got a lovely touch.'

'Thanks a million.'

When the security man had gone, Sam peeked out of the grubby window. The yard at the back was of cracked concrete surrounded by bricks blackened by decades of pollution. Two small children played on rickety tricycles while their mother watched listlessly. All three were black and very beautiful. Somali or Ethiopian, Sam guessed. Refugees from the sort of injustice he'd spent his life fighting. A fight which Julie Jackman had sabotaged with a single flick of an eyelash.

He moved back from the window and contemplated the plain, peeling walls of the stale-smelling bedroom. His mind flashed back to the cell in Baghdad two years ago, his fate then also determined by a woman.

He flipped open the suitcases and was impressed. Bennett's girl had chosen sensibly. He would need one of the bags for Vienna, so began hanging some of the clothes in the cheap wardrobe. When he'd done, he sat on the bed to gather his thoughts.

Vienna. A city of spies, where twelve months ago an elusive Russian called Vladimir Kovalenko had conned a gullible trader called Harry Jackman into shipping nuclear weapons to Arab terrorists, telling him the boxes contained a fool's gold known as red mercury. Vienna, where a few years earlier an old Stasi spymaster called Günther Hoffmann had set up his retirement home because he wanted to be away from the witch hunts in his newly united homeland, and to be close to his beloved opera. Two men who held answers to most of the questions hammering in his head.

Hoffmann would be the easier to find. He'd chosen a sedentary life after the winding up of the Staatssicherheitsdienst. Sam had last met him a few years after his move to Vienna, by which time he and his wife had been well settled in their small apartment. He'd claimed to have turned his back on his old world – an assertion that wasn't entirely true, Sam had discovered a short while later. In exchange for being spared further investigation by the German authorities, Hoffmann had agreed to spy for them on former KGB contacts setting up businesses in Vienna. Sam was crossing his fingers that Kovalenko might have been one of them.

He had little doubt that the 'Johann' who'd blackmailed his father was none other than Hoffmann himself. A field officer in a foreign land was exactly the sort of job he'd have been doing twenty-seven years ago. And it would have been typically pretentious of him to have used a composer's Christian name for his legend. Also characteristic to have taken such a personal interest in the fate of his victims – the man had an odd compassionate streak.

It was as a direct consequence of the dismantling of the former East German spy network that Sam had met Hoffmann. Stasi documents uncovered by German counter-intelligence in 1991 had revealed the existence of 'Papagena', a female informer who'd operated inside British Rhine Army headquarters during the last decade of the cold war, her controller being Günther Hoffmann. Sam had been sent to Berlin to sit in on the interrogation of him being conducted by the German BfV counterintelligence service, but the man had refused to reveal Papagena's name or position, saying that to identify her would wreck her marriage and alienate her children. His concern for her well-being had seemed strangely decent in a man who'd exploited people so ruthlessly for so many years. Only when Papagena developed a terminal illness in 1995 had Hoffmann agreed to name her.

Sam's sporadic contacts with the old spy had spanned the best part of five years. He'd even grown to like the man, a clever, cunning foe from a nobler era when spying had been fuelled by ideology rather than cash. Sam had pondered whether to telephone him to arrange a meeting, but had decided it wiser to turn up unannounced. The German had a knack of avoiding confrontations when he knew one was coming.

Sam extracted the telephone from his rucksack, intending to ring the airlines about flights to Vienna. When he switched it on, he saw the message icon flashing.

'Damn!' He kicked himself for not asking Bennett for a replacement SIM card. Julie Jackman or Tom Craigie had probably sold his number to every media outlet in the country by now. There'd be invitations from *Newsnight*, offers from the tabloids. Full of trepidation, he dialled into voicemail.

'*You have two new messages. First message: Mr Foster – Simon – it's probably mad of me to ring . . .*'

The wind left his lungs. The voice was Julie Jackman's.

'*I just wanted to say I am terribly sorry about what happened.*'

Sam's eyebrows shot up. 'Sorry?' She soon would be if he had anything to do with it.

'*I just got in a total muddle over my father. And I let myself be bullied by the press. I realise I've put you in a terrible position. I'm really, really sorry. I shouldn't have done what I did.*'

Sam listened hard, searching for some give-away in the voice. Something to back his suspicion that there was a press man at her elbow.

'*If you'd only let me see you again, I'd try to explain.*'

'Of course, sweetheart. Any bloody time you like.' The submissive tone she'd injected into her voice incensed him.

'But I don't imagine for one moment that you'd agree . . .'

'Too bloody right.' The woman was out of her tiny mind.

'But just in case, you can reach me through e-mail. I'm avoiding phones at the moment.' She rattled off a web address. 'Well um . . . goodbye. And again please accept my apologies.'

He erased the message and disconnected the line. The second message could wait. He leaned back against the wall savouring what he would do to the woman if by some chance they met again. The dark side of his nature fancied murder, but the more reasonable part simply wanted to shake some sense into her. To make the silly bitch understand once and for all that he hadn't killed her father.

The phone trilled. He froze, imagining it was her again. He let it ring until the system diverted to voicemail. A couple of minutes later he dialled in.

'You have two new messages. First message: Hi. I've been thinking of you all day. Give me a ring if you get the chance.'

Sam smiled. Good old Steph. A friend in need.

'Second message: Ring me will you? I'm in your neighbourhood and we need to meet.' Duncan Waddell, sounding like he had a ferret up his arse.

Sam rang straight back. His controller was parked round the corner from the Arcadia Hotel.

'I'll be there in five,' he told him.

'Make it four. The clock's ticking.'

Sam stood up, collected his thoughts for a moment, then left the room, locking the door behind him.

Waddell had found a parking meter on the main road a couple of hundred yards away. There was ten minutes on the clock. Sam got into the car, which smelled overpoweringly of Waddell's deodorant.

'We'll keep this short,' his controller snapped, not looking at him. 'I can tell you there's been blood spat today. There are even people washing their mouths out after talking about you.'

'Do me a favour . . .' Sam complained. The car rocked as a bus passed, its brakes squealing as it approached a stop.

'The point is this, laddie. If it were simply Jackman's word against ours on Bodanga, the FCO would have walked it. But with your guilty-looking mug shot in the paper, the opposition's been given a huge shove up the ladder.'

Sam let his head fall back against the rest. 'So? What's the verdict?'

'Still making up their minds.'

'About?'

'Whether to stuff your corpse in an incinerator, or to invite you to find a new job on the other side of the world.' Waddell spat out the words, still staring straight ahead.

'Thanks, Duncan.'

'I can tell you that my vote was for the former,' the Ulsterman added without a trace of humour.

'Of course.'

'Heavens above, man! D'you ever stop to think how much easier your life would be if you followed your instincts instead of your gonads?'

'For me sex *is* an instinct, Duncan.'

Waddell let out an explosion of air. 'But one to be kept separate from your professional activities, for Christ's sake! Anyway, this isn't getting us anywhere.'

'No. Look, perhaps we can hurry up with the execution. I've got a plane to catch.' Sam had already told Waddell about Hoffmann and Vienna, when they'd spoken on the phone from Glasgow.

'The truth is there *were* two options,' Waddell went on, calmer now. 'One plan was for you to make yourself available to the press and proclaim your innocence. The other was for you to keep well out of the way until the media get bored with the story.'

'And?'

'The latter. Nobody trusted you to pull the first option off.'

'Quite right too. Duelling with lions isn't my thing.'

'So get yourself over to Vienna, but make it a quick in and out. I need to be able to produce you if I have to.'

'Why?'

'For the politicians. The PM's on holiday in Italy, but the opposition's stirring like crazy. Determined to make Bodanga and Harry Jackman's death the scandal that gets them back from the wasteland.' Waddell tapped his fingers on the steering wheel. 'Vienna,' he murmured. 'Seems to be the centre of the whole damned universe all of a sudden.'

'How d'you mean?' Sam turned to stare at him.

'Our American cousins have heard unconfirmed reports that Kovalenko's back in town . . .'

'Ah . . . But no actual sighting of him?'

'Not yet.'

'Anything more on the backpack nukes, or bin Laden?'

'Nothing. However it *is* still the favoured view of what this Jackman business is all about.'

'And the other Vienna connections?'

Waddell turned to face him at last. 'You may find this rather interesting.' He watched for Sam's reaction. 'Julie Jackman was there when her father struck the red mercury deal with Vladimir Kovalenko a year ago.'

'*Was* she, by God?' Sam blinked. He was suddenly remembering the words in Jackman's letter. *Kovalenko knew about you, Julie.* Now it made sense. 'The lying little minx.'

'We found their names on the hotel records,' Waddell continued. 'Denise Corby and a Special Branch officer worked her over yesterday morning. Julie claimed she'd been there for an HIV conference. Said being there at the same time as her old man was just a coincidence.'

'Bollocks. Nothing's a coincidence with that woman.'

'Actually her story checks out,' Waddell assured him. 'There *was* an HIV conference. And Denise's view is that she probably *didn't* know what deals her dad was sewing up there.'

Sam shook his head. There was no room for charity in his heart. 'If I've learned one thing about Julie Jackman, it's not to believe a sodding word she says.'

There was a sharp tap on the window. Sam flinched. When he turned to look it was a couple of black schoolgirls not more than ten years old giggling and making faces at him. A bit of fun on the way home. He made as if to open the door and they quickly ran off.

'Ever get the feeling the whole fucking world's against you?' he muttered.

'When you're around, quite often,' Waddell assured him. 'Now you'd better be running along before those kiddies tell the cops you tried to abduct them. Touch base with the station head in Vienna. His name's Patrick de Vere Collins. You'll be okay there. He's not as posh as you'd think from the name. And we've filled him in. Keep in regular touch with me. Every few hours. And for God's sake keep your head down. And,' he added as an afterthought, 'keep your goddam dick in your trousers.'

Sam decided against hitting him. He had a nasty feeling that inside the Intelligence Service, Waddell could well be the only friend he had left.

Stockholm, Sweden

About a thousand miles north-east of London, in the Swedish capital, a thirty-two-year-old schoolteacher with straight, fair hair that flopped forward across his forehead locked the filing cabinet in the staff room where he'd been working late, then crossed to the door, latching it as he left. There'd been a spate of vandalism in the school in recent months with pupils' personal files being doctored and teachers' property being stolen or destroyed.

The young teacher had spent the past hour marking his class papers for a history test which he'd set that afternoon, its subject being Gustav II Adolf, the seventeenth-century Swedish king who'd died in action battling to victory over the Germans. A compelling leader of dazzling abilities who'd turned Sweden into the strongest power in Europe, he was a man every Swedish child had to know about before completing their education. The Lion of the North. A character the teacher admired.

The school was in Stockholm's western suburbs, an area where the fabled prosperity of this neutral nation was not particularly obvious. As he drove down the road towards the home where his wife and young son would be looking forward to his return, the teacher glanced at a group of youths on the pavement who were darker skinned than his fellow countrymen. Turks or Albanians, he guessed. The sight of them made him bristle with dislike. Being a rational man, he'd often tried to analyse why he felt afraid of these swarthy foreigners. As a tourist he'd seen them in their own lands, so it wasn't a fear of being attacked by them. It was a cultural matter, fear that their alien ways would spread through his land like knotweed, choking the native customs into extinction.

He turned off the main road into a recently built shopping centre, finding a parking space easily. Most shops would be closed by this hour of the afternoon. He removed the radio and locked the car, checking nothing thievable had been left lying on the seats. A neatly paved path led him to the retail area and to the café where he planned to take a quick cappuccino before returning to his family. The girl behind the bar beamed in recognition, taking his money for the drink and for the use of the computer. He watched her pull at the lever on the espresso machine, then squirt steam into a jug of milk. An attractive girl, dark haired and round hipped, with disturbingly perfect teeth. As the milk hissed and boiled she flashed him a smile. When she'd done her business he carried the cup and saucer to the PC at the end of the row where the screen would not be overlooked by others.

While the machine dialled its way onto the net, he sipped at the coffee, glad she hadn't made it too hot. Then, checking he wasn't being watched, he connected with Hotmail and found two messages waiting for him. The first was the usual spam from a porn pedlar, but the second was the one he'd been expecting. A message in English from a man he'd never met, a man who called himself Simon.

Comrade! The Revolution is under way. The time has come for you to act. The comrades in England, France and Germany have already shown their strength. Now it is your turn!

Always the exclamation marks.

You will not be alone. All across Europe this weekend, men of right minds will stand up to be counted. It is war, comrade! We must fight for what we believe in, a Europe preserved for the people who have inherited it from their ancestors!

Are you ready to commit yourself to the Lucifer Network? You have talked bravely of your intentions. Will you act this weekend?

The target and the method are for you to choose. I'm sorry it has not been possible for my people to bring you weapons. Our resources are limited, but they will grow as our campaign of action grows.

Remember! It is only the acts of extreme violence which attract the attention of the media and the politicians. There must be deaths! There is no other way if the revolution is to gather pace and the enemy is to be defeated.

I wait to hear from you. To know you are with us and that you are not a coward. That you will join in the action this weekend which will shake the pillars in Brussels.

The teacher picked up his coffee cup and drained it. He looked towards the counter. The girl sat behind it on a stool, reading a paperback. Coward. In truth he feared he was one by nature. If not he might have made some effort to chat up that beautiful creature with the perfect teeth. To capitalise on her inviting smile.

But now there was a much greater reason for him to show his mettle. A chance to help change the political direction of the European continent. A dream that could only become reality if hundreds like himself were ready to fight for what they believed in, so that thousands, then millions would be inspired to join them. He turned back towards the screen and clicked on 'New Message'.

Yes, he typed. *We are ready. The enemy will suffer losses this weekend.*

He looked at what he'd written then added an exclamation mark at the end.

London
9.00 hrs

Sam climbed the stairs to his second-floor room and let himself in. The air inside smelled stale and sad. Morbidly he imagined some miserable refugee sitting here contemplating suicide, even carrying it out. Or some homeless, redundant car salesman wanking himself to sleep. He would be glad to leave this place.

After finishing with Waddell he'd booked a seat on a flight to Vienna for first thing the next morning, then phoned Stephanie. She'd had half an hour to spare before picking up her man Gerry from a Paris flight at Heathrow. They'd sat in her car round the corner from the hotel, eating greasy hamburgers while she commiserated over the media coverage and told him about the interview with Julie Jackman that morning. He'd found her more preoccupied than usual. The Southall bomb investigation was getting nowhere, she'd said, describing the detective in charge of the investigation as a brain-dead moron.

'But something big's starting,' she'd confided. 'I can feel it in my water. There's something very nasty going on. The deaths in Southall are the tip of an iceberg. Before long we'll all have our work cut out.'

When their time was up she'd kissed him on the cheek and wished him well.

And now he had to pack. Then he needed to catch up on some sleep if he wasn't going to stumble round Vienna like the undead.

'Damn!'

He'd wanted to take his file on Hoffmann with him, a dossier compiled over his years of dealings with the man. To jog his memory. The papers were in a safe in the flat in Brentford. He pulled Bennett's card from his trouser pocket, thinking he'd get him to send his girl back. But it was after ten. It'd take an age to find someone to do his bidding.

He decided to go himself. A foolish idea on the surface, but the more he thought about it the more it appealed. He'd take a look first to see if the snappers were still hanging around. If they were, he'd give up on the plan – or else treat it as a challenge to get in and out without being spotted.

He dug into the suitcase which he hadn't emptied. The headquarters girl had packed some of the scruffier clothes he used for disguises. He put on a pair of old jeans and some grubby trainers, then slipped a faded fleece over a grey sweatshirt and found a knitted hat to pull down over his hair. With a shuffling gait and a surly stare, he'd be the sort of street trash sane people avoided eye contact with.

He caught a bus to Ealing Broadway, then another to Kew Bridge – at this hour it was mostly youngsters travelling, heading for a late night out. As the bus passed the block where he had his flat, he looked for evidence of people waiting for him, but saw none. He got off on the bridge and walked slowly back, keeping to the shadows. Fifty metres short of the block he loitered in an office doorway and watched. A police car cruised by, its occupants eyeing him. The vehicle stopped for a better look, then drove on.

Sam decided to move. He'd considered entering the block by the fire escape, but remembered it was alarmed. He would use his card and go in the front. There were no security staff in the building at night, the place being watched on CCTV by a control centre half a mile away.

With one last check for press men, he slid his pass through the reader and pushed on the door as the lock clicked. The lift took him to the floor below his own, then he used the emergency stairs for the last flight. The fire door onto the main landing creaked as he opened it. He peered through the narrow gap and looked along the full length of the passageway. Doors to the flats on either side, all closed. No one waiting by the lifts. He walked swiftly and silently to his own front door and let himself in.

Inside, he used the torch he'd brought, the beam shaded by his fingers. With windows everywhere, turning on lights would be a give-away. In the living room he removed the small painting from the wall above his computer. Behind it was a wall safe, which he opened with a key. He pulled out a plastic folder containing a photograph of Hoffmann and several pages of biographical notes, then closed the safe again.

He felt pleased with himself. He looked across at the drinks cabinet, tempted to sink a whisky or two, then remembered the damned thing played a tune that would be audible through the walls – a heads-up to all those neighbours who'd taken bags of silver from the media. He'd got what he came for, so after a quick check of the security camera, he slipped back into the corridor.

The emergency stairs took him all the way down to the underground garage. His dander was up by now and he'd decided to take the car. He paused in the doorway, eyes probing the dimly lit cavern that reeked of petrol and rubber. Then, convinced he was the only human there, he stepped towards the Mondeo, pulling his keys from his pocket.

Suddenly he heard a click.

His heart stopped. He spun round, saw the glint of the knife, then the face of the man holding it. His mind tumbled back two years. The grimacing visage inching towards him was last seen in the catacombs of Odessa. The man was a *shpana* – a mafiya bodyguard Sam had all but killed when he'd rubbed out his boss. Cold, unblinking eyes boring into his, checking, checking that this was indeed the man he'd been sent to murder.

Sam made a feint towards his car then darted back to the door he'd just come through. The assassin was fast and agile despite the bullets Sam had put in him two years ago. As he pounded up the stairs, he heard the man's trainers crunch behind him. He kicked a wastebin into the path of his pursuer, then shouldered the bar of the fire exit and burst into the garden, blind terror powering his legs.

The gate to the towpath was locked. Sam swiped his card and tugged, slipping through. He clicked the gates behind him just as the knife slashed down, then melted into the darkness of the towpath, telling himself the killer would have a gun, to be used if the blade proved ineffective. He ran, weaving from side to side in anticipation of a bullet. Legs brushing nettles and willow herb, he heard the clang of wrought iron as the Ukrainian climbed the railings, then a light thud as he landed on the path behind him. To his right converted barges glowed with light. Geese honked.

Sam's feet hit rock. He pitched forward, his knees slamming into something hard. Clutching the Hoffmann folder with his left, his right hand felt bricks. He remembered builders had been working on a wall here. He struggled to stay on his feet but the ground rolled away beneath him. Scaffolding poles. He crashed on his back beside them, his hand grabbing, fingers closing on a pipe that proved mercifully short. The *shpana* loomed above him in the gloom, a faceless shape lunging down with the knife. Sam rolled and swung the pole, enjoying the thump of steel against bone. He heard a gasp and a scrabbling on the ground as the killer looked for his weapon. Sam clambered to his knees, gripping the steel tightly. He jabbed forward into the darkness, heard teeth break and a howl of pain. Then he was running again.

Ahead were the lights of the bridge. Cars passing. Behind him a couple of shots cracked out. The *shpana* was getting desperate. Weaving, he reached the steps to the roadway. A bullet chipped the stonework as he pounded up them, his head tucked below the balustrade. He flagged down the first vehicle that came his way.

'Stop, for fuck's sake,' he hissed. 'Get me outa here!'

But he was still holding the scaffolding pole and the car swerved and accelerated. Realising he must look like an escapee from an asylum, he ran across the road and skittered down the steps on the far side of the bridge to a low road running parallel to the river. A glance behind showed no sign of his pursuer. Dumping his weapon in a hedge, he dived into a side street. He knew his way around here and prayed that his assailant wouldn't. Left, then right, then left again and he was on the main road. A bus was disgorging a passenger at a stop thirty paces away. He ran, waving wildly, shouting to it to wait.

'Thanks, mate,' he panted as he swung himself aboard.

'Where to?'

'Anywhere, chum. Absolutely anywhere. Just close that fucking door and drive.'

'Not until you pay. Where you goin' to?'

Sam restrained his desire to reach for the door lever himself and dug into his pocket for coins. 'Two stops,' he croaked, having no clue where the bus was heading. He fired a wild glance over his shoulder.

'Sixty pence.'

Sam took his ticket and slumped in a seat, conscious of other passengers looking at him. No holes in his body. No blood. A miracle. He began to tremble, the shock catching up with him. For two years he'd lived with the threat of a revenge attack by the Voroninskaya. Now it had happened. And why? Because a pretty but malicious woman had caused his picture to be plastered all over the media.

He leaned his head against the window glass. The dark side of his soul had taken over. No room for compassion any more. He needed to hurt Julie. To hurt her badly in whatever way it took. To damage her life, to perch it on the edge of a precipice in the same way she'd done to his.

13

The Adriatic Sea, off the coast of Montenegro
Wednesday morning

DEEP BELOW THE surface of the Adriatic Sea, some 200 kilometres east of the Italian coastline, a long black shape sped westwards, unseen, unheard and undeclared. HMS *Truculent* – 280 feet of two-inch-thick welded steel, filled with men and electronics – was moving towards a spot on the chart where a helicopter would meet them after dark that evening. The submarine's mission to eavesdrop on the rapidly developing conflict in Kosovo was over and there was a bagful of interception tapes to be offloaded. Inside the nuclear-powered hull, 130 souls had lived in artificial light and scrubbed air for two and a half months. The end was in sight, however. By Friday night they'd be in Crete for some much-needed shore leave with wives and girlfriends, before the long haul back to Britain through the Strait of Gibraltar.

On the uppermost of *Truculent*'s three decks, just forward of the control room, five blue-shirted sonar specialists listened on padded headphones to the newly detected clatter of a diesel engine a few miles to the north of their course. The sound room was small. If one man moved, others had to bend their backs. A dozen raster screens filled two sides of the space, the herringbone patterns and green smudges on their displays logging every detectable sound in the water around them.

One of the two leading artificers manning the 'waterfall' screens for the bow sonar swung round in his seat. 'One shaft, three blades, chief.' The youth was little over twenty, his accent from Plymouth, *Truculent*'s home port.

Behind him on a tall stool his watch leader nodded. 'Fishing vessel,' he confirmed, pressing the headset microphone against his lips and clicking the transmit switch. 'Ops, sonar control.' He spoke in a high, clear voice.

Beyond a thin bulkhead, in the submarine's control room, watch officer Lieutenant Harvey Styles heard the intercom call and swung his seat to face the screens of the Submarine Automated Command System known as SMACS.

'Bearing zero-five-seven, one shaft, three blades, diesel engine audible,' the sonar controller announced. 'No evidence of trawl. Suggest small merchant vessel, range outside ten thousand yards.'

'Thanks, sonar control.'

No threat to them at that range, but one to keep an eye on. Nets were a submariner's nightmare.

'Cut it through.'

'*Cut*. Track eight-six-seven.'

A small green square appeared on the SMACS VDU, showing the fishing vessel's position relative to the submarine. A thin line indicated its heading.

'We have that, sonar. Thanks,' the SMACS chief acknowledged.

'If he stays on that course we don't have a problem, men,' Styles announced. 'But if he comes any further south to catch his squid then I can't promise to stay friends with him.' They were due at periscope depth in twenty minutes to receive a scheduled radio broadcast.

Harvey Styles was the submarine's Tactical Systems Officer, a short, broad-shouldered man in a sand-coloured shirt with a fuzz of fair hair and brown eyes. As he crossed to the navigator's station to check the chart, he spotted the captain emerging from his cabin.

'We've got a fishing vessel at more than ten thousand yards, sir, on green zero-five-seven.'

Commander Talbot nodded and strode over to the command seat.

'I don't see any conflict at this stage, sir,' said Styles, following him.

'Thanks, TSO.'

Truculent's captain was a stocky, dark-haired man with a deceptively mild expression, who wore a white, open-necked shirt with his rank insignia on his shoulders. Talbot let his gaze wander round the control room. Millions of pounds of electronics were packed in here, controlled by men whose minds were beginning to cloud with testosterone in anticipation of the upcoming 'run ashore'. Brains in going-home mode could easily lose concentration. They needed to know he was watching them. He stared hard at the Command System screens, breathing down the necks of the operators. Then he stood up again.

'You have the submarine, TSO.'

'I have the submarine, sir.'

Talbot made his way forward past the conning tower access hatch and into the sound room.

'Let me hear what you've got,' he announced, clamping on a pair of headphones.

The bow sonar operator swung the beams through the three main targets on the screens.

'The heavy beat is the US carrier the *Theodore Roosevelt*, sir,' the sonar controller told him. 'Ten miles to the south. The louder three-blader's a small merchant vessel heading for Dubrovnik and the lighter beat's the fisherman to the north of us.'

HMS *Truculent* was a 'special fit' Trafalgar class submarine, whose primary role was intelligence gathering. She had experimental sonar processors on board as well as a sophisticated signals intercept suite.

Talbot removed the headphones. 'You all happy bunnies in here?'

CPO Smedley eased round on his stool and slipped his own cans halfway towards the back of his head.

'Shall be, sir, so long as I trap in Souda at the weekend.'

'Shouldn't worry, chief. You usually do.' Smedley had a reputation for finding women ready to perform for him. 'The wife's not coming out, then?' he needled.

'Hates flying, sir,' Smedley answered, poker-faced.

Talbot suppressed a smile. 'Just watch out for that ouzo,' he cautioned. No one drank alcohol on board, but they all made up for it on a run ashore.

He left the sound room, stepping into the tiny 'trials shack' opposite, where the men from GCHQ did their stuff, huddled over scanners and frequency analysers, picking the interesting bits out of 'enemy' radio transmissions. For most of the mission *Truculent* had loitered at periscope depth a short distance from the Yugoslav coast, with her highly sensitive domed intercept mast poking above the surface. All transmissions picked up that were deemed significant had been taped for shipment to Cheltenham and a more detailed analysis. The last batch was packed up ready for the rendezvous with the helicopter in a few hours' time.

There were six GCHQ specialists on board, each with a knowledge of Russian and Serbo-Croat. For much of the past two months they'd manned their scanners around the clock, but at this moment just one of them was in the trials shack. Communications Technician Arthur Harris sat on a padded bench with a map spread out on his knees.

'What're you up to, Chief Harris?' Talbot demanded. 'Your war's meant to be over.'

'Planning my next summer holiday, sir,' the CT answered without a moment's hesitation. Then he stood up, holding out the sheet of paper. 'Actually, to be honest, I was hoping for one last bite of the cherry.' He pointed to an island marked on the map, which was a large-scale sheet of the Adriatic coast. 'When we come up to periscope depth for the broadcast, sir, we'll be about fifteen miles south of Lastovo island. There's a naval base there. Just a small one, but I'd be glad of the chance to listen in.'

'Don't want to dick around here for long,' Talbot warned him. 'Mustn't be late for the budgie.'

'Twenty minutes would be better than nothing, sir.'

'I'll see what I can do.' He turned towards the door, then hesitated. 'Oh, just a thought. If you happen across any cricket scores when you're listening in, do pass them on.' It was an old joke, wearing a little thin at this end of the tour.

'Certainly will, sir.'

Talbot stepped back into the control room. They were cruising at fifteen knots at a depth of eighty metres, halfway between the surface and the sea bed. In a few minutes he would slow down and bring the boat shallower, ready for the raising of the periscope and radio mast – and now the intercept mast too.

Arthur Harris folded his map, deciding to fetch a smaller-scale sheet which showed all the known telecommunications sites on the Adriatic islands. He walked briskly through the control room, down the companionway to 2 deck and along the passageway leading forward. As he passed the galley he caught a whiff of pastry baking.

A few paces short of the forward bunk spaces where the junior rates had their berths, an open hatch gave onto a ladder down to the 'bomb shop', the weapons compartment that had been the living quarters for himself and the other CTs for the past ten weeks. He swung himself onto the rungs, taking care not to bang his head on the hatch handle, and dropped down to the deck below. Long black Spearfish torpedoes and Harpoon anti-ship missiles lay strapped on racks behind the polished brass caps of the launch tubes. Some of the weapons bays were empty, however, fitted instead with bunk pallets. Feet protruded from a couple of them. In the gangway between the weaponry were boxes of spares and recording tapes for the myriad sensors on board. One of them contained the CTs' maps and manuals. To get at it Harris had to remove two others.

He was of average height with a thick shock of dark hair and a narrow, expressionless face. He was unmarried, though not by choice, but at sea he invented a wife to deter comments from the more homophobic senior rates.

He glanced up. Feet were descending from the deck above. They belonged to a young, dark-haired sailor whose pretty-boy looks prompted regular ribbing from some of the older men. The youth's name was Griffiths. Not more than eighteen, Harris reckoned.

'Sorry to disturb you, chief. Got to clean the place.' Griffiths spoke softly so as not to disturb those sleeping.

'That's all right. I'll be gone in a moment.'

Harris reached the box he was looking for and opened the lid. The orderliness with which he and his team had begun their mission had rather fallen apart. There was even an old paperback in there that he'd finished reading a week ago.

'What's the book, chief?' Griffiths had come up beside him as he made his way to the aft end of the compartment looking for anything on the deck that shouldn't be there.

'Clive Cussler. It was okay.'

'Never get the time, me,' Griffiths complained. 'Only reading I do is manuals. I've got a promotion exam when I get back to England.'

'Good luck with it.'

'Thanks.'

Griffiths moseyed on down to the end of the compartment, then finding nothing amiss made his way back to the torpedo tubes and began rubbing their brass caps with a cloth. Harris remembered hearing that the lad had got some girl pregnant back in Plymouth and was intending to do the decent thing. Married at eighteen. The thought of so much responsibility so young made him shudder.

Suddenly the hull began to tilt. They'd begun the transition to periscope depth. He found the map he'd been looking for and replaced the storage box under the others that had covered it. He had no particular reason for wanting to listen in to the Croatian naval base on Lastovo, but he hated wasting an opportunity when it was there. He squeezed past the boxes, then climbed the ladder back to 2 deck.

In the control room, the TSO crossed to the navigator's position and nudged his fellow lieutenant aside so he could look at the chart. From beneath the navigation table a dot of light shone, marking their position on the chart as plotted by the Ship's Inertial Navigation System. The TSO jabbed his finger at it.

'Plus or minus how much, Vasco?' The SINS had been drifting of late.

'A mile at the most. When we stick the mast up we'll get a GPS correction.' A mile of error wouldn't matter in the open sea and the Global Positioning System satellites would quickly locate them to within a few metres of their exact position.

Styles liked to throw his weight around when he was officer of the watch. He knew he'd make a damned good skipper when he'd passed his 'Perisher'. Fail the stressful commander's course and he would never serve in a submarine again. Pass and he should have his own boat to drive within five years, so long as the captains he served under didn't take against him. Flag rank was what he was aiming for. A vice-admiral's job at least. Maybe even the very top.

He crossed the control room to check data on the small screen next to the Command System panel. A graph recorded changes in salinity and the biological condition of the water around them as they came up from the depths, all of which could affect the way sound waves reached them. A sharp kink in the trace showed they'd passed through a layer that could have blanketed out noise from the surface directly above them.

Commander Talbot had seen it too. Warily, he ordered eighteen metres – periscope depth – and a speed of three knots.

Styles hovered by the search periscope ready to seize its grips when the order came to raise it.

'New contact, sir!' An alert from the sound room.

'Damn!' Talbot grunted. The submarine was at its most vulnerable just below the surface. 'Bearing?'

'Red zero five. One shaft, five blades. Large merch.'

'Damn! Starboard thirty,' Talbot ordered. The planesman pulled hard on his wheel.

'Moving left.' The sonar chief again. 'Range five to seven thousand yards.'

'That's better,' Talbot muttered. Far enough for safety and moving away from them. Everyone in the control room relaxed.

'Three minutes to the broadcast, sir,' Styles cautioned. If they missed the slot it'd be four hours before they could try again.

The boat began to wallow in the surface swell, the planesman riding his controls to keep her level.

'Ops, control. No more contacts.'

'Thanks control. Raise the search periscope.'

The stainless steel shaft hissed up from its well. Harvey Styles pressed his face to the soft rubber of the eyepiece. Water splashed silently against the outer glass of the sight. Overhead the sky was overcast. The slate grey sea heaved and chopped in a stiff breeze which flicked spray from the wave crests. Styles checked the horizon. Satisfied it was clear ahead of them, he swept the sight through a full 360 degrees.

'No visual contacts, sir.' He began a second sweep to make sure. 'I estimate visibility at five thousand yards.'

'The Radar Warner has low level E and F band,' another voice shouted. Civilian radars. No threat. 'Risk of detection nil.'

'Good.' Talbot relaxed. 'Raise the comms mast and the intercept mast. Let's make the CTs happy.'

Three minutes later the signals officer reported that the satellite broadcast from London had been taken in successfully.

'Excellent.' Talbot beamed. Apart from routine operational matters the signal should include the solution to yesterday's *Telegraph* crossword. He stepped across to the periscope as Styles relinquished it. 'Nice sailing weather up there?'

'Depends on your stomach, sir.'

A few feet from the control room, Arthur Harris and two of his fellow communications technicians hunched over the racks in their shack. Harris's knowledge of Serbo-Croat was basic, Russian being his main skill. He was due to attend a course in the language when he'd completed his leave at the end of this patrol. His two companions were fluent, however.

This far from land their expectations of intercepts were low. A week ago they'd been close in to the mainland, monitoring tactical chat between Serb units in the Kosovo mountains to the north of them. Harris watched the squiggles on the spectrum analyser, randomly selecting transmissions to dip into. Dull stuff, mostly. Marine band VHF – the ramblings of local boatmen. If the Croatian Navy was active on Lastovo, it was being damned quiet about it. Harris kicked his shoes off. His feet had been itching of late – some fungal infection between the toes that seemed resistant to athlete's foot powder.

Suddenly a new spike appeared on the VHF display. He tuned in quickly, activating filters to minimise the background hiss to the voices he was hearing. The transmitter must have been on low power or at the limits of its range.

Then he sat bolt upright, pressing the headphones to his ears, his interest galvanised. What he was listening to wasn't Serbo-Croat. It was Russian.

Coming from a place where no Russians ought to be.

Vienna

Sam's flight touched down at Schwechat Airport just after midday. The attack by the *shpana* from Odessa had left him badly rattled. Stumbling into ambushes seemed to be becoming a habit. Last night after escaping from the mafiya killer, he'd phoned Bennett with a description of his assailant, but they'd both known the chances of his being found were slim.

Sam walked from the arrivals gate past a long line of overpriced boutiques. He was dressed in his light grey suit. A bored official on the EU passport counter waved him through, then while waiting for his bag, he queued at the tourist desk and booked a room in a small pension near the Ringstrasse.

When he'd phoned Hans Kesselring his German intelligence contact yesterday to check on Hoffmann's whereabouts, he'd asked for an update on the man when he got to Vienna. The response was waiting outside the arrivals door, a copy of *Spiegel* magazine clutched in his fist.

'Fischer,' said the fair-haired German, introducing himself. He was a centimetre taller than Sam and wore a dark blue suit. 'I am in post at the Embassy here in Vienna.'

'Packer' said Sam, happy that the man's English was okay. His own German had become rusty through lack of use. 'Good of you to meet me.'

They headed towards the exit and waited until they were in the car heading in to the city before talking again.

'May I ask why you still have an interest in Herr Hoffmann so long after he retires?' Fischer asked.

'History,' Sam replied. 'We think he can throw light on something that happened in Britain twenty-seven years ago.' Sam didn't feel the need to elaborate further.

Fischer's eyes narrowed. 'So long ago . . . We know little about him at that time. Many of the oldest Stasi files were destroyed during the days before the wall came down and Herr Hoffmann is not a man who gives information unless he absolutely must.'

'I'm well aware of that. It took me four years to get a name out of him.'

'Ah yes. Herr Kesselring told me about "Papagena", the woman in the British army headquarters. So what exactly do you want to know?'

'Anything you can tell me about him. Is he still active?'

'I think that he is not. Or not very. Herr Hoffmann is nearly seventy. He lives with his wife in the Karl-Marx Hof. They are lovers of music and fresh air. They go to concerts and for long walks in the Wienerwald.'

The answer was too glib. 'You don't *think* he's still active? You mean he's not sending you reports any more?'

Fischer's jaw hardened. Sam suspected he wasn't sure how much he was allowed to reveal. 'Herr Hoffmann still has good contacts,' he replied enigmatically. 'And he still informs us about certain people who do business in Vienna.'

'People like Vladimir Kovalenko . . .'

Fischer glanced sideways and ventured an awkward smile. 'Except we don't think Kovalenko *is* in Vienna at the moment. Everybody is looking for him. You too?'

'That's not the reason I'm here, no. But d'you think Hoffmann ever dealt with Kovalenko?'

'I have not seen his name in Herr Hoffmann's reports. The truth is that we don't hear often from him. The arrangement we made when we ended his interrogation was a good idea but it has not proved very useful. Herr Hoffmann has many loyalties, but they are not to us.'

'Loyalties to his old friends, you mean. I know about that.'

Fischer nodded. 'Papagena,' he murmured.

'But let me get this straight. D'you think he's done business with his old Russian chums here in Vienna? Like worked with them on some of their scams?'

'It is possible. Herr Hoffmann has good connections in the German speaking world. He could be very useful to Russians.'

'And they would pay good money for those connections?'

'As I have said, we only know what he tell us, Herr Packer. If he make money from these people, then he keeps it well hidden.'

'No private Schloss in the Tyrol . . .'

Fischer smiled. 'No private anything. Herr Hoffmann has strong political principles. Still very much a socialist, I would say. Puts the national interest above personal comfort. The apartment where he lives has only three rooms. He passes a lot of time at the Staatsbibliothek – the national library – studying the history of the German peoples. Every Saturday afternoon and other days also. His only big expense is the Opera. If he was making big money he would use it for some cause that he believed in, not spending it on himself.'

'When did you last see him?'

Fischer pursed his thin lips. 'Maybe two month ago.'

'He contacts you, or you contact him?'

'The first. As I said, we don't expect much from him these days. He is too old. The Russians in Vienna are most aged thirty to forty.'

Sam glanced out of the window as they crossed the wide, brown streak of the Danube. He smiled, remembering Hoffmann saying that only a musician could have convinced the world that Vienna's river was blue.

'So you think he's on the same side as you now?' Sam suggested.

'Or on no side at all,' Fischer answered briskly. 'How long do you stay in Vienna?'

'For as long as it takes. It'll be my luck to find that Hoffmann's gone away this morning.'

'Your luck is not that bad. He is still here. One of my assistants telephoned him one hour ago to check.'

'What? And mentioned I was coming?'

'Of course not. He was pretending to offer financial advice. Here in Austria there are many companies that make such calls.'

'Makes a change from double glazing.'

Ten minutes later Fischer dropped him at his hotel. He handed Sam a business card.

'Please, before you leave Vienna, you will tell me if you learn anything interesting?'

'Of course.'

Brussels

Commissioner Blanche Duvalier called the meeting to order. It was already mid-morning, the session having been delayed by the late-arriving flight from Vienna bringing in Anders Klason, head of the EC's new racial equality unit. Klason was scheduled to give the opening address, so the day's programme couldn't start without him.

Blanche Duvalier watched Klason settle down at his place in the horseshoe of the Salle Bertrand at the Commission headquarters. His bearing, his bright blue eyes and golden skin made him a godlike figure. A Nordic Adonis. If the opportunity arose she had every intention of adding him to her list of lovers. This morning however there seemed to be something wrong with him. He was frowning a lot, as if trying to catch up with himself. Unsettled by the delayed flight, she decided. She would give him a moment to compose himself.

It was an important meeting this morning. The European Union faced a punishing influx of refugees from the war-torn Balkans and the bankrupt states of Eastern Europe. And matters were worsening, with experts predicting a catastrophe in Kosovo. The vast majority of European citizens had been tolerant of the new arrivals in their midst, but there'd been demonstrations of intense xenophobia by fascist groups in several member states, culminating in the violence of last weekend. Blacks, Asians and Jews had also been subject to renewed hostility in many parts of the continent. What the meeting today needed to achieve was a strategy for dealing with the issue, so that ministers could discuss it at their next council session in three weeks' time.

Blanche Duvalier looked around her. A pleasantly spacious conference room with glass panels at the far end behind which the linguists sat, ready for their gruelling stint of simultaneous translation. There were twenty-six delegates seated at the horseshoe, most of them appointed by member governments, many of them academics well used to theorising and pontificating, a good half of them with an excessive fondness for their own voices. Her task would be to keep them ruthlessly to the point. If she didn't, then the chances of anything useful coming out of the two-day session were remote.

Thank God they had Klason here to kick things off, she thought. Anders was one of the most down-to-earth men she'd ever met.

Anders Klason, however, felt very peculiar this morning. It had started when he woke up. For a few moments he hadn't known where he was, even though it was his own bed with Nina's warm nakedness beside him. At first he hadn't been able to remember what it was he had to do today. Then, later, on the journey to the airport, he found he couldn't remember which airline he was flying with and had needed to look at his ticket. Other things had stayed perfectly clear in his head. The speech he was to give, and the fact that by making this journey to Brussels he was avoiding one of his mother-in-law's visits. But there were gaps. As if someone had bored holes in his memory.

'Ladies and gentlemen, dear colleagues,' Blanche Duvalier began, speaking her native French. 'May I welcome you to this meeting and wish us all success in formulating ideas for countering the resurgence of racism in Europe which we all fear.'

Anders Klason gaped. The sounds from her mouth weren't words to him at all, but strange animal twitterings. He searched the faces of his fellow delegates. Attentive. Listening. Pretending, all of them. Pretending things were normal when they so obviously weren't. A smile flitted across his face. This was laughable. The woman at the desk bridging the two ends of the horseshoe, whom he thought he knew but now couldn't quite place, was playing some extraordinary game. And everyone else was conniving at it. Like the Emperor's new clothes. Everyone except him. Then he looked closer at the faces around him and realised there wasn't a single soul here that he recognised. An assembly of strangers. He'd made a terrible mistake. Gone through the wrong door. He pushed the chair back and levered himself to his feet.

Suddenly he heard his name. Spoken by the woman at the head of the table. He stared at her. How did she know him? They were all looking at him. Expectant faces. Total strangers into whose midst he'd suddenly been dropped. He had no recollection of how he'd come to this place, or why. No idea where this place was. He stared down at the desk, his vision strangely tunnelled. There were papers there with words that made no sense. He felt desperately tired. He knew he must lie down.

'Anders?' Concern and curiosity on the woman's face.

Klason wanted out of there. Back to bed, away from this mistake. No. He wasn't all right. His legs suddenly gave way.

Blanche Duvalier stood up in horror. 'Call an ambulance, someone!' She walked round the back of the horseshoe to where Anders lay, his mouth goldfishing, eyes fixed on nothing. His face was ashen, a tail of saliva dribbled from the corner of his lips.

'He's had a stroke,' she whispered. She'd seen it before. A French government minister with whom she'd had a long affair. She screwed up her face. 'Anders! Can you hear me? Say something.'

But he couldn't. They didn't know it then, but Anders Klason would never speak again.

HMS *Truculent*

Commander Talbot ordered the boat to eighteen metres for the second time in an hour. The periscope slid up. The sea around them was clear. They were safe, at a distance of about five miles from Lastovo island.

He'd diverted from his track towards the evening's rendezvous with the helicopter at the request of Communications Technician Arthur Harris. The direction-finding equipment in the intercept mast had located the source of the Russian voices as being east of the island, in an area of rocky outcrops which the charts on board described as uninhabited. The biggest of them and the most likely source of the transmissions was called Palagra. They still had a hundred metres of sea beneath the keel. Any closer in and the waters became significantly shallower.

Talbot had been reluctant to deviate from his original course. He'd wanted a steady, risk-free transit to their rendezvous with the Lynx from the frigate HMS *Suffolk* in six hours' time. The tapes of the last ten days of intercepts of Serb and Kosovan military communications were urgently needed back in the UK. They still had a hundred miles to run to the pre-arranged point in the ocean. Four hours was the minimum at a full-power dash, but their sonar would be degraded by noise at that speed. He preferred a more modest cruising rate. He'd told the CTs they could have an hour to play with. At a pinch he would give them two.

Lt Harvey Styles was studying the chart, familiarising himself with waters they'd not explored before. One more hour on duty for him before the watch changed. He noted the arrival of the captain's lean deputy, Lt-Commander Martin Hayes, the only man on board apart from the skipper who'd passed the command course.

The captain saw him too and stretched. 'Keep the CTs on a tight rein,' he cautioned as Hayes took up position by his elbow. 'Don't want them delaying us so we end up blowing a gasket trying to make the RV with the Lynx.'

Styles overheard and moved closer to the two senior officers. 'The First

Lieutenant's a demon on the exercise bike, sir. Hook him up to the shaft and we might get a few more revs out of the propulsor.'

Talbot smiled and slid off the command seat. 'I shall be in my cabin. You have the submarine, First Lieutenant.'

'I have the submarine, sir.'

Martin Hayes had the race-bred looks of a greyhound, a body on which there was not an ounce of flesh that wasn't sinew. Keeping fit was hard for submariners. Life on board for most of the men revolved around work, sleep and large meals. There was an exercise bike in the swelteringly hot machinery spaces aft of the reactor, and a running machine on the lower deck next to the coxswain's office. Hayes used them both whenever he could, but most of the crew didn't.

In command of the boat for the next couple of hours, he began to take stock of their position. The Command System screen showed half a dozen small contacts off the coast of Lastovo, none fast moving and all more than three miles distant. He crossed to the chart table as Styles vacated it to take over the periscope from the ship control chief. Clear of these islands the Adriatic was deep, but if they ever had to go in amongst them great care would be needed. The bottom shelved to less than the sixty metres which was their normal operational minimum.

Styles's quip about the exercise bike had irritated him. An innocent enough witticism to the others, but to Hayes it was just one more jibe. Six months ago his relationship with the TSO had become unpleasantly personal, when the girl he planned to marry switched allegiance. From the moment this patrol began, Styles had lost no opportunity to talk about his 'delightful' Frances whenever Hayes was in earshot. A Chinese water torture of deliberate insensitivity.

Hayes brushed past Harvey Styles and stepped into the trials shack. Seeing the First Lieutenant walk in, Arthur Harris removed his headphones. 'They're not sending at the moment, sir. Quiet as the grave.'

'What exactly did you pick up earlier?' Hayes asked, perching on a stool.

'It appeared to be comms between a boat called the *Karolina* and someone ashore. Two men, the first saying they'd be alongside in five minutes. Complaining about how many boxes he had on board and how it wasn't his job to hump them all. The complaint seemed to work, because the other man said he'd be at the landing stage to help.'

'Holidaymakers bringing in fresh supplies of slivovitz,' Hayes suggested.

'That's not impossible, sir,' Harris conceded. 'But a little unlikely. The Russians go for jazzy resorts like Limassol where they can flash their money around, not remote Croatian rocks.'

'Well whatever, we can't hang around for ever waiting for them to transmit again.'

'I know that, sir.'

Hayes stood up again. 'Keep me posted.'

'I will, sir.'

Vienna

The air in Vienna was hot and dry, a wind known as the *Föhn*, blowing in from the Sahara, a fickle breeze, said to induce migraines in the susceptible and to drive the suicidal towards their ultimate ambition. When Sam had come here last, three years ago, it had been early winter, before the snows had iced the roofs, but with a fetid fog clinging to the dank waters of the Danube. Sam had bought Hoffmann a *Viertel* of new wine in a *Heurige*, then been taken back to his flat in the Karl-Marx Hof to be told at last the real name of the woman who'd spied on the British Rhine Army headquarters.

Sam left his bag at the *pension* off the Ringstrasse, then boarded a U-Bahn heading north from the baroque city centre. Fifteen minutes later, the almost empty train emerged from its tunnel, passing factories and oil storage tanks before terminating at the suburb of Heiligenstadt on the edge of the Wienerwald. Facing Sam as he emerged from the station was the monolithic, ochre and terracotta apartment complex built with tax levies by Red Vienna's socialist administration at the end of the 1920s. He remembered Hoffmann being proud of his new home's history.

He waited for a bus to pass, then crossed the road and walked through one of the building's wide arches into an enclosed garden on the far side of the block. Young women lounged and chatted on a bench while their children swung perilously on a climbing frame. He turned to stare up at the building. Social realist statues looked down from their keystones. It had puzzled him how Hoffmann had been able to move from Berlin and immediately find a flat here. Accommodation was hard to secure in Vienna – Austrians even joined political parties in an attempt to bump their way up the housing lists. He'd come to the conclusion that thirty years in the Stasi must have given Hoffmann a thick file of Austrian contacts to pressure and cajole.

Sam found the staircase he needed and made his way to the third floor. He remembered Hoffmann's wife as being a homely woman of indeterminate shape with drawn-back hair, the sort it was impossible to imagine being young. She'd worked as a schoolteacher in East Berlin, he recalled, but had been forced to retire after the fall of the wall because of her inability to separate history from dogma. Sam remembered her stiff greeting in the small hallway, the doors to all rooms except the lounge firmly shut. She'd brought them coffee and cake, then retired to some other part of the flat. He'd imagined her listening in to their conversation on headphones.

It was a shared love of the sea that had got him close to Günther Hoffmann. The old spy stemmed from Greifswald on the Baltic coast and had inherited a small family house there in the fourteenth-century Altstadt. Hoffmann told how he and his childless wife would spend weekends there in the summer, sailing their elderly ketch. It was a coastline Sam also knew, having spent a summer in the 1980s sailing from Denmark to Leningrad. Accompanied by an unnervingly virginal WREN and equipped with two Irish passports, they'd observed Warsaw Pact harbours from the cockpit of a sloop.

The stairwell he was climbing smelled of disinfectant. Somewhere nearby a cleaning bucket clanked. On the small third-floor landing were four front doors. Number 12 – Hoffmann's place – was the only one without a name. A glass spyhole was set into the panel above the bell push. Sam pressed it, then turned his face away, far from sure his visit would be welcome.

He heard no sound from inside and pressed the bell again, holding the button for longer. He could still visualise that living room where Hoffmann had talked with pride and sadness about Papagena, who was by then close to death. There'd been a wooden model of their Baltic ketch on a bookcase, and above it a perfect copy of a work by the German Romantic painter Caspar David Friedrich, done by a Stasi forger.

With still no response, Sam tried a neighbour's bell. The door opened a crack, held back by a chain. He saw a bespectacled eye, a beak of a nose and caught a whiff of cats.

'Grüss Gott,' he smiled.

'Grüss Gott. Wer sind Sie?' The woman's voice scratched like a broken quill.

'Ich suche Herr Hoffmann . . .' Sam inclined his head towards her neighbour's flat.

'Weiss nicht.' She made to close the door, but Sam's foot prevented it.

'Sorry . . . Entshuldigung. Wissen Sie wo . . . ?'

'Nein. Weiss nicht wo er iss. Die Frau ist neulich tot.'

Sam blinked, unsure he'd understood aright. 'Frau Hoffmann, she's dead? Frau Hoffmann tot?'

'Letzte Woche. Wer sind Sie?'

'Ein Freund. A friend.'

'Englisch?'

Sam nodded.

'Später. Versuchen Sie später. Come later.'

The door pressed against Sam's foot and this time he removed it.

'Vielen Dank,' he murmured as it clicked shut. He turned to find that an elderly couple making their slow way up to the floor above had paused to listen.

'You look for Herr Hoffmann?' the man asked.

'His woman dead,' his wife added. 'Letzte Woche.'

'You know where he might be?' Sam queried, glad of their English.

'Im Friedhof,' the woman suggested.

'The funeral was yesterday,' the man explained.

'Do you know which cemetery she's buried in?'

'The Zentralfriedhof, I believe.'

'Thank you.' The couple continued on their way. 'Danke schön,' he called after them, two portly figures, as puffed as the cream cakes they'd probably just been consuming at a local *Konditorei*.

He made his way back downstairs, then extracted a map from his pocket. The cemetery was on the other side of town. He headed back to the U-Bahn.

HMS *Truculent*

Arthur Harris sat spellbound. Suddenly after nearly two hours, his screens had sprung to life. A string of spikes like an earthquake. The same frequency as before. VHF on a band not normally used in this part of the world.

One of the voices was the same as before, a whingeing litany of complaint in a Moscow accent. The other speaker was from further east. This time the moan wasn't about lifting boxes. There was a major drama unfolding. A search was under way. A search for a man.

Harris checked the tape machine was recording, then balanced an A4 pad on his knees, making shorthand notes and logging key words against time codes. The transmissions were uneven, breaking up. Hand-held walkie-talkie sets, he guessed, with a range of a mile or two normally. Given a clear line of sight over the sea, the intercept mast was picking it up at more than twice that distance.

Suddenly a new voice cut in. Harder. More authoritative. Urging the others on to find their quarry. A voice that to Arthur Harris sounded chillingly familiar. Holding his breath, he jotted harder.

Find the bastard! Check the Karolina is secure. He may use the boat to escape.

Circle the island on foot, two men in each direction.

No violence. We need him back alive.

Harris felt a hand on his shoulder and jumped. The First Lieutenant stood beside him tapping his wristwatch then drawing a finger across his throat. The window was closing. HMS *Truculent* was about to dive again.

'Five more minutes, sir?' Harris pleaded. 'They're sending.'

'No can do. Sorry. The masts are coming down now.'

As he said it, the voices in Harris's ears turned to hiss. He pulled off the headphones.

'In that case, sir, I have a most exceptional request to make.'

Lt-Commander Hayes raised a far from co-operative eyebrow. 'Try me.'

'When we surface for the rendezvous with the helicopter I would like to transmit what we've just recorded direct to London.'

'God! The captain won't like that,' Hayes cautioned. There'd be no chance of keeping their position secret with their satcom mast radiating like a beacon. 'How much tape have you got?'

'About five minutes, sir.'

'Why can't you ship it with the others? It'll be in Cheltenham within twelve hours.'

'Because it can't wait that long, sir. I believe I recognised one of the voices. There's a man at my HQ who can confirm it.'

Hayes frowned, intrigued suddenly.

'Who is this bloke?'

'Well actually, sir, if it's the man I think it is, he's a top Russian scientist. A biological warfare expert specialising in viruses. And a man known to have something of a cash flow problem. The bastard's been offering his skills on the open market to anybody prepared to pay his price.'

14

Vienna

T HE TRAM STOPPED directly outside the number 2 entrance to Vienna's vast central cemetery. When the doors hissed open, half a dozen souls got off before Sam, all making for the main gates. On the far side of a wide, cobbled yard stood a row of flower stalls. At the sound of the tram's arrival, four pinafored proprietresses had emerged from their separate huts and bustled towards the visitors like an operetta chorus line, arms brimming with blooms for sale. On the opposite side of the courtyard, cut-price gravestones were on sale – 50 per cent off for ends of lines. To Sam it seemed he'd arrived at a supermarket of death.

Passing through the cemetery entrance, tree-lined avenues fanned out into the distance. At the far end of one stood a huge domed church. Sam realised that if Hoffmann were in this graveyard, he would need a grid reference and a GPS to find him. He spotted an administration office. Inside, a helpful young woman looked up the Hoffmann name on her computer and directed Sam to plot D 175. 'It's up towards gate number 1,' she told him. 'Close to the Israeli section.'

Israeli. He blinked at her use of the word.

'Thanks.'

He found signposts pointing to zone D and followed them. To his left and right, mausoleums in marble and blackened bronze held the remains of Vienna's great and good. Further on the plots became less presumptuous, but some screamed their presence with gaudy displays of red and pink begonias. Large labels stuck into the turf advertised the companies that maintained the graves. But the commercial neatness of the cemetery ended abruptly at the Jewish sector. Here, stones were crooked and untended, their messages obscured by moss. Plots had lost their shape to the weeds, and footpaths were overgrown from lack of use. A red deer using the area for grazing took off at Sam's arrival.

He read off some of the names – Adler, Goldstein, Kohn. The dates of death were all before 1938, the year many Austrians had lined the streets to welcome Hitler in. These graves looked like they'd been unattended ever since, abandoned, he assumed, because the families that would have cared for them had vanished in the Holocaust. A moment ago the admin girl had referred to this as the Israeli sector. He pulled from his pocket the tourist map of Vienna. There it was in print. *Israelit Abteilung* – Israelite sector, as if the nation had taken a conscious decision to forget that the Jews buried here had been Austrians.

He turned away. Zone D was back in the vast Christian sector, down a gravel track running along the edge of this abandoned ghetto. Here the stones and plots set amongst trees looked new. Dates were from this year and the last, some freshly planted, others still bare earth. Sam rounded a bend in the path and stopped. There, some twenty metres ahead of him sat a dark-suited, silver-haired figure, his backside straddling a folding canvas stool, his chin supported by his hands as he gazed forlornly at a mound of earth.

Sam held his breath. It felt an invasion of privacy to approach the old spy at such a time, but he reminded himself that this same man had abused the sanctity of his own father's life without the slightest compunction.

Sensing his presence, the leathery face turned towards him. It bore a defeated look, as if life had been deprived of its meaning. For what felt like a full minute, Günther Hoffmann stared at him, his expression one of puzzled half-recognition. Eventually he made the connection and his eyebrows lifted. Then for a moment his face registered fear.

'Herr Maxwell . . .' he exclaimed. 'Was machen *Sie* denn hier?'

Maxwell. Another pseudonym for another time.

'Herr Hoffmann.' Sam closed the gap between them. 'Your wife . . . I'm very sorry.'

'Ja.' The German stood up with a grimace, then extended his hand. He was a tall man, aristocratically handsome, though age had turned his face into a relief map. His eyes were as slate grey as the Baltic in winter. 'It was a big shock for me, Herr Maxwell.'

'Of course.'

Hoffmann frowned. 'But you are not here because of Ilse.' He bent down to fold up the chair.

Sam could see the man's brain whirring, trying to guess what undeclared aspect of the Papagena case might have emerged unexpectedly from the woodwork.

'No. But I could have chosen a better time, perhaps.'

'Ach, Herr Maxwell, we do not *choose* time,' Hoffmann responded, philosophically. 'Time chooses us.' He shot a last look at the mound of earth. 'And for Ilse this choice came much too soon.' He sucked in his cheeks, holding in his grief. 'They will plant flowers here tomorrow.' He seemed embarrassed by the plainness of the grave. '*Komm*. We will go from here. Perhaps I must be grateful to you. If you didn't come I would stay here until the night.'

'It was sudden, her death?' Sam asked as they began to walk.

Hoffmann took a cigarette pack from his pocket and lit up. His fifty-a-day habit had turned his slicked hair yellow at the temples.

'It was her heart. She have two attacks before this year . . .' He shrugged, as if the rest was obvious.

'I'm sorry.'

'Ja . . .' Hoffmann sounded dismissive. 'But we all must die, Herr Maxwell.' A largish stone lay in the middle of the path and he moved it aside with his foot.

'She wanted to be buried here? Not in Germany?'

'Because she was born in Vienna,' he explained. 'And brought up.'

'I see.'

Hoffmann paused to tuck the folding stool into a carrier bag. He pointed to the wilderness on the far side of the path. 'Jews.'

'I know,' said Sam. 'It's a mess.'

'Austrians have never felt they must conceal their anti-Semitism,' Hoffmann explained, matter-of-factly. 'They weren't re-educated after the war like we Germans. The Allies chose to believe that Austrians were innocent victims of the Nazis instead of collaborators. So there was no pressure for a change of attitude.'

The old man sounded almost envious of Austria's freedom to be prejudiced. They carried on walking, a silence developing between them. Overhead a jumbo jet growled powerfully as it climbed to altitude from the airport a short distance to the east of them. Hoffmann scowled up at it.

'I hate those things,' he muttered, grouchily. 'I never fly these days.'

When they reached a T-junction the German's curiosity finally became too much for him. He looked at his watch – it was nearly five – then squared up to Sam.

'Why you have come, Herr Maxwell?'

For a couple of seconds Sam let him sweat, enjoying the discomfort in Hoffmann's eyes. 'Because of Jo Macdonald,' he told him eventually.

Hoffmann blinked. He took a small step back. Then as quickly as he'd reacted, his face was still again, calm and expressionless. The steady gaze of a poker player.

'Jo Macdonald,' he murmured, as if the name were new to him.

'She knew you as Johann, I believe,' Sam prompted.

For a few seconds Hoffmann remained as still as a statue. Then without replying, he took Sam by the elbow and they began to walk up the long avenue of poplars towards gate number 1. Red squirrels darted across the stones in front of them. After a minute Hoffmann stopped again and studied Sam's face with a new intensity.

'You know, Herr . . . *Maxwell*.' He laid an ironic stress on Sam's cover name. 'At this time of the afternoon in Vienna, it is customary to visit a café. You have a saying in English: *when in Rome* . . . So, if you want to talk about things that happened a very long time ago, then we should find somewhere more *gemütlich* than a graveyard.'

'As you wish.'

They walked more briskly towards the gate.

'You still have your boat?' Hoffmann asked.

'Unfortunately not. Lack of time,' Sam explained. Time was what Hoffmann was playing for, he realised. Giving himself space to think.

'You miss it, of course,' Hoffmann insisted.

'Yes.'

'I too. Vienna is a long way from the smell of the sea.'

They reached the gate and crossed into the middle of the road to wait at the tram stop.

'But Vienna has its compensations for you,' Sam continued. It was a nonsense conversation which he longed to abandon. 'You go to the opera a lot.'

Hoffmann rambled on for several minutes about the variable standards at the Staatsoper, then, to Sam's relief, a tram came. On the ride back into the centre of the city, they hardly spoke. At one point when the machine stopped at traffic lights, their view was blocked by a political poster – the smiling, film-star face of a charismatic politician called Jörg Haider on which a small, black moustache had been daubed.

'They have elections here next year,' Hoffmann commented, pointing to it. 'I think maybe this country will see big changes.'

'To the right, you mean?'

'*Ja*. This Freedom Party says in public many of the things that Austrian people think inside their heads. Particularly about foreigners. *Überfremdung* they call it. Too much immigration. They want to stop it. Even I as a German am not always welcome here.'

'You mean the Austrians didn't all support Hitler's invasion . . .' Sam remarked.

'No. Of course not. But Germans are more acceptable here than most foreigners, so if I feel some hostility, what must it be like for people from other countries?'

The tram sped on, transporting them to Schwarzenbergplatz where they found a secluded booth in a café smelling of fresh-baked cakes which overlooked the Russian war memorial. They ordered *mélange* and small glasses of schnapps.

'So . . . You came because of Jo Macdonald,' Hoffmann sighed.

'She showed me your letter,' Sam explained.

'And you think that I was Johann.'

'Yes.'

He paused, then let a little smile play on his lips, like a child caught cheating but who didn't care. 'You are correct, of course . . .' He examined Sam's face with the intense eye of a portrait painter trying to get the mouth right. 'You know, Herr *Packer*, it is strange that in all the times when you and I are meeting, I never make the connection. You look so like him.'

'So people keep telling me.'

'A remarkable coincidence that I use the father to help protect communism, then I *am* used by the son when it failed.' He smiled grimly. 'You call it *turning the table*, I think.'

'Something like that.'

Hoffmann nodded reflectively. 'Please, tell me about Jo.'

'She's terminally ill.'

Hoffmann's face crumpled. 'I feared it. Because she will not reply to my letter. You have seen her?'

'Yes. She's not expected to last much longer.'

Hoffmann nodded sombrely. Then he frowned. 'How did you find out about her?'

'It's a long story which began with one of your old Russian buddies defecting to America with a list of names.'

'So you began to investigate your father's life . . .'

'. . . and found a photograph of him with Jo.'

Hoffmann licked his lips. 'But why you have come to see me?'

'To hear your side of the story. I always try to be professional.'

The waiter arrived with their coffees, a slender young man with a single gold earring and a bearing that was overtly gay. Hoffmann fixed him with a look of loathing, then stared down at his coffee as if it had been contaminated.

'Such men disgust me,' he hissed, after the waiter had left them. 'We must be grateful for AIDS – don't you agree?'

Sam was surprised by his vehemence. He ignored the comment.

'I want to know what information my father gave away,' he said.

Hoffmann shook his head. 'For that you must ask the GRU. Twenty-seven years ago I was only their messenger boy.'

'But a persistent one, according to Jo.'

'I also have always tried to be professional,' Hoffmann countered.

'Jo Macdonald told me the GRU weren't satisfied with the stuff my father handed over.'

'They said it was old,' Hoffmann confirmed.

'And they sent you back for more.'

'*Ja*. But then he became sick, your father, so I told the Russians he was no more use to them. Jo . . . she didn't explain this to you?'

'She did, but I wanted to hear your version.'

Sam felt disappointed. He'd expected more from Hoffmann. He watched the old spy sip his coffee then throw the schnapps back in one.

'You know, I really don't understand you.' Sam's remark made the German look up. 'You had no qualms about ruining a man's life, yet you cared enough about him to send flowers to his funeral.'

'A good general cares for his soldiers,' Hoffmann countered, 'however rough he must use them to fight his war.'

'And Jo Macdonald? Why did you write that letter of apology to her?'

'Because in war we always do things we feel bad about after.'

'But she was just my father's girlfriend . . .'

There was mockery in Hoffmann's eyes. Sam groaned inwardly. The camera in the bedroom that had caught his father *in flagrante*. Jo Macdonald's wide-eyed bafflement as to how it got there.

'It was not very original,' Hoffmann apologised. 'Using a prostitute to catch Navy men.'

'You'd recruited her first,' Sam grunted. Hoffmann nodded. 'For money, or were you blackmailing her too?'

'Not blackmail,' Hoffmann protested. 'She was afraid of nuclear war. So I could persuade her that if she helped me get information about how the British would launch an attack, then it could help prevent one. And yes, I paid some money. Expenses.'

'So she was never in love with my father?'

'Oh yes. She fell in love. She even wanted to tell him what she has done, but I warned her it would make her his enemy. Better to live with a lie . . .'

'. . . than for him to die knowing the truth.'

Sam didn't blame her for deceiving him about her involvement with Johann. She'd had precious little dignity in her life, without being branded a traitor at the end of it.

He glanced around the café. The other customers were mostly twenty-somethings in office clothes, making a pit stop after work. Gabbing. Spinning the little untruths that made the world turn.

Hoffmann looked at his watch. Half-past six.

'You like opera?'

'Some . . .'

'Tonight it is *Traviata*. The ticket I had bought for Ilse – if you would like . . .'

'Why not,' Sam murmured. He needed more time with Hoffmann. There was another pressing matter to pick his brains about. A matter of far greater significance to world security than the Packer menfolk's unfortunate predilection for women who deceived them.

Brussels
19.10 hrs

Nina Klason arrived at the University Clinic of St Luc by taxi. She'd come straight from the airport, numbed by what had happened and with no idea what to expect. It had been early afternoon in Vienna before she'd learned about her husband's sudden illness. The Commission staff had tried to reach her from mid-morning but she'd been out of the house taking her visiting mother shopping.

The hospital's reception desk sent her to the tenth floor. When she stepped out of the lift she was met by a nurse, whose grim face spelled the worst. Suddenly it all became too much and Nina began to cry.

'Please, the doctor will explain everything in a few minutes.' The nurse addressed her in English and ushered her into a small consulting room. 'Please wait here. He will not be long.'

Nina clung to her arm. 'Is Anders dead?'

'No, Mrs Klason. But he is very ill. The doctor will tell you.'

'I want to see him.'

'I'm sorry. You must wait for the doctor.'

The silence of the room after the nurse left was broken only by the sound of her heartbeat. She'd left Vienna in a panic, putting her reluctant mother in charge of the children. The Commissioner for Racial Affairs had told her Anders had an unidentified brain infection. Surely by now they'd know what it was.

A couple of minutes later the door opened again. She knew how long it had been, because she'd been staring at her watch from the moment the nurse left. She looked up to see a very white coat topped by a very black face.

'Madame Klason, vous parlez Français?'

'*Non*. But English.'

'I'm Dr Gouari.' They shook hands, then the medic sat down in the chair opposite her. 'Your husband is very ill, Mrs Klason.' He spoke clearly, but with a heavy African accent.

She knew Anders was very ill. Why did they keep repeating it?

'At this moment we still don't know what is causing his illness. His blood shows viral antibodies, but we haven't been able to identify the virus yet.'

'I don't understand. Can't you do tests?'

'Tissue cultures take time. The laboratory is working on it.'

'I want to speak with him.'

'It's not possible. His brain function has been severely impaired by the infection.'

'I . . . I don't understand,' she stammered. 'He *will* be all right?'

The Congolese doctor hesitated. 'Until we know what the infection is . . .'

'I want to see him now, please.' She stood up, pushing back the hank of dark hair that had fallen across her thin, pale face.

'Please, Mrs Klason. You can see him soon. But first you must understand some things.' He held out his hand, indicating she should sit down again.

She complied, but reluctantly. Nina's compelling desire to be out of that room was not simply because of her desire to see her husband. Although she espoused the idea of racial equality and was married to one of its champions, she felt deeply uncomfortable with black men. She'd been brought up to think of them as savages and had a physical fear of them. The fact that her husband's fate depended on the competence of one of them was hard to come to terms with.

'The first thing I should tell you is that you won't be able to touch your husband, Mrs Klason.'

'Why not?'

'Because he is being barrier nursed. Inside a plastic tent where the air is kept at negative pressure so that the infection is contained.'

'But I'm his wife,' she protested.

'This disease may be dangerously infectious.'

Nina began to panic. Maybe she and the children had been infected already. 'How . . . how could he have caught this illness?'

'That's what we must find out. As soon as possible. I'd like to ask you some questions.'

'Of course.'

'Has your husband been in contact with animals?'

'I don't think so.'

'You don't have a dog at home?'

'No pets at all. My son is allergic to cat hair.'

'Your husband hasn't been bitten by an animal recently?'

'No.'

'Or by some insect?'

'I don't think so. He is very thin and mosquito bites always show on his body. I would have seen. Why? What is it you think he has?'

The doctor clasped his hands together. 'His symptoms are not consistent with any known illness, but some of them resemble rabies. And the rabies virus enters through a break in the skin. A bite or a cut, normally.'

Nina felt her face burning. 'A *cut*,' she whispered.

'Yes.'

Her lips moved silently at first. Then the words came. 'On . . . on Sunday he was cut.'

The doctor's eyes widened. 'By an animal? A scratch with a paw and then a lick perhaps?'

'No, no. No animals. It was a little piece of glass.'

'Glass . . .' The doctor looked disappointed.

'It was caught in his towel – we were at the lake, for swimming.'

'There would have been animals around. The towel had been on the ground?'

'Yes but there were no animals where we were. I am always so careful where we put our things, because of dog dirt. The children can get sick. So I looked carefully. The ground was clean and there were no animals that I saw. But there were two people who came and talked to us, a man and a woman. They said the children were too far out in the water. I was distracted by what they were saying, but I think they could have put the glass on Anders's towel. When he came out of the water he cut himself when he dried his back.'

The doctor frowned. 'I don't understand. You mean this piece of glass was on the ground? It got caught in the towel when he picked it up?'

'It's what we also thought at first. Then after, we realised the glass piece must be on the top of the towel, not on the underside. We don't understand it because the towel had just come out of the wash machine. Then we remembered the strangers. We wondered if they had put it there. Like crazy people, you know?'

The doctor sat very still, digesting what she'd told him. 'I see. And this man and woman you mentioned, you don't know who they were?'

'No. We never saw them before. And after, they drove quickly away, like they were criminals.'

Dr Gouari rose slowly to his feet.

'Please wait here, Mrs Klason. Just a little longer. There is a telephone call I need to make.'

London

'Peter' had said the next attack should be on Saturday, but that was the wrong day for what Rob Petrie had in mind. This time his target wasn't to be blacks or Pakis but ZOG – the Zionist Occupation Government whose tentacles spread through the northern hemisphere controlling the white race's lives in ways the average guy in the street would hardly credit. Sure, the Lucifer Network needed simultaneous action across Europe, but the Sabbath was a bad day for killing Jews.

It had crossed his mind to bomb a synagogue full of the bastards, but he'd ruled it out. Attacks on religious sites were distasteful to the British, even to the right wing whose political voice the network needed to mobilise. So he would hit them at work. At the places where they wielded their power, where they accumulated their wealth. And for that it would have to be Friday.

His first thought had been to secrete the bomb on the directors' floor at the Golding Brothers headquarters on Bishopsgate, revenge against the Zionists who'd sacked him eighteen months ago. But it was too obvious. Too personal. And anyway, it would have been impossible to get in and out of the building without being seen by someone who would recognise him.

This afternoon he'd dressed in a suit for the first time in months, camouflage for penetrating the streets of London's financial centre. He exited from the tube at Bank, headed down Threadneedle Street, then into the courtyards where the wine bars were doing good business. It was the first time he'd been back here since the sacking and it hurt. They all looked so damned cocky, the peer group he'd been a part of, strutting to the bars with their wallets full of twenties and plastic.

He needed a target that was overtly Jewish. He walked on through the paved squares and narrow lanes to Bishopsgate, forcing himself to look up at the edifice of brown bricks and glass where he'd worked for eight years. Nearly a decade of bonus cheques – the sky the limit until it fell on his head. Sandra had been with him for the last of those years, impressed by his lifestyle as much as by him. Holidays in Phuket, dinners at Marco's and loads of sex under a mirrored ceiling in a fifteenth-floor Docklands loft with river views and gold-coloured taps in the bathroom. Then he'd lost it all and Sandra had been forced on to night shifts because the pay was better.

Suddenly it became patently clear to him that he'd made a mistake. He was in the wrong place. A bomb in the City would be crazy. Yes, there were Jews and Asians here, but the majority were like him. The focus for the attack had to be sharper than that if the thick-heads in the press were to understand its meaning.

He quickened his pace away from the Golding Bros building, heading back to the tube. A new thought had occurred to him. He knew precisely where he needed to go.

Stepney

Sandra Willetts stepped out of the lift on the twelfth floor of Windsor Court carrying a couple of Tesco bags. It annoyed her that Rob was so useless about shopping for food. He spent most of the day hanging round with nothing to do, so why couldn't he bloody well buy the groceries instead of leaving it to her to do on her days off? She walked along the concrete landing then dumped the bags on the ground while she stuck her key in the lock, psyching herself up to have a go at him when she got inside the flat.

'Rob?'

No reply. She stepped into the tiny kitchen and put the bags down on the draining board. He'd left an empty beer can on the breakfast bar and a greasy lunch plate in the sink. The place stank of burnt fat.

There'd been times lately when she'd wondered why she stuck with him. The main reason was pity, she'd decided. He'd been a real turn-on when they first met, and she hadn't forgotten it. She'd tried to convince herself that if he could only get a decent job he'd be his old self again. Relationships were like the stock market, he'd said to her once. You don't dump your best shares when the price drops. You hang on in there until it goes up again.

But of late she'd begun to doubt whether it ever could. Being sacked had changed Rob into a bitter no-hoper, a change that felt permanent.

Sandra was five foot six. A few years back she'd had an all-over suntan she could afford to maintain right through the winter, which looked great with her blonde hair. In the Docklands days she'd gone to a gym three evenings a week. Rob used to say her tits were well up to page three and the sight of her bum could give a dead man an erection. But in the last eighteen months she'd put weight on in the wrong places, her skin had turned pasty and most of the time her roots showed. Rob used to take it for granted that she loved him; nowadays he kept needing to ask. She always said yes, but she didn't really know any more.

And where the hell was he? They'd had breakfast together – a rare event with her shifts – and he'd said nothing about going out.

Listlessly she unpacked the groceries then went to the bedroom to change into trainers. She'd been on her feet all day, clothes shopping in Oxford Street. Just looking. The only place she could afford anything these days was at charity shops. Although it was nice to have a break from work, she almost dreaded these days off, tending to find reasons to go out because Rob got on her nerves if she stayed at home. He'd started playing heavy metal, which she couldn't stand. And in the evenings they both drank. Not for pleasure, but so that when they went to bed they were too pissed to think about why they weren't having sex any more.

She wandered into the living room and was about to switch on the TV when she noticed he'd left his computer on. She stared at it. The screen was black – it turned off automatically – but the power lights glowed on the tower. He never left it on when he was out normally. The computer was his private world. She never used it – couldn't because you needed a password to start it up. She knew how computers worked, though. One of the girls who shared the night shift had a laptop which she brought in sometimes. Sandra walked over to the trolley, listening to the soft whirr of the machine's cooling fan. Listening too for the sound of Rob's key in the lock.

Timidly she reached out and touched the mouse. The screen hummed and came to life. She'd half expected to see pictures of girls showing their fannies – he spent hours on the Internet when she was out. She knew that, because whenever she rang to say hello, the line was engaged. But on the screen it was his e-mail program. Her friend on the ward had the same software on her laptop. One very quiet night they'd dialled into the net from the ward extension for a few minutes, totally against the rules, because her friend wanted to show her what it was all about.

The main window on the screen said Inbox. There was a list of e-mails he'd received, many from people called Peter. Different surnames, but always Peter. Odd. She turned away. This was wrong. Rob was entitled to his privacy. She thought of shutting the computer down, as he himself must have meant to do before going out, but there was so much about him she didn't know now. Like that cupboard of his on the wall which he always kept locked.

She swallowed her fear, put her hand on the mouse and ran the cursor up the list of mail. The last one received had been two days ago. She glanced over her shoulder. Through the open living room door she could see into the hall and to the glass-panelled front door. Nobody there. Nobody about to come in.

It couldn't harm. He'd never know.

She double clicked. The letter appeared in the bottom half of the screen.

Congratulations!

She began to read.

After she'd read it once she sat down, covering her mouth with her hands. It had to be a joke, this. Some game. Some piece of cyberspace role playing.

Then she read it again and began to feel sick. Sick at what it might mean and sick with guilt. Quickly she stood up, closed the screen window, then shut down the computer. She was finding it hard to breathe, as if she had a heavy weight on her chest.

Suddenly there was a shadow outside the front door. Metal grated on metal as the key went in. Rob . . .

Sandra ran for the bathroom. She locked the door behind her and turned on the taps.

Vienna

In the third act of *La Traviata*, as Violetta lay dying upon the stage, Sam became aware that Günther Hoffmann was overwhelmed by grief. He half turned and saw by the light spilling from the set that the old spy was holding a handkerchief to his face and his shoulders were shaking. A few minutes later as the final applause died and the audience got to their feet, Hoffmann remained where he was until a silk-gowned lady to his right made it rudely clear that she wanted to pass. It wasn't until they'd filed out into the cream and gold lobbies that Hoffmann could bring himself to speak.

'It was Ilse's favourite opera,' he confided hoarsely.

The departing audience carried them through the main doors and out onto the Ring. Once in the fresh air Hoffmann shook his head like a dog.

'*Um Gottes willen!* I need a drink.'

'Better than that,' said Sam, 'I'll buy you dinner.' He'd begun to feel sorry for the old spymaster, but told himself to get a grip.

The night air was stickily warm. They squeezed onto a tram for a couple of stops to get away from the opera crowds, then found a restaurant which Hoffmann said was good for schnitzels. To a muzak track of Strauss waltzes they ordered food and a large carafe of Wachauer Riesling. Hoffmann said it was better than the usual Grüner Veltliner. The wine arrived quickly. When he took a mouthful he puckered his lips.

'Ach. This is not so good.'

'No, it's pretty vile,' Sam concurred.

'You know, in German we have a name for such a wine,' Hoffmann told him, a twinkle returning to his slate grey eyes.

'Something like rats' piss, you mean?'

'Ja. Similar. We call it *Hemdzieher*. You know why?'

Sam frowned. 'Shirt-puller?'

'Ja. Because the wine is so *sauer* it suck the shirt up your backside.' Hoffmann smirked at his own crudeness. 'We would have been better with the Veltliner. We can change it.'

Sam shook his head. 'As rats' piss goes, I've tasted worse. The second mouthful was better than the first.'

He wanted to broach the subject of Vladimir Kovalenko, but decided it was wiser to do so obliquely. 'Will you stay in Vienna now you're on your own?'

Hoffmann ruminated for a moment. 'It is too soon for such a question.' He picked up a beer mat and tapped its edge on the table. 'But . . . when it is my time to die, then I would like to be at home.'

'Home?'

'Greifswald. The house of my parents it is still there. Someone rents it now, but perhaps in a few years I will go back. It depends.'

'On what?'

'On how it is in Germany then. What sort of country it has become.' His eyes flared for a moment, then he looked away as if to hide some secret passion. 'But most of all when I die, I want to smell the sea,' he added quickly. 'Like Caspar David.'

'The painting in your apartment . . .'

'Ah. You remember. Caspar David Friedrich he was born in Greifswald. He wanted his last days there, but must die in Dresden, because of no money for the journey.'

'You won't be in a hurry to move from Vienna, surely?' Sam suggested, edging the conversation to where he wanted it to be. 'You must have many friends here.'

'Some friends, yes,' Hoffmann replied cautiously.

'Old contacts passing through . . .'

Hoffmann grew wary, suspecting new ground was being broken. 'I lose touch with people,' he answered firmly.

'Even with Vladimir Kovalenko?'

Hoffmann blinked, then quickly got his face back under control. 'Kovalenko . . . ?'

'He's lived in Vienna almost as long as you.'

'Why do you ask about him?'

'Oh, because there are a lot of people trying to find him. Including the Kremlin. He disappeared for a while, but I'm told he's back in town.'

Hoffmann's leathery face became a mask. 'So, you had another reason to come here.'

Sam shrugged, as if it didn't matter that much. 'Have you seen him?'

'Kovalenko . . . I met him once.' His expression was as blank as fresh-washed paint. 'A *playboy*. Why do you want to speak with him?'

Sam was saved from answering by the arrival of their schnitzels, vast slices of meat that filled the plates, with side dishes of potato salad and lettuce.

'Guten Appetit!' said the waiter, checking they had all they needed.

'It is not easy to starve in Vienna,' Hoffmann mused, surveying the plates. He looked up again. 'Why you are looking for Vladimir Kovalenko?'

'Because of something he was involved in a year ago. Supplying dangerous materials to terrorists.'

Hoffmann stopped in mid chew, his eyes widening. He put down his knife and fork and took a swig from the glass. 'What materials?'

'Something pretending to be red mercury.'

The eyes stayed rock steady. 'Red mercury does not exist.'

'It's not what the *label* said,' Sam countered. 'It's what was inside that we're worried about.'

'What do you think it was?' Hoffmann asked, unblinking.

'Something nuclear.'

'Ah, yes.' The German nodded. 'And you know who is the customer?' His question was studiedly casual.

Sam shrugged. 'We have an idea he spoke Arabic.'

For some reason Hoffmann appeared relieved.

'You know where Kovalenko is?' Sam pressed.

'A man such as he have many reasons why he don't want to be found,' the German said, swirling his glass as if to sniff the wine's bouquet, then thinking better of it.

'You ever work with him?' Sam prodded. 'Give him introductions? Contacts?'

'*I?*' Hoffmann looked pained. 'I am an old man living on my pension.'

And I'm the Queen of Sheba, thought Sam.

Hoffmann cut another chunk from his schnitzel and chewed it thoughtfully. 'You know why we can never live in peace with the Arabs?' he asked suddenly.

'I can think of a few reasons.'

'Because their music is strange to us.'

'That's one I hadn't thought of.'

'If they like Brahms and Puccini then we can live together with them. In Europe each country is different, but because we like the same music so we can be friends. But Islam makes a sound which hurts our ears. It makes people here afraid of them. And when people are afraid of foreigners they get angry. It was like that in the Nazi time.' He stopped, as if deliberating how far to pursue the point.

'And like that in Austria today?' Sam prompted. 'Is that what you're saying?'

'This is a small country,' Hoffmann explained philosophically. 'Keeping their race pure is always important for such peoples. And with the Balkans on their borders they fear being drowned by refugees. It is the same in Germany. And in your country. It is why so many people want that the refugees are sent back.'

'Europe is drifting towards the right . . .'

'It is inevitable. In France, Germany and England there are socialist governments now, so the next swing will be in the opposite way. People can feel sorry for the victims of the Serbs but . . .'

'. . . won't want them in their own back yards.'

'Exactly.' He ate another mouthful. 'I agree with them. Don't you?'

Sam shrugged. He didn't want to get into a debate about refugees.

'But you ask about Kovalenko,' Hoffmann said, returning to the point. 'I cannot help you to find him.' He said it with a galling finality that brought the topic to a close.

As they finished their food they chatted about the meanderings of European politics since the collapse of communism. Eventually Sam paid the bill and Hoffmann asked the waiter to call him a cab.

'For you too? They come usually very quick.'

'Thank you, but I'll walk. My hotel's not far.'

They made their way outside to wait for Hoffmann's car. The night air was still muggily warm. When the taxi came, Hoffmann reached out his hand.

'It was a pleasure to meet you again. Please give my regards to Jo.' With that he ducked inside and the vehicle sped off.

It was nearly midnight. Sam heard a church clock striking early. Trams still lumbered past, but he guessed they'd be heading for their depots. He began to walk, returning to the Ring and then eastwards towards the 3rd District and the Pension Kleist. He needed to be on the other side of the road. He paused in front of the luxury Marriott Hotel, where there was a pedestrian crossing controlled by lights.

Suddenly, as he waited for them to turn green, a limousine brushed the back of his legs as it swung into the bay in front of the hotel entrance.

'Hey, watch it!' he yelped, stepping quickly out of its way.

It was a chauffeur-driven car, a fat silver Merc, which halted under the Marriott's canopy. The rear door opened before the driver could get to it. A woman in a blue dress got out, followed by a man in a dark suit. She turned as if to say goodnight to him, her face towards the road.

It was Julie Jackman.

15

THAT VILE WINE must have got to him. This had to be an illusion. He shook his head like an idiot, but the image didn't change. Julie was dressed in something blue and satiny, with jewels at the neck that could have been diamonds. She was got up like a goddam princess, her hair pinned back with a shiny clasp.

Behind him the crossing light ticked, evenly at first then more rapidly as the green light flickered its way to red. He stood motionless, unseen by the couple standing in the hotel entrance who were engrossed in a tense conversation. After a matter of seconds the car that had delivered them swished away again and they went inside, the man's hand pressing against Julie's back as if forcing the issue. Some completely irrational part of his brain told Sam that this was Vladimir Kovalenko that Julie was with. But the height was wrong and this man had hair.

His mind began to fizz. He felt a strong impulse to hurl himself into the lobby and get his fingers round that slender neck, but he suppressed it.

There was a reason she was here and it couldn't be coincidence, he decided. Some hack must've spotted him leaving Heathrow that morning. She was here because *he* was, and the man with her had to be another sodding journalist.

A tram bell clanged behind him – he'd inadvertently stepped into the road. He hopped back onto the pavement then gingerly approached the hotel's entrance, keeping to the shadows. Through the glass he observed the pair standing by the lifts, Julie gleaming like a kingfisher, but keeping at arm's length from the man. Sam saw his face for the first time. Older than her by about twenty years. Dark, straight hair. Well-built and upright. The lift doors opened and closed and the couple were gone.

On the right-hand side of the lobby was a row of booths. He passed through the doors and picked up the house phone.

'Could you give me Miss Jackman's room number, please?'

'Three-two-eight. I connect you?'

'No thanks. It's late. I'll call her tomorrow.'

'From the lobby phone you dial one first, then the room number.'

'Thanks.'

He stepped smartly back into the street, crossed over to the outer side of the Ring, then looked up at the hotel's third floor. Half a dozen rooms had lights on. A new one lit up, then went off, then lit up again.

He'd thought of another possible reason why she was here. Julie had visited Vienna a year ago when the red mercury deal was set up – Waddell had told him. She might have come back with a warning that enquiries were being made, perhaps for the man he'd just seen her with. He stopped himself. Guesses were pointless. He needed certainties.

He stood there trying to decide what to do. From his own personal point of view he had a score to settle, apart from the multitude of questions he wanted to ask. A siren sounded somewhere to his left. He looked along the Ring and saw blue lights approaching. An ambulance screamed past; his eyes followed it automatically. When it disappeared he looked back at the hotel again.

There was movement at the glass doors. A man was emerging. He paused to light a cigarette. Sam moved a few feet along the pavement so he could see more clearly – there were parked cars in the way. The male stepped out uncertainly, like someone who hadn't expected to be on a pavement at this time of night. It was the same dark suit, the same straight back. Sam's pulse quickened, almost certain it was Julie's companion.

The man looked both ways, smoking nervously, searching for a taxi as he moved slowly along the kerb. On the other side of the road Sam kept level, then walked quickly to the next lights, crossed the Ring again and turned back towards the hotel. When the man glanced in his direction he stepped into a tram shelter so he could watch without being seen. It *was* Julie's companion, striding along with the bruised, semi-defiant stare of someone who'd just lost an argument. And it wasn't a cigarette he was smoking but a small cigar. He had a long, narrow nose almost sharp enough to cut paper and was dressed in the manicured style of a banker or politician. As Sam watched, a taxi pulled up for him.

When it had driven off, Sam re-emerged from the shelter and walked towards the hotel. His conviction that this was a journalist had lost its strength, and his theory of a link with Jackman's business dealings was on hold. All bets were off. As he neared the Marriott's glass doors there was only one thought on his mind.

Harry Jackman's daughter would now be alone in her room.

★   ★   ★

Julie sat at the beechwood dressing table in room 328, staring at her weary reflection in the mirror as she undid the clip holding back her hair. A large glass of brandy stood comfortingly in front of her, chosen because it was the strongest drink in the minibar. The evening had left her wrecked. She'd got through to Max in the end, but it had been an uphill struggle. He'd made light of her wish to end the affair, assuming she was after a bit of extra cosseting and would succumb in the end. Rather than risk a scene in the lobby, she'd let him come up to the room. Once inside, he'd turned the lights off in an infantile effort to get her in the mood, but when she'd told him no and he'd realised she meant it, his face had crumpled like a bag of crisps. Then he'd kissed her forehead once and once only, and let himself out. That had been it. She felt relieved it was over, but empty too. Yes, the affair had been unsatisfactory, but at least it had existed. What she'd replaced it with was an impossible dream.

As soon as Max had gone, she'd taken off the blue dress he'd given her in Paris the last time they'd been together. The frock had been a part of their relationship and she'd needed to feel free of it. She was considering leaving the thing behind when she returned to London, but wasn't sure she could, the garment being of a style and quality well beyond her normal budget. She'd slipped on the white towelling robe that hung on the back of the bathroom door, then found herself a drink.

She took a big mouthful of the brandy and let it burn its way down her throat, feeling its almost instant effect on her head. The mirror showed the tension round her eyes and mouth. She tried a smile. The lips moved as intended, but the eyes stayed sombre and sad.

There was a sharp tap at the door.

'Oh God,' she gulped. Max had come back. She froze. No idea what to do.

A second tap, louder this time.

'Who is it?'

'A fax for you, madam.'

Relieved that the voice wasn't Max's, she stood up. The accent was vaguely European. She tried to connect it with the faces of the hall porters downstairs. A fax? Who from, for heaven's sake? No one knew she was here – apart from Max.

'Could you slip it under the door?'

'You must sign for it, please.'

Nervously she slipped the latch. To her horror the door kicked inwards with a force that knocked her backwards.

'Simon!' she gasped, clutching her hands to her throat. He'd followed her from London bent on revenge.

Sam banged the door shut behind him, then swung her round, gripping her from behind with an arm across her neck and a hand clamped over her mouth.

'Don't make a sound!'

He pushed her into the room, checking no one else was there. 'You and me are going to have a little talk.'

His voice grated in her ear like a stonecrusher. Julie's brain turned to spaghetti. When he'd burst through the door there'd been murder in his eyes. She felt his fury radiating like fire. It had been insane to imagine he could ever forgive her for what she'd done. His wristwatch pressed on her windpipe and she was finding it hard to breathe.

Sam hustled her further into the room and tightened his grip. The feel of her soft, bathrobed body against his own was stimulating him in a way he didn't want. And her smell, a musky mix of perfume, alcohol and sweat, was shooting straight up to his brain.

'Fucking bitch!' he fumed, angry at the effect she was having on him. His mouth was inches from her neck. Her hair brushed softly against his face and the curve of her behind pressed against his groin. For a mad moment he thought of stripping the towelling off her and doing what he'd wanted to do ever since he first clapped eyes on her. Then she started choking and he came to his senses.

'No dramatics,' he warned, removing his hand from her mouth and transferring his grip to her shoulders.

'No dramatics,' she coughed.

'We're going to talk.' He manoeuvred her into the chair by the dressing table. 'Or rather *you* are.'

'Yes.'

'The truth.'

'Anything you want.' She noticed for the first time that he'd shaved his beard off. And looked even better as a result. Her attraction to him was stronger than ever, despite the coldness in his eyes.

'First question. What are you doing in Vienna?'

'Look, I'm sorry about last Sunday,' she gabbled, desperate for him to understand she meant it. 'I made a dreadful mistake. Please believe me that I'm very, very sorry.'

'Answer my question. What are you doing in Vienna?'

'I came to see someone,' she explained.

'Who?'

'His name's Max Schenk.'

'When did you see him?'

'This evening.'

'What's your connection with him?'

'There isn't one any more. He'd been a boyfriend . . . of sorts.'

'The sugar-daddy sort by the look of him.'

His comment startled her. He must have been watching her for hours. Watching and waiting until Max left.

'You could say that,' she admitted.

Sam turned away, noticing the room itself for the first time. Standard hotel layout. Chinese print on the wall behind the king-size bed. A dark cover on it that matched the curtains. A single armchair and a table scattered with tourist literature. Beside the bed was a drawer unit with a phone and an address book. He picked it up. Open at S for Schenk.

'That's private,' Julie protested, then bit her tongue.

He ignored her, flicking through the pages. Women's names, mostly. UK phone numbers. He searched under K, but found nothing for Kovalenko. Max Schenk's was the only overseas number she had. Not even one for her father. Damn the woman. If she *was* involved in her old man's shenanigans, she was covering her tracks with skill. He closed the book and patted it against the palm of his left hand.

'Okay. So why did you do it, Julie?'

'You mean . . . ?'

'Why did you set me up?' His eyes roamed the room, still searching for something that didn't fit.

Julie sighed. She'd thought long and hard about how to explain. 'This is going to sound pathetic.'

'I'll be the judge of that.' He prowled over to the wardrobe. Inside was the blue dress he'd seen her in earlier, hanging next to a brown skirt and dark cotton trousers. A smell of cigar smoke left on her clothes by her companion's habit. It had been the same at the flat in Acton. Smart, black shoes sat on the floor beside a pair of trainers. Shelves empty. She'd left the rest of her clothes in her suitcase. 'I'm listening.'

'I was in a state, that's all I can say. Confused to bits. My father had just been murdered.'

'Not by me.'

'No . . . No, I accept that now.'

Surprised by her easy capitulation, he turned round. This was what he'd needed to hear, but it washed over him because there was no way of knowing whether she meant it. He pushed open the bathroom door and shot a quick look inside. Towel on the floor from the shower she'd had before going out. Empty Badedas bottle lying in the tub.

'What are you looking for?' she asked as he re-emerged.

He didn't know. Something to say that she hadn't come to Vienna simply to see a lover. Her suitcase sat on a folding stand with its lid open. He fiddled through the contents. Clothes, women's things. A paperback with an airport receipt sticking out of it – *Men are from Mars, Women are from Venus*. And a leather box with the necklace he'd seen earlier – they certainly *looked* like diamonds.

'You say it's over with this Max Schenk bloke. Who ditched whom?'

'I was the one who ended it.'

It fitted with what he'd seen. He ran his fingers inside the pocket in the lid of the suitcase and pulled out an air ticket. Her return flight was on Friday. He checked the picture in her passport. Prettier in the flesh. Much prettier. Which had been the whole damned trouble. His anger flared again and he turned on her, pressing his face to within a few inches of hers.

'Have you any idea what you've done to my life?' he snarled.

She looked down at her hands, biting her lip. 'I'm sorry.'

'*Sorry* . . .' He leaned forward and flicked her chin up with his finger. 'Because of you, someone tried to kill me last night.'

Julie blinked, trying to grasp the enormity of what he was saying. 'I don't understand.'

'They found out where I lived by watching the TV news.'

'Who did?'

Sam pulled back, shaking his head. He'd said too much. 'And don't you dare pass that little tit-bit on to your media friends.'

'They're not my friends,' she demurred. 'There was just the reporter from the *Chronicle* that I talked to and I had no idea it would lead to all this.'

'*No idea* . . .' Sam mouthed. 'Pay well, do they, the *Chronicle*?'

Julie closed her eyes, realising the impossibility of redeeming herself with him. 'It wasn't for money.'

'What, then?'

She took in a deep breath and let it out again. 'I did it for my father. Because it was his last wish. I felt . . . I felt a duty to him.' She arched her eyebrows in exasperation at herself. 'God knows why. He never felt one to me.'

Sam stood with his back to the curtained windows, arms tightly folded. Julie shot him a quick glance then stared at the floor, bunching together the lapels of the dressing gown.

'I wish there was *something* I could do to make it up to you,' she whispered meekly.

Sam looked at her sitting there. She was infuriatingly attractive and convincingly contrite. He suspected that if he told her to take her clothes off she would comply. But it was something even more potent than sex that he wanted from her. Somewhere in that cotton wool mind of hers was, he suspected, a piece of information that could peel open her father's secrets. He kept remembering Jackman's dying words. *Julie knows.* And something about the certainty with which the old rogue had said it made him feel it wasn't just because of the letter that he knew would be sent after his death. There'd been some other reason. Something to do with Julie being here in Vienna a year ago when the deal with Kovalenko was struck.

'How long have you known Max?' he asked, fumbling for a bigger picture.

'We met last year. Here in Vienna. I came over for a conference.'

Everything seemed to have happened a year ago. Too many simultaneous events to be coincidental.

'And to see your father,' he reminded her.

'That was incidental.'

'Are you sure?'

'Yes,' she hissed. 'As I've said a million times, I have never had anything to do with his business activities.'

'How did you meet Max?'

'He's a doctor. Has his own clinic. The hotel I was staying in was full of medical people. For the conference.'

'So you met by chance. Locked eyes with him at a seminar and that was it?'

'Not exactly.' Julie straightened her back and pulled the robe's belt tighter round her waist. She had no wish to get into all this, but didn't see an alternative. 'Max was delivering a conference paper on viral mutation. I was just a lowly scientific officer, brought along by my boss to try to pick up tips about laboratory techniques. Max and I weren't exactly moving in the same circles at the conference. But everyone was staying at the Intercontinental. And so, coincidentally, was my father. Most evenings there were social events connected with the conference, although I did manage to spend one with my father and his girlfriend – I told your colleagues.'

'I know. Go on.'

'Well, after dinner, I'd said goodnight to Dad and gone up to my room. Then a little later I realised I'd left a folder somewhere with my conference papers in it. I came downstairs to look around the bar and that's when Max spoke to me. He knew my name. Said he'd seen me around and had made up his mind to get to know me. I was flattered. And he had my folder in his hand. Said he wouldn't return it unless I had a drink with him.'

'And the rest is history.'

'Well, yes. He impressed me. He'd done his homework. Knew a lot about me. Pressed the right buttons. He's a nice man, actually. And I'd reached a point in my life when I was ready to meet one.' Still was, she thought to herself.

'How come Max knew so much about you?'

'I don't know. I never really thought about it. Too busy enjoying the warmth of the attention he was giving me.' She frowned. Delicate tramlines spread across her broad forehead.

Sam's antennae twitched.

'What sort of things did he know about you?'

'I don't really remember.'

'Try.'

She shrugged. 'Well . . . he seemed to know – or sense – that I'd had some bad experiences with men.' She grimaced, unhappy about the way that had come out.

'Where would he have got that from?'

'I don't know.'

'Professor Norton?'

'No way. I'm not even sure he's aware that I have a child.'

Julie knows – Jackman's words still niggled. Could it be, Sam wondered, that she didn't yet *know* that she knew? But that her father had thought she did?

'Is it possible your *father* could have told Max about you?' he suggested, the words emerging simultaneously with the thought taking shape in his head.

Julie looked at him as if he'd just appeared from outer space. 'Max had no connection whatsoever with my dad,' she said dismissively.

'You quite sure?'

'Totally.'

Then the frown came back and Sam realised he'd got her thinking. She wasn't sure at all. Not any more. He perched on the end of the bed and leaned towards her.

'The men your father was doing business with a year ago – you told Denise Corby that you met some of them.'

'*Met* is too strong. They just happened to be sitting in the same corner of the bar. I don't remember anything about them.'

Sam narrowed his eyes. 'So, if you don't remember anything about those men sitting in the bar with your father, Max Schenk might have been one of them.'

Julie blinked as if blinded by what he'd just suggested. 'I can't believe that . . .' she whispered.

Sam stroked his chin. The trail he was following had no logic to it. Even if Schenk *had* for some reason been able to quiz Harry Jackman about his daughter it was hardly likely he'd have been the gun-runner's partner in the illegal shipment of nuclear materials. The man was a doctor. He ran a clinic.

But it was a lead. And one which made sense, if Jackman's dying words had had more meaning to them than a reference to a letter not yet sent.

And, if there was even the smallest chance that Max Schenk and Harry Jackman had been in conversation at the time the 'red mercury' deal was struck, then it needed investigating. Sam leaned forward and took hold of Julie's hands.

She saw that his eyes had become as soft as chocolate again. She had a nasty feeling she wasn't going to like the reason for it.

'A few minutes ago, Julie, you said you wished there was some way you could make up for what you did to me last weekend.'

'Yes,' she croaked, certain now that what he was about to ask of her was going to hurt.

'I want you to see Max Schenk again.'

16

HMS *Truculent*
Thursday

THE SUBMARINE HAD rendezvoused on time with the Lynx from HMS *Suffolk* at midnight local, surfacing under a starlit sky at a point on the chart precisely defined by the Global Positioning Satellites. The helicopter, its nav lights off, had homed in on their fin, using its thermal imager for guidance. The winch line had snaked down with a bag of mail, then jerked up again with the sack of tapes destined for GCHQ. Ten minutes. Another five for the satcom transmission of the voices detected by Arthur Harris and their sojourn on the surface had been completed. Now the boat was deep again, heading south to Crete and the crew's first break ashore for ten weeks.

Arthur Harris was troubled. For him the game was being abandoned prematurely. There was more to be uncovered. Four hours to the east of them a drama was unfolding, the outcome of which he was desperate to know. His gamble was that when the tape of the Russian voices was played back at Cheltenham the bosses would want to know it too.

He lay on his mattress in the bomb shop surrounded by torpedoes, quite unable to sleep. In *Truculent*'s proper bunk spaces little curtains closed off the narrow shelves that passed for beds, keeping out the light, but here the fluorescent tubes in their shock-proof mounts between the loading rails blazed day and night. But it wasn't the light that was keeping him awake, it was the memory of the voice he'd heard coming from that small island east of Lastovo.

He was almost certain he'd heard it before in one of the small Cheltenham listening booths used for updating CTs before a patrol. Most of the tapes played to them for this mission had been in the rough-tongued Serbo-Croat of Balkan military commanders, but dropped in amongst them like a pinch of spice was a long-distance phone conversation recorded by the Echelon satellites of the US National Security Agency at their base at Menwith Hill.

The recipient of the call had been sitting in a small, single-storey house in Maryland, a Russian scientist who'd made the leap into the American economy three years earlier. The call had originated in a Moscow phone booth, placed by a disgruntled biochemist who'd rung his friend to test the water. 'It's impossible here,' Harris remembered him saying, the voice heavy with disgust. 'One way or another I'm going to leave Russia. But I need a job, Yuri. Don't forget me. Otherwise I'll go to the people we all know about that none of us wants to work for. I have to eat, Yuri. I have to have a life.'

Chursin. Igor Chursin. An assistant director at the Russian State Research Centre of Virology and Biotechnology, known as VECTOR, based in Novosibirsk in Siberia. At the end of the Soviet era the laboratory had been the Moscow government's main centre for biological weapons research. The work continued today, but in even greater secrecy.

It had been the head of the Biological Warfare desk at GCHQ who'd slipped the tape into the briefing session. He'd done it as a 'heads up' to alert them. As far as anyone knew Chursin was still in Russia, but if he decided to carry out his threat to leave then he'd be a prime catch for any renegade nation looking to develop biological weapons. Iraq and Iran had been obvious candidates, but with Serbia suspected of preparing for war against NATO, it made sense to cast the net wide. However, the last place in the world any of them expected Chursin to turn up was on a barren lump of rock in the Adriatic.

Which was why Harris had a sneaking suspicion that he could have been wrong. That it hadn't been Chursin's voice on the VHF. Cheltenham would know for sure. And in four hours' time when they came back to periscope depth to receive the broadcast, the submarine would know too. There was nothing he could do until then. He turned his face away from the light and made a determined effort to sleep.

Vienna

Sam Packer was woken by the phone. He fumbled groggily for the handset.

'Mmm?'

'Sam Packer?'

'Yes.'

'Oh dear. *Sorry* if I woke you up.'

'Who is this?'

'The name's de Vere Collins.' The SIS head of station in Vienna. The accent was surprisingly downmarket. 'A friend in London told me where to find you.' Waddell – Sam had checked in with him when he arrived in Vienna. 'And since I didn't hear from you yesterday I thought I'd save you the trouble today.'

He was being reprimanded for failing to make contact.

'Good of you,' Sam grunted. 'My apologies.' He should have rung.

'Accepted. Now look, there's been a development overnight. It stands everything on its head, rather.'

'What's happened?' He was suddenly wide awake.

'May I suggest we discuss it in the privacy of breakfast?'

Sam focused on the bedside clock. It was just before nine. 'Where?'

'The Intercontinental does a good spread. It's not more than ten minutes' walk from where you are.'

The hotel where Julie had met Max Schenk. Wouldn't do any harm to look the place over, he decided. 'Fine. Say half an hour?'

'Spiffing, old chap.' De Vere Collins said it fake posh. 'I'll be in the coffee shop. In the far corner, reading a copy of *Newsweek*.'

Sam showered quickly and ran a shaver over his face.

He tried to second-guess what development Collins might be talking about, but couldn't concentrate, his mind preoccupied with last night's encounter with Julie Jackman. To have such a strong urge for intimacy with someone who'd done him so much harm was a contradiction he was finding hard to rationalise.

He dressed in the business suit he'd worn the day before. There were things to be done before Julie saw Max Schenk again – assuming she managed to tempt him into another date. He intended to ask Collins to find out if Austrian security had a file on the doctor. As he straightened his tie, the phone rang once more. This time it was Duncan Waddell.

'Thought I'd better warn you the screw's tightening,' he cautioned. 'I don't know what you've done to the women of this world, but they're out to get you.'

'What's happened now?' Sam sighed, sinking onto the bed.

'The *Daily Chronicle*'s struck again. This time it's your real name up in lights. Not only that – the subjects you were good at at school, your favourite food at around the time your father started spying for the Russians . . .'

'Bloody hell!' The story about his father had finally leaked. 'Where the hell's all this personal crap come from?'

'From your loving sister, mostly.'

Sam groaned.

'But the real culprit's a man called Craigie who picked up a couple of grand for telling the *Chronicle* you'd been in Scotland looking for pictures of your father.'

Sam put his head in his hands. He should have accepted the SIS security man's offer to have the Scotsman taken out.

'After getting that little tip-off, the hacks started digging,' Waddell continued. 'They traced your sister and she poured it all out like sick. She must really hate you.'

'Yes, but it's not personal.'

'Must hate your dad too.'

'That part *is*.'

'So, in a word, I'd say you've been stuffed again.'

'Thanks a million.'

'The government's been "no commenting" ever since the first editions appeared. I'm afraid you're not exactly popular with the bloke at Number Ten. Brains a lot bigger than mine are still trying to work out what to do with you. Best thing is to stay where you are for now. Ring me again around midday. And don't go giving interviews to anyone.'

'That I can't promise,' Sam replied sarcastically.

'Oh. By the way. What did our friend Günther have to say for himself?'

'Very little. His wife's just died.'

Sam outlined their conversation, saying that everything Hoffmann had said served to confirm his father had *not* given away anything sensitive.

'Glad to hear it,' Waddell grunted.

'And Duncan . . . I met someone else last night.'

'Not the man whose name begins with K?'

'No. A woman whose name begins with J.'

'Good God!' There was a stunned silence at the other end. 'What the hell's she doing there?'

'Kissing goodbye to a sugar daddy, apparently. Someone, it turns out, who may just possibly have had some connection with her dad.'

Another short silence. 'You don't mean a connection of the nuclear kind . . . ?'

'I don't know yet.'

'Jackman had many irons in the fire,' Waddell warned. 'Anyway, what d'you propose to do about it?'

'I'm making further enquiries. With Julie's co-operation.'

'*Co-operation?*' Waddell spluttered. 'What *is* going on over there?'

'The girl's said sorry.'

'I shouldn't pay too much attention to that,' Waddell warned. 'You're sure there's no media around?'

'As sure as I can be. Anyway, I propose to rope Collins in. I'm meeting him for breakfast in a few minutes.'

'Make sure you explain exactly what you have in mind. He's a stickler for doing things by the book. Which at this stage in your career is no bad thing.'

'Point taken. By the way, he said there'd been a development overnight. What's it about?'

Waddell cleared his throat.

'Nothing's come across my desk,' he replied cagily. 'Ring me when you've spoken with him.'

'I will.'

He reached the Intercontinental by 9.35. To the left was the bar where Jackman must have sat with his cronies a year ago and where Julie had met Max Schenk. Clusters of armchairs around low tables. He turned his back on the bar then paused at the news-stand in the lobby in case the London papers were in. They weren't.

Collins had secured a remote table for two in the brasserie overlooking the Stadtpark. He recognised Sam and held up his magazine as a signal.

'Pat Collins.' They shook hands. 'You've seen this, have you?' He passed Sam a faxed copy of the morning's *Chronicle* story.

'Just been told about it,' Sam grimaced. He skim-read a few paragraphs then put it aside. 'If I read the rest it'll ruin my breakfast.'

'Why don't you do the circuit,' Collins suggested, pointing to the buffet, 'then we can talk.'

Sam took himself off to the servery and helped himself to a plate of fruit and some scrambled eggs and bacon.

De Vere Collins was an untidy-looking man with a reddish, pock-marked complexion and straggly hair. He'd finished eating, leaving the tablecloth in front of him covered in crumbs. Their table was in a corner, out of earshot of the others. Collins poured himself another cup from a cafetière, then glanced round to check nobody was standing near them. He leaned forward.

'There's been a pretty startling development in the Jackman case,' he murmured. 'That theory the Yanks had about him shipping atomic demolition munitions to Osama bin Laden – it doesn't stand up any more.'

Sam blinked. 'Why not, for Christ's sake?'

'The ADMs have been found, that's why.'

'Good Lord! Where?'

'Still in Moscow. An undercover police squad raided a Chechen mafiya hideout yesterday looking for drugs, and there they were. Still in component form. The nasties hadn't found anybody to reassemble them, it seems. And there were a few key bits missing.'

Sam let out a gust of air. Their house of cards had collapsed. Back to square one. Then he frowned. 'But I've just spoken to Duncan Waddell. He didn't mention any of this.'

'He may not know it yet. I got it from a friend at the US Embassy.'

'Well . . .' Sam gulped, thrown into confusion. 'Where the hell do we go from here?'

'Makes it more important than ever that we find Vladimir Kovalenko and persuade him to tell us what Jackman shipped for him,' Collins reminded him. 'Trouble is it's only been rumours so far that he's back in Vienna.'

Sam had little faith in Kovalenko ever being found, which made it vital to know whether Julie's friend Max Schenk had been a business contact of Harry Jackman's.

'There is one other avenue I'm pursuing,' he ventured cautiously. 'It may not take us anywhere, but it'd be mad not to explore it now we don't have any other leads.' He explained about stumbling across Julie Jackman last night, and his suspicion that her boyfriend could have been a contact of her father's. When he'd finished, Collins wrote Max Schenk's name in a notebook.

'I'll see what Austrian security have on him. Sometimes they're helpful, sometimes they aren't.' He puffed out his cheeks and gave Sam a sideways look. 'How come the little bitch talked to you? I thought she considered you the devil incarnate.'

'Believe it or not she's apologised for what she did. Claims she got it all wrong.'

'Wonders'll never cease!'

Sam finished eating and glanced around. The coffee shop was built like a conservatory. Sleek men in suits were scattered amongst the potted plants. He tried to picture it a year ago, full of woolly-haired scientists discussing the idiosyncrasies of HIV.

Collins's mobile phone bleeped. He dabbed the button. 'Yes?'

Suddenly his eyes bored into Sam's. 'Bloody hell!' He jotted something on a paper napkin, grunted a couple of acknowledgements and ended the call.

'What's happened?' Sam demanded.

'Vladimir Kovalenko.'

'He's been found?'

'He certainly has. The Kriminalpolizei were called to an apartment in the second district first thing. The bugger's been murdered.'

Collins's embassy car was waiting outside the hotel. The driver refused to break the law and took them through the traffic at regulation speed. Collins tapped his knees impatiently.

'First Harry Jackman gets it and now Kovalenko,' Sam murmured, in a voice low enough for the driver not to hear. 'Somebody's making damn sure we don't find out what was in that shipment out of Moscow.'

'There may be no connection, of course,' Collins warned. 'There's a whole string of people who wanted Kovalenko dead.'

They crossed the brown streak of the Danube Canal and turned right by the Prater amusement park with the giant Ferris wheel towering above them. Then they hit a traffic jam. A tram had had a minor altercation with a car. The police were sorting things out.

'Shouldn't be long,' their driver commented. 'Doesn't seem to be much damage.'

Sam noticed a copy of the *International Herald Tribune* on the seat next to the driver. Anxious to know whether the allegations against his father had reached the international press, he picked it up.

'Mind if I have a look?'

'Help yourself,' the driver told him.

He checked through the pages but found nothing. Then Collins pointed to an article headed MYSTERY VIRUS STRIKES EU OFFICIAL.

'That one's getting interesting,' Collins told him. 'The bloke had some sort of brain meltdown and they think he was infected deliberately.'

'How d'you mean?'

'Bio-terrorism with a racist motive. The victim was the head of the EU's anti-racism centre here in Vienna. Infected with a virus no one's ever seen before. Through a cut with a chip of glass, they think.'

Sam turned to him. 'Any connection with the Southall bomb and the other racist incidents in Europe?'

'Nobody knows. But that's what they're working on.'

Sam stared fixedly through the windscreen. Max Schenk was a virologist . . .

He shook his head. No good getting ahead of himself.

The traffic began to move again and soon they were passing the Messegelände, Vienna's huge International Trade Fair site. Beyond it, monolithic apartment blocks lined the road. The driver turned left then pulled up outside a drab-fronted building where four police vehicles already stood. The street was curiously empty of onlookers.

'If this were London, there'd be rubbernecks everywhere,' Sam murmured.

'The Viennese tend to keep themselves to themselves,' Collins explained.

They got out of the car and Collins gave his name to the uniformed officer guarding the door to the apartment house. After a few words into his walkie-talkie he saluted and told them the Herr Inspektor was on his way down.

When the plainclothes officer appeared, Collins greeted him as an old friend, then introduced him to Sam as Inspektor Pfeiffer. The security policeman led them up a stone staircase that smelled of some undefined unpleasantness. He had the ruddy complexion of a Tyrolean mountain guide and spoke reasonable English.

'The police were called by a neighbour at five of this morning,' he told them. 'She heard much noise from the apartment next door. Like a fight.'

They reached the floor where the incident teams were at work. The apartment was small and in severe need of refurbishment.

'Our high-living friend had come down in the world,' Sam murmured. There were three doors off the narrow hall, all open. From one of the rooms came flashes of light as a police photographer captured the scene.

'At first the officers thought it must be a robbery. That the thieves were discovered by the victim and killed him. But one look at the body and it was clear this was a planned murder.'

'Because of the way he was killed?' Collins asked.

'Yes. They used a garrotte.' Pfeiffer raised his eyebrows. 'Quite special, I think. Come. I show you.'

The bedroom he led them into looked as if a hurricane had passed through. The cheap bedside table and lamp were overturned and a wardrobe door had been wrenched off its hinges. Books and clothes were strewn round the floor. In amongst them lay the prostrate figure of a man sprawled on his side on the brown carpet, the blue of his distended face almost matching the indigo of his silk pyjamas. Round his neck was a thick metal strap with a thumbscrew at the back.

'Jesus. That's medieval,' Collins gasped. He turned to Sam. 'Recognise him?'

'It was years ago,' Sam whispered. 'And I only saw him from a distance.'

'How did you identify him, Herr Inspektor?' Collins asked.

'The crime officers found six passports in a suitcase, including his original Russian one with a photograph taken before he had the cosmetic surgery to change the way he looked. That's when I was called in.'

'Any idea how long he'd been living here?'

'Four weeks only. The woman in the next apartment, she saw him arrive with two bags.'

'Alone?'

'Yes. And she say he never have visitors.'

'Because he knew that if he did, they'd probably kill him,' Collins commented.

'So it looks. But this garrotte, I have never heard it to be used by criminals in Vienna. The people who do this are not from here, I think.'

Sam stared miserably at the remains of the witness they'd placed so much store in finding. 'Have you found any other papers in the apartment?' he asked forlornly. 'Diaries, business contracts, notebooks?'

The Inspektor shook his florid head. 'Only the passports and some plastic cards. We already make investigation about the bank accounts he have.'

A forensic specialist had begun dusting the furniture for the attacker's prints. Sam guessed there wouldn't be any.

Collins turned from the room and pulled Sam with him. 'That garrotte's the sort of toy the KGB used to play with,' he whispered. 'My guess is the Kremlin's behind this. Kovalenko knew too much about the people at the top.'

Inspektor Pfeiffer had followed them out into the hallway and overheard. 'I think you can be right. The FSB have wanted to find Herr Kovalenko very bad since six months. Every week we speak about him with Moscow. We had new information that he had been seen back in Vienna, but in the west of the city, not here.' There was a bullishness about his manner which Sam interpreted as contentment. One more undesirable foreigner out of the way.

'How fat is your dossier on Kovalenko's activities?' he asked.

'*Fat* I would not say. Such people are not easy to check. There are so many like him in Vienna. And they all have some legal business to hide their activities. Many are in joint venture with Austrian citizens. We don't have enough officers to watch them as close as we would like.'

'What about in the last twelve months?' Sam checked.

'For most of this year he has not been in Vienna. And before that we had nothing for many months. What I want to know most importantly is how the killers found him here.'

'A man like Kovalenko would never function totally alone,' Collins stated. 'He'd have used someone local to find him the apartment and watch his back. But such a person normally works for money, not loyalty. So if a better payer comes along . . .' He shrugged.

The explanation was tidy, but it was the timing of the murder that disturbed Sam, as much as the killing itself. Kovalenko had been eliminated just a few hours after he'd told Günther Hoffmann why they were looking for him. He shook his head. It had to be coincidence. It couldn't be anything else.

He looked at Collins and they nodded at one another. There was nothing to be gained from hanging around this morgue.

They thanked the Inspektor and left.

Out in the street they paused by the car without attempting to get into it.

'I'm going back to the Embassy,' Collins told him. 'Drop you somewhere?'

Sam thought for a moment. He'd arranged to meet Julie Jackman at lunchtime to hear what she'd arranged with Schenk, but he had a couple of hours to kill. Time enough for another word with Hoffmann.

'I saw a metro station close to that Ferris wheel. If you can drop me there it'll do me fine.'

'No problem.'

They got back into the car. Sam drummed his fingers on his thigh, thinking hard.

Harry Jackman ships a mysterious cargo out of Russia after setting up the deal with Kovalenko in a hotel full of virologists, one of whom was Dr Max Schenk. A year later a virus is being used as a weapon . . .

'I've been having some more thoughts about the rendezvous Miss Jackman's trying to arrange with her former lover,' Sam announced.

'Go on.'

'I want her to wear a wire.'

'That's a little OTT, isn't it?'

'She'll be under a lot of stress. Can't expect her to remember everything that's said. She might forget something important. And I'd like to hear his voice.'

'I take your point.' Collins chewed it over for a moment. 'Well, fine. There's a bloke I use occasionally who could help with that. Give me a ring this afternoon when you know when and where it's to happen.'

'Thanks. I will.'

Ten minutes later Sam was on a train heading for Heiligenstadt again. When he reached the third-floor apartment in the Karl-Marx Hof, he found the door to the neighbouring flat open and the beak-nosed woman cleaning the threshold. A couple of her cats were curled up on the rug behind her. He gave her a courteous smile.

'You again!' she remarked in German. 'You always come when he's out.'

He pretended not to understand and knocked at Hoffmann's door anyway.

'There's no point,' she commented. 'He's in the hospital.'

'What?'

'Last night. An ambulance came.'

Sam gaped. He had visions of another murder. *Hoffmann's* neck with a strap round it this time.

'Heart attack,' the crone went on, gleeful at the drama that had come into her tedious life. 'That's what they said. Like his wife. *Unheimlich, nicht?*'

Uncanny indeed. Sam asked when it had happened and she told him it was around midnight. Which would have been shortly after the man had got home.

'He didn't seem too bad,' the woman concluded. 'He could still talk. Told me not to worry.'

Sam asked which hospital he'd been taken to but she didn't know.

He thanked her and made his way downstairs again, making a mental note to try to trace the clinic later and check on his condition.

One thing was clear. If the old spy had been hospitalised last night, he could hardly have been connected with the death of Vladimir Kovalenko.

Brussels

On the tenth floor of the University Clinic of St Luc, two of the four twenty-five-bed units had been turned into isolation wards. In the past twelve hours the Brussels police had traced and brought to the hospital every person known to have been in contact with Anders Klason since his arrival in the Belgian capital the previous day. Thirty of those who were now sitting on beds or standing around chatting had been involved in the conference where Klason had collapsed. Sitting alone at the far end of the second unit was a scared, uncomprehending Turkish taxi driver, the man who'd brought the Swede from the airport to the city centre.

In a room on her own lay a terrified Commissioner Blanche Duvalier. When she'd heard about Klason's incident with the broken glass at the Austrian lakeside, she'd told Dr Gouari about her own confrontation with a sharp object outside the Commission building three days earlier. Within minutes she'd been isolated. Since then she'd been questioned thoroughly by the police and subjected to hourly blood tests administered by a masked nurse with coldly observant eyes. Klason, she'd learned, was still alive but little more than a vegetable. She knew too that her description of the woman she'd collided with bore similarities to the one provided by Nina Klason. Something evil was under way in Europe and the two of them were its first victims. She'd sent word to Paris where her daughter worked for UNESCO. Annette was on her way. She'd been praying to God that she would arrive in time.

In the last hour she'd begun to feel confused, as if parts of her memory were being unplugged and then reconnected. She remembered Anders Klason disintegrating before her eyes in the Salle Bertrand. Remembered his fear. She was experiencing panic interspersed by patches of incomprehensible calm. One such more restful moment was engulfing her now. Her lips widened in a smile at the irony of it all. All along she'd been hoping for a closer relationship with the tall blond Swede, but not in separate beds.

The door to her small room opened. She didn't recognise the three who came in because their faces were masked. They were carrying equipment which they began to set up. A roll of transparent plastic. Stainless steel frames. Drips, tubes. To her it looked like the paraphernalia of death.

One of the masked faces came closer. A black face that she was quite certain she had never seen before. And it spoke.

'Je suis desolé, madame.'

Nina Klason was also occupying a single room. No masks for the medical staff here though, because her blood tests had shown none of the viral antibodies now surging through the veins of the Commissioner for Racial Equality. The African doctor's initial assessment was proving the most likely one. That the virus was like rabies and needed broken skin to enter the body and attack the brain.

A small table had been brought to her room for the plain-suited, Neanderthal-faced Belgian police officer to set up his laptop. He liaised with Interpol, he'd said, and had been showing her disks full of photographs. Men mostly, hard faces with shaven heads. A few sour women too. A cast of hundreds from a half-dozen nations, all with a record for racially motivated crime.

Nina Klason shook her head for the hundredth time. None of the faces was familiar. None matched the couple who'd crouched next to Anders's beach towel less than a week ago. By now she was numb with exhaustion. No sleep last night and a day of talking today.

She'd spoken on the phone to her mother in Vienna, who was at the end of her tether coping with the Klason's two attention-seeking children. The woman had agreed to hold the fort for one more day on the understanding that Nina made alternative arrangements after that. Nina was torn about what to do. The Congolese doctor had told her that if her blood tests were still negative the next morning, she would be free to go home. The children needed her, but so did Anders. The doctors had warned her he could die, and deep down she'd already accepted it. She wanted to be there when it happened, whether or not he was aware of her presence. But someone had to look after the children. She'd tried three of her Viennese neighbours. All had expressed concern that whatever infection Anders had been hit by, the Klason infants might be carrying it.

'Es tut mir leid,' she whispered, apologising to the policeman for not recognising the last of the faces presented to her. The Flemish officer had been conversing with her in German.

'Thank you for trying, Frau Klason,' he replied, powering down the computer and shutting the lid. 'I didn't expect anything, to be honest with you. Most of these are football hooligans. The people who attacked your husband are in another league.' He stood up and shook her hand. 'I hope the doctors can do something for him.'

Only if they can work miracles here, thought Nina Klason. Only if they can work miracles.

HMS *Truculent*

Arthur Harris was lunching in the senior rates' mess. In the corner of the small, beige-panelled space a couple of chiefs were looking through a box of video cassettes, trying to decide which films would bear watching for the umpteenth time this patrol.

Harris had resigned himself to the idea of playing no further part in the 'Russians on the Rocks' mystery, as the affair was being referred to on board. The boat had been due to take in a broadcast at six that morning. He'd slept through until nine, but if there'd been a follow-up he was sure he would have heard about it.

There was a different atmosphere on board today. An end of term feel, yet one the men were reluctant to grasp. The operational phase was over, but it would be three weeks before they saw the lights of Plymouth again. Meanwhile the weekend lay ahead. Many of those with partners coming out to Crete were suffering from nerves. Sitting beside Harris was one of the 'back aft' chiefs, a nuclear reactor technician.

'It's like starting again every time I get back with the wife,' he complained.

'I know what you mean,' Harris affirmed, living his small private lie.

'They say being married's like riding a bike. You don't forget how to do it. But each time you get back on top you ask yourself if anything's changed. Any bits broken or worn out. Anybody been oiling it while you've been away . . .' The chief picked up his empty plate. 'Shouldn't have fucking said that,' he muttered, returning it to the serving hatch. 'Got meself all worried now.'

Harris drank down the remains of his coffee and stared absently into the corner. He would miss this companionship when he got back to Cheltenham. The only regular company he had at home was his mother, whom he'd moved down from the north after his father died.

The sonar chief Brian Smedley dropped into the chair opposite with a plate of spaghetti, which he began to devour.

'You stopping in Crete before heading home?' Smedley asked, tomato sauce sticking to his lips.

'No. Got a flight booked for Saturday night. The CTs' job is over.' No need for the GCHQ team to stay on board for the long underwater transit to the UK. 'Looking forward to Souda?'

'Not much, to be frank,' Smedley confided. 'Have to behave meself now there's a spy on board.'

'How d'you mean?'

'That pretty-boy lad with the panda eyes.'

'I'm not with you. You mean Griffiths?'

'Yes. Bloody Griffiths. It were *my* daughter he got pregnant, the dirty little rascal. I'm gonna be his bloody father-in-law in a few months' time. Can't have him reporting back to the wife.'

'I had no idea,' Harris breathed, trying not to smile. 'Cramping your style a bit then.'

'Just this once, yes. Won't happen again. The coxswain's getting him transferred to another boat.' Smedley stuffed his face with another forkful. 'Mind you, we mightn't even get to Crete, the way things are going.'

'How d'you mean?' Harris's hopes soared suddenly. Perhaps they were going Russian-hunting again after all.

'We detected a bloody submarine this morning. Went into the ultra-quiet state. Didn't you hear the pipe?'

'Must've slept through it,' he mumbled disconsolately.

'Just before six, when we were going to PD for the broadcast. Had to go deep again. We thought it was one of the Yugoslav boats at first. Turned out to be an Italian way out of his box.'

'So what happened to the broadcast?' Harris asked, his hopes rising again.

'Lost it. Had to stay deep. Next access time is about now.'

They both glanced at the depth repeater on the mess bulkhead.

'Thirty metres,' Smedley nodded. 'We're on the way up again.'

Commander Anthony Talbot nodded with satisfaction as the sound room reported no new sonar contacts.

Earlier, when the first trace of that other submarine had been picked up, the control room had gone electric. He'd marched into the sound room to listen to the rustling noises that Chief Smedley assured him was the water flow round a submerged hull. With no NATO boats scheduled in the area, he'd had to assume it was a potential enemy which they needed to identify. They'd diverted from their course south to track it. From his own point of view he'd have been delighted to have missed the run ashore in Souda Bay if it meant a bit of action. For the most part, this mission had been tediously routine and it was his last patrol before a staff job ashore. But when the 'enemy' boat's signature was identified as an Italian Sauro class submarine, the relief on the faces of the crew told him that if he'd cancelled the weekend's leave he might have had a mutiny on his hands.

'Twenty metres.' The planesman had shouted the depth every ten metres as they came slowly up.

'Keep eighteen metres,' Talbot ordered. He got to his feet, standing behind the ship control panel. 'Revolutions for three knots.'

As the submarine's fin grazed the surface of the sea the boat began to wallow, the planesman pushing forward to decrease the ascent angle, then pulling back sharply to stabilise the response. Riding the bubble, they called it.

A red figure 18 appeared on the digital depth gauge and stayed there.

'Depth steady at eighteen metres, sir.'

'Thank you, ship control. Raise the search periscope.'

Watch officer Lieutenant Harvey Styles grabbed the handles as the shiny tube slid upwards. When it locked in place he walked the sight all the way round.

'Nothing visual, sir.'

'Raise the WT mast,' Talbot ordered. Two minutes to go to the broadcast.

The periscope video camera showed a grey morning up above, with large waves splashing foam over the optics. The boat rolled uncomfortably. Submariners' stomachs weren't used to surface motion. They'd want to go deep again the moment the broadcast was in.

Talbot noticed Arthur Harris hovering by the chart table, waiting to know if there was a reaction to the recording they'd transmitted twelve hours earlier. A man obsessed by a voice.

In the W/T room LED displays flickered as bursts of data were sucked in from the satellite 24,000 miles above them.

'Broadcast reception successful, sir,' the operator announced a few seconds later.

The signals officer broke off a strip of punched tape containing the day's code and fed it into the reader. A few seconds later the dot-matrix printers perched on top of the equipment racks purred into life. The officer fingered the leading edge of the paper to read the heading.

TO HMS TRUCULENT. FOR THE CAPTAIN'S EYES ONLY.

Arthur Harris stood by the chart table staring down the passageway leading aft. The W/T office was off it. He noted the rating emerge with his clipboard and followed him with his eyes as he approached the captain. Talbot took the sheets of signals. He read the heading, then ordered Styles to take the boat to thirty metres again. Frowning, he walked towards his cabin.

Once inside with the curtain drawn across the doorway, Talbot sat at his tiny desk and began to read. As he did so, his heart sank. Then almost simultaneously he experienced a surge of excitement.

The shore leave at Souda Bay had been cancelled. They were to return to the waters near the island of Lastovo and prepare for a special forces mission. There'd be action after all.

He sat quietly for a moment, thinking. Selling the idea to the crew would have to be done with care and compassion. Expressions of regret over the loss of leave, rather than being too gung-ho about their new task.

After a couple of minutes he stood up and returned to the control room, pausing by the navigation table. He looked at the chart, measuring their distance from Lastovo with a pair of dividers.

Lieutenant Harvey Styles came and stood beside him.

'We're going back,' Talbot told him. 'On full power.'

Styles pursed his lips but didn't say anything. In a few moments the captain would need to make a pipe, a task he didn't envy him.

Talbot saw Arthur Harris standing by the door to the trials shack. 'You win, Chief Harris,' he grinned. 'We're going back for your Russians.'

Arthur Harris allowed himself a smile.

Vienna
12.25 hrs

As Julie Jackman walked from the Marriott Hotel to the café where she'd agreed to meet Sam, she was in a state of perplexity. Stuffed into her shoulder bag was a copy of that morning's *Daily Chronicle*, bought at the stall in the hotel lobby.

The midday sun beat down strongly, but she hardly noticed it. After a night of bad dreams, she'd woken this morning in a cold sweat at the thought of what she'd agreed to do. Deciding that delaying the dreaded phone call would only make it harder, she'd rung Max at the clinic soon after nine to tell him she wasn't sure she wanted to end their relationship after all. Sounding remarkably unsurprised by her change of heart, he'd suggested they meet for a drink in the late evening 'to talk things through'.

Julie had agreed to set up the meeting with Max partly because she owed it to Sam after making such a mess of his life, but more importantly because in the restless small hours she'd come to the conclusion she was definitely falling in love with him. But now as she approached the café everything was up in the air again. This latest article in the *Chronicle* painted him as a thoroughly suspect character, a man just as untrustworthy as all the others she'd fallen for over the years.

When Sam saw Julie walk into the café, her appearance touched him. Her face was ashen with worry. Her glasses had slipped a little, giving her the forlorn look of a fresher student still trying to work out where the library was. She was dressed in a pale grey T-shirt and her dark trousers were baggy with cargo pockets. He felt an urge to hug her, until he reminded himself of the havoc she'd caused him.

As she approached the table, he stood up. It was an old habit from his Navy days.

'Hello,' he smiled.

She nodded a greeting but avoided his eyes.

'Is it fixed with Max?' he asked softly.

'Tonight at ten,' she whispered, putting her shoulder bag down on the floor. 'Sort of.'

She cast a glance around the café, looking anywhere but at Sam. The place was large and open and only half full. There were hat stands in the corners, big windows onto the street and black-jacketed waiters ignoring the customers.

The 'sort of' had worried him. Sam saw the newspaper poking from Julie's bag and guessed why she was reluctant to meet his gaze. He cleared his throat.

'I gather your media friends have been having fun again.' He spoke aggressively, deciding to confront the problem head-on.

Julie rounded on him. 'They're not my friends!' She didn't like the way he was staring at her. Not the bruised look of someone cruelly misrepresented in the media, but the calculating glare of a manipulator. She pushed her glasses up the bridge of her nose, as if to sharpen the focus of this different view she was having of him. She straightened her back. His catty gibe about her relationship with the press had decided things for her.

'I've changed my mind,' she announced, returning his glare. 'I won't be seeing Max this evening after all.'

Sam gritted his teeth. He should have expected something like this. The woman was as dependable as a chocolate teapot. He waved an arm at the waiter and ordered two beers without bothering to enquire what Julie wanted to drink.

'May I ask why you've decided that?' he demanded, when the waiter was gone.

'I have to return to London this afternoon,' she insisted stonily, her resolve strengthened by his chauvinism over the drinks order. 'I spoke to the lab an hour ago and they need me urgently.' She lifted her chin, daring him to challenge her veracity.

'Your ticket's for tomorrow,' Sam countered, determined to make her change her mind again. 'It's an unchangeable reservation.'

'They're paying for a new one,' she retorted. It was a lie. All the lab had said when she'd spoken to them that morning was that they would welcome her back as soon as she could make it.

'And why do they need your presence so urgently?' he prodded. 'I thought you'd been suspended.'

Her face reddened. 'Because of the Brussels virus. They're working flat out to identify it and develop a vaccine.'

'Brussels virus?' Sam asked, slow to make the connection.

'You must have read about it. It's been in the papers. Two EU officials ill with a brain disease nobody's ever seen before.'

He narrowed his eyes. 'Yes, I've read about it. But the story I saw only mentioned one official.'

'There's been another taken ill this morning. A woman – the European Commissioner for Racial Equality, or something . . .'

Sam felt a buzz of alarm. Something very nasty was developing, making it more important than ever to discover whether there was a Jackman connection.

'If the problem's in Brussels why's your lab involved?'

'Because Professor Norton is big in genetic engineering. The theory they're working on is that someone's combined rabies with another virus so that it gets into the brain faster.'

Combining viruses . . . Wasn't that the same as viral mutation, the subject Dr Max Schenk gave a paper on a year ago? Sam rubbed his forehead. 'Explain that bit, would you?'

'Human skin is an effective barrier to most viruses,' she explained. 'But when there's a break in it – a cut, or whatever – then rabies can enter. It gets into a nerve fibre and makes its way up to the brain, moving very slowly. It can take weeks before it gets there and destroys cells. But combining rabies with another infection which reaches the brain through the blood instead of a nerve means it could be got to work within a couple of days, before any vaccine has a chance to fight it. That's the theory, anyway.'

'Devilish,' Sam murmured. 'What sort of skills would a person need to do that?'

'I don't know. Somebody who specialised in genetic engineering, I imagine. Viral mutation, all that sort of stuff.'

'Someone like Max Schenk.'

Julie's jaw dropped. 'That's ridiculous,' she gasped.

'Is it? We don't know what your father shipped out of Russia, Julie.

Nuclear, biological . . . All we know is that the whole shipment was shrouded in secrecy, with a cover story floated saying it was red mercury.'

'But Max never met my father. I'm sure of it.'

'Ask him, Julie. This evening. It's important.'

Julie felt her resolve crumbling, but she was still furious with him. The nub of the issue was that he hadn't been straight with her. Not at all. Not when they'd first met. Not when he'd come to get the letter in Woodbridge. Not last night. All this time he'd pretended to be someone else and she wasn't going to stand for it.

'Look. I know it's my fault all this stuff about you has come out in the press, but what the hell am I supposed to believe?' she blazed, pulling the *Chronicle* from her bag and slapping it on the table. 'I mean, it turns out you're not called Simon Foster at all but Sam Packer. And it says here your father spied for the Russians, for heaven's sake! And your sister seems to hate you so much she's prepared to tell the whole world what a two-faced rat you are.'

Sam didn't answer. He sensed that she didn't want to believe what had been written about him, but convincing her wouldn't be easy.

'I mean, I just don't know what to make of you,' Julie went on, her fears about him pouring out. 'I . . . in my own life I work with *normal* people who don't have to lie about what they do. But *you* . . . I mean, first you lied to me about being a businessman – okay I never really believed you on that one. But now I find that your name was a lie too and that you come from a long line of liars and cheats.'

'Hold on a minute,' Sam protested. 'If you think bad blood is passed from generation to generation like red hair, then you'd better worry about your own salvation.'

'Okay, okay,' she conceded, 'we all know about my father. What I don't know about is *you*, Simon – *Sam*. You're asking me to spy on Max. But who's it for? What *are* you, for God's sake? You've got to be straight with me.'

Sam knew he'd have to bend the rules. Knew he would have to open the door into his life. Just a crack.

'Okay. My real name *is* Sam Packer, and I do work for the government. And that stuff you've read this morning about my father having been recruited by the Russians has some truth in it. But you've got to understand there are many, many things I simply can't talk about.'

'Why not? Everybody else is,' she goaded.

'There are laws . . . Official Secrets Acts.'

Julie bit her lip. She *wanted* to believe in him. Still wanted *him*, but she had to be able to trust.

'There is something I need to know, Sim—' She shook her head at her confusion. A wisp of hair settled on her lips and she brushed it away.

The waiter came with the beers and surlily suggested they order food while he was there. They chose omelettes and salad.

Julie waited until he was out of earshot then repeated her demand. 'There's something I must know if I'm going to help you.'

'What?'

'The full truth about why you were in Africa with my father.'

Sam felt her eyes bore into him. He remembered Waddell's warning not to give interviews.

'*You* need to know? Or is it your friends in the press?'

Julie closed her eyes momentarily, wondering what she had to do to convince him she wasn't in league with the media any more. She took in a deep breath.

'Is it true or not that you paid my father to supply guns to the Bodanga rebels?'

Sam ground his teeth.

'I really can't get into that . . .'

'Look. If you're not prepared to be straight with me, then I *am* going to stand Max up tonight.'

Her mouth set in a thin line. Sam felt a silly urge to kiss it into a more friendly shape. He leaned forward, his brow furrowing as he prepared to concede more ground.

'The things your father wrote to you about MI6 and Bodanga,' he said in little more than a whisper, 'that's only half the story.' He glanced round to check no one could overhear and to underline the confidential nature of what he was about to tell her. He described the background to the Bodanga coup attempt, carefully pointing out that if it had succeeded people would have been singing the government's praises instead of damning it. Then he told her how her father had been using his inside knowledge of the coup to blackmail Whitehall into giving him immunity from prosecution for a whole host of unnamed crimes.

Julie listened intently. When Sam had finished, she rubbed her forehead. It all fitted. What he'd said had an awful ring of truth about it. She guessed that whatever deceptions Sam/Simon may have indulged in during his life, it was small beer compared to what her father had got up to.

'Thank you for telling me all that,' she whispered. 'It won't go any further. I promise.'

Sam trusted her as much as he trusted a wet paper bag, but if it made her deliver Max Schenk to him this evening then the risk of telling her these things would have been worth it.

Their food arrived. The omelettes were undercooked but the surliness of the waiter deterred them from sending them back.

'I'm sorry,' Sam murmured, indicating her untouched beer glass. 'I didn't have the courtesy to ask what you wanted to drink. Was that all right for you?'

'It's fine,' she replied taking a sip.

He left it for a few moments before asking her what her arrangement was with Max.

'Ten o'clock tonight. He's got a dinner to go to first, but he'll pick me up from the Marriott. I've asked to go somewhere quiet for a chat.'

'How did he sound?'

Julie lifted one eyebrow. 'I got the impression he thought it perfectly natural that I'd come crawling back to him.' She shivered.

'You'll be okay,' Sam reassured her. 'We're going to protect you tonight.'

'How?'

'I want you to wear a wire.'

'A *wire*? What's that?'

'A small microphone the size of a pinhead attached by cable to a little box hidden in your clothes. It'll relay your conversation with Max. We'll be in a car nearby.'

Sam saw that he'd terrified her. Her composure crumbled before his eyes.

'It'll be okay, I promise.'

'I can't do this. Any of it,' she whispered. 'I'm no good at pretending things.'

He grunted in astonishment. 'You did all right in that café in Chiswick.' He wasn't going to let her off the hook. He noticed that she had the grace to blush.

'But what on *earth* am I going to say to him?' she whined. 'He thinks I want him back.'

'Up the stakes to a level he won't go for,' Sam suggested. 'Tell him you want to go on seeing him but only if he divorces his wife.'

She looked aghast. 'Suppose he agrees? No way.'

'It's just for one evening, Julie.'

'What else am I going to talk about? I can't just plunge straight in and say, "Were you involved with my father in something smuggled out of Russia which he called red mercury."'

'He's talked to you about his work in the past?'

'Yes. From time to time.'

'Well, get him to do it again and then pop the question about what sort of business he was doing with your father.'

'*Pop the question.* Anyway it's only your paranoid suspicion that he was connected with my dad.' She was desperate to devalue the plan. 'I'm far from convinced.'

'Paranoid suspicions are what my trade is all about,' he reminded her. 'What *has* he told you about his work?'

'He's talked about the clinic. How he and his brother built it up.'

'Where does the virology come in?'

'It's his special interest. Or used to be. He worked as a physician in one of the main labs in Vienna when he was younger. And he established a state-of-the-art virology lab at the clinic when they set it up four years ago. He still takes an interest, although these days at the clinic he's more of an administrator. His brother was killed in a skiing accident eight months ago. Hansi was older. The financial brains. Max runs the place on his own now.'

'They'd been close?'

'I get the impression his whole family is. They own a big estate in southern Austria somewhere. Max told me once that his grandfather bought it for next to nothing from some Jews who wanted to flee the country when Hitler moved in. After the war they tried to get it back, but the courts blocked them. It happened quite a lot in Austria, Max said.'

Sam felt the back of his neck bristling. 'He told you this with *pride*?'

'Well . . . he didn't seem embarrassed by it.'

'What are his politics?'

'Oh, I don't know. That sort of stuff doesn't interest me. He did talk about some new Austrian nationalist party or other once. It's getting stronger, apparently. But I used to switch off when he got on to politics.'

'Ever talk about there being too many foreigners in Austria? Ever use the word *Überfremdung*?'

Flustered, Julie knitted her brow. Sam had taken on the intense look of a terrier. 'I don't remember. He seldom used German words with me. But I know that it's not just Austria he's concerned about. He thinks the whole of Europe should be keeping the foreigners out. Turks, Bosnians, Albanians, gypsies . . .'

Sam swallowed, reminding himself it wasn't only active racists who held such views. He let his eyes wander from Julie's troubled face and over to the window. He felt like a hound that had scented the fox. The smell was still weak, but it was definitely there.

'It's going to be okay tonight, Julie,' he said, giving her hand a squeeze. He felt a strong urge to give her a hug. 'Just a matter of eliminating Max from our enquiries. And don't worry about it. I'll be within shouting distance. I'll look after you. I promise.'

She looked doubtfully at him. It was a promise men always made – and, in her experience, one they never kept.

17

London. St Stephen's Hospital, Stepney
19.45 hrs

SANDRA WILLETTS ARRIVED a little earlier than usual for her night shift on the elderly care ward. There were grey bags under her eyes from lack of sleep. She hadn't dared confront Rob about the e-mail she'd seen on his computer, but the thought of it had filled every waking moment during the past twenty-four hours.

St Stephen's Hospital was an old Victorian building of blackened brick, scheduled for replacement within the next couple of years. Inefficient, draughty and lacking in modern facilities, but Sandra found it a pleasant place to work because the staff were nice. The night shift wasn't what she wanted to do. Lack of daylight didn't suit her. But nights paid better. So did caring for the elderly.

Sandra climbed the stairs to the third floor. She always walked up when she arrived for work because the lift was out of order half the time. Also she was overweight. She was fifteen minutes early this evening, but had been desperate to get out of the flat. Rob had become even more withdrawn and uncommunicative, too wrapped up in himself to realise how uptight she herself was.

'Hi, Mary,' she breezed, stepping into the nursing office and putting her black leather shoulder bag down in a corner.

Staff Nurse Mary Cowan was alone in the little room and peered pointedly at her watch. 'What's with all this keenness, may I ask?'

'Misread the time,' Sandra lied. 'How's the day been?'

'Not so bad. We've six empty beds this afternoon, which must be a record. Two new patients. A woman with a broken hip and a man who's just been catheterised. They're considering him for a transurethral prostatectomy tomorrow.' She frowned. 'You look as if you could do with a good lie-down yourself. What's up?'

Sandra shook her head. She longed to tell someone about it, but held back.

'It's Rob, isn't it?'

Mary Cowan was a small Irishwoman with dark hair and a thin, watchful face. They'd known each other for years and often chatted about their partners during these handovers. Mary was married to a policeman.

Sandra nodded.

'Up to something, is he?'

Sandra tried to shrug it off.

'They usually are,' Mary stated. Then she became concerned. She could see this was no ordinary tiff. 'What's it about? I mean I know I'm being nosy, but . . .'

Sandra looked away. She felt loyalty to Rob, yet was desperately scared about what he'd got himself into.

'You think he's seeing someone?' Mary persisted in a soft, low voice.

'Another woman? No.' Sandra shuttled her head. 'Although how would I know what he does in the evenings when I'm on shift? All I know is that the bed's left in a mess and smells of him when I get home in the mornings. No. It's not that.'

'What, then?'

Sandra looked towards the door. It did seem remarkably quiet out on the ward.

'He's doing stuff on the Internet,' she mumbled.

Mary Cowan looked a little dismissive. 'What, like porn and that?'

'No. Well . . . I don't know. He may be for all I know, but that's not what I meant.'

'Go on.'

'Well, yesterday – I'd been out shopping and when I got back to the flat he'd left his computer on. He was out, see. Now, he always turns it off, normally. Never lets me see what he's looking at on the net. So . . .'

'So you thought you'd give it the once-over. Don't blame you.'

'It was e-mail.'

'It's like picture postcards, isn't it? If you leave 'em lying around, you've only yourself to blame if other people read them.'

'Well . . . yes.'

'So, what did it say?'

Sandra bit her lip. Rob would kill her.

'It was a message from somebody who was congratulating him. Talking about the "effort on Saturday" all across Europe. Thanks to Rob and the other comrades, it said some network has been established.'

'A network?' Mary wasn't getting the drift at all. 'About football, was it?'

Sandra shot a guilty glance behind her, almost as if she expected to see Rob there. 'Not football, Mary. The message called it the Lucifer

Network. You remember what happened last Saturday? Here and across Europe?'

Mary frowned. Then suddenly her eyes were as big as marbles. 'You don't mean . . .'

'I mean Southall, Mary . . .' Sandra gulped.

'No! But why, in the name of God? Why d'you think that?'

'Well, to be honest, Rob's always been a bit of a racist . . .'

'So's my Colin and he's a copper, but blowing people up . . .'

'I know. It's crazy, isn't it. My mind's gone doolally thinking about it.'

'But that *is* crazy, Sandra. You can't seriously think that Rob . . .' They held each other's look for several seconds, knowing that men were capable of almost anything. 'Have you asked him?'

Sandra laughed bitterly. 'You have to be joking. He'd knock the breath out of me if he knew I'd read the stuff on his screen. I never used to be scared of him, Mary, but I'm petrified of him now.'

'But hang on a minute . . .'

'Look. All I know is he's up to something he shouldn't be. And it's serious. I've never seen him so uptight, so secretive.'

'But that bomb in Southall . . . That was *murder*,' she gasped.

'I know,' Sandra moaned. 'It couldn't *really* have been him, could it?'

Mary didn't answer. It wasn't for her to judge. 'What're you going to do?'

'I don't know.' She was about to tell her friend about the last part of the e-mail, the bit asking him to select a target for the coming weekend, but a buzzer sounded.

'Duty calls,' said Mary Cowan as she bustled from the room.

Duty. For the past twenty-four hours Sandra had been trying to work out where hers lay.

HMS *Truculent*

The submarine passed at periscope depth through the channel between Lastovo island and the rocks a few miles to the east. The tiny piece of land named Palagra where the Russian voices had been detected was now just two miles distant, in a wide stretch of inter-island water known as the Lastovski Channel.

'Depth under the keel?'

Talbot had been pacing nervously between the navigation table and the planesman's position. Charts of this part of the world weren't famous for their accuracy.

'Thirty-eight metres, sir,' the navigator reported, reading off the echo-sounder.

They were navigating with every means at their disposal. GPS, bottom contour analysis and visual sightings through the periscope. They had the attack mast up on this moonless night, slimmer and less visible than the search periscope and equipped with a thermal imager which produced ghostly outlines of the islands around them.

'Single flash, five seconds, bears *that*,' barked Lieutenant Harvey Styles, his face pressed to the periscope sight. He swung the optics to the east, where another light was visible. He counted the flashes and timed the pause between the bursts. 'Flashing five, thirty seconds, bears *that*.'

Talbot stalked to the chart again. The navigator had noted down the bearings and was pencilling in the plot. Everything matched. Just as it should.

On a small monitor behind the ship control position the periscope's thermal imager showed the stumpy, flat-topped outline of Palagra island dead ahead: 300 metres long and about 100 wide, it was uninhabited, according to the preliminary archive research done in London. The submarine's task was to approach as close as they dared and photograph it from every angle to find a landing place for the reconnaissance team London was sending out.

Depth would limit how close they could get. The chart showed sixty-two metres a mile off shore, perilously close to the minimum for a submerged nuclear submarine. Talbot also feared uncharted rocks and fishing boats. Getting snared in a net or going aground well inside Croatia's territorial waters would be an embarrassment of world-shattering proportions. He marched into the sound room and hovered. Every man concentrating, every sensor straining for some noise that shouldn't be there.

In the trials shack, Arthur Harris also had headphones clamped to his ears, but there'd been nothing on the frequencies the Russians had used. Disappointment was written on his face. Disappointment and annoyance. Time had been lost when the boat had headed for Crete. Precious time, which if they'd returned to the surveillance straight after the rendezvous with the helicopter, might have given him another piece of the jigsaw.

He checked the digital time display at the top of the equipment rack. It was after 11 p.m. local. An inactive hour. The broadband frequency analyser showed a flat trace, apart from the blip from two fishing boats on marine band VHF. He lifted off the headphones, and nudged the CT wedged next to him on the bench. He was going for a leg stretch. As he emerged into the control room, a voice rang out from the intercom speakers.

'New contact bearing red zero-five.' Chief Smedley's voice.

The control room was electrified.

Talbot marched into the sound room and craned his head towards the bow sonar screens, staring at the thin green trace that had suddenly come up.

'Contact is track number nine-zero-one,' Smedley called.

'Cut it through.'

'Cut.'

'Motor boat, sir.'

'Somewhere near the island,' the captain growled, hurriedly returning to the control room. He stopped by the periscope. 'See anything, TSO?'

Harvey Styles had the optics on full magnification. 'Yes, sir. Small boat just visible, heading left to right.'

'How small?'

'Fifteen, twenty metres at a guess, sir. Looks like there's a little harbour at the east end of the island.'

There was nothing on the chart to indicate it. 'Let me see.'

Styles relinquished the eyepiece.

The craft was a powerboat, moving at a good speed, judging by the bow wave. As he watched, Talbot saw it turn and settle on a course heading straight towards them.

'Starboard twenty,' he barked, handing the periscope back to Styles. The risk of their mast being seen in the black of night was minimal, even if the powerboat passed close, but he would take no chances. He returned to his command seat and watched the video screen as the craft veered away to their left. Styles switched the sight to full magnification. The front half of the boat filled the frame. There was lettering on the bow, barely distinguishable on the thermal imager.

'I think there's a "k" and an "l" there, sir,' Styles commented. 'Could be the *Karolina*.'

Talbot glanced round and saw Arthur Harris hovering by the conning tower access hatch. He beckoned him over and pointed to the monitor.

'I have an awful feeling, Chief Harris,' he opined softly, 'that those are our Moscow birds in that boat. And if so, they may have just flown the coop.'

Vienna
22.10 hrs

The dark blue Passat had been rented by a twenty-six-year-old Cambridge graduate called Malcolm who had the shoulders of a rowing blue and the nervous enthusiasm of a teenager. Through the windscreen, Sam and he watched Max Schenk double-park his Audi outside the Marriott, then walk quickly into the hotel.

'Off you go,' Sam murmured.

Malcolm pushed open the driver's door, hurried over to Schenk's car and crouched by a rear wheel arch, pretending to tie a shoelace. Fifteen seconds later he was back.

'Okay?'

'Yep. He'll only see the transmitter wire if he goes looking for it.'

Sam opened the portable computer on his lap, waiting for the red dot to appear on the screen which would tell him the tracer was working. It came up a split second before Schenk re-emerged from the hotel with Julie.

'Well done, Malc. We're go for launch.'

Harry Jackman's daughter wore a jacket and skirt and looked drawn and tense. Sam caught her glancing about to see if she could spot him.

The Audi started up and turned onto the Ringstrasse. Malcolm swung the Passat out to follow it. On the roof of the rented car a small additional antenna had been fixed by magnets to pick up the transmissions from the car in front. The lead from it came down through a gap in the window and connected to a small receiver the size of a Walkman. Sam put on a pair of headphones and listened, praying the system would work. Malcolm kept glancing at him to check.

Sam gave a thumbs-up. As they progressed through the evening traffic the signals broke up now and then, which was to be expected. The transmitter taped to the inside of Julie's jacket was low powered, its output weakened by the metal shell of Schenk's Audi.

Sam had spent most of the afternoon with Collins planning the operation. The station chief had remained sceptical about a link between Jackman's cargo and the Brussels virus and was insisting on keeping a diplomatic distance from his activities. He'd offered the assistance of a junior, however, a man who worked for a British bank in Vienna, but freelanced for SIS. According to Collins he was reliable and knew the city well.

The kit they were using was commercial, bought by Malcolm at a 'spy shop' that afternoon. Sam had taken it to the Marriott at around eight to wire Julie up. He'd hidden the tiny microphone in the lapel of a dark blue blazer which she'd bought after their lunch together, taping into the lining the slim transmitter box and a credit-card-sized digital recorder that would provide back-up if there was a failure of the radio link. He'd warned her to be careful not to snag the thin wire antenna that hung down the inside of the jacket.

'Wherever you go, I'll be right behind you,' he'd told her, less confident than he sounded. He'd shown her the small black object half the size of a matchbox they would attach to Schenk's car. 'It's a tracer which sends a tiny signal to a satellite.'

'Will it take my pulse?' she'd quipped, momentarily allowing humour to lighten her terror.

The car braked suddenly, Malcolm mouthing expletives. A tram had turned at a junction in front of them, cutting them off from the Audi. 'You have to watch these bastards,' he hissed. 'They've got priority and they use it.'

Seconds later the headphones died. 'Now we've bloody lost them,' Sam snapped. Then the traffic lights went red, compounding their problems.

'Damn!' Malcolm banged on the wheel.

The notebook computer on Sam's lap was linked through the car's cellphone to a satellite terminal in the Embassy. Its glowing screen showed a street map of Vienna. Superimposed was the flashing dot of the tracer. Waiting for the lights to change, Malcolm leaned over to look.

'He's going for the Franzen bridge, then towards the Prater,' he opined, pointing out where he meant. When the lights turned green he jammed his foot down, glancing in the mirror for police cars.

Sam had become anxious about what he was putting Julie through this evening. If Max Schenk discovered that wire, he might not be the gentleman she thought he was. A fresh crackle in the earphones brought some relief. They were getting back in range.

'. . . *taking me* . . .'

'. . . *nice and quiet. We can* . . .'

Tantalising but useless. Sam loathed so-called hi-tech devices that promised more than they delivered.

'Catch up, for Christ's sake,' he fumed. 'I'm getting sod all.'

They accelerated past a bus, then braked for a fresh set of lights turning amber.

'God, you're no bloody Schumacher, are you?'

'Look. If the police stop us because I jump a light it'll be game over,' Malcolm protested, his hands fidgeting on the wheel.

More headphone crackles.

'. . . *changed your mind?*'

Sam winced. Schenk had started to question her.

'Which way at the Praterstern?' Malcolm asked, glancing down at the screen then back up at the lights.

Sam checked. 'Looks like they've gone straight ahead.'

'Show me.'

Sam swung the laptop towards him.

'Okay. No problem. I know that road. We can still catch them.' The green came up and he zoomed off.

Collins had been full of praise for Malcolm's navigational skills that afternoon. *Knows Vienna better than the shape of his own wedding tackle* was the way he'd put it. He'd better, thought Sam. He'd bloody better.

To their right the sky flashed and flickered with the lights of the amusement park, the spill from them illuminating the cabins of the giant Ferris wheel as it ground slowly round. They were close to where Kovalenko's corpse had been found that morning. It would have taken two killers to slay a man with a garrotte, Sam had calculated, one to restrain the victim while the other screwed the cutting bolt into his spinal cord. Two people of a very special mindset. The same kind, he realised, as might use a virus to addle a man's brain.

The trouble was, everything they had was supposition, not fact. The link between Jackman's death and Kovalenko's, the connection between Max Schenk and Jackman. And his suspicion about Schenk had weakened after Collins's enquiries with the Austrian Security Police had turned up nothing on the doctor.

He was due some luck, but tonight they weren't getting any. The earphones had gone dead again and the tracer dot was streaking away from them. His anxiety began ratcheting up.

'Bloody move it, Malcolm. If you get booked, I'll pay the fine.'

'It's not the money, Mr Packer, I can assure you of that.'

Malcolm was a nervous driver, hunching over the wheel. He drove with a jerky unevenness that made Sam want to retch. Goaded by the drumming of Sam's fingers on the dashboard he suddenly swung out to overtake a bus, putting his foot hard down.

Ahead was another junction. More lights. 'Oh Jesus!' Sam moaned as they clicked to amber. Malcolm dabbed the brakes, but Sam swore at him and he trod the accelerator again. 'Good man . . .' His voice trailed away. Out of the corner of his eye he'd seen a small shape dart from a side street. 'For fuck's sake!'

Malcolm swerved, but too late. The motorcyclist skidded, wobbled and banged against their rear wing.

'Shit!'

Malcolm swung over to the kerb. They looked back. The bike was on its side in the middle of the road, its rider getting gingerly to his feet.

'He's okay, Malc,' Sam insisted, glowering at the laptop and its winking red dot. 'Forget him. He's okay . . .' But he heard the door open and Malcolm sprinting back. 'Bloody hell!'

He was imagining the worst by now. Schenk's arm round Julie's shoulders. A groping hand slipping inside the jacket. The unexpected feel of wires and metal against the back of his fingers . . .

He wrenched open the door. '*Malcolm!*'

A few seconds later the young man was back, checking the rear wing before slipping behind the wheel again.

'Pissed, thank God,' Malcolm muttered as he crunched in the gear. 'Unhurt. And fortunately the bugger thought it was his own fault.' He accelerated away. 'Where does the tracer put them?'

'In Germany,' Sam snarled. He would have words with Collins later, to tell him Malcolm's knowledge of his own genitalia was winning hands down.

'Seriously.'

'They've crossed the Danube already.'

'Floridsdorf Bridge?'

'If you say so.'

'Then I've a bloody good idea where they're headed.'

'Where's that?'

'Stammersdorf. It's a village right on the edge of the city. There's a street full of *Heurigen* there. You know, wine taverns. Not like the tourist traps in the Wienerwald. It's where the locals go for a quiet jug.'

They had no chance of catching up. Schenk was driving fast and had been luckier with the lights. But Malcolm had guessed right. Ten minutes later the red dot ceased moving in Stammersdorf. Three minutes after that they arrived there too, a pretty village whose straight main street was lined with pastel-painted hostelries. Halfway down they spotted the Audi, parked by the kerb and empty. They pulled up near it.

Sam's nerves were like crushed bamboo by now. They should have been picking up signals from Julie's wire again, yet they weren't. They looked up and down the narrow, lamplit street. There were at least half a dozen taverns close by.

'Any ideas?' Sam demanded. Malcolm shook his head.

Sam slipped the Walkman-like audio receiver inside his jacket and they began to move, praying for a sudden earphone crackle to tell them they'd got near.

'Shall I try this one?' Malcolm suggested, pushing at the door of the first tavern they came to.

'Might as well.'

Within a couple of seconds he was out again.

'Closing. And the place was empty.'

The next they came to was the same. Then Malcolm touched Sam's arm and pointed across the road. The zumphing sounds of an accordion wafted through an archway which formed the entrance to a cream yellow tavern with bottle-glass windows.

'That one's got life in it.'

They crossed the road. Beyond the arch was a vine-bedecked, cobbled courtyard set with tables and lit by coloured lights in the trees.

'Check it out,' Sam ordered. 'If Julie's in there and sees me it'll put her off her stroke.'

As Malcolm walked in, a waitress came up to him, tapping her watch. 'Looking for a friend,' Sam heard him say.

Suddenly he jumped. The headphones had come alive. A male voice, crisp and close, with a strong Germanic accent. Schenk. And he was angry.

'*You tell me on the telephone you have a new thought about us. That you change your mind from last night. But now you say you don't want to make love. You must explain to me, Julie.*'

'*I told you in the car. I just want to talk.*'

Sam was extraordinarily relieved to hear Julie's voice. She seemed okay, if understandably tense.

'*I just felt I should give us another chance,*' she went on, unconvincingly. '*We've been seeing each other for a year, yet I hardly know you. I've no idea what you think about a lot of things. We never talk about anything important.*'

'*Important? What d'you mean?*'

'*Well, personal things. I don't even know where you live. Is it a house, a flat? Large, small? I know you have a wife called Cara. I know you have children, but you've never given me their names or their ages.*'

'*These things you have no need to know,*' he answered, icily.

'*You know a lot more about me. Even when we first met, you seemed to know loads already. I've no idea how.*'

Sam heard a fluffing noise that sounded as if the microphone was being banged.

'*No, Max! Get off me!*'

He imagined Schenk trying to remove her blazer.

'*N'ja Julie. Why do you want to know such unimportant things?*' There was a kissing sound and Schenk's nasally breathing. '*You enjoy it with me. That's what matter. I don't believe you have been pretending when we are in bed.*' Another clunk on the lapel mike. '*You cannot have all of my life, Julie. A part of me belongs to other people. You know that. It is our understanding.*'

More grappling noises, then a squeak of protest.

'*No, Max. I . . . I'll only have sex with you if you tell me some things I want to know.*'

Sam winced. Her commitment to his cause was beginning to astonish him.

'What things?' Schenk's voice had turned into a menacing growl. 'What is it you want to know?'

'How you knew so much about me when we first met?'

There was no reply. Somewhere in that room they were in a clock was ticking.

'Was it from my father?'

Another silence. Even Schenk's breathing had stopped.

'Why do you think that?'

'Oh, because I know he used to talk about me a lot . . . Even to strangers, sometimes.'

If there'd been a pin in that room Sam would have heard it drop.

'I didn't meet your father, Julie.'

Sam's heart sank. Was that it? All over. End of story.

'Didn't you?' Julie persisted. 'That's odd. I could have sworn I saw you with him earlier that evening.'

Sam perked up again. She wasn't giving in easily.

'Well, you were wrong,' Schenk told her with a little laugh. 'What is this game you play with me, Julie? What is it? Mmm? What do you want, you funny little girl?'

More rustling against the microphone. Much more. Then a sharp intake of breath.

'Hands off, Max. I do not want to go to bed with you.'

'But I have answered your question.'

'I don't know if you were telling the truth.'

Schenk exploded with rage.

'Get off!' Julie squealed.

Sam whirled round, trying to use the receiver as a direction finder, but the level was almost constant wherever he pointed it.

'You play some game this evening. What it is?' Schenk repeated, gravel voiced.

Sam looked about wildly. Blank walls everywhere. She was only a few paces away yet he didn't know where.

'Take me back to the Marriott,' Julie begged. 'Please, Max.'

'Oh no. I don't take you anywhere yet. We are not finished. Perhaps you don't understand what we have been doing for the past year.'

'What d'you mean?'

'I think maybe you have never understood.'

'I want to go back, Max.' Julie's voice was beginning to crack. 'Please let go of me. I'll get a taxi.'

'We are not finished.'

'Yes, Max. It's over. I love someone else . . .'

Schenk snorted in surprise. Then he chuckled.

'Well then, I am happy for you. I too love someone else. But what you and I have done this year, it has never been love.'

'That's true.'

'And we didn't pretend so.'

'No.'

'Because it was just business, yes?'

'Business?'

'I give you airplane tickets, clothes, good food and wine, take you to beautiful places. And . . . in return, you give me what I want. It is simple, Julie. We have been like customer and supplier for each other.'

No response. Sam knew what was coming next.

'And you still owe me for this time, my little Julie.'

'Look, Max, I'll pay you for it.' Her voice trembled. 'The flight, the dinner, the hotel. I'll write you a cheque . . .'

All of a sudden Malcolm emerged from the *Heurige*, shaking his head. 'Not here,' he grunted.

Sam held up a hand to silence him. 'They're in a bedroom,' he snapped. 'Which of these places lets rooms?'

Malcolm peered round looking for ZIMMER FREI signs. 'I'll ask inside.'

'Be quick, for Christ's sake.'

Sam heard more rustling of clothing near the microphone, then Julie's voice, much more frightened than before. 'All right, Max. Fine. We'll do it. But I have to go to the bathroom first.'

'No. First I undress you.'

'I don't want you to.'

'It doesn't matter what you want . . .' His hiss tailed away suddenly. Then he grunted with surprise. The mike banged and grew muffled, as if fingers had closed over it.

'What is this?'

'Please, Max . . .'

Sam heard a slap, then a whimper of protest. There were sounds of the jacket being wrenched off.

'Verdammt!'

Then silence. Total electronic death. Not even a hiss. The antenna or microphone ripped from its socket. Sam's throat was blocked by a huge lump. He'd promised to protect her.

He began walking, listening for raised voices from behind the windows closest to him. Seconds were ticking away. Soon they'd be minutes and Schenk was doing God knew what to her.

Suddenly there was a bang from the other side of the road. He shot a glance at the tavern opposite. Curtains moved in an upstairs window. A dark-haired head was being shoved back against the glass.

226

He ran, bursting in through the bottle-glass door. Ignoring the protests of the landlord, he saw some stairs and pounded up them. At the top was a pine-floored landing with a handful of doors. Thumps and muffled sobs came from behind one of them. He tried the handle. Locked, but it gave way to his shoulder.

Inside, it smelled of Schenk's vile cigar habit. Julie was cowering on the bed, her shirt half off, one small and vulnerable breast pulled free from the bra. Schenk was whipping her, her handbag bunched in his fist like a lash. At the sound of Sam's entry he lurched round, face white with rage and fear. Then he flung the bag at Sam's head and barged towards the door.

Sam ducked low and went in with a tackle, but Schenk showed a surprising agility and twisted from his grip, hammering both fists down. Sam staggered from the blow to his head. By the time he could steady himself, Schenk was out of the room.

Sam grabbed Julie by the shoulders, mouthing apologies. Her face was red with slap marks, her lower lip split and bleeding. Eyes locked shut, her body shook with sobs. He pulled her shirt back on, then held her in his arms and hugged her.

And it had all been for nothing. The secret of Harry Jackman's damnable deal was as obscure as ever.

He heard feet on the stairs. The landlord appeared at the door.

'N'ja. Was geht los hier?'

'Can you walk?' Sam asked. Julie nodded. 'Then let's get out of here.' He draped the torn blazer over her shoulders, then gathered up her bag and the pieces of bugging equipment that lay scattered on the floor.

Malcolm was at the foot of the stairs as he helped her down. 'Schenk came crashing out of the place like a mad bull,' he announced breathlessly.

Behind them Sam heard the landlord remonstrating.

'Got any money?'

'Some,' Malcolm answered.

'Give it to me so I can pacify mine host. Then get in that damned car and see where Schenk runs to.'

Malcolm thrust a wad of notes into Sam's hand, then left, jangling the car keys.

'Sit down a sec, while I sort this out,' Sam whispered, helping Julie to a chair.

He apologised to the landlord in the best German he could muster and counted out notes until the man was satisfied. Then he asked about taxis and was told there were usually a couple waiting fifty metres down the road.

He took Julie into the street, and found one. He helped her onto the back seat and slid in beside her, ordering the driver to take them to the Marriott.

'Tell me you're all right,' he croaked, putting an arm round her shoulders.

But she told him nothing. Instead she stared blankly ahead, stunned by the fact that the world as she knew it had irrevocably changed.

'I'm sorry,' said Sam, helplessly. His prime concern was to ensure she was okay, but at the same time he was desperate to know if she'd learned anything useful. 'I heard Max say he hadn't met your father. You think he was telling the truth?'

She still didn't answer. He had the feeling she wasn't registering what he was saying.

She couldn't stay at the Marriott tonight, he realised. Not with Schenk running amok. He thought of ringing Collins to ask if he and his wife had a spare room they could let her use, but remembered the station chief's insistence on being kept out of play.

'Look, it won't be safe for you at the Marriott tonight.' He shot her a glance. She blinked. The first indication that she was hearing him. 'I'll find you some other hotel, okay? I'll ring round.' He began to think of the modalities, wishing he had a mobile with him. 'Or there's the *pension* where I'm staying,' he suggested cautiously. 'They may have a room free. If not you could use my bed. I'll sleep in a chair.' She blinked again. Then after a few moments' consideration nodded her assent.

Julie didn't look at him again during the rest of the time it took to drive back into central Vienna. Her eyes were wide open but they weren't seeing anything. Nothing except the black misery of knowing at last how abjectly she'd been used.

'Do you want to see a doctor?' Sam asked, suddenly fearing Schenk had done her some serious injury that he couldn't see.

She shook her head.

They turned onto the Ring. The Marriott loomed ahead.

'Give me your key card and I'll get your things.'

She didn't respond at first, her mind in turmoil.

'Julie? D'you have the key card?'

When at last she turned her puffy red face towards him, he flinched at the hurt he saw in her eyes.

'Give me your key card and I'll collect your things from the room,' he repeated.

She pointed to the blazer he was holding.

'In the pocket,' she whispered.

It took him a little over five minutes to pack her case and check with the front desk that the bill was being settled by Dr Max Schenk. Outside by the car again, the taxi driver took the suitcase from him and slipped it into the boot.

The Pension Kleist was unstaffed at night, which Sam was grateful for. Arriving with a bruised woman would have brought the police round. Inside the hotel, when they got into the small wood-panelled lift, Julie kept her eyes averted. Sam assumed she was blaming him for what had happened.

When they reached his room he asked her again about her readiness to make do with his bed. She nodded, then made straight for the bathroom. He heard a stifled sob as she saw for the first time what had happened to her face. When she emerged, her hairline was wet from the water she'd splashed on her swollen cheeks.

'This place doesn't run to minibars,' Sam apologised. He was in bad need of a drink and imagined she was too. He kicked himself for not raiding the fridge at the Marriott.

She ignored him, walking towards the bed. She slipped out of her shoes, then lay down on her side, pulling a pillow over her head.

Sam watched her shoulders begin to shake, telling himself it was good for her to cry. He sat on the edge of the bed, and put a hand on her arm, but withdrew it when she gave no sign of wanting it there. He got up, moved to the chair by the dressing table and flopped into it. It *had* been a good plan this evening, he told himself. The fact that it had gone wrong and produced nothing was bad luck. The same bad luck that had dogged his whole fucking life since the death of Harry Jackman.

Her handbag was on the end of the bed, together with the blazer she'd been wearing and the bits of equipment he'd retrieved from the tavern bedroom floor. To occupy himself, he began to reassemble the pieces. It wasn't long before he realised the back-up recorder was missing. He felt inside the jacket where it had been taped, running his fingers along the lining in case it had slipped. Eventually he found it and turned it over in his hands, examining it.

Julie seemed to be withdrawing further and further into herself. She had her knees tugged up and her arms wrapped round them. Sam was beginning to think she was making a meal of it. Turning a crisis into a drama.

Then, it dawned on him that her extreme distress could have been caused by something that had happened in the couple of minutes between Schenk ripping out the antenna and his bursting into the room. A couple of minutes' conversation he hadn't heard. He peered at the credit-card-sized recorder, trying to work out how to play it back. It was Malcolm who was the expert on the gear, and Malcolm was chasing Schenk's car. Turning it over, he found a socket for a headset and a cluster of tiny control buttons. He plugged in the phones from the Walkman and put them on. Then, holding the device under the dressing table light, he began prodding at the controls with the point of a pen.

It began to play. The first part of the recording was disjointed, the in-built, voice-activated mike only cutting in when words spoken in the Audi rose well above the background noise. Two minutes from the start of the replay they were at Stammersdorf. Car doors slamming. Schenk's steel-tipped heels on the pavement. Stilted, awkward words spoken. A hard edge to Schenk's voice, nervousness in Julie's. There was the noise of them entering the tavern, Julie pointing out a nook where they could sit in private. Then Schenk telling her to follow him. More footsteps, clumping on wooden stairs. Julie saying she wanted to sit in the *Stube*, Schenk telling her the room upstairs was paid for and the champagne chilled.

Then came the conversation Sam had already heard. He listened again to the way she'd led Schenk down the path that he'd asked her to pursue.

The slaps to her face when they came had a digital crispness, as did her cries for him to stop. He heard Schenk ripping into the blazer lining, the snap of the transmitter wire, the straining to pull the microphone from its cable.

'*Why you do this? Who is this for?*'

Another slap when she didn't answer.

'*You will tell me . . .*'

Julie gasped as Schenk did something unspeakable to her. She began to cry, then between gulps spat out her reply.

'*For me! It's for me, Max. I was going to blackmail you. For money . . .*'

Sam closed his eyes in admiration and humility. She could so easily have said that she'd been forced into it, but instead she'd covered up for him.

Two more smacks followed.

'*You greedy bitch.*' Schenk's voice was acid-edged. '*Greedy like your shit father . . .*'

The words hit like a punch to the stomach. Sam stopped breathing.

'*My father,*' Julie gasped. '*So you did . . .*'

'*Yes. Yes, it was your father who told me all about you.*'

Sam stared at the crumpled figure on the bed and understood her despair.

'*He gave you to me. You can have her, he said. I will help you get her.*'

Sam put his head in his hands.

'*You remember those conference papers?*' Schenk's relentless voice continued. '*You leave them in the restaurant when you have dinner with your father and Linda. After you go upstairs he comes looking for me in the bar and gives them to me. Play your cards right and she'll do a number for you, he said. His words, Julie. His own words. Your own pimp father.*'

'*No . . .*' she whimpered. '*This isn't true . . .*'

'He said you look for a new relationship. Something uncomplicated with an older man with money who will be nice to you. He tell me about your past affairs. All those useless young men. He tell me what you didn't like and what you did. He told me what interest you.'

'I don't believe you,' Julie moaned, but Sam could hear that she did. 'Why?' she howled. 'Why would he do that?'

'Business, Julie. As I just tell you. You and me, our relationship has always been business, nothing more. He . . . your father – I was buying something from him. His price was too high. I make him come lower, but not low enough. Then he say he will fix it for me to have you as my mistress. As part of the deal. Like the salesman gives you the sun-roof when you buy a car.'

'It's not true . . .' she repeated, so low Sam could barely hear.

'I didn't believe it also,' the Austrian answered in a bitter chuckle. 'I thought it was a joke. Or some trick and you were part of it. Then when we talk in the bar, I realise how innocent you are, Julie. So naïve. Everything he tell me about you was right. He made it so easy for me. You were so ready for someone like me. You remember how long it was before we went to your room? Forty minutes, Julie. Forty minutes after we first speak we have our first fuck.'

Sam bit his lip, willing her to have the strength to ask the vital question – what it was that Schenk had bought from Harry Jackman.

But a new sound began to swamp the recording. A thin, high howl like an animal in pain. The awfulness of what her father had done had broken through. Then came the clatter of a fight. Schenk firing off German expletives. More smacks. Grunts and stifled screams, then finally the crash of the door breaking in and Sam's voice shouting.

He pulled off the headset.

Julie *knows*.

She did now. Knew that the man who'd been her lover for the past twelve months had done business with her father. And something far worse than that – she'd learned the depths to which her father would sink to achieve his ends.

Sam looked up and let out the breath that he seemed to have been holding for ever. Julie had raised herself onto one elbow and was staring at him, her eyes blurs of bewilderment.

'Julie,' he croaked. 'I heard it, love. Heard it all.' He walked over to the bed and sat on the edge of it. 'I'm so sorry.'

Sorry. A useless word. Always inadequate. A word with no power to reveal the feelings behind it.

He tried to think of something to say which might ease the pain of discovering that the man she'd spent a lifetime trying to please had sold her like a bag of sweets. But, if such words existed, they weren't in his vocabulary.

Slowly and stiffly, Julie swung her legs round until she was sitting next to him. She turned to face him, her eyes begging for answers.

'Am I really worth so little, Sam?'

He took hold of her hand. It was feverishly hot.

'No, Julie. You're worth millions,' he told her. 'The whole fucking bank.'

He moved closer and touched his mouth against her swollen lips. She flinched from the pain, but hooked an arm round his neck, resting her forehead against his.

'Could you please turn the lights out,' she whispered. 'I'd prefer it if you can't see me.'

They sat without moving, digesting the thought of what was about to happen.

'I will,' he answered eventually, 'but you'll have to let go of me first.'

Reluctantly she uncurled her hand from the back of his head. He turned off the switch by the door, leaving the room bathed in the soft orange glow of the street light that was filtering through the net curtains.

When he returned to the bed she was lying on it. He knelt beside her and she took his hand and slipped it under her shirt.

'Will you show me, Sam? Show me what you think I'm worth?'

He leaned down and kissed her neck just below the mole that was half hidden by the lobe of her ear. Then as he freed her from her clothes piece by piece, he kissed the rest of her feverish body until it began to move and sway like a field of corn.

18

Vienna. Schwechat Airport
Friday, 09.00 hrs

A T VIENNA'S INTERNATIONAL airport the departure hall was seething. Sam stood to one side of the check-in desks, studying every face within pistol range as Julie presented her ticket. First thing, he'd switched her to an earlier flight from the one Schenk had booked her on. He was taking no chances. The last thing in the world he could allow to happen was for the killers who'd eliminated two of those who'd known about Jackman's sinister deal to turn it into a hat trick.

Julie's suitcase disappeared down the conveyor and she returned to Sam's side with her boarding pass in her hand and her handbag over her shoulder. Thick make-up covered her bruises. They walked without speaking towards the Departures sign. She'd been lost in thought that morning, hardly exchanging more than a dozen words with him. Just before the barrier, she stopped and touched his arm.

'There's something I want to say,' she whispered, turning to him. Her eyes were as dead as stone and stayed focused on the middle of his chest.

'Okay,' he replied. But nothing came. She seemed to be trying to pluck up the courage. 'What is it?'

She bit her lip. 'It's this. I'm glad that my father's dead.' She said it without any emotion. A statement of cold fact. Slowly she lifted her head and looked him in the eye. 'Glad because it means he can't betray me any more. And,' she added, letting out a long sigh, 'if the same thing were to happen to Max . . . I wouldn't mind at all.' One of her thin eyebrows lifted, then she turned away.

Sam swallowed uncomfortably. She was telling him that if he had after all orchestrated the death of her father and were to mete out the same treatment to Max Schenk, she would consider it a service to mankind. He reached out an arm, intending to put her straight, then decided there was little point.

Julie glanced towards the passport check. Although eager to get away from

Vienna, she was dreading saying goodbye to Sam. Having made him a part of her life last night, she had a horrible feeling he would lose interest in her now she'd delivered Max to him.

'I'd better go through.' She turned back to face him, taking hold of the hands that had caressed her back to sanity last night. 'Do you . . . d'you know when you'll be back in London?'

'No.'

She searched his eyes for some clue as to what he was thinking, but found nothing. The blank mask of a man who seldom gave anything away.

'Will I . . . will I see you again?' she asked plaintively.

'Would you like to?'

'What do *you* think . . . ?' She fingered the lapel of his jacket.

He kissed her mouth, careful to avoid the part of her lip that was split. 'Then you will,' he murmured.

'*Au revoir*, then.' She backed away.

'I'll ring you. Take care of yourself.'

Sam watched her disappear through the security barrier, then turned towards the exit doors. There was nothing more he could do to ensure her safety and he had to move on.

Earlier he'd phoned Collins to alert him to the fact that Schenk *had* done business with Jackman. The station chief would soon be at the Embassy, wanting a full rundown on last night before he contacted the Austrian authorities.

As he walked out towards the taxi rank, Sam was remembering the intensity of Julie's hunger for him last night. The first sexual climax when they'd joined their bodies had been quick for both of them, a cathartic release of the tension that had wound them as tight as clock springs. Later, after they'd sated themselves further, Julie had clung on as if he were the only thing in her life preventing her from sinking. They'd fallen asleep bodies touching, but she'd stirred many times in the night, crying out unintelligibly.

When they'd awoken this morning she'd been awkward with him, as if embarrassed at the weakness she'd shown in the face of Max's revelations. She'd used the bathroom first, spending a while fixing her face. Some time later, when Sam emerged from it after shaving, he'd caught her looking through his file on Günther Hoffmann, which he'd left in his suitcase. The lid had been open. She'd turned quickly away, pretending not to have seen anything and he hadn't pursued it.

It was obvious she hadn't wanted to talk this morning, so he'd turned the TV on, finding Sky News. The saga of the Albanian refugee family was continuing. The camera crew had followed them to Germany where they'd been received without much enthusiasm in some northern town whose name he didn't catch.

Outside the terminal there were half a dozen people queuing for taxis but no shortage of cars. He slipped onto the back seat of a cream Mercedes and gave the driver the Embassy's address in Jauresgasse.

Sam wasn't at all sure what to make of Julie. A part of him was a little in love with her, another part felt pity. What he *was* certain of was that their coitus last night had fulfilled him in a way that he hadn't experienced for some considerable time.

St Stephen's Hospital, Stepney, London
07.40 hrs

Considering that the ward had six empty beds in it, the night shift had been unusually busy for Sandra Willetts. It hadn't helped that she'd been bog-eyed from lack of sleep when she'd arrived for work twelve hours earlier, nor that two of the patients had developed chest pains which wouldn't respond to their angina medication. Now, just before handing over to the day shift, she'd finally managed to complete the toilet round.

The one good thing about being so busy was that it had left her little time to think. But as she sat in the ward office updating the patient notes and preparing for the handover to the day team, her worries about Rob began to bite again.

Twenty minutes later with the new shift settled in, Sandra pulled on her raincoat and set off for home. She'd heard the rain beating against the windows in the ward and was glad of the telescopic umbrella she kept in her bag. It was a seven-minute walk to the flat, against a trickle of bleary eyes coming the other way, people living on the estates heading for work. The people who had jobs, that is. It unnerved her that Rob had stayed unemployed for the last eighteen months. He could have found something if he'd tried, but it wasn't *any* job he wanted. It had to be back in the City, a high-rolling post that would let him look his old mates in the eye.

She and Rob were both East End kids. They'd known each other since school but only started going out three years ago, following a blind date. A good piece of matchmaking which, three months later, had seen her moving into his classy Docklands flat with its picture window views down the river.

She reached the foot of the grim tower that had replaced it as their home and had to wait a couple of minutes for the lift. When it came, a black girl emerged with three children under five. Sandra smiled wanly at her. Seeing the joyless struggle of most of the mothers in this block was putting her off having kids.

The door to the flat was double-locked, which meant Rob was out. She heaved a sigh of relief. She'd been dreading having to look him in the eye.

'Blimey!' she breathed when she got inside. The bed had been made. The place was tidy. His breakfast things had been washed up. Then she saw the note.

Her heart flipped as she picked it up from the small table in the kitchen, her instant thought being that he'd left her.

Out for the morning. Back 2ish.
Howsabout we go out for a pizza before your shift?
See ya. R.

She felt unbelievably relieved. He was making an effort. He wanted to communicate for once. Recently it had been down to her to engineer the occasional meaningful conversation.

A chance to talk.

Then a dreadful thought occurred to her. That his sudden wish to speak was because he'd found out she'd read his e-mail. Found out and wanted to sort her out for it.

HMS *Truculent.*

Commander Anthony Talbot read the new signal from London in the privacy of his cabin. They'd been given just under twelve hours in which to prepare and it would be no mean feat to achieve the deadline. The last time the submarine had trained for such a mission was six months ago and there was much brushing up to do. He looked at his watch. Twenty minutes to his Heads of Departments meeting in the wardroom when the responsibilities for the mission would be defined. But before that he needed to talk to the men. There was bitter resentment at the loss of shore leave and he needed to fire up the crew for the task ahead.

He walked the half-dozen paces to the control room where the First Lieutenant was in command, standing by the chart table. Hayes looked up expectantly.

'We're go for tonight,' Talbot told him. 'What's happening up top?'

They'd moved well to the west of Palagra island to use their communications mast. Now they were heading east again to continue their reconnaissance. But daylight was making it difficult for them.

'Looks like there's a sailing flotilla up ahead, sir. About a dozen yachts. I've altered course to the north to try to keep clear of them, but there are small boats all over the shop.'

'It's vital we're not detected,' Talbot reminded him unnecessarily. 'One of those craft could have our Russians on board.'

They'd detected no further activity on the island since spotting the powerboat leaving it last night. The radio channels the Russians had been using had remained silent.

'I'm going to do a pipe,' Talbot announced, stepping over to the command seat and unhooking the microphone that hung on a rack behind it.

'D'you hear there,' he began. 'This is the captain speaking. I have just received our new orders from the Ministry of Defence.'

Out of the corner of his eye he saw Arthur Harris emerge from the trials shack.

'As you know, the CTs recorded some VHF comms from the island of Palagra and one of the voices belonged to a Russian biological warfare specialist. Defence Intelligence in London thinks he may have set up a germ warfare factory on the island. With trouble brewing in Kosovo and with a heavy contingent of NATO forces in Bosnia, the commanders-in-chief are very concerned. If BW stocks are being produced on Palagra, then they're a potential threat to our servicemen and women.

'In just under twelve hours' time a special forces team will parachute into the sea about thirty miles west of the island. We will bring them back to the waters off Palagra and insert them some time in the early hours of tomorrow morning.

'That's a tight schedule. But understandably tight considering the nature of the threat being investigated. I realise we're all pretty rusty when it comes to this sort of op, so once the heads of department have been briefed, all the relevant sections of the crew will close up for training.

'The next twenty-four hours will be some of the most testing and challenging any of us have ever faced, gentlemen. But it's the sort of job we all joined the Navy for. I know you will all acquit yourselves brilliantly. And remember, if our efforts help prevent some Balkan madman murdering our troops, then we can be justly proud of the personal sacrifices we've all made to achieve it.

'That is all.'

The First Lieutenant nodded his approval. 'Well put, sir.'

Suddenly there was a shout from the watch officer at the search periscope.

'Surface contact bearing *that*. Looks like a small ferry.'

The bearing he indicated was to the west. Coming up behind them out of the haze.

Talbot took his decision. They had enough data on the island to furnish the marines with landing information. Continuing the observation in daylight in a tourist area was a mug's game. He touched the First Lieutenant on the arm.

'Take us to thirty metres and keep us out of trouble until sunset. We'll have time for a last recce in darkness before heading west for our RV with the special forces.'

Hayes nodded. 'Yes, sir.'

Arthur Harris watched the goings-on in the control room with an intense feeling of satisfaction. So much of his working life was spent sucking up trivia for others to analyse. This time he'd made things happen all by himself. But he felt anxious, and humbled too. As a result of what he'd done, other men would soon be risking their lives.

Vienna, the British Embassy

Patrick de Vere Collins's cratered face was anxious and solemn when he collected Sam from the embassy reception desk. He led him in silence up to the SIS suite which was separated from the rest of the diplomatic quarters by a door controlled by a swipe card.

'Malcolm tells me it all blew up on you last night,' he said, offering Sam a chair in his chronically untidy office. 'Hope to God the fallout's not going to blow my way.'

'You're safe enough,' Sam replied, 'thanks to Julie telling Schenk she was intending to blackmail him. Did Malcolm catch up with him?'

'Eventually. Your target fled Vienna and took off at a rate of knots to his family seat near Klagenfurt. That's at least four hours away. Malcolm's sleeping it off somewhere. Now . . . what *exactly* do you have on the man?'

Sam placed a plastic bag on Collins's desk. 'Here's the kit.' He put his hand in and extracted the recorder. 'This is the piece that matters.' He ran through in detail what it had picked up.

'Fascinating,' Collins muttered when he'd finished. 'I'll get a transcript done for my Austrian friends.' He frowned. 'What state's the poor girlie in today?'

'Recovering,' Sam told him. 'On her way back to London.'

'Safest place for her.' He rubbed his lumpy forehead. 'You think Schenk believed her story about the bugging device being for blackmail purposes?'

'Initially yes, but the sight of me turning up may have changed his mind for him. Which could be why he got out of Vienna in such a hurry.'

'Hmm. He didn't say *what* it was he bought from Jackman, I suppose?'

'Unfortunately not. Julie's questioning of him rather fell apart at that point.'

'Understandably.'

'But Max Schenk is a specialist in the mutation of viruses, Pat. The Russians were up to their necks in that type of research. It is utterly possible that Jackman's cargo contained viral material of some sort and that Schenk was the customer.'

'Oh we certainly can't ignore that possibility,' Collins replied cautiously, 'but it's still a hell of a hop, skip and jump to tie it in with the bug that hit those two EU officials in Brussels. And I'd have preferred something firmer to go on before trying to persuade my Austrian colleagues to pull the man in for questioning.'

Sam snorted with frustration. 'Well if they won't quiz him then *I* bloody will.'

'No you bloody won't,' Collins retorted. 'This is a sovereign country. We can't go around interrogating Austrian citizens. Have to use the proper channels, squire.' He tried in vain to flatten his haystack hair. 'But don't worry. They should bite. There's enough circumstantial stuff in Schenk's past to make them curious.'

'Meaning?'

'That the Security Police have been looking a bit further into his family background. They've found a strong tradition of Fascism there. Max's father Heinrich was an active anti-Semite. Served in the SS. When the Jews were driven out in 1938 he took possession of a couple of their houses – Julie told you this, you said.'

'Yes. Max volunteered it.'

'Well, what he didn't tell her was that the houses were stocked with significant works of art. The original owners perished in the gas chambers, so old Heinrich thought he was sitting pretty. But twenty years after the war, some Jewish relatives turned up to demand their property back. Old man Schenk managed to produce documents showing that the houses and their contents had been legally acquired and a court dismissed the relatives' claim. But the whole affair left a bit of a smell – and, once the paintings were sold, enough capital in the family coffers for Max and his brother Hans to set up one of the swishest clinics in the city.'

'Interesting.' Sam locked his hands together and flexed the joints. 'What do they know about Max's own politics? Any evidence that *he's* been involved in racism?'

'He's a member of the conservative Volkspartei, which doesn't mean much. Political organisations in Austria are like masonic lodges in Britain. People join for the sake of their businesses. And no – he's never done anything that's overtly racist.'

'What's known about his immediate family? His wife's called Cara.'

'And he has two children. She's from Croatia. Zagreb, they think. The link between her family and the Schenks is an old one, dating back to the Habsburgs when Croatia and the rest of Yugoslavia belonged to the Austro-Hungarian empire.' Collins flattened his hands on the desk. 'Look, let me have a word with my friends at the Interior Ministry. In the meantime use the link to Vauxhall Cross. Duncan Waddell's eager to talk to you.'

Sam was shown into the shielded communications room with its secure channels to SIS headquarters. Within a minute he was through to his controller.

'Take me through it, Sam.' Waddell sounded distant. Thoughtful.

Sam told him everything that had happened and everything that had been going through his head. When he'd finished there was a prolonged silence at the other end.

'You still there?' Sam checked.

'Very much so,' Waddell muttered. Then after a short further pause, he added, 'You know, what you're suggesting about the nature of Jackman's cargo is not altogether preposterous.'

Sam's eyebrows shot up. Waddell was usually deeply suspicious about hunches.

'I'll tell you a little story,' Waddell went on. 'It's about seafaring folk. One of Her Majesty's submarines has been bugging some Russians on a tiny island in the Adriatic. One of the voices picked up belonged to Igor Chursin, a senior scientist with VECTOR. The suspicion is he's been paid a wad of dosh to set up a biological warfare lab on this little piece of Adriatic rock.'

Sam sat bolt upright.

'Picture a map of that area,' Waddell went on.

'Doing that.'

'Then you'll quickly realise that from Rome, where Harry Jackman's famous shipment supposedly ended up, it's only a few hours' drive to the east coast of Italy. And only a short hop from there by powerboat to the islands of the Adriatic.'

'Indeed it is,' Sam purred. The pieces were falling into place.

'There is an investigation under way. Being run by Defence Intelligence. Their own spin on the BW lab – if that's what it proves to be – is that it could be producing germ stockpiles for one of the Balkan military factions. Serbs, presumably. The NATO military committee fears that if they have to put soldiers into Kosovo in the coming months, they could face attacks with anthrax and botulinum toxin.'

Sam scratched his head. This was a different scenario and not implausible. 'So what are the military doing about it?'

'The MoD is sending in the SBS to take a look.'

'When?'

'Tonight.'

Sam looked at his watch. 'There's something else you ought to know. Schenk's wife is Croatian.'

'Is she now . . . ?' There was a prolonged silence again. Then the sound of a deep sigh. 'You know, the trouble with "booties" is that they have a one-track mind,' Waddell mused, as if talking to himself. 'They'll be looking for whatever their military guvnors tell them to look for and nothing else.'

'Yes.' Sam's pulse was beginning to race.

'So from our point of view I think it might be wise if we sent someone with them. Someone who knew this Jackman case inside out. A bloke with his mind set on proving once and for all whether our little theories have any substance. Don't you think, Sam?'

'I couldn't agree more, Duncan.'

Another pause. Sam needed Waddell to come out with the idea that was in both their minds. As much as anything else in order to show that despite the PR disasters of the past week he was still on the team.

Waddell cleared his throat. 'Ever jumped out of an aeroplane, Sam?'

London
11.40 hrs

Rob Petrie left his ancient Ford Escort in a residential turning off the main north London shopping street of Golders Green Road. Slipping on the sunglasses and baseball cap which he'd worn in Southall, he walked past suburban houses until he reached the shops. In his right hand was the Tesco bag containing the second instalment of his contribution to the Lucifer Network's campaign for ethnic purity. It would be a day earlier than Peter had wanted, but circumstances dictated it.

When he'd come here two days ago to choose his target, being amongst these people had made his skin crawl and it was doing so again today. The sinister men with black felt hats and stringy beards, the dark eyed, ringleted children, the rectangular foreign script in the windows of the shops: he'd stepped into an alien culture which sat like a cancer in his own land, an inward-looking community that was a part of the great Zionist conspiracy. These were the faces of ZOG.

The door to a hairdresser's opened in front of him and a man stepped out dressed in a long, black satin frock-coat, the crown of his newly trimmed head covered by a skull-cap. He pulled up the aerial on a mobile phone and punched in a number as he hurried down the street. Petrie shivered with loathing.

The first thing he'd looked for on his recce on Wednesday were the video cameras the police had mounted on tall masts all over the capital. He'd seen two in the High Street up towards the tube and bus station, but down this end where the kosher delicatessens were, none was visible. Rob Petrie wore dark trousers and a light blue sports shirt. He kept his head low as he moved towards the target, the peak of the baseball cap pulled firmly down. He paused by the kerb to let a delivery van go past, then crossed the road towards a bagel bakery and a small shop called Treasures of Jerusalem, its windows full of Menorahs. The shopping centre was drab, a line of between-wars, redbrick commercial developments with flats above. A trading site that had been deprived of business in recent years by nearby shopping malls.

He slowed his pace to avoid attention. He was almost there. He glanced up at the sign – Segal's Kosher Restaurant. He'd noticed on Wednesday the first floor level had been popular at lunchtime, the tables by the windows the first to be occupied. Outside on the pavement was a rubbish bin lined with green plastic, five metres from the windows whose splinters would slice through the diners when the bomb went off.

Petrie faltered. Suddenly his nerve went. He felt a thousand eyes on him.

He marched on, needing to distance himself from the scene of his forthcoming act of war. The line of shops and restaurants ended at a public library. Outside it was a bench. Petrie sat on it, wedged the carrier bag between his feet and pulled out a newspaper. He pressed his ankles against the hard metal of the biscuit tin containing the killing device.

He stared at the tabloid's headlines, seeing them but not reading. He was conscious of a crocodile of primary school children chattering past, being ushered into the library by a pair of watchful teachers. He glanced up at their faces.

'Now remember to speak softly when inside, children,' he heard one of the teachers say. 'Libraries are places where people go for a bit of quiet.'

A quiet that would soon be shattered by his bomb. He looked at his watch. Five past twelve. The timer was set to detonate at a quarter to one. Although he had faith in the technology, having the device between his legs was making him uncomfortable.

His stomach fizzed and bubbled like a sulphur spring. If he didn't get it over with quickly he would shit himself. He stood up, stuffed the newspaper loosely into the top of the bag to make it look like rubbish, then walked back along the pavement and dumped it in the bin outside Segal's.

As he made his way back to his car he murmured. 'Enjoy your meal, Yids.'

Vienna

Before Sam left the Embassy, Collins got a positive response from the Austrian Security Police. Max Schenk would be interviewed as soon as he could be contacted, if he agreed to it.

'They say our suspicions are nowhere near strong enough to justify an arrest,' Collins explained.

'A mistake, in my view,' Sam muttered, his gut instinct telling him that Schenk needed to be detained as soon as possible, in a cell with thick iron bars. 'But it's better than nothing.'

He shook hands with Collins, leaving him with the task of finding out if the family of Schenk's wife happened to own a small island in the Adriatic.

He'd booked a seat on a 13.30 flight. A taxi took him to the Pension Kleist to collect his belongings. As he was stuffing his clothes into the suitcase, he suddenly remembered his promise to Fischer, the German intelligence officer who'd briefed him when he'd arrived. He picked up the phone and persuaded him to drive him to the airport so they could talk.

In the heat of the last twenty hours, he'd had no time to check on Günther Hoffmann's state of health. The old spy's heart attack was the first thing he mentioned when Fischer picked him up. The German expressed surprise.

'It is the first I hear. It must have been a false warning,' he suggested, cutting through a side street to join the main route out to the airport. 'Because I saw Herr Hoffmann yesterday afternoon and there was nothing wrong with him.'

'Really?' Sam was nonplussed. 'He contacted you?'

'Yes.'

'May I ask why?'

Fischer looked uncomfortable. 'He felt it advisable to report to me your visit.'

Sam bristled. 'Why, for God's sake?'

'Because of the murder of Vladimir Kovalenko,' Fischer continued stiffly. 'He said you had been asking for his help to find him.'

Sam stared through the windscreen. A tram was blocking the road in front of them.

'And he showed me an article in a British newspaper which linked your name with a situation in Africa,' Fischer went on, clearing his throat.

'The old bastard,' Sam grated. 'Don't tell me he actually suggested that *I'd* taken out Kovalenko?'

'He didn't exactly say it . . .'

'But it was the gist of his message.'

Fischer nodded.

Sam was flabbergasted. Why go to the trouble of sowing suspicion about him?

'For the record, my friend, my aim was to question Kovalenko, not kill him. I wasn't involved in his death or that of Harry Jackman in Zambia.'

'I am pleased to hear this.' The tension seemed to slip from the BfV man's shoulders. 'And your discussions with Herr Hoffmann?'

Sam described his meeting at the cemetery and their subsequent conversations.

When he'd finished, Fischer clucked his tongue. 'It is odd that Herr Hoffmann did not tell me his wife had died.'

'I get the feeling he's quite selective about what he does tell you,' Sam commented.

'Yes.' Fischer reflected. He pursed his lips for a moment before continuing. 'Oh, there is some more information about his career in the Stasi which came to me yesterday. It might interest you. You understand it has been a slow process to uncover the full story of the former GDR's state security activities.'

'Too many people with too much to lose.'

'Of course. But we have recently learned that for two years in the middle 1980s Herr Hoffmann was in control of the Stasi section which monitored Austria. The Czechs let the Stasi have a listening post in Bratislava. As you know, it is just across the border from Austria, only fifty kilometres from Vienna. From Bratislava they monitored the telephones of 270 Austrian politicians and businessmen.'

'No wonder he knew how to jump the housing list,' Sam remarked.

'Yes . . .' Fischer paused reflectively. The car turned off the autobahn onto the airport approach road. 'And because of this information I think it may be very possible that Herr Hoffmann has been more active in Vienna than I told you when we first met, Herr Packer,' he added with a degree of discomfort.

They pulled up outside the terminal. Sam thanked the German and ran inside, making the check-in just as they were closing the flight.

Was it spite, he wondered as he marched briskly to the gate? Hoffmann spreading suspicions about him as some sort of revenge for Sam uncovering his relationship with his father?

Later, as the plane taxied to the end of the runway, he opened the newspaper he'd picked up when he boarded. The story in the bottom right-hand corner leapt off the page at him.

DEATH OF A SCOTTISH MATA HARI.

With a heavy heart he began to read.

A statement from the Home Office late last night confirmed that Mrs Jo Coggan (née Macdonald), who died yesterday in a Scottish hospice had co-operated with Russian military intelligence in the early 1970s in an attempt to blackmail a British submariner into betraying his country. Her victim, Chief Petty Officer Trevor Packer, whose involvement with the Soviet Union was revealed yesterday, died in 1971. The Home Office statement said there was no evidence that any significant naval secrets were lost as a result of the activities of Mrs Coggan and CPO Packer.

Sam put the paper down and stared at the ceiling. So now it was official. His father had *not* betrayed his country. To see it there in black and white had come as a relief. But he felt sad for Jo Macdonald who'd hoped to die in obscurity. If it hadn't been for him digging up the past she'd have kept her shameful secret to the end.

North London

Inside the children's reading corner at Golders Green Public Library the two young teachers bustled round their brood, urging them to replace their books neatly on the shelves. It was time to get back. The children's lunchboxes were waiting for them in the classroom, lined up like soldiers along the back wall.

'Come along now.' The young teacher had fair hair tied into an old-fashioned ponytail and wore a red pullover above blue jeans. Her companion was darker haired and broad hipped.

They trooped out of the library and turned left.

'Keep away from the kerb, children,' the plumper teacher ordered, bringing up the rear of the crocodile. 'No straggling. Keep up with the ones in front.'

They were a tightly bunched little group as they passed Segal's. The blast from the wastebin bomb lifted most of the tiny bodies completely off their feet. A good half-dozen of them were fired like soft bullets through the plate glass windows of the restaurant.

It was mid-afternoon when Rob Petrie closed the garage door with the Escort safely inside. He'd been sick a couple of times after hearing the report on the radio, throwing up into a spare shopping bag lying on the floor at the back of the car. According to an ambulance service spokesman, one of the little girls from St Mary's Roman Catholic Primary School had been sliced in two by a jagged shard of glass. The children had taken the full force of the blast, cushioning its effects on the diners. The Jews he'd intended to kill had sustained cuts and shock, but eight of the children were dead.

He carried his bag of sick to the rubbish skips behind the lift shafts. He needed to hide. To bury his head and pretend it hadn't happened. How he could face Sandra he didn't know, but home was the only place he could go.

He pressed for the lift and waited. He'd told himself that in a war, accidents happened. That you had to turn your back and move on. But he'd seen those kids. Remembered their faces as they walked into the library. Eight little lives snuffed out.

He'd had his war now. He knew he couldn't go through this again. It would be down to others to take up the fight.

The lift came. As he raised his finger to the button he heard a shout, then running feet. His heart began to race but it was only a kid wanting him to hold the door. A black girl, fourteen, fifteen. White teeth, big lips, woven hair, wearing the navy skirt and sweatshirt of a school uniform. She lugged a small rucksack, heavy with books.

'Thanks, mister,' she whispered, fingering the button for the sixth.

Petrie pressed himself back against the wall and held his breath. A week ago he might have imagined the kid naked and spread out for him, bound with ropes, but today she was something to fear. She was a part of the enemy that would want its revenge.

'Thanks, mister,' she repeated as she stepped out.

On his own landing, the sound of children's voices wafted up from the playground below. He clutched the rail and gagged again, but there was nothing left to come up. Recovering, he reached his door, put his key in the lock and turned it.

As he stepped across the threshold he sensed all was not well. The door to the living room was closed, which it never was. Very quietly he shut the front door behind him, listening.

Suddenly a large man in body armour stepped out of the kitchen, pointing a pistol at his head.

'Don't move, Rob. Not so much as a fucking eyebrow.'

19

RAF Lyneham, Wiltshire
Friday, 16.30 hrs

THE HANGAR SMELLED of kerosene. At the far end two Hercules transports stood like lowering beasts, their engines stripped to their innards. The eight men from No.2 Special Boat Section stood just inside the huge folding doors which were open the width of a truck. Identically dressed in black rollnecks, with trousers tucked into thick socks, some were crouching, all were concentrating as they checked the kit laid out neatly on the floor. There was a lot of it. The four largest waterproof canisters contained the inflatable boats and their outboard engines. Four smaller bags were for weapons and four for special clothing.

Sam stepped out of the Land Rover that had brought him from the front gate and walked into the hangar. Bennett's girl had met him at Heathrow with clothes to change into from his suit – dark trousers, a blue sweatshirt, pullover and trainers. The marines turned to look at him, their faces solemn and expressionless. None wore rank insignia, making it impossible for Sam to tell which was the lieutenant in charge. He was about to ask when a short, ginger-haired man in his mid-twenties stepped forward.

'Mr Packer? I'm Willie Phipps.'

'Hello. Glad to meet you. Sam's the name.'

He felt the pale blue eyes size him up, knowing full well how reluctant the SBS would have been to include an untested stranger in their mission.

'You made good time,' Phipps remarked. 'We've just finished checking the gear. In fact, once we've got you sorted, we'll be ready to roll – that's if the RAF can get their act together. When was your last jump?'

'Eight or nine years ago. Before I left the Navy.'

'And never into the sea.'

''Fraid not.'

The lieutenant sucked his teeth. 'In that case we'd better do some talking.' He took Sam to one side to introduce him to his kit. 'Immersion dry suit.' He held up a drab green one-piece with thick waterproof zips and soft rubber seals at neck and wrists. 'We don't put them on until fifteen minutes before the drop, otherwise it gets like a sauna inside. You'd better try it for size.'

Sam forced his feet down the legs and tugged at the zips until the neck seal fitted snugly across his throat.

'Could have been made for you,' Phipps commented briskly. He picked up a short plastic tube attached to a strap. 'Cyalume,' he explained. 'Fix this to your wrist. If we lose you in the oggin, snap the tube and it'll glow like a beacon.' Sam was familiar with the chemical lights from his service days. The lieutenant handed him a lifejacket, then, when he had it in place, helped him on with the parachute harness and adjusted the straps. 'We'll be on a static line, so the chute'll open automatically. Never fails. If it does, you've got your reserve,' he added drily, clipping it across Sam's middle. 'We'll be jumping low, so be ready to yank the ring damned fast if the main chute doesn't deploy. Soon as you're sure it's open, ditch the reserve, otherwise the weight of it'll sink you when you hit the water. Use your torch to see when you're about to get wet feet and release the main harness immediately. Same problem as the reserve. Get rid of it fast or it'll drag you down with the canopy on top of you. You'll sink several metres anyway because of your own body weight, but the lifejacket's self-inflating and will pull you back up.' He handed Sam a nose clip. 'Happy so far?'

Sam had never been less so, but he nodded.

'The met men say it'll be as dark as a cow's insides tonight,' Phipps continued. 'No moon and one hundred per cent cloud, so no stars either. If you don't see anyone else near you in the water, stay put. We'll find you. Shout from time to time. The submarine will be watching on thermal. They should have a Gemini ready to pick us up and tow the gear alongside. Glad you joined?'

'Scared to death.'

'So am I. You'd have been lying if you'd said anything else. One final piece of kit.' He handed Sam a small metal canister with a line attached. 'Underwater beacon. Clip it to the ring on your lifejacket. If you really think you're lost and the world's forgotten about you, turn the switch to the green, unwind the line and let it dangle beneath you. The sub will get a bearing on it.'

They turned at the sound of a diesel engine and watched a grey, covered lorry reverse into the hangar.

'Okay, boys,' the lieutenant said, rubbing his hands, 'we're on our way.'

Rob Petrie stared at the grubby red carpet in the boxy living room. He'd been back a couple of hours, but the police hadn't told him how they'd found out about him. Not told him anything. He knew it was to do with Sandra. She'd been acting oddly with him for a couple of days. Withdrawn. Uncommunicative. Suspicious and hostile. As if she'd got wind of what he was involved in. He'd guessed she'd read his computer files somehow. He hadn't seen her since he arrived home, but could hear her voice in the kitchen. The police had mugs of tea which she'd made after letting the bastards in.

Four of them were in the small living room. Three men – one in uniform – and a woman who'd only arrived twenty minutes ago and who had a quiet authority the others lacked. The armed policemen weren't visible any more. He guessed it was their voices he could hear talking with Sandra. The computer was on in the corner, a young officer with steel glasses operating the keyboard as if it was a natural extension of his fingers. One by one they'd dug out every e-mail he'd ever sent or received in the past few months. All the items he'd thought were deleted. All the secrets he thought he'd buried for ever.

They'd also taken his keys so they could remove the Escort from the garage and pull it apart. By now they would have found the third bundle of explosives and detonators the Lucifer Network had provided. And they'd taken all his clothes away for forensic tests, ignoring his request for a blanket or a towel. He sat on the sofa naked, his hands cuffed behind his back.

A few minutes ago someone had brought in a video tape to show him – the Golders Green massacre as filmed by the London Fire Brigade. Vile scenes, so horrific they would never be shown on TV. It was true about the little girl who'd been cut in half by glass. Seeing the bloodied bits had made Rob throw up again, retching onto his knees until they brought a bucket. But he still told them nothing.

A detective chief inspector from Southall CID had been firing questions about the bombs – where he'd got the explosives from, who his contacts were, how many people were involved with him? But Rob had told them nothing.

They'd browbeaten and insulted him, calling him arsehole and scrote. Shown him the e-mails telling the whole story of his relationship with

'Peter'. The different names used. The string of addresses to prevent tracing. The encryption keys. It was all there. Where to go to pick up the bomb kits. His message describing the targets he'd selected. The reports of mission accomplished and the congratulations. Everything they needed to put him away for life. But he still wouldn't talk. However much he regretted Golders Green, he consoled himself with the knowledge that mistakes were made in the most professional of conflicts. A battle had been lost, but the war would go on. He himself had fallen, but others in the Network wouldn't. Not while 'Peter' still functioned as leader of the white revolution that was now firmly under way in Europe.

'Tell us about him, Rob. It might go in your favour,' the DCI from Southall urged, struggling to curb his exasperation.

Petrie kept his eyes averted and his expression blank. Then the woman officer who'd been hovering by the computer screen moved directly in front of him. He didn't look up, but felt his privates shrink under her contemptuous glare.

'You've never met Peter, have you, Rob?'

It was the first time he'd heard her speak. He closed his eyes as if bored.

'You don't even know what country he's from, do you?' To Stephanie Watson the e-mails had made it as clear as day.

It was true. Petrie knew precious little about the man, except that he had the power to inspire.

'Did you two ever discuss using germs to kill people?'

Her question surprised him. He'd seen the story in the morning papers about the two Brussels officials hit by a brain virus, but hadn't made the connection. The fact that she'd asked him suggested they thought the Lucifer Network was behind that too. It excited him to think the people he'd been involved with had such resources and he was tempted to say 'yes'. To rub her nose in the fact that she was up against an enemy of substance.

'You didn't know what you were getting into, did you, Rob?' There was a softer edge to her voice, now. Not quite pity, but close to it. 'Liked what you read on the Internet and just went along with it. Yes?'

There was an element of truth in what she'd said. He'd never envisioned being responsible for what had happened at Golders Green.

'All a bit of a game to you.'

Game? He bristled at the word, but it made him think. Yes, he'd got a buzz from taking part. From being involved.

'Then it went wrong.'

It had today. Horribly.

'You never meant to kill those kids, we know that.'

No. But Jews, yes. He *had* meant to kill them. Wanted them dead. Wanted his London cleaned of the ZOG.

'So . . . Tell us about it. Get it off your chest.'

Stephanie looked down at the lumpen, deflated figure in front of her. She found his nakedness and his spew-smeared thighs revolting. The broad shoulders were fleshy rather than muscular and had dark hairs sprouting from them. He'd been a turn-on once, according to the woman in the kitchen who'd loved him. Cocky, confident and well paid. Now the sullen cropped head with its putty nose looked as if it had come straight off the hooligan end of a football ground. A thug. A creature from the arse-end of humanity. He lifted his face to look her coldly in the eye and she knew there was no soft spot in this man. She turned away and nodded to the detective from Southall. *All yours*, she indicated.

'You know, Rob, your girlfriend says you've lost it,' the man goaded, his mouth twisting with frustration. 'Says that limp apology for a sex organ that you're hiding between your thighs – you can't get it up any more. Not with her, anyway.' He paused to let the insult take effect. 'Going with fellers now, are you?'

Petrie flinched. The extent of Sandra's betrayal of him was something he would never have imagined possible. Only days ago she'd told him she loved him and would support him through thick and thin.

'Hitler was a fairy, you know,' the detective sneered. 'That what you're trying to be? Fucking Adolf Hitler?'

Petrie smiled. If only . . .

The detective snorted in disgust.

'Know what happens in prison to toerags like you? They'll give you a cell with a nigger. He'll have a knob as big as a baseball bat and fists the size of frozen chickens. You'll be all shit and blood before you've had your first slop out. Your own mother won't recognise you. Not that a bastard like you's ever had a mother.'

Rob felt a ripple of fear. He'd never thought about what prison would be like.

Suddenly the CID man turned to the uniformed officer guarding the door.

'Get a track suit on him for fuck's sake and take him out of here. The smell's getting to me.'

Stephanie had stepped back to her position behind the wizard at the computer. She folded her arms as Petrie was led from the room.

'Waste of fucking breath,' the Southall man fumed, after Petrie was gone.

'Yes, but everything we need's on that hard drive,' Stephanie told him.

'Open and shut,' the DCI agreed.

'However, I would like a blackout on the arrest,' she told him firmly.

The Southall man got to his feet, hands on hips. He had an Asian community to pacify. 'Why's that?'

'Because if we tell the whole world we've nailed the bomber, we'll never hear from Peter again. Leave it twenty-four hours and there's a chance of another e-mail.'

'Why bother? We've more than enough for a conviction,' the detective insisted, sourly. This was *his* investigation. To him Special Branch were snooty elitists.

'Sure. *Petrie* will go down,' Stephanie agreed, 'but what about the bloke who's pulling the strings? He's the one we've got to nail.'

'What makes you think he'll send another message?'

'Because Petrie's owed one. You've read the e-mail he sent last night?'

'Moaning about how his girlfriend's become suspicious of him?'

'That's the one.'

The detective scratched his chin. 'Odd show of weakness, don't you think? Why would he tell Peter about it?'

Stephanie pushed a hand through her straight brown hair, then retrieved the relevant message from the sheaf of printouts next to the PC. She re-read it, trying to think of a sensible answer. There was something almost plaintive about it. *Don't know what's come over her . . . Always been loyal before . . . As if she's got wind of it . . . Can't think how . . . Never given any hint . . .* Almost as if seeking guidance from his mentor.

'I suppose Peter was the only bloke in the world he could talk to about it,' she concluded. 'His only friend. And even a loner needs one sometimes.'

New Scotland Yard
19.55 hrs

Two hours later, Stephanie Watson sat in the Fraud Squad's Computer Crime Unit at Scotland Yard, watching while the hard disk from Rob Petrie's PC was examined file by file. As she'd expected, there'd been a certain amount of pornography scattered across it, the random pickings of a man who'd let his curiosity have its way on the World Wide Web. Petrie had a catholic taste, she'd noted. There'd been a selection of well-hung erect males amongst the heterosexual and girl-on-girl images.

Slowly, item by item, the specialists in this section of SO6 would build up a detailed history of Rob Petrie's obsession with white supremacy. Already they'd identified half a dozen white power sites that he'd frequented. The analyst working on the drive was the same bespectacled civilian who'd made the initial exploration of the computer at the Stepney flat. He'd volunteered to work through the night in an effort to find a clue to Peter's identity.

Stephanie realised there was little she could do except wait for the results of the analysis. As soon as anything significant turned up she would get a call.

As she made her way back to the sixteenth floor, it was an earlier phone conversation that kept going round in her head. Sam had called. He was back in England, but on his way to some place that he couldn't talk about. He'd explained how little Miss Jackman had made up for her earlier misbehaviour, and then sketched out his suspicion of a link between Harry Jackman's so-called 'red mercury' and the Brussels virus. It worried her that he seemed to have little firm evidence for his suspicion.

The conversation had done two things for Stephanie. It had reminded her how pig ignorant she was about viruses in general and it had made her intensely curious to have another look at Julie Jackman.

As soon as she reached her office she put in a call to the St Michael's Hospital virology centre which she knew was working round the clock.

St Michael's Hospital
20.45 hrs

Julie Jackman was alone in the laboratory, continuing the tests begun by her colleagues earlier in the day when the latest blood serum, stool and saliva samples had arrived from Brussels. She'd volunteered to carry on until midnight, despite feeling numb and exhausted after Vienna. The near certainty that the virus could only be passed on through broken skin meant that work on the samples could be done at a low level of containment. No need for the plastic suits with hoods and respirators and sealed Level 4 cabinets with their remote handling mechanisms.

Laboratories in four European countries were co-operating in the race to isolate the virus and to develop an antidote. She sat at her bench, a white coat over her slacks and shirt, injecting enzymes into tubes containing serum and viral antigen. Research would accelerate if one of the patients died, yielding up brain tissue packed with the virus.

Julie was glad to be back at the lab, needing the distraction of it. The discovery of the way her father had used her was still eating at her soul. Sam's lovemaking had brought her back from the brink, but the feeling of worthlessness that Max's revelations had filled her with could best be countered with work, she'd decided.

There'd been two letters waiting in Acton when she'd got back to the flat at midday, both from tabloids offering five-figure sums for her story. She'd lit a match and burned them. Later in the afternoon when she arrived at the lab, Ailsa Mackinley had handed her a sheaf of phone messages. Most were from the media, which Julie had dumped in the bin, but one was from her St John's Wood confidante Rosemary. Yes, she wanted to talk to her again, but not for a few days. She needed to get her head straight first.

Sam had told her he would ring. That they would see each other again. And in her heart she badly wanted that. Since making love, her longing for him was strong, but her head was still full of uncertainties. She wanted a soul mate, not just a lover. Someone to be open with. Sam had a life boxed into compartments, most of which would stay closed to her.

She kept telling herself to stop thinking about him. That the chances were he wouldn't even contact her again. But she hoped he would, and very soon. Because there was something she needed to tell him. Something about what she'd seen in that hotel room of his in Vienna.

Suddenly she sensed she wasn't alone any more. She looked up. Professor Norton was watching from the doorway. He pulled a tense smile and walked over to the bench, clasping and unclasping his hands.

'There's someone here,' he told her. 'She wants to talk to you.'

Julie tensed, suspecting some media type had broken through the professor's defences.

'From Special Branch,' he explained. 'A Detective Chief Inspector Watson. She says you know her.'

Julie guessed it was the woman who'd questioned her at Paddington Green along with Denise Corby.

'I'm in the middle of this assay at the moment,' she protested.

'Then it can wait until you've finished pipetting. I'll tell her.'

Julie blinked. 'D'you know what she wants?'

'To understand more about viruses, she says.'

'You're the expert, professor.'

'I've filled her in on the basics, but she's asked to see how the tests are done.'

Julie shrugged. 'Well, all right.'

'I'll bring her along in a few minutes. I've told her not to touch anything.'

Julie bent her head back to her work, loading and injecting the multi-pipette until all the tubes were full. As she dropped the last of the used nozzles into the wastebin, the policewoman walked in.

Julie pulled off her thin rubber gloves and discarded them, deliberately ignoring her. She wasn't ready to forget the hard time the two women had given her at Paddington Green.

'Hello again.' Stephanie reached out a hand, then withdrew it, remembering the warning not to touch. 'I'm sorry to disturb your work.'

Julie noted the humbler tone this time, but wasn't reassured. 'What is it you want?' she asked.

'First, to say that I'm aware of what you went through in Vienna, Julie. I've spoken with Sam.'

'Oh.' Julie was taken aback. She felt herself colouring, wondering exactly how much Sam had revealed.

'Secondly, I wanted to say that as an investigating officer on this case we're very grateful for the help you gave the authorities in Vienna.'

Authorities . . . Yes, she realised. That's what Sam was. 'Yes, well . . .' Julie felt utterly wrong-footed. She'd expected a slap on the face and was getting a pat on the back.

'And apart from that,' Steph continued, 'I'm keen to understand the processes you go through to track down a virus.'

'Yes. Well I suppose it's a little like detective work,' Julie gabbled, relieved to be getting away from personal matters. 'How much do you know about viruses already?'

'The professor's been blinding me with science,' Stephanie smiled. 'But it'd be best if you imagined you were explaining things to a four-year-old.'

'Okay. Well . . . viruses are extremely small, that's the first problem. One hundredth the size of bacteria. Some are visible on the electron microscope, but many are too small even for that. And they come in different shapes. So, when we start our search for a virus whose effects we don't recognise, it's worse than a needle in a haystack, because we don't even know what the needle looks like.'

A sparkle had come into Julie's eyes which made Steph understand exactly why Sam had gone for her. From her coy reaction when she'd mentioned his name she guessed that they'd slept together.

'In a case like this,' Julie went on, 'we start by studying the defences the body puts up to fight the infection. That way we hope to narrow it down to a particular family of viruses. There are various tests we can do . . .' She indicated the array of tiny tubes which she'd just filled. 'These I've just started on. Excuse me a moment.' She pulled on a fresh pair of gloves, picked up the samples, placed them in a covered tray and set it on the vortexer so the contents would mix. After a few seconds she removed it and pushed it into a temperature-controlled cabinet. 'The assays are kept at body heat and in a couple of hours we'll have a set of results which may or may not get us any closer to the mystery.'

'Professor Norton mentioned something about growing the virus.'

'That's right. On tissue samples from rhesus monkey kidneys or human embryos. Aborted foetuses, in other words.'

Stephanie recoiled.

'I know. It's not a nice thought to be working with jars full of dead babies, but you get used to it.'

'You'd have to,' Stephanie murmured. 'So, if you manage to grow the virus, you can identify it under the microscope? Oh, no. You said some are too small.'

'That's right. We look under the light microscope for any changes to the cells. That shows us the virus is there, even if we can't see the virus itself. We isolate its nucleic acid and use PCR – polymerase chain reaction – to multiply it.'

'I'm sorry. You've lost me.'

'I'll go back a step. Viruses are tiny pieces of genetic material – DNA or RNA – that are programmed to do one thing and one thing only, which is to replicate themselves. They can only do that inside the cells of plants or animals. And each different type of virus is programmed to seek out a different type of cell in which to multiply. As I said, the shapes vary. Some are round with knobs on, others are like tiny threads. The rhabdoviruses – and that's what we think this is – are normally rod shaped. Like little bullets. The problem with the Brussels virus is that it seems to have been modified. It behaves like rabies, but may look very different.'

'Like a terrorist dressed as a nun,' Steph suggested.

'Exactly. The disguise carries it swiftly to the target cells in the brain, then it sheds its outer shell before dividing and multiplying and finding more cells to take over.'

'Sounds like viruses want to conquer the world.'

'That's the nightmare. That one day some new virus will emerge, cross from animals into human beings and rip through an unprotected population.'

'Like Marburg and Ebola might have done if they hadn't been contained.'

'Precisely.' Julie shuddered at the thought that her own father and the man who'd been her lover for the past twelve months might have been involved in such horrors.

Stephanie watched Julie's face closely. She was coming across very differently from the silly, out-of-her-depth creature she'd interviewed three days ago. And her calm explanations had given no hint of the horrors she'd been through twenty-four hours earlier. Steph noted the swelling to her lip.

'How're you feeling?' she asked, gently. 'I mean, inside.'

Suddenly Julie became tearful. The dreadfulness of what had happened twenty-four hours ago came back in a rush. She shook her head and looked down.

'I'm sorry. Shouldn't have asked.' Steph touched her arm. 'You're a brave girl.'

'You'd better wash,' Julie whispered quickly. She pointed to the sink by the door. 'The risk of picking anything up from my coat is minimal, but the professor would kill me if I didn't make you do it.'

Stephanie crossed to the basin and washed her hands with soap.

Julie went with her. 'I'd better get on. There's a lot more I have to do.'

'Of course.' Stephanie dried her hands. She sensed Julie wanted to ask her something. 'You've been so helpful. Is there anything I can do for *you*?' she checked.

Julie shook the hair back from her face. 'You said you'd spoken to Sam . . .'

'Yes.'

'He's here in London?'

'I don't know where he is. It was on the phone.'

'Ah.'

Steph saw the disappointment on her face and guessed it was because Sam hadn't rung *her*. 'You wanted to talk to him again?'

'There's something I need to tell him. Quite urgently.'

Steph had a good idea what it was. She wondered whether to warn the girl about her old friend. To tell her that plenty of other women had fallen for the rogue, then been ditched for the sin of trying to get too close to him.

None of her business, she decided.

'Will you be talking to him again soon?' Julie asked.

'Quite possibly. If I do, I'll ask him to call you.'

'Thanks. It is quite important.'

Love always is, thought Steph, stepping back into the corridor.

On board RAF C130 Papa Victor Zulu Golf

There was a smell of hot oil inside the back of the Hercules, which was doing nothing for Sam's stomach. The aircraft had dropped below the cloud layer, flying a thousand feet above the ink-black water and descending steadily, hammering through the turbulent air like a jeep over potholes.

They had their full kit on, ready for the drop. The headphoned dispatcher, a blonde woman in shapeless overalls but passably good looking, held up a hand with fingers for five minutes. The voice in her ears said the cockpit had contact with HMS *Truculent*. Lieutenant Willie Phipps sat next to Sam on the webbing seats along the edge of the huge cargo space, part of which was taken up with extra fuel tanks so the aircraft could return to the UK without landing. Phipps turned and mouthed 'All right?' Sam nodded, grim-jawed, glad of the deafening noise, which prevented the possibility of speech. He was as nervous as a kitten.

When the dispatcher signalled two minutes, the rear ramp clunked its latches and began to open, swirling cold air into the cavernous cabin. Sam and the marines stood up. Two crewmen released the tie-downs on the pallets holding the marines' kit, then the drop team lined up behind the gear. Sam clipped his parachute release line onto the overhead wire and clamped on his nose clip. As he sucked in air through his mouth, he tried to close his mind to what was about to happen. There were men in front to follow and men behind to push him if he froze. The plane bucked and wallowed, threatening to knock them all off their feet. Phipps gestured for them to crouch.

One minute to go. Sixty excruciating seconds, each a lifetime long. It didn't help knowing that the hard cases he was wedged between were also plagued by fear. No matter how many times you did this, the risks were the same. Their lives would be hanging by threads.

Red on.

They stood again, hands grasping the man in front. Sam's heart hammered. Beyond was a big square void.

Green on.

'Go!' A yell split his ears, whether from behind or from his own throat he didn't know. The pallets rolled and were gone. Then one man, two, three. A jab in his back and the slipstream hit him. Cold air that took his breath away. Then the bang of the harness opening. He hung from his straps. The reserve chute clung to his stomach like a fat blister. His lifesaver if anything went wrong, but it had to go now the main canopy was open. He pulled the release and felt it fall away.

The night was as black as death. Not a speck of light. He'd forgotten to count. Phipps had said ten. Sam shone the torch down, searching for a reflection off the waves.

Six, seven, eight . . . Breath held, hand on harness release. The water hit as soon as he saw it. He yanked at the D-ring and felt the harness let go of his crutch. Then he went down beneath the water. It felt like for ever. At last, with a hiss, the lifejacket cuddled his neck.

Thirteen, fourteen, fifteen . . . An eternity of gurgling ears, then air suddenly. He could breathe again, but not see. He flinched, anticipating a wave pounding down.

A light came on. Beside his head. The lamp on the lifejacket, reliable as paint drying. Enough light to show a gentle swell. Waves of no consequence. He turned his head. Wherever he looked, more lights twinkling. Like fairy dust. A couple of the men had cracked the cyalume tubes too.

'Sam?' A shout off to his left where several lights were grouping together.

'Here!'

'Okay?'

'Yep.'

He checked he was free of the canopy lines, then swam towards the voices. They were further off than he'd thought and progress with the lifejacket was slow. After a few minutes, a pencil of light reached out from the darkness, sweeping across them, pausing when it picked out a figure in the water. HMS *Truculent* had surfaced close by. Sam looked away to preserve his night vision and kept swimming.

As he neared the cluster of bodies, he saw that something was wrong. Five of them together, a daisy chain round one man at the centre who wasn't moving.

Lieutenant Willie Phipps held up a waterproof radio, telling the submarine of their casualty.

'Hit by something . . . Unconscious . . .' The lap of the water broke into his flow of words. He acknowledged Sam with a nod.

'Stick close. The submarine's coming over. Don't get anywhere near the stern. Those propulsors can chop up torpedoes.'

The submarine doused its spotlight. Sam looked towards the vessel and saw the flicker of torchlight on the casing.

'They don't have a Gemini out, but there'll be a diver to help you,' Phipps told him. 'There'll be a scrambling net to get onto the casing. Look after yourself, okay? I'm busy.'

'No problem.'

The submarine switched on a deck light so they could see it more easily. It had stopped some fifty metres away. Sam struck out. He saw water splash as a diver from the boat jumped in to help.

The man waved an arm. 'Over here!'

Sam reached him.

'You the civvy?'

'Does it show?'

'Not what I meant. You're on your own, that's all. Follow me to the casing. Feel for the net with your hand.'

'Thanks.' Sam banged against the hull, scrabbling along its smooth surface until he touched the thick rope of the net. He jammed his toes in and struggled to raise himself from the water. His limbs were like lead. Hands reached down and pulled him up onto the casing.

'Welcome on board, sir. Name, please?' asked a brisk, efficient sailor in white rollneck, clutching a clipboard.

Sam gave it.

'Straight down below please, sir.'

A hand took his elbow and guided him firmly to an open hatch. He felt an updraught of warm air, the stale warship smell that he'd once known so well. A CPO met him at the bottom and helped him remove his dry suit.

'Any injuries or immediate needs?'

'Yes to the second. A stiff drink.'

The chief smiled. 'There's hot tea in the senior rates' mess. The lad here'll show you down below. The bomb shop's been cleared for you.'

Sam nodded at a young sailor with spots on his chin and a label on his chest that said Griffiths.

'We're hot bunking to make room for you lot,' the youth complained as he led Sam down the companionway. 'We had a full complement already.'

'Sorry to inconvenience you,' Sam muttered.

In the chiefs' mess a mug was pressed into his hands and he gulped the tea gratefully while the rating waited outside for him to finish. When Sam rejoined him in the passageway leading forward, he seemed eager to make it clear that he hadn't been complaining.

'I didn't mean it were an inconvenience having you on board,' Griffiths explained awkwardly as they reached the ladder down to the weapons storage compartment. 'Most interesting thing that's happened all trip. You okay now, sir? Got to go for the others.'

'Fine. Thanks.'

Sam looked round at the packed stowage area. In his years in the Navy he'd never served in a submarine. He noted the bunk pallets fixed onto empty torpedo racks, but knew there'd be no time for sleeping.

Over the next fifteen minutes the rest of the landing party gathered. There was little chat amongst the marines, just the clipped grunts of men used to working closely together.

Last down was Lieutenant Willie Phipps, stepping off the bottom rung as the pipe announced they were diving again.

'That's a bugger,' he murmured. 'Macko was our linguist. Fluent Russian and Serbo-whatsit.'

'How is he?' Sam asked.

'Severe concussion, by the look of it. The MO's got him in the sick bay. How's your Russian?'

'Not good enough.'

'Then I'd better ask if there's anyone on board who can come ashore with us.'

'When do we go?'

'In about two hours.'

They heard footsteps on the ladder and turned to see a lieutenant commander's epaulettes emerge below the hatch.

'Everybody comfy?' the First Lieutenant asked as he reached the bottom. He had a folder clutched under his arm.

'Like pigs in shit,' growled a voice from the back.

Hayes grinned. 'Okay. Happy for me to brief you now?'

'Sooner the better,' Phipps told him.

'Fine.' Hayes set his folder down on one of the boxes where the GCHQ team stored their tapes. 'We're currently about thirty miles west of Palagra,' he explained, opening a chart of the Lastovski Channel. 'We'll be in position to surface again in about ninety minutes.' He pointed to a circle on the chart. 'There's only one easy way onto the island as far as we can see.' He spread out a small-scale plan that had been faxed from London. 'A natural inlet at the eastern end, sheltered from the northwesterlies. The rest of the coastline is rocks and cliffs about ten metres high with thick scrub on top.'

'When we left Lyneham, the intelligence picture was like a fog in the Channel,' Willie Phipps interjected. 'All they said was the island's *supposed* to be uninhabited. Nothing about what's on it.'

'We can do better than that now. The place used to be lived on by monks, until Tito's communists turfed them out so the big man could use their monastery as a guest house for his cronies. When Yugoslavia broke up, the place was reclaimed by the Church, but, strangely enough, they couldn't find any young men wanting to shut themselves away there. So they leased the building to an Austrian religious foundation as a retreat.'

'*Austrian* foundation,' Sam repeated, his interest sharpening. 'D'you have a name for it?'

'Sorry. Nothing more than that.'

'The monastery's the only building on the island?' Phipps asked.

'There's one other house, occupied by a Croatian family. They run goats and chickens and have a few patches of maize, peaches and vegetables. Used to supply food to Tito's guests when they were in residence, and when they weren't, they'd look after the place for him.'

'How many bods on the farm?'

'Don't know. A "family" is all it says on the signal.'

'Okay. So tell us about the Russians?'

'The CTs picked up four different voices. There may be more. Our assumption is they've been occupying the monastery. And not for a prayer meeting. The last transmission monitored suggested panic. Something had gone badly wrong and a manhunt was under way on the island.'

'But they may have all left,' Phipps prompted. 'A boat was seen leaving?'

'That's right. A cluster of people on board. Hard to tell numbers. At least four, maximum six. We'll show you the video.' He pointed beyond the line of gleaming torpedo tube hatches where a small monitor and video player had been set up.

'No police or Croatian armed forces on the island?' Phipps queried.

'We don't think so. There's no reason for them to be there.'

'And what's the met picture?'

'Cloud cover may break up after midnight Zulu – London time. If it does there's a moon.'

'A new moon, thankfully,' Phipps told him. 'Not so bad.' Total darkness suited them best because their night vision gear was brilliant. 'One thing . . . That casualty of ours – Macko – he was our linguist. We'd like a Russian and Serb/Croat speaker with us if possible. Anybody on board who could fill in?'

'Will he have to swim?'

'No. We'll carry him on our backs if he can tell us what we're listening to.'

Hayes scratched his chin. 'I could try the CT who identified the voice of Igor Chursin. He'd be ideal if I can persuade him.'

'Good.'

'He's racked at the moment, but coming on watch in an hour or so. I'll give him a shake when we've finished our briefing.'

'Fine. Let's have a look at your pictures.'

Martin Hayes crouched in front of the recorder as the SBS team bunched closer to the screen.

'Okay. These first shots are of the boat seen leaving the island.'

Sam peered over the heads of the marines. A modern glass–fibre utility boat, with a forward wheelhouse and cabin and a long open stern section for passengers or goods. Ideal as a work boat for someone running a covert laboratory. Two figures visible behind the wheelhouse windows, with more on the open deck.

'As you can see, an accurate head count is hard.' There was a grunt of affirmation from Phipps. 'The next bit of tape is our circumnavigation of the island. I'll speed through. You'll soon get the message. Pretty unapproachable because of the cliffs and dense woodland. You could get ashore that way, but it'd take an age.'

The marines' eyes drilled the screen. 'Can you see any of the buildings from the sea?' one of them asked.

'Nope. The trees are too tall.' The First Lieutenant cleared his throat. 'And now we're back at the inlet.' He slowed the tape to normal speed.

'I've done some hard-copy printouts which you can study at your leisure. As you can see, there's what looks like a quay there. Perhaps "quay" is too generous. It's rocks cemented together.'

'Freeze it, could you?' Phipps spread his fingers and thumb and measured the image on the screen. He estimated fifteen or twenty metres of landing space. 'When was this taken?'

'Twenty-four hours ago.'

'There's a family living at the farm, you said?'

'Yes, but I've no idea how current or sound that piece of intelligence is,' Hayes cautioned.

'If they're still there, they're bound to have a boat too, that's all,' Phipps added ruminatively.

'Out fishing?' Hayes suggested. 'Or gone across to Lastovo for supplies. Probably find it back there when we arrive.'

'How close can you take us?'

'Half a mile at a pinch.'

Sam looked at his watch. A quarter to eleven Zulu. Nearly one in the morning local. Ninety minutes until they neared the island. Fifteen minutes to get the boats loaded and off the casing once they'd surfaced. Two hours ashore at the most before the approach of daylight forced them to withdraw.

'It's essential the submarine stays undetected,' Hayes told them, 'and that *you* do too. NATO does not want to find itself at war because of this operation. Weapons for self-defence only. Absolute last resort. If we have to leave you ashore overnight to prevent detection of the submarine, then so be it. We'll collect you the following night. Or else you could become tourists and make your own way back.'

The thought of being stranded in the Adriatic horrified Sam. His instinct was to be back in Vienna as soon as he could, snapping at the heels of Max Schenk. As the briefing continued he detached his mind from it. Phipps and the First Lieutenant were on to technicalities – communications frequencies and procedures for every balls-up imaginable.

Sam perched on the edge of a bunk pallet watching the faces of the marines, his unease growing. They were a tight-knit group of men, all under thirty. Single-minded and with a clear agenda, but one that was different from his own. *Their* mission was to look for signs of biological weapons being prepared for use against NATO troops, but their priority was to remain unseen. They'd keep their distance. Observe from afar, as they were trained to do. *His* need was to gather the sort of hard evidence that might only be found by taking the place apart. He wanted tangible proof that this rock was where Harry Jackman's shipment had ended up. And confirmation that what had been produced here was now being used by European racists. To get it could well mean becoming very visible indeed. It might even come down to sticking guns in the Russians' mouths to encourage them to talk.

And unless he could persuade them otherwise, the men he was travelling with would do all in their power to stop him.

Stockholm
After midnight

Twelve hundred miles to the north of where HMS *Truculent* was making her preparations, a Saab 900 drove through a western suburb of Stockholm. The vehicle was stolen and so were its plates.

Although the centre of the Swedish capital stayed abuzz until late on a Friday night, out here, where many immigrant families had settled close to one another for support, the streets were empty after midnight and the apartment windows for the most part dark.

The history-loving schoolteacher behind the wheel wore a long, brown wig over his straight, fair hair, and heavy-framed spectacles without any lenses in them. It was a cold, wet night in eastern Sweden, justifying the parka he'd put on. He drove slowly through a bleak, run-down commercial centre, scanning shopfronts. Buildings of three floors – business premises at street level, with apartments above.

It didn't take him long to spot the doner kebab house on the opposite side of the road that he'd checked out a couple of days before. He slowed the car and glanced up at the apartments. To his relief, the windows were in darkness or curtained. No one to see him. He stopped a little way down the road.

He'd thought about this moment for days, doubting he would dare go through with it. *I wait to know that you are not a coward.* The words of the e-mail had lingered in his mind like a stain. He wasn't brave by nature. But on this issue he was determined. Determined that something had to be done to stop the contamination of Europe by the dispossessed from other lands.

He swung the car in a U-turn and drove slowly back to the takeaway, stopping outside. He pulled the parka's hood over his head, then got out. From the boot he removed a sledgehammer, a Molotov cocktail and a can of petrol, hurrying them over to the shop before he could change his mind.

He unscrewed the lid, lit the rag in the half-filled bottle with a Zippo, then swung the hammer at the glass, shattering it easily. Snatching up the bomb, he hurled it down on the stone floor inside. Flames splattered as the petrol/sugar mix spread, licking up the legs of the handful of chairs and tables. He slung the petrol can after it, then ran for the car as flames leapt up behind him.

Foot hard down on the accelerator, he put some streets between himself and the scene of his crime. Then, fearing a heart attack if he didn't calm down, the schoolteacher slowed the car. Concentrating, he drove carefully so as not to draw attention to himself, his mind reliving every moment of what he'd just done.

Eventually he spoke. Not to himself, although anyone watching would have thought so, but to the man who called himself Simon, a man whose face he'd never seen.

'You see, comrade? I did it. I am not a coward. And I *am* with you.'

20

HMS *Truculent*
Saturday, 01.40 hrs Zulu

COMMANDER ANTHONY TALBOT sat glued to the attack periscope monitor as the marines made their preparations on the casing aft of the fin. He had a deepening sense of dread about the mission.

The monochrome thermal images were crisp and clear, the men's warm faces and hands showing up white. Bulky in their kit, the ten marines were grouped round the Geminis, inflating them with compressed air from bottles and attaching the silenced outboards to the transoms. Beyond them, where the casing slipped into the sea, the submarine's rudder swung slowly from one side to the other like the tail of a basking whale. Standing a little apart from the SBS men, looking ill at ease, were the two 'passengers' on the mission, Sam Packer and Arthur Harris. It hadn't taken much to persuade the CT to step in as translator, but Talbot knew he'd be more scared now than at any time in his life.

His misgivings concerned the other man, however. Harris was military and would obey the lieutenant's orders, but Packer was a civilian, and a shady character judging by the press summary that had been included in the last broadcast from Northwood. It wasn't at all clear why the man had been sent. No explanation from London except 'security reasons'. But whatever they were, the man had his own agenda, which meant the mission had split aims, something naval commanders were trained to avoid.

The periscope swung away as the watch officer scanned the sea around them. Fishing boats were what Talbot feared most. If there was a danger of being discovered by one inside Croatian territorial waters then he would have to abort.

Lieutenant Harvey Styles aligned the periscope sight with the Palagra shoreline and cranked up the magnification to check the landing inlet again. The work boat they'd seen leaving a day ago was back at the jetty. They'd expected to spot a second vessel there, belonging to the family who farmed on the island, but there was no sign of it.

He switched back to wide-angle and focused on the casing again. Drum tight and loaded with their kit, the inflatables were being shoved towards the edge ready for the off. As the control room watched the monitors, two of the men unzipped their dry suits to urinate, their warm flow creating a white arc against the darker background.

'One for the album, sir,' Styles commented before swinging the scope away for another all-round look.

Standing next to the captain, a young signaller had been monitoring the VHF from the landing party. Suddenly he began hopping like an electric toy. 'Signal from Sunray, sir. They're ready for off.'

Outside, the night was black, the cloud cover not yet broken. Good SBS weather.

'Fine.' Talbot stood up. 'Shut and clip the engine room hatch. Clear the bridge. Officer of the watch, come below, shut and clip the upper lid.'

A few seconds later his order was acknowledged.

'Bridge cleared. Conning tower upper lid shut and clipped. Engine room hatch shut and clipped.'

'Ship control. Open one and four main vents.'

'One and four main vents open, sir!'

Air roared from the ballast tanks. On the monitor they saw a blow of spray from the outlet in front of the rudder. Slowly, as the submarine settled, the sea began to wash over the casing. Catching a surge, the SBS launched their wallowing craft into the water and flung themselves on board, yanking the outboards into life. Both Geminis swung their bows away and began to motor.

As Talbot watched them go he crossed his fingers behind his back.

'God bless,' he murmured.

The drum-tight tubes smacked gently against the waves. There was a light wind from the north-west. Sam crouched on the floor of the inflatable, gripping a webbing strap. A holstered Browning pistol pressed heavily against his thigh. The sound from the silenced engine was a burble, which Phipps had assured him would be inaudible from the shore. Above, breaks in the cloud were just beginning to appear, leaking light from the new moon, just enough for him to make out the vague shape of the other boat twenty metres to their left. Arthur Harris sat stiff-backed between two squat marines.

Willie Phipps lay in the bows of Sam's boat, a monocular thermal imager on his head that gave him the look of a Cyclops. They were making straight for the harbour. No alternative if they were to get on and off the island fast. With the naked eye Sam could make out little of the shore. He realised they were getting near when the marines cut the engines and began to paddle.

They rowed a few strokes, then drifted. Rowed a few more, then paused to listen.

Suddenly a shot rang out. It chilled their blood and flattened them to the neoprene. Then two more. Heavy bangs echoing briefly through the pines that crowned the island. Not the supersonic crack of bullets aimed at them, they realised with relief, but some act of violence being perpetrated in the middle of the island.

Safety catches clicked. The soldiers scanned the shoreline through the night sights of their MP5s.

Then came a sound which stopped their breath. A scream, splitting the night – a wail more animal than human. Three more shots followed, silencing it.

'Fuck . . .' A low expletive from somewhere in the Gemini.

They drifted, listening and watching, then Phipps ordered them to don respirators and gave the signal to paddle again. In close to the low cliffs, they hugged the shore for the cover it gave them, inching towards the inlet and the jetty. As they closed with it, they saw a wooden landing stage grafted on at the end of the stone pier where the work boat was moored.

As the marines secured the painters to a ladder and scuttled ashore, Willie Phipps reached back and put a hand on Sam's arm.

'You and Chief Harris wait in the boats. I want people around me who know what they're doing.'

'Okay, but not for long,' Sam cautioned. 'I've a job to do too.'

'I know. We'll check what the fuck's going on here and come back for you.'

With that, the lieutenant joined his men on the jetty. The sky had cleared further, giving enough light for Sam to see a couple of the soldiers conceal themselves amongst the rocks. The rest went with Phipps, heading silently up the stone track that led inland.

A light swell rolled into the anchorage, causing the rubber boats to nudge against one another. Arthur Harris was just inches away from him.

'What d'you think?' the CT asked, his voice nasal with nerves beneath the rubber of the respirator. The scream they'd heard had been a woman's voice.

'Sounds like they're killing people,' Sam answered inadequately, trying to stifle a worry that events might prevent Phipps from coming back for him.

Harris's breath was coming in short, uneven bursts. 'I've not done this sort of thing before.'

'Everybody's scared,' Sam assured him. 'But these boys know their business. Just do what they tell you.'

'I realise that.' Harris fell silent again, but Sam could tell there was more. 'I simply wanted to say that if you see me not reacting right, or doing something stupid, then tell me. Okay?'

'No problem.'

As the minutes passed, they didn't speak again. There was no more shooting, but at one point they heard voices, too far away to make out the words or the language. Finally, after an age, Willie Phipps reappeared, his rubber soles moving silently over the stones.

'Quick!' he hissed, pulling them onto the jetty.

'Tell me,' Sam growled, frustrated at having been out of the loop.

'This is plague island, by the look of it.' Phipps kept his voice low as he led them up the hill. 'Whatever these witches were brewing, they seem to have screwed up. At the old monastery there's a guy in a respirator removing stuff from the building and stacking it for a bonfire.'

Sam cursed. 'We've got to stop him, Willie. That's evidence he's destroying.'

Phipps paused and put a hand on Sam's shoulder. Then he pressed the mouthpiece of his respirator close to his ear.

'We can't stop anybody doing anything, Sam. Understand that. My orders are to stay covert. If these jokers are shutting the place down, that's fine by NATO. It'll save the cost of a Tomahawk. Intervention by us, in any way, means a change of rules.'

'Well bloody call London on your satcoms and get them changed,' Sam snapped, despairing at the thought that proof of Harry Jackman's connection with Palagra might go up in smoke at any moment.

'I've called already . . .'

'And?'

'I called because of what's going on at the farmhouse,' Phipps explained, reluctant to elaborate.

'Go on.'

'They're sick bastards,' he said eventually. 'Two arseholes with AKs and wearing respirators have shot dead the couple who live there. Two lads, teenagers – could be the couple's sons – are being forced to dig a pit to bury them in. Fucking animals!'

They both knew what would happen to the boys when the digging was done.

'We asked Command if we could intervene and the answer was no,' Phipps added bitterly.

'Remaining undetected matters more than the lives of two Croatians.'

'That's the implication.'

Sam swore under his breath. 'Willie, we're supposed to be finding out what's been happening on this rock.'

'*Observing* what's happening. That's the key word.'

'But if we let them burn the evidence, we'll never know.'

'I hear what you say. But I'm paid to obey orders. And for as long as you're with me and my men so are you, Sam.'

They began to move and Phipps warned that they shouldn't talk any more. The track narrowed into a natural gully between outcrops of rock. They were getting close.

Sam decided the MoD's rule book was going to have to be bypassed. He hung back a little, then pulled Arthur Harris close to him.

'Whatever happens, stick to me like glue, Arthur. I'll watch your back.'

The answering grunt from beneath the mask was noncommittal.

Soon they heard the rumble of a generator up ahead and saw the soft glow of lights. Two more shots rang out, off to their right. They dropped to a crouch, sickened at the thought of two young men slumping forward into the hole they'd dug, their blood mingling with their parents'.

Arthur Harris tasted vomit in his throat. It was the closest he'd ever come to the act of death. Despite the supportive words from the SIS man, he was far from sure he could handle what was happening here. He'd thought of saying so, down by the boats, but knew that if he'd refused to leave the safety of the harbour, he would never be able to look Navy men in the eyes again. Swallowing for all he was worth, he watched Willie Phipps press a hand to his radio earpiece as a report came in from one of his squad.

Sam edged forward to where Phipps was crouching.

'They've done it, the bastards,' the marine muttered softly. 'Killed them. Why? That's what I want to know.'

'The answer'll be at the monastery,' Sam growled, his respirator nudging the other's ear. 'On that bonfire.'

Phipps half turned to him. 'You bloody stick to the rules, Sam.'

Sam nodded. He'd stick to them all right. His own. Only one thing mattered to him – learning the secrets of that building before they went up in smoke.

They moved to the crest of a rise, using trees as cover. The one-time monastery stood fifty paces away, its white walls glowing eerily in the moonlit blackness. It had a pitched, tiled roof and shuttered windows. The upper floor was in darkness, but at ground level, double doors stood open and lights were on inside. From behind the building they heard the sound of breaking wood.

Phipps led them to some bushes from where they could see into the yard at the back, a space protected from the northerly winds by a high wall. Light spilled from the rear of the house. A bonfire stack had been built of old wooden bed frames. Books, papers and bedding were strewn beneath the timbers, ready to be ignited. But whoever had done it was inside the monastery again.

They flattened themselves to the ground. Sam sensed other marines were near, but couldn't see them.

A man in a respirator emerged from the house, his arms full of cardboard boxes. Tall and thin, he wore a grubby white coat. He tipped the boxes onto the stack, then pulled a cigarette lighter from his pocket.

'Willie . . .' Sam mouthed, desperate to get the marine on his side. 'Your rules are fucking *wrong*.'

The lieutenant didn't reply at first. Sam could almost hear the clicks of the calculations going on in his brain.

'We *can* go overt,' Phipps whispered, as if talking to himself, 'if something happens that puts our lives in danger . . .'

Sam swallowed. He'd got the message. It was down to him. He turned to Arthur Harris. 'Come on, chum. We've got work to do.' He jerked the reluctant translator to his feet. Phipps made no effort to stop him.

Harris felt a protest rise in his throat, but it stuck somewhere behind his teeth. He stumbled after Sam like a lemming.

The man in the white coat looked up in horror at their sudden emergence from the darkness. He thrust his spare hand into a pocket as if going for a gun.

Sam already had the Browning out of its holster and levelled it at his chest.

'Stop!'

His yell was muffled by the rubber of his respirator. The man saw the pistol and froze.

'Put that flame out! Tell him, Arthur. Translate, for Pete's sake.'

Harris tried, but his breathless Russian was inaudible beneath the mask.

'Louder,' Sam hissed. 'It's what you bloody came for, man.'

Harris filled his lungs and released a stream of invective. But instead of stopping the lab man in his tracks it galvanised him into action. Ignoring the threat of being shot, he tossed the lighted Zippo into the base of the stack then whipped out a VHF handset from his pocket, shouting into it in Russian.

Seeing that things were about to get dangerously out of hand, Willie Phipps sprang forward, his MP5 pointing like a bee sting. The Russian stared at them, eyes like whirlpools behind the lenses of his mask. Then, suicidally, he began to move towards them, his arms spread wide in an effort to block their advance for long enough for the flames to take hold.

Phipps swung the gun against the side of the man's head and felled him. Then Sam threw himself at the fire, pulling away the bed-frame timbers before their ends had a chance to light. He kicked at the papers burning at the base, but it was too late. The blaze had caught.

'Shit!' He leapt back to prevent his dry suit catching fire.

Suddenly there was the sharp crack of a bullet by his ear and he flinched. He saw a puff of dust from the monastery wall behind him where it had thwacked into the stucco.

'Down!' Phipps yelled, swinging round to face the way they'd come. The shot was from beyond where the marines lay hidden. Sam flattened himself next to Arthur Harris as more rounds smacked overhead. Beyond the scrub he could see muzzle flashes in the darkness as two men hurled themselves towards the monastery, firing wildly.

Phipps opened up with the submachine-gun, prompting a fusillade from the marines in the bushes. The gunmen fell. A couple of the soldiers emerged from cover to check the men were disabled. They stood over the bodies and loosed off rounds to finish them off. Sam sensed their relief at doing what they'd wanted to do at the farmhouse ten minutes before.

Behind him the bonfire crackled and spat as the flames spread across its base. He heard the ping of glass exploding. Bottles and vials from the lab, he guessed. Vital evidence going up in smoke. He scrambled to his feet to attack it again, pulling whatever he could from the flames. The heat was intense, the blaze now fuelled by bed sheets and blankets. He grabbed a piece of bed frame as a probe, trying to beat out the conflagration, but the heat defeated him.

'Water,' he murmured, spinning round in the vain hope of seeing a convenient hose. There was nothing, and searching the place would waste precious time. He'd saved what he could from the flames. What mattered now was the information inside the Russian's head.

Harris still lay motionless on the ground, his hands over his ears. Sam tapped him on the shoulder.

'It's okay. The war's over.'

Harris scrambled to his feet, relieved that he'd survived his baptism of fire.

'Make this fuckwit talk to us, Arthur.'

Eager to take charge again, Willie Phipps wrenched the Russian's hands behind his back and secured them with nylon ties. 'Let's see what's inside this creep's head,' he snarled, pulling the prisoner to his knees and pressing the gun barrel into the back of his neck. A couple of his soldiers ran past, their belts heavy with grenades. They flattened themselves against the outside wall of the monastery, one each side of the open door, then swung inside, searching with their guns.

Harris began his questions. The responses were muted. Pretence of ignorance, whines of complaint. The Russian was playing for time.

'You're getting up my nose, scrote,' snapped Phipps. He grabbed the man's respirator, as if to pull it off.

The Russian writhed and pleaded.

'He's begging you not to take that off,' Harris translated.

'You don't say . . .'

'Says he'll co-operate.'

'Then he'd better be quick.'

Harris repeated his questions, listened to the responses, then probed further. For a couple of minutes the Russian talked, his words now punctuated by gulps of shock.

'There's a biology lab inside the house,' Harris confirmed eventually. 'Set up over a year ago. He says they've been experimenting with viruses. Several kinds. Smallpox was the main one.'

'*Smallpox?*' Sam interjected. 'Not rabies?'

'Hasn't mentioned it,' said Harris quickly, not wanting to lose the thread of his translation. 'There were three of them running the lab. All Russians, all ex-VECTOR. Igor Chursin was in charge. His number two was Yuri Akimov – not a name known to me, but it's likely they'll have heard of him at Cheltenham. And this fellow's called Sasha Koslov. He's the lab assistant. The two men you just shot are Croats. Security guards. The word he used to describe them was pretty contemptuous. Translates roughly as "pond life".'

'Okay, but what happened here?' Sam pressed. 'Why the carnage at the farmhouse?'

Harris questioned some more. Koslov seemed reluctant to answer.

'He's muttering something about an escape,' Harris explained. 'Being evasive. Doesn't want to talk about it.'

'Tosser!' growled Willie Phipps, wrapping a big, square hand round the Russian's filter and wrenching it upwards. The rubber mask separated from the man's skin with a sweaty, sucking sound. Koslov squirmed and writhed, trying to push his face back into it. His pinioned hands tore uselessly at their ties. He pressed his lips shut and flattened his nostrils, his eyes swelling with the strain of holding his breath.

'Let's have a look at your miserable, evil little face,' Sam murmured, twisting the man's apoplectic visage towards the light of the fire. Broad forehead, Slavic eyes popping from their sockets. Muted squeals from the throat.

'Whasthat you're saying? Speak up.' Sam turned to Harris. 'Smallpox'll make a terrible mess of his looks before it kills him. Tell him, Arthur. Then ask him about the escape again.'

When Harris repeated the question, the reddening face nodded frantically, eyes pleading for the mask to be restored.

Phipps pushed it back down, easing the rubber over the man's chin and checking the seal on his neck. The Russian sucked in great gasps of filtered air before speaking again.

As he talked, Willie Phipps met Sam's look. They'd reached the same conclusion. For Koslov to be so terrified of exposure, the air around them had to be a soup of infection. They glanced at the bonfire and nodded to one another. The most lethal stuff could well be on it. Putting distance between themselves and the flames made sense. But as they prepared to move, Harris held up a hand.

'Hang on. He's describing the escape.'

Sam listened hard. His knowledge of Russian was rusty but he understood Koslov to be talking about a 'boy'.

'My God.' Harris sounded shaken by what he was hearing. 'They used human guinea pigs to test their vaccines.' His voice was flat. 'It was the Croats' job to keep the lab supplied.' He pointed to the men on the ground a few feet away. 'Says that when Chursin and Akimov needed someone to experiment on, the Croats took the boat to Split or Dubrovnik to look for people sleeping rough. Refugees – Bosnians, Kosovans. Or druggies. They'd kidnap them, bring them here and keep them chained up while trying out new viruses on them – the word he's using is "mutated" viruses. I don't know what that means exactly.'

Sam knew precisely what it meant. And he knew of an Austrian doctor who was an expert on the subject.

'The main aim of the research was to develop antidotes,' Harris continued. 'Most of their vaccines didn't work, so the people died.'

'How many, for God's sake?' Sam asked.

'He thinks around thirty over the past year. He says the people themselves were rubbish. Refugees. Nobody missed them.'

'Except their mums,' Phipps suggested.

'What about the escape?' Sam prodded.

'It was a few days ago. One of the prisoners had been infected with a new smallpox variant. He says it's a strain which the world's stock of vaccine can't touch.'

'And they lost him?'

'Yes.'

'Jesus . . .'

The man was a walking timebomb.

'By the time they'd discovered he was missing the boy had got to the farm and taken the farmer's daughter hostage. The girl was mentally backward, Koslov says. The boy took her off in the farmer's boat. To Lastovo, they think – they assumed he was heading for the ferry to the mainland. Chursin, Akimov and a couple of the Croats went over to Lastovo to look for him, but there was no sign. Chursin panicked. He feared the boy would contact the police and the game would be up. So he sent the Croats back with this man, with orders for the lab to be burned and the farmer and his family to be killed. All trace of what they'd been doing here to be removed or destroyed. That's it. That's what he said.'

'And a vaccine for this new smallpox?' Sam demanded. 'They'd developed one?'

Harris checked. The Russian shrugged again.

'That's what they were testing on the boy. He says find him and we'll know if it works.'

'Christ,' Sam whistled. 'If it doesn't, we've got a lunatic wandering around infecting people with an untreatable plague.' He posed the most crucial question of all. 'Who were they doing this for, Arthur?'

Harris asked the Russian, but the man just shrugged. His own confidence growing, Harris himself threatened to remove the man's mask and throw it into the fire. But the answer remained the same.

'He says he doesn't know,' Harris translated. 'Chursin never told him.' Phipps grabbed at the mask again, but Harris put out a hand to stop him. 'No. I really think he's telling the truth.'

'Course he bloody knows . . .' Phipps insisted. He clamped his hands round the Russian's neck and squeezed. 'See if a lack of air helps him remember.'

There were two more key questions Sam still wanted answers to. The rabies-like virus used against the two EU officials in Brussels – had it been produced here? And had a Mr Harry Jackman supplied the scientists with their raw materials?

He decided to wait a moment before asking them. To see if the onset of suffocation would persuade the man to name his employers.

They watched for some sign of a readiness to co-operate, but all they saw through the steaming up lenses of his mask was some unexplained horror in his eyes. Eyes which stared past them, looking at a point high up on the wall of the old monastery.

Sam suddenly understood. But too late. As the warning yell took shape in his lungs, the head that Willie Phipps was so forcefully gripping burst apart like a rotten fruit. He twisted his face away in horror, catching a glimpse of smoke at the upstairs window from where the shot had been fired.

Sam's stomach rebelled but he managed to swallow back the vomit before it filled the mouthpiece of his mask. Harris scrabbled frenetically across the stony ground, desperate to get away from the appalling sight of the Russian's brains spread across Willie Phipps's torso. Ignoring the gore, the lieutenant raised the MP5 and loosed off rounds towards the monastery window.

Sam flung himself sideways, rolling away from the line of fire, then got to his knees to run for cover. Arthur Harris was nowhere to be seen. He darted for the corner of the monastery, crouched, looked again and saw the translator lying prostrate a few feet away, his hands clamped to his head.

'Arthur!' Sam shouted. 'Over here! Quick!'

But Harris didn't move. There was blood oozing through his fingers.

'Jesus . . .'

Sam peered out from the shelter of the wall. From the upstairs window came the thunder of a grenade. As suddenly as the shooting had started, it came to an end. There was a gruff shout from inside the building.

'Secure!'

Sam ran over to the translator and dropped to his knees.

'Arthur . . .'

Harris didn't move.

'Shit!' In the firelight he could see two wounds. The back of the head and the shoulder. 'Willie!'

Phipps joined him, wiping off the Russian's brains with a fistful of dry grass. He bent to listen, to see if Harris was still breathing. Mouth to mouth would be impossible with the masks on.

'Dressings,' he breathed. 'Pouch on my belt.'

As Sam tugged at the Velcro flap, Phipps lifted Harris's hands from his head.

'Bad?' Sam asked, peeling the wrapper from a dressing.

'Can't tell. But anything to the head's bad.' He took the sterile wad and pressed it on the wound. 'Rip his suit open at the shoulder while I tie this on. Got a knife?'

'No.'

'There's one strapped to my ankle.'

Sam found it and cut the blood-clogged, rubberised cloth away from Harris's shoulder. 'Flesh wound,' he announced.

'Then he may have been lucky. Know how to do it?'

'Yes.' He opened another pack, and pressed the dressing on hard.

'Have to get him to the surgeon,' Phipps mumbled.

They both looked up as one of the soldiers dropped down beside them.

'The building's clear, boss.'

'Who *was* that fucker?'

'Some Croat with a name with no vowels in it. Found a driving licence in his pocket.'

'How come you missed him?'

'Hadn't cleared that far, boss. Simple as that. We'd checked downstairs first. We were on the way upstairs when he opened up. Sorry.'

Phipps slipped fingers under Harris's respirator to feel for the carotid pulse.

'Still there,' he whispered.

Sam stared helplessly at the translator. That head wound needed a specialist. And they were a long way from any. He visualised a wife and kids for Harris. Elderly parents. The whole damn agony of grief.

Phipps stood up and detailed three of his men to get Harris to the jetty. 'Take one of the boats back to the sub. Tell 'em the rest of us'll be out of here in twenty minutes.' Then he strode towards the house.

Sam followed a few paces behind, shaken that Harris had been hit – he'd told the man he'd watch his back. But he told himself not to dwell on it. There was still work to do.

The former monastery was L-shaped, a main block with a long extension at one side. As Sam stepped through the door he found a high-ceilinged hall running from front to back, its floor taken up by refectory tables with benches for a couple of dozen people. One of the tables was stacked with supplies – drinking water in plastic bottles, boxes of tinned food. Another had been used for work. A laptop computer sat with its screen up and Sam recognised the bulky black box beside it as a satellite phone. He made a mental note to take the PC with him.

Willie Phipps was being briefed by one of his sergeants. Sam listened in.

'Upstairs in the wing, two rooms used as bedrooms, three others empty. Downstairs two rooms are laboratories, three others are like cells. Bare beds and fixings in the walls with chains attached.'

'What's in the labs?' Sam asked.

'Loads of equipment. Test gear, incubators, cabinets. The usual. Haven't done a thorough check.'

'Sounds a good place to start,' Phipps decided.

Sam strode with him into the wing. The two labs were very similar, although in the second the fridge had been emptied, its contents on the bonfire, he guessed. One of the lieutenant's men produced a camera and snapped off some flash shots. Then they closed the doors. This place needed to be looked at by scientists. He wished Julie were here. She'd have an idea what monstrous diseases they'd been experimenting with.

They walked further down the corridor peering into the bleak cells the sergeant had talked about. Sam ran upstairs to check the first floor, but there was nothing. Nothing whatsoever to link this place with Max Schenk, with Harry Jackman, or with the virus attacks in Brussels. They'd come too late. The Russians had covered their tracks. As he re-emerged into the hall, so did Willie Phipps.

'We're off,' he announced. 'All that shooting, someone's bound to take an interest soon.'

Sam zipped the computer into its case and tucked it under his arm, hoping against hope that its contents would reveal something. He looked round the long hall, staring into corners, looking for some last thing they might have overlooked.

'Five more minutes,' he pleaded.

'No chance. If we're not buttoned up inside the sub within half an hour she'll leave without us. And there's no way we're going to stay the night here waiting for the Croat police to turn up.'

They stepped out into the yard. The bonfire had collapsed into a heap of glowing ash. That's where his proof had been, Sam told himself, ruefully.

Phipps beckoned to Sam. 'Come on. We're going back to the boat.'

At the far side of the yard amongst the scrub, marines were checking the ground with torches, picking up cartridge cases to eradicate evidence of their having been here.

Sam had a long last look round. Suddenly he spotted something. 'Hang on a minute.'

'I said come on!' Phipps was losing patience with this troublesome civilian. He grabbed for his arm.

But Sam began to run, down to the far end of the small courtyard where an outhouse nestled against the windbreak of a wall. The door hung half open, its bottom hinge broken. Black as pitch inside. He dug in his pocket for a torch. The beam lit up an old wheelbarrow, spades and a pickaxe. He heard feet sprinting across the stony ground. Phipps was coming for him. Then the flashlight beam lit on something shiny. At the back, half covered by fragments of ply. He reached for the wood and pulled it clear.

'Oh boy . . .'

Containers. Five of them. Like small milk churns. Metal-cased with handles. Necks with screw tops wide enough to suspend samples inside.

'Harry Jackman,' he breathed. 'You little devil. You gave yourself away . . .'

Sam felt the lieutenant's hands on his arm.

'Come on, chum, for Pete's sake.'

'Look!' Sam pointed gleefully at the storage flasks. '*Like Ali Baba,*' he whispered. '*Like bloody Ali Baba . . .*'

'What're you on about?'

'It's how they got the viruses here, Willie. In liquid nitrogen.'

'So?'

Sam bent down. Something written on a piece of the plywood had caught his eye. He snatched it up. Blocky, stencilled lettering sprayed on when the wood had still been a packing case.

'Willie . . .'

'Come on, for fuck's sake.'

'But this is it, man. It's what I came for.'

Six simple words that told him everything he needed to know.

Property of the Government of Zambia.

21

HMS *Truculent*
Saturday, 05.40 hrs Zulu

T HE EASTERLY SKY was becoming uncomfortably bright as the hatches
were sealed and the submarine slunk back to its deep water habitat.
In the sick bay Arthur Harris had already been examined by the surgeon-
lieutenant and pronounced not in immediate danger. The wound to his
head was more superficial than it had looked to the amateur eyes of the
Royal Marines lieutenant.

Sam sat in the wardroom at one end of the dining table. Next to him was
Willie Phipps. The notebook computer salvaged from the old monastery
was open in front of them, plugged into the submarine's mains supply.
Sam pressed the power button. The drive purred into life and 'Windows
loading' appeared on the screen.

Phipps had borrowed another PC from the First Lieutenant and while
waiting to see what emerged from the Russians' computer was preparing
his mission report.

'I'm going to have to tell it like it was, Sam,' he announced, apologetically. 'There's no other way I can explain getting into a fire fight when
the orders were to avoid one at all costs.'

'Fine by me,' Sam rumbled. 'If your general wants to file a complaint
to Vauxhall Cross, then I think we can handle that.' As far as he was
concerned, the mission had achieved its goal.

The notebook computer from Palagra had a standard keyboard. He
hadn't noticed it back at the monastery and had been fearing having to cope
with a Cyrillic text. He opened Windows Explorer and 'My Documents',
then ran the cursor down the long list of files. Most were identified only
by code letters. He double-clicked on the first to see what it contained. It
loaded into Word. Three pages of scientific gobbledegook that appeared
to be an analysis of a virus trial, something the brains at Porton Down
would wet themselves over. What *he* needed, however, was something in

plain language that showed a direct link between the laboratory and the rabies-like virus used on the two EU officials. And something that pointed to Max Schenk.

Suddenly he saw it. One complete word standing out from the acronyms on the file list.

VIENNA.

He double-tapped. The file loaded in Internet Explorer. It was a download of a timetable, the schedule of flights between the Croatian coastal town of Split and the Austrian capital.

'Brilliant! Bloody brilliant.'

'What've you found?' Willie Phipps leaned over.

'Something that could prove to be a crucial piece of the jigsaw,' Sam replied cryptically.

On the deck above, Commander Talbot was dog tired. He'd been in the control room for the best part of eight hours. The special forces men were their own masters, but he'd felt a responsibility for them. On board, they'd kept track of the operation by listening in to the marines' secure communications and had been intensely relieved to get them back on board without loss. Now the submarine was thirty metres down, heading south at fifteen knots for the channel between the rocks that would lead them into safer depths and international waters. Talbot crossed from his command seat to the chart table.

'Four-point-three miles to the one hundred metre contour, sir,' the navigator informed him. 'About seventeen minutes.'

'Thanks, Vasco.'

Beyond the hundred metre line the sea bed shelved away steeply. Once across the contour he would take the boat to sixty metres and, with the trawl-net danger passed, would push up the speed to eighteen knots. He stepped past the conning tower into the sound room. The waterfall screens showed thin herringbone traces of boats nearby.

'There's two fishing vessels to port and one to starboard, sir,' Chief Smedley told him. 'Small time, working the rocks. Nothing closer than fifteen cables.'

'Any bio?'

'A school of porpoises followed us when we dived, but they've given up and gone home.'

'Let's hope they weren't working for the Croat Navy,' Talbot quipped.

'They sang "Rule Britannia" when they left us, so I think we're in the clear, sir.'

Talbot smiled and returned to the control room. As he rounded the periscope housing he saw Lieutenant Commander Hayes appear at the top of the companionway with the SIS man. Hayes introduced him to Talbot and they shook hands. It was the first time they'd met. Personal contact with the special forces team on board had been left to the First Lieutenant.

'Mr Packer has a request to make, sir.'

Talbot took quick stock of this man whose formerly secret life had been so thoroughly ventilated by the UK press.

'Better come into my cabin and tell me what's on your mind,' he said. 'Officer of the watch, you have the submarine.'

'I have the submarine, sir,' Styles responded.

Talbot told Sam to sit on the small settee that doubled as his bunk. Hayes left them to it.

'What's your problem, Mr Packer?'

'I've a very urgent need to speak to my controllers in London, Commander,' Sam explained.

'Well at this point that's quite impossible, I'm afraid. We're still well inside Croatian waters.'

'They were experimenting with smallpox on that island,' Sam stressed. 'A new variant, for which there's no vaccine. Stocks may already have been shipped to Europe to be used for mass murder. If I delay passing on the information, hundreds may die who might otherwise have lived.'

Talbot gulped. 'I appreciate your concern, but you must also appreciate mine.' He pulled a chart from the shelf above his desk and spread it out.

'We're here,' he explained, jabbing a finger at it. 'There are fishing boats in the area and there's a Croatian naval presence on Lastovo. If I stick a mast up to transmit, there's a serious risk of detection. So far as we know we've got away with being here. When that bloodbath on Palagra is discovered, there should be nothing to say that NATO forces were involved and I won't do anything to jeopardise that.' He said it with absolute firmness.

Sam nodded. He understood perfectly. No point in arguing.

'So when's the soonest I can talk to London?'

'We have a scheduled rendezvous with HMS *Suffolk* in three hours from now, in international waters close to the Italian coast. If we crank the speed up, then once we're beyond the Croatian territorial limit I could come up to PD to transmit and still make the rendezvous on time. Five minutes long enough for you?'

'It'll have to be. When d'you expect that to happen?'

'In about an hour's time. It's the best I can do for you.'

Sam looked at his watch, which he'd left on Vienna time. 7.15 a.m. London an hour earlier.

'Then let's just pray we're not too late, Commander.'

'Amen to that.'

Vienna
08.30 hrs

Igor Chursin stared out of the window of the hotel. It was in a mixed residential and business area close to one of the main railway stations in Vienna, a city he'd been to only once before. On the street below, the day's activities had begun. A van was delivering confectionery to a corner shop. An elderly man was exercising a small dog which yapped at a postman. He relished the intricacy of the scene after twelve months of isolation on Palagra.

Chursin had breakfasted in his room. He was a jowly man of forty-five, who'd had a tendency to put on weight before his appetite was blunted by the diet served up by the Croatian they'd hired to cook and housekeep for the past twelve months. His fair hair, once straggly, had been cropped short by the same, multi-skilled young man.

The flight from Split had delivered him to the Austrian capital the previous evening but he'd not yet had his instructions from 'Peter'. Last night, after a short tram ride from his hotel, he'd found an Internet café that stayed open late and had sent him an e-mail to break the news about the enforced closure of the laboratory in the Adriatic. He'd remained on-line for an hour, hoping for instructions on where to deliver the vials of lethal serum that he'd brought to Vienna, but the café had closed before an answer came. The bottles which he'd transported so perilously in his hand luggage had spent the night in the refrigerator in his hotel room, but if they weren't used or chilled properly within a few days, the virus was going to die.

To some extent, that was what he wished to happen. A year ago when he'd accepted the invitation to work for a handsome salary instead of a poverty-line wage which was seldom paid, he'd turned a blind eye to the motives of his new employers. Since then, he'd stifled his conscience and partaken in acts of unimaginable inhumanity in the interests of attaining the new life he dreamed of. But now that he was delivering the products of his labours, he was experiencing a guilt he was finding hard to suppress.

It was the development of the vaccine that had taken them so much time. Without it, the administration of the modified smallpox virus would be potentially lethal to anyone bent on using it. Although the project had been prematurely terminated, Chursin was convinced he had a triumph on his hands. The youth who'd been injected with the vaccine had been infected fourteen days before he absconded. Normally by that time the fevers and pains would have developed, but the youth had been clear. All Chursin lacked was proof.

He looked at his watch. The Internet café would open again in fifteen minutes. He took the plastic bucket from on top of the fridge and filled it with ice from the machine at the end of the corridor, then dumped it into the insulated coolbag he'd used for transporting the vials from Split. Finally, he extricated the bottles from amongst the whisky miniatures in the minibar and put them in the bag. The last thing he wanted was for the maid to discover them while he was out.

A tram came after a five-minute wait at the stop. He arrived at the café just as the doors were being unlocked. He logged on, but to his dismay found no response to his e-mail to Peter. He ordered another coffee and sat down to wait. There was nothing else he could do.

The Adriatic Sea
09.15 hrs Zulu

First to be winched into the Sea King was Arthur Harris, strapped to a stretcher. He'd regained consciousness and been able to make enough sense to ask for morphine.

Two hours earlier the submarine had put up a mast to burst-transmit Lieutenant Phipps's written report to London and for Sam to be patched through to his controller. Waddell had spent the night at Vauxhall Cross, waiting for news.

In the interests of speed Sam had trimmed the detail of what had happened on Palagra.

'The bottom line is that we have a clear link to Harry Jackman and to Vienna,' he'd concluded. 'The circle's been closed, Duncan. It *has* to be Schenk.'

'You'd have thought so. Unfortunately the Austrians are having no luck in making anything stick. Schenk agreed to be interviewed by the security police last night, but he changed his story. Claims never to have met Harry Jackman. Says he made up what he said to Julie, to hurt her.'

'He's lying.'

'We've no proof of that. And finding a Vienna flight timetable on Chursin's computer doesn't provide us with any.'

'What about Schenk's Croatian wife?' Sam had asked, exasperated at the failure to nail the doctor. 'Any connection between her family and the island of Palagra?'

'Nothing recorded. We're hamstrung here. Can't make too many obvious enquiries without attracting suspicion that we had something do with the bloodbath on Palagra. So we're having to rely on the Austrian security police for now. There are several key links still missing, Sam. We need something with Schenk's name on it. We also need something that links Palagra to the rabies variant used against the EU officials.'

'I'm still hoping to find that on the computer,' Sam had told him. 'Where's Schenk now?'

'Back in Vienna.'

'Under surveillance?'

'The Austrians are tapping his phone and Collins has somebody watching him. Of course, after what you've come up with, we'll urge the Austrians to interview him again. By the way, the Met's caught the London bomber.'

'Brilliant! And?'

'A loner, by the look of it. Being run through e-mail by some racist mastermind calling himself Peter. And before you ask, there's nothing we've uncovered that suggests that Peter is Schenk.'

'Damn. Any new racist attacks?'

'Yes. A firebomb in Stockholm last night. A Turkish family burned to death. An eyewitness saw one man throwing petrol into a takeaway. The family lived above it.'

'God, what a bunch of bastards. So what've we got?'

'Looks like an international network of lone wolves, being directed by a central puppetmaster. If we can take him out, then the whole structure'll probably collapse. And for my money, the place for you to be is still Vienna, even if the evidence is circumstantial. The RAF are helicoptering you and the marines to Gioia del Colle – that's the Italian air base the RAF use for Bosnia operations. There's an HS125 waiting. It can drop you off in Austria before taking the rest of the party back to Lyneham.'

'Excellent.'

Sam was last to be winched up to the Sea King. As he was dragged backwards over the sill, he looked down and saw Commander Talbot wave briefly from the top of the fin. Sam gave a thumbs up. His old service had done them proud.

The helicopter banked away. As he looked back, fine jets of spray erupted from the bow and stern. The submarine was losing no time in returning to the invisibility that was her natural element.

London

The morning call from the Computer Crime Unit came at a quarter to ten, shortly after Steph had arrived in the Special Branch offices on the sixteenth floor at the Yard. She'd heard about the Stockholm bomb on the radio at 7 a.m.

'Your friend Peter's gone verbal again.' The voice belonged to the analyst who'd been working on the hard disk the previous evening. Didn't computer nerds need sleep, Stephanie wondered.

'I'll be right over.'

She took the lift and was there in three minutes.

'What's he saying?' she asked, dropping into a chair. She saw a camp bed in the corner of the room and understood how the technician had survived the night.

'For a fascist he sounds eerily kind and thoughtful,' the computer specialist commented. 'Full of concern about our friend's personal problems. Look.' He pointed at the screen. 'Read for yourself.'

Stephanie wheeled the chair in closer.

> *Anthony,*
>
> *I have seen on television what happened at Golders Green. At such difficult times we must find all the strength we have within ourselves. On the path to great achievements there are always tragedies. You must not blame yourself. In war there are many accidents.*
>
> *Of course for now there must be a delay before your next mission. A few weeks perhaps. And your next target must be chosen with such care that a mistake is impossible.*
>
> *You told me you were worried about Sandra. Take some time to find out what she knows. If she cannot support what you and I believe in, then it cannot be right for her to continue to share your life. You must be brave about this. I also have must to make such a sacrifice.*

Stephanie blinked. The last sentence contained the first full error in what had been almost flawless grammar. A simple typo? Or a clue to the man's nationality? She tried to hear a voice in the words. An accent. Trying to find a match with the Austrian doctor Sam suspected.

'No way of knowing where this man lives?' she checked.

'It could be anywhere on the planet. The mailbox is registered under the name of Vino Blanco, with a fictitious address in Liechtenstein.'

Stephanie looked at the screen again. There was one more paragraph.

Courage, my friend. Protect yourself in whatever way you must. If it is safe for Sandra to live, then make the separation quickly and be kind to her. If it is not safe and she must be silenced, then it is possible I can help you with that.

'Blimey,' Stephanie exclaimed, reading the last line again. 'Is he offering to kill her for him, or what?'

'Like I said,' the technician smiled. 'He's thoughtful. And the sign-off's a gem.'

Stephanie gaped at it.

Chin up! Peter.

'That's almost Woosterish,' she mouthed.

'Eh?'

'Never mind.' The lad was too young to understand. 'Print it for me, would you? I'm going to think of a reply. Something to entice Peter into the open. That's if I can persuade Southall crime squad to keep mum about Petrie's arrest for a little longer.'

'You'll have your work cut out,' the analyst told her. 'You heard the nine o'clock news this morning?'

'No.' Steph's heart sank. 'Tell me.'

'There was a report from Stepney. Neighbours talking. How Rob Petrie seemed a decent enough guy. Kept himself to himself . . . All the usual stuff.'

'Bloody hell! How did it get out?'

'No idea.'

Steph snatched up the phone and dialled Southall, demanding to speak to the DCI in charge of the investigation. She had to hold on for a couple of minutes.

'Who's been blabbing?' she demanded when he came on the line.

'Not us,' he assured her. 'But one of the other residents of Windsor Court works for the local BBC.'

Steph groaned. 'Has Petrie told you anything?'

'Not a word.'

'Charges?'

'This afternoon, probably. Tomorrow morning at the latest.'

Steph grasped her forehead and rubbed it. 'Have *you* said anything to the media yet?'

'No, but the Yard press office has had to confirm that we're questioning a man.'

Steph sighed. 'Thanks.'

She rang off. The hard copy of Peter's e-mail which the computer analyst handed her would be the last communication they got from the man. However little it told her about his identity, she was going to have to make the most of it. And so was Sam. Wherever the hell he was.

Vienna

It was after eleven before Igor Chursin got the e-mail response he'd been waiting for. By then his heart was palpitating from all the caffeine he'd consumed. He took careful note of the instructions, then returned to the hotel to vacate his room before the midday checkout time. By the end of the day if all went to plan, he would be well away from here, with his final payment filling his briefcase and his dream of a new life coming closer to fruition.

He had no luggage with him. The few personal items he'd possessed on Palagra had been left there. By now they would have been burned by Sasha and the Croats. He'd worn the same shirt for three days now and it smelled of sweat.

The instructions from Peter told him to take a tram to the Währingerstrasse U-Bahn station then telephone a mobile phone number and give the code word *Prinz*. He would be told where to go for the rendezvous. The tone of the e-mail had been cool but understanding, ending with the philosophical words, *on the path to great achievements there are always setbacks*.

The trams round the Ring were frequent and Chursin reached his destination quickly. He took the escalator down to the subway station which doubled as a tram terminus for routes heading west towards the Wienerwald. The first phone box he tried was broken, but the second worked. The mobile phone number rang four times before it was answered, in German.

'This is *Prinz*,' he responded in English.

'*Ja*. You must to take the Strassenbahn *Nummer achtunddreissig*, number mmm . . . thirty-eight, you unnerstand?'

'Strassenbahn?'

'Streetcar.'

'Number thirty-eight . . .'

'*Ja.* To Grinzing. It is end station. You wait and we will come.'

'How will I recognise you?'

But the line had already died. He was unfazed by all this subterfuge. It had been the same on his previous visit a few months ago and he well understood the need for it. They would be watching to make sure he wasn't being followed – for his protection as well as for theirs. The people he was working for had treated him fairly up to now and he had faith they would do so until the end. He replaced the receiver, collected some change from the refund recess, then looked round at the tram stops, reading the numbers. A thirty-eight was waiting for the off.

He'd bought himself a twenty-four-hour transport pass when he'd arrived at the airport last night, so took his seat without recourse to the ticket machine behind the driver's cab. Within a couple of minutes the tram was grinding up the slope to street level and humming its way north through residential districts of the city. There was a comfortable orderliness to much of the Austrian capital that reminded him of Russia in better days.

The journey to Grinzing took twenty-five minutes. On the last stages of the route, the tram climbed steadily. Most passengers seemed to be tourists with cameras round their necks and when they reached the terminus Chursin saw why. Grinzing was a pretty village of mellow yellow houses, souvenir shops and taverns. He stepped down from the vehicle and stood to one side as the other passengers dispersed. The tram trundled round a loop line to head back into the city and he was alone on the pavement, the coolbag full of smallpox dangling from one hand and a plastic shopping bag from the other.

He waited for a good five minutes before an elderly Volkswagen Golf pulled up and a dark-haired woman leaned out from the driver's window.

'Herr Prinz?'

'Yes.'

'Please.' The rear door of the car opened for him to get in. Chursin slid onto the back seat and the woman drove off. The car wound through the village, climbing steadily. Next to the woman driver was a brown-haired man who kept his eyes on the road as if not trusting her ability to avoid the kerbs. His head was like a small dog's, wiry and pointed. Neither of them spoke as the car left the built-up area and headed into woodland interspersed with vineyards. Their silence made Chursin uneasy.

After about ten minutes, the woman swung the car into a lane which quickly became a rutted track, ending at a small, darkly painted wooden house with a barn behind it. The large doors were open. The woman drove in and switched off.

Still without speaking, she got out and indicated he should do the same. Chursin was uncomfortable with this couple. It had been more straightforward with the professional-sounding man he'd dealt with last time. There was something sinister about this pair. A cold efficiency about their actions that was not entirely human. And the garage had a faint smell of chloroform about it.

'You will show us what you have brought,' the man told him, walking over to a workbench and indicating that Chursin should open his bag on it.

'You have money for me?' he checked, defensively.

'Ja, ja. Alles in Ordnung,' the man grunted, opening a drawer in the workbench and pulling out a fat brown envelope.

Chursin's eyes widened at the thickness of it. He unzipped the seal on the coolbag and removed four bottles.

'These contain serum,' he explained, holding up the two larger ones. 'Infected serum. Other two bottles are vaccine.'

'It is good?' the terrier-faced man asked him. 'It will protect us?'

'One hundred per cent.' Mentally Chursin crossed his fingers as he said it.

'We must use the vaccine how long before?' the woman checked.

'Any time before infection.'

'And for the virus you have . . .' She didn't know the English word. '*Eine Spritze?*'

Chursin picked up his plastic shopping bag and pulled out an insecticide spray with a pump handle and a reservoir tank.

'You see, it is made special so the droplets are right size,' he explained. From their frowns he wasn't certain they were following his English properly.

'First you mix serum with water. Fifty–fifty. Understand?'

'Ja. We understand.' The couple looked at one another and nodded. 'Alles in Ordnung.' The man handed him the envelope. When he smiled he revealed a wide gap between his front teeth. 'Your money. You must to count it.'

Chursin felt intensely relieved. He slit open the envelope with his thumbnail and pulled out a sheaf of $100 bills. As he concentrated on them, dividing them into tens, he failed to notice the man walk round behind him. The notes were crisp and new. Like the life he envisaged they would buy him.

Suddenly a bag was pulled over his head. Dark, smelly plastic. He went rigid with shock, tightening his grip on the cash and swearing in Russian. Then his elbows were wrenched behind his back and pinioned. He struggled but was pulled off balance. His wiry assailant had the strength of a bear.

He breathed in sharply, air that smelled of manure. He felt outraged and foolish, but when he tried to protest again his voice failed, as if some part of him realised there was no point in speaking. He seemed to be standing outside his own body, watching a process as relentless and terminal as when a spider traps a fly. He felt fingers unbutton his shirt in the middle of his chest, then a probing to locate the base of his sternum, followed by an excruciating pain in his heart.

'Aaagh . . .' He felt he'd been impaled. His pulse faltered like some seized engine. The stench from the sack was choking him. His head began to spin and his legs gave way. He sank backwards into the steadying arms of his attacker. Then his mind went black.

The woman finished emptying the horse syringe into Igor Chursin's heart and withdrew the needle, leaving a tiny hole in his white skin from which a thin rivulet of blood trickled. After a few seconds it stopped of its own accord. The man lowered Igor Chursin to the ground. The two of them stood side by side, observing the end of another life, watching the onset of death in the quietly satisfied way that they'd done many times before in the last twenty years. Ending people's lives was an art they took pride in, using skills their Stasi trainers had inherited from the Gestapo and refined under the tutelage of the KGB.

In the corner of the barn was a stone sink with a brass tap. The woman took the veterinary syringe over to it, washed it out and replaced it in its container in the workbench drawer. Then from a box on a shelf behind it she retrieved two disposable syringes in sealed plastic packs, opened them and filled them from one of the vaccine bottles. The man bared his upper arm and she plunged in the needle. When she'd done, she rolled up her own shirt sleeve for him to do the same to her. Finally they transferred the bottles of infected serum to a thermo-electric camping coolbox which they placed on the floor at the back of the car, connecting its power cable to the cigar lighter socket.

The man knelt beside Chursin to check that his pulse was flat. Then the two of them lifted him into the boot of the car, folding down half of the rear seat to make it easier for his legs. They covered the body with a blanket, and dumped two suitcases on top of it.

The pair nodded at one another. The job was done. Their next mission awaited. They got into the car and reversed from the barn, locking the doors behind them.

They had a long journey ahead.

On board an RAF HS125 *en route* to Vienna

Unlike the exhausted marines, Sam had forced himself to stay awake during the flight, checking and rechecking the computer files. He'd done a word search on every document, but Schenk's name hadn't registered. Nor had rabies. If Schenk was to be nailed, then somehow they were going to have to get him to admit his involvement.

He kept thinking of what Julie had gone through with Schenk thirty-six hours ago. He felt a strong wish to see her again. Almost as strong as a longing.

Thirty minutes later the small jet touched down at Vienna's Schwechat Airport and taxied to the business terminal. Willie Phipps stirred from his slumbers to bid Sam goodbye. He shook his hand warmly and wished him luck. After a brief passport check, Sam was taken to the city by the same cautious British embassy driver who'd been so meticulous about speed limits on the day of Kovalenko's murder.

Once beyond the airport perimeter, the driver handed him a phone. 'Mr Collins thought you might want to get up to date with what's been happening in London,' he suggested.

Sam rang Waddell's number first, but finding him unavailable, dialled Stephanie's line at the Yard. She sounded unusually harassed.

'Where the hell are you?'

'Vienna.'

'He calls himself Peter. The mastermind.'

'I know. Waddell told me.'

'Is it Schenk?'

'Everything points that way. There *was* a biological weapons lab on Palagra and we have found links to Vienna. But I can't prove it's Schenk. Tell me about the bloke you've arrested.'

'Aged thirty-two. Former securities trader with no previous convictions. Shacked up with a nurse. No known associations with racist organisations, but his computer hard disk was stuffed with downloads from white power websites and he'd failed to erase a whole bunch of e-mails from his leader.'

'Waddell said they gave no clue to his identity.'

'Not so sure about that. There's been a new missive this morning. Tell me something. How good is Schenk's English?'

'Pretty fluent. Makes the odd error.'

'Would you recognise one?'

'Try me.'

'The e-mail's full of sympathy about the mistake Petrie made in Golders Green – blowing up a crocodile of schoolkids rather than a restaurant full of Jews. All written in near perfect English until the end when he says *I also have must to make such a sacrifice*. Ring any bells?'

Sam pondered for a moment. 'No. But it does sound sort of German. What was the precise context?'

'He seems to be talking about having to sacrifice partners who don't support the Lucifer Network's views on life . . .'

'*Lucifer* Network?'

'Seems to be the name of the organisation. There was reference to it in one of the other e-mails we found. Want me to read the whole text?'

'No. Fax it to the Embassy in Vienna. For the attention of Pat Collins. I'm on my way there now.'

'Okay. I'll tell you one other thing, though. It ends with the words *chin up*. Is Schenk a fan of P.G. Wodehouse?'

'God knows.' *Chin up*. He'd heard someone else use the words recently, but couldn't remember where. 'Ask Julie.'

'I will. Oh, I saw her last night. She's keen to talk to you. In fact I get the impression she's rather keen altogether.'

He ignored her innuendo. 'Where is she?'

'In the virology lab at St Michael's Hospital. She told me she'd be working there all weekend.'

The car turned into Jauresgasse and stopped outside the British Embassy.

'D'you happen to have the phone number?'

'You mean you *don't*?'

'Leave it out, Steph.' She gave it to him. 'Thanks. And we'll do that curry soon. Right?'

'Right. *If* Miss Jackman can spare you . . .'

He handed the phone back to the driver.

Chin up.

He walked into the Embassy still dressed in the crumpled trousers and sweatshirt that he'd worn under his dry suit. And judging by the way the secretary who escorted him upstairs wrinkled her nose, he wasn't smelling too fresh any more.

Inside the SIS offices Collins was on the phone and waved him to a seat. The station chief's ruddy forehead bore a perplexed frown.

'Vielen Dank.' He rang off, puffing out his cheeks with surprise. 'Well . . . there's a turn-up,' he exhaled. 'I think you may have had a wasted journey.'

'Why? What's happened now?'

'Austrian security pulled Schenk in for questioning again just before lunchtime today, to confront him with your evidence of the link between the germ warfare lab and Vienna,' Collins gabbled, spluttering. 'And, wait for it – Schenk confessed.'

'*What?*' Elation swelled inside him like a balloon.

'But not to what we wanted him to confess to.'

The balloon burst. Sam clasped his scalp with both hands. 'Explain.'

'He's admitted doing a deal with Harry Jackman.'

'Fantastic.'

'But not the deal you have in mind. He categorically denies being involved in biological terrorism. And to prove it he's shown Austrian security what it was he *did* buy from Jackman.'

'Which was . . . ?'

'Medical equipment. Some quite flash stuff. Gear donated to a hospital in Africa by a European aid programme. It had been sitting in some flyblown storeroom for a year and a half because the locals didn't have anybody who could operate it. Then money changed hands and the equipment quietly disappeared, turning up in Schenk's clinic at half the price he'd have paid if he'd bought it through the usual channels.'

'The little shit.' Sam sank back in the chair in disbelief.

'And this was no fantasy on his part. The serial numbers on the gear in his clinic match with those of the equipment sent to Africa.'

Sam rested his head on the back of the chair and stared at the ceiling. It was too pat. Too well-prepared an excuse for someone who only a few hours earlier had denied ever meeting Harry Jackman.

'What makes you think this is the *only* deal Schenk did with Jackman?'

'Because we have no evidence of any other. Nothing connecting him with Palagra.'

Sam stared at the ceiling again. Every fibre of his body told him Schenk was guilty of something far more sinister than receiving stolen property.

'If Schenk is unscrupulous enough to deprive Africans of life-saving equipment, he could easily have been involved in racist murder too.'

'Of course he could,' Collins concurred. 'Trouble is, his denials have been very convincing.'

There was a tap at the door and a secretary handed Collins a sheet of paper.

'What's all this?'

'A fax.'

Sam looked over his shoulder. 'If it's from Scotland Yard and the text of an e-mail, then it's for me.' Collins gave it to him.

Sam sat down again, rubbing his forehead as he read. The caring tone of

'Peter's' message intrigued him. He was reminded of Hoffmann's homily about a good general caring for his troops. He lingered over the penultimate paragraph.

If she cannot support what you and I believe in, then it cannot be right for her to continue to share your life. You must be brave about this. I also have must to make such a sacrifice.

What sacrifice? Had the maniac killed his own wife?

Then *Chin up*. It annoyed him that he couldn't remember where he'd heard it.

'Mind if I use your phone?'

'Help yourself. Nine for an outside line.'

He rang the London number Stephanie had given him. It was a male voice that answered. He asked to speak to Julie.

'May I say who's calling?'

'Sam Packer.'

There was a teeth-sucking sound at the other end. 'I'm not sure that . . .'

'Just tell her I'm on the line and that it's important.'

He heard a clunk of the handset being laid down and the squish of rubber soles on polished floors. A couple of minutes later Julie's voice came on.

'Sam? Are you all right?'

'Fine. Look I've got some questions about Max.'

'Okay.'

'How did you two communicate? Was it ever by e-mail?'

'Oh no. Max is a Luddite when it comes to new technology. He can't even use a keyboard.'

Sam's heart sank. 'You sure about that?'

'Totally. I've seen the way his eyes glaze over when confronted by a computer.'

'Never mentioned something called "the Lucifer Network" to you?'

'Nope.'

'One other question.' It was his last hope. 'Did he ever say *chin up*?'

There was hesitation at the other end. For a moment Sam thought he'd struck gold.

'Absolutely not,' she told him. 'His English was terribly Germanic. Utterly devoid of phrases like that.'

'Damn . . .'

'You sound so disappointed.'

'I am.'

She made sympathetic noises. 'What's happened?'

'I've a nasty feeling I've done my maths wrong, that's what. Two and two may not make five after all.'

'Sam, I . . .'

'Look, I've got to go. I'll ring you again when I'm back in London.'

'Sam!'

'What?'

'There was something I wanted to tell you.'

He felt uncomfortable under Collins's penetrating glare. 'Yes, but perhaps now isn't the best . . .'

'I've seen him before, Sam.'

He felt an icy finger down his back. 'Who?'

'The man in your folder.'

Sam screwed up his eyes, trying to latch onto what she was talking about.

'What folder, Julie?'

'In your room at the *pension*,' Julie explained. 'There was a folder with a photograph in it.'

Sam swallowed, not trusting himself to speak. He remembered emerging from the bathroom and seeing her poking around in his suitcase.

'Somebody Hoffmann,' she went on, breathlessly.

'Hoffmann,' he croaked. The world was turning upside down.

'The face seemed familiar, but I couldn't think where I'd seen it. I've been puzzling over it ever since and come to the conclusion there's only one place it could have been.'

'Where, Julie? Where've you seen him before?'

'The Intercon bar. I'm 99 per cent certain he was one of the men my father was chatting to when I joined him for a drink that evening a year ago.'

Yes, thought Sam. Harry Jackman had been right.

Julie knows.

22

T HE CLUES HAD been there and he'd missed them.
Peter's paternalistic concern for the problems of his foot-soldiers –
it bore Hoffmann's signature. Kovalenko's murder, done KGB style – *Stasi*
style. The supposed heart attack that had left Hoffmann hale and hearty the
next day – a carefully created alibi. And *chin up*. Sam remembered where
he'd heard it now. At Jo Macdonald's bedside. It had been 'Johann' who'd
told the Scotswoman to keep her chin up when his father was dying.

The embassy car hurtled round the Ring, the driver threatened with
an unpleasant personal injury if he didn't push the speed over the limit
this time.

Sam sat alone in the back, reliving his meeting with Günther Hoffmann
three days earlier. His brain kept singling out other indicators he'd missed
– the man's envy of the Austrians' freedom to be anti-Semitic – his blatant
homophobia – his dislike of Arabs because of their music – his sympathy
with those who wanted to keep Europe free of dusky foreigners. Taken
separately, each had been a small thing, the mutterings of an elderly grump.
But together they spelled out a man with the mindset of a Nazi.

And there were other clues. Fischer's comment that Hoffmann had
been more involved with Russian businessmen in Vienna than they'd first
thought. And his view that if Hoffmann was making money from Russians,
he would have been doing it to fund some cause he believed in.

And what a cause.

Sam groaned. Hindsight was a wonderful thing.

It was another of Fischer's snippets that was driving him now. The tip
that Hoffmann spent most Saturday afternoons 'researching German history'
in the National Library.

The car swung through the neo-classical gateway of the Hofburg, the
palace of the Habsburgs. To each side of the broad, gravelled road lay
Heldenplatz, the square to the heroes of the Austro-Hungarian empire.

Horse-drawn fiacres lined one side of the highway, their bowler-hatted coachmen holding the beasts' bucking heads while tourists clambered on board. Sam's embassy driver turned right and stopped beneath a statue of a prince on a prancing horse that was streaked with green. He nodded towards the curved, grey, colonnaded block facing them.

'That's your Staatsbibliothek. Want me to wait?'

'You bet.' Sam pushed open the door and slammed it behind him.

'By rights I'd need permission to park here . . .' The driver's plaintive moan was lost to the breeze as Sam climbed the steps to the library.

One half of the barred bronze portal stood open. Beyond it a cavernous, stone-floored hall. At the far end were glazed doors made of carved oak, topped by a coat of arms. He hurried through into the library itself, a light and airy space, with a black-and-white tiled floor, stately marble columns and ficus trees in tubs. He felt the hair twitch on the back of his neck. He was getting close.

There was a security office on the left. A red-faced, potato-shaped guard leaned on his desk, eyeing all new arrivals with suspicion. Next to his window a display board listed departments. Halfway down was the name of the one Sam had guessed would be here. On the lower ground floor.

There was a warm, leathery smell about the building. A sign pointed to a spiral staircase. At the bottom was the book collection centre. Readers who'd placed orders were waiting on benches for their tomes to be retrieved from the vaults. Several glanced up, disturbed by Sam's hasty and breathless arrival. He stopped, looking for some sign pointing to where he wanted to be. Finding none, he asked at the collections counter. The middle-aged woman behind it indicated a corridor to the left. He hurried through a pair of swing doors and found the library's communications centre. Faxes and photocopy machines lined one wall. There was a desk manned by a grey-suited official, whose fingers clicked at a keyboard. Beyond the desk was the place Sam had guessed would be here, the Internet room from where 'Peter' had controlled his small network of activists.

He stopped in his tracks. About a dozen PCs sat on tables, only one of them in use.

The old Stasi man sat hunched over the keyboard, his deeply lined, deceptively noble face sombre with concentration. For a split second Sam felt sorry for the man. He'd had a dream and it was about to end. Sam crept past and came round behind him. Over his shoulder he could see the Hotmail screen. Hoffmann was typing a message. Sam hovered, trying to see the words, but the text was too small.

Suddenly, sensing danger, Günther Hoffmann lifted his eyes above the screen and saw that the official behind the payment desk was looking intently in his direction. Not at him, he realised quickly, but at someone standing behind him. He swung the chair half round, completing the turn with his head.

Hoffmann took in a sharp breath. The steeliness was gone from the slate-grey eyes. Sam saw a look of defeat. Then the old man swung back to the monitor and grabbed the mouse to block off the text on the screen.

'No way,' Sam growled, springing forward to prevent him erasing what he'd written. He yanked at the chair, swinging it round again, jerking the mouse from Hoffmann's hand.

'How's the heart, Herr Hoffmann? Or should I say Lucifer?' Their faces were inches apart.

Suddenly the German butted forward. Sam felt his nose crack. His vision exploded in stars. He reached blindly for Hoffmann's shoulders but the chair was already empty. He felt warm liquid trickle down his upper lip and pressed a sleeve against his nostrils. As his eyes cleared, he set off after Hoffmann, yelling at the official behind the counter not to touch the computer. The man grabbed a phone and began dialling.

Hoffmann was only seconds ahead of him. Back in the book collection room Sam saw the door to the staircase swing shut. There were gasps from the waiting readers at the blood spattering his front.

Once on the staircase, he heard Hoffmann's wheezy breath above him and caught a glimpse of his back in the curve. The old spy was showing a surprising turn of speed for a man of his age.

'Stop!'

In his confusion and anger the German words weren't coming to him. Sam was furious with himself for letting the rogue get the better of him.

Up on the ground floor level, Hoffmann ran full pelt for the exit. He shouted something to the security guard in his hutch by the door and pointed back towards Sam.

'Fuck . . .'

The blob of officialdom emerged from his cubby-hole, arms out-stretched. Sam swerved to avoid the man but his bulk blocked the doorway.

Sam's tongue seemed to swell in his mouth as he sought the words which would make the man understand. But before he could form them, huge arms folded round him like a clam shell, enveloping him in an odour of armpits and stale smoke.

'Na, ja . . .' the guard grunted, turning him round like a pot on a wheel and pinning his arms behind him. He gabbled on in a Viennese accent that Sam found incomprehensible.

'Sie verstehen nicht,' Sam croaked. 'Er ist Mörder! Sie müssen ihn . . .'

'Ja, ja ja . . .' the guard clattered. Sam made out the word 'Polizei'.

He was manhandled into the security office. The man's strength was

phenomenal. Other staff had gathered, alerted by the sound of the com-
motion. The blood and the fact that he was a foreigner fuelled their
hostility.

He was slammed onto a chair and held there by the guard while a woman
in glasses dialled a number. He heard the word 'Polizei' again.

Then suddenly they were there. Not in response to the call, but because
Patrick de Vere Collins had promised to tip off Austrian security about Sam
going after Hoffmann. Two uniformed officers came running in through
the entrance doors, closely followed by the Inspektor who'd been in charge
of the Kovalenko murder case.

'Herr Packer . . . You seem to be in some difficulties.'

'Inspektor Pfeiffer, that's an epic understatement,' Sam coughed as the
library guard reluctantly released his grip. 'Did you get Hoffmann?'

'I do not know how he looks,' the Inspektor answered, frowning.
'Explain to me please.'

'I will. Outside. Follow me quickly.' He pushed through the doors into
Heldenplatz, the police close behind him.

There was no sign of Hoffmann. Sam checked with his embassy driver.

'See anybody come running from the library?'

The man shook his head. 'Wasn't looking,' he mumbled. Illegally parked,
his anxiety at the arrival of the police was tangible.

Sam clicked his tongue with annoyance. The nosebleed was stopping.
He quickly filled Pfeiffer in.

'The computer, it still have the Internet connection?' the Austrian asked,
grasping the situation immediately.

'It did a few minutes ago.'

They ran back inside and down to the communications centre. The grey-
suited official was hovering by the PC that Hoffmann had been using.

The Inspektor ordered him not to touch it. The official protested that
the time paid for had run out. Sam pulled a 50-schilling note from his
wallet and thrust it into the bureaucrat's hand.

They sat at the screen. The message Hoffmann had been writing was
still blocked off but hadn't been erased. The words were in English to
someone with the moniker 'Gustaf Adolf'. Praise for a firebomb attack
last night. Sam assumed it was Stockholm. Then a warning. The Lucifer
Network cell in England had been closed down by ZOG activity. It was
time to lie low for a while.

'It is better we don't touch this,' the Inspektor breathed. 'I will send for
computer specialists to examine everything.'

'We must find out where Hoffmann's gone,' Sam insisted. 'The answer
may be here.'

He clicked the mouse on the mail 'folders' and opened up 'sent messages'.

One e-mail there. In German this time. Sam and the Inspektor read it together.

It warned the recipients that the opposition was making progress against them and it begged them not to fail. It talked of the twelve months of preparation they'd already put in. And it described the next attack as the most important of their whole campaign.

You must succeed. None of us can know how long we have in this life and I want to die in peace knowing that my homeland will be safe.

The Inspektor pointed at the screen. 'He use the word *Heimat*.'

'Homeland. So the smallpox attack is to be in Germany,' Sam deduced.

'But *Heimat* can mean a place more particular. His own home. His own part of the country. You know where that is?'

'He lived in Berlin for most of his life,' Sam told him. 'But . . .' Suddenly he stood up. 'I've just thought of something.'

He strode to the service counter and asked the official if he had international phone directories. The man handed him a CD and pointed to a PC next to the photocopiers. Sam loaded the disc into the machine and looked up the number of Sky News in London. He rang it from a booth and a couple of minutes later emerged grim-faced.

'Greifswald,' he announced. 'That's where the attack will be.'

Pfeiffer looked quizzical.

'Sky News has been following an Albanian refugee family,' Sam explained. 'The broadcasts have been shown all over Europe. Yesterday morning they filmed them settling into a hostel in northern Germany, a place already full of Balkan refugees. And the town was Greifswald – that's where Hoffmann was born, Herr Inspektor. No wonder this target's so important to him.'

The policeman got to his feet. More of his men were arriving. He ordered them to seal off the communications area and to keep the Internet connection open until specialists arrived from his headquarters. Then he turned back to Sam. 'I will quickly contact my colleagues in Germany,' he told him. 'And we will put out Hoffmann's description.'

'How would he get to Greifswald?' Sam asked.

'Why? You think Hoffmann goes there himself?'

'In that e-mail he talks about dying. He told me once he wanted to end his days in Greifswald.'

The Inspektor stared at him.

'Then I must warn the airport. He would first fly to Berlin.'

'No.' Sam put out a hand to stop him. 'He hates planes. Told me he never flies these days if he can help it.'

'The train, then. Come. We will go to the Westbahnhof.'

Outside, Sam told his driver to return to the Embassy, then piled into one of the police cars with the Inspektor. With the blue light and siren going, they powered their way through the traffic, reaching the station in less than five minutes.

Sam and the policeman ran inside, checking the indicator board for trains to Nürnberg where, according to the phone conversation with rail enquiries which the Inspektor had had in the car, Hoffmann would pick up a connection to Berlin and Greifswald. There was one leaving in twenty minutes.

'Number seven,' the Inspektor grunted.

They hurried onto the platform. Several of the train doors were open and a few passengers were already boarding. Sam stepped into the first carriage with the Inspektor right behind him. He looked the length of it, checking faces, then passed swiftly through to the next.

It was in the fourth carriage he spotted him. Sitting alone at a table at the far end of an otherwise empty compartment. Günther Hoffmann began to rise when he saw Sam, but flopped back into the seat when the Inspektor thrust a hand under his jacket and pulled out a Glock pistol. Hoffmann's grooved cheeks seemed to hang loosely from his skull. As they closed in, he placed his hands flat on the table.

'Aufstehen!' the Inspektor ordered, the gun sight levelled on the centre of Hoffmann's forehead.

The old spy rose, head held high, back straight, his eyes looking past them as if at some distant goal that he still intended to reach. The Inspektor told him to put his hands on his head then frisked him. There was nothing in his inside pockets other than a wallet and a pen.

'Where is it, Günther?' Sam hissed. 'Where's the smallpox?'

Hoffmann glared contemptuously at him. 'You know me for too long time, Herr Packer, to expect me to answer your questions.'

'You're an evil bastard,' Sam blazed. 'Lucifer. The name suits you.'

'It does. But not in the way you mean. You misunderstand, Herr Packer. To the Romans, Lucifer was the morning star. The bringer of light to the world.'

Sam saw a touch of insanity in his eyes. 'And you planned to emulate Lucifer by murdering people and creating a climate of fear . . .'

'You cannot have morning light without first having the darkness of night,' Hoffmann rejoined, sitting down again stiffly.

'The Sikhs and the Jews in London. The Turks in Sweden. Albanians in Germany.' Sam counted off the targets. 'Vladimir Kovalenko . . .'

'He had, as you say in English, passed his sell-by date,' Hoffmann interrupted, allowing himself a little smirk.

'After providing you with the wherewithal to let loose a plague.'

Hoffmann pressed his lips together.

'There'll be children dead in Greifswald,' Sam stressed. 'Like in Golders Green. Only this time it'll be hundreds. Is that what you want?'

He saw a flicker in the eyes. A reminder that despite Hoffmann's insane ambition his compassion might still be stirred by its consequences.

'Little bodies aflame with blisters. Raging fever. No treatment possible that could stop their screams. You want *that?*'

Hoffmann wet his lips and sniffed. But his jaw was still defiant.

Sam remembered Peter's e-mail which Steph had faxed from London – the suggestion that he too had had to sacrifice a loved one.

'Ilse . . .' Sam murmured, not quite believing what he was thinking.

The leathery head turned to look at him, eyes as lifeless as lead.

'She found out about you. Was that it?'

There was no response. Sam realised he was looking at a monster.

'You feared she would betray you . . . So you killed her. For the sake of your dream.'

The old German's eyelids drooped. He took in a breath deep enough to have been his last, then let it out again. He looked broken.

'Well your dream is over Herr Hoffmann.' Sam placed his hands on the table and leaned forward. 'But you can still stop it turning into a nightmare. The smallpox. Tell us where it is. Tell us who's got it.'

Slowly Hoffmann pulled himself up straight. It was clear he'd made a decision. 'Give me some paper,' he croaked. 'I will draw you a map.' He reached into his jacket.

Seeing the movement, the Inspektor raised the pistol again, then lowered it when the hand emerged with the pen. He produced a notebook from his pocket and passed it across.

'I am like a painter or a poet,' Hoffmann declared wearily. 'My only weapon is my pen.'

He held it in both hands then, staring into the middle distance, slowly unscrewed the lid. He shuddered involuntarily, like someone about to have his teeth pulled. Sam saw the eyes tighten. Then the pen stabbed downwards. Hoffmann plunged its tip into his thigh and pressed hard on its end. They heard the click of a spring being released and watched the lined face contort with pain as the needle fired its lethal charge into his leg muscle. Sam lunged forward, but the syringe had already emptied itself.

'Shit!'

The Inspektor got on his mobile to call for an ambulance.

Hoffmann shook his head. 'There is no point,' he breathed. 'Three minutes and I shall be with my wife again.' He panted for breath, as if drained of all energy. Then he turned to Sam. 'So . . .' he whispered.

'Because of you, I shall be like Caspar David Friedrich. I will not smell the sea again before I die.'

Sam seethed at his own powerlessness.

'Damn you, Günther.' He grabbed the German by the shoulders. 'Who's got the smallpox? Max Schenk?'

Hoffmann reacted as if he hadn't heard.

'Tell me and save your sodding soul.'

It was pointless. Sam let go of him. Three minutes, he'd said. One gone already. He sat down in the chair opposite.

'Was Schenk in this with you? *His* clinic you went to with your fake heart attack?'

Hoffmann frowned as if puzzled. 'I don't know any *Schenk*,' he declared.

Sam read the man's eyes and drew a blank. Hoffmann's ability to claim black was white had been perfected over a lifetime. Impossible to tell if this was the truth.

'Tell me about Harry Jackman, then. How much did he know?'

'Harry. Poor Harry,' Hoffmann mocked.

'Did he know what was in the flasks?'

'Of course. He had to make special arrangements for the flights.'

'And calling it red mercury . . .'

'. . . was his idea.'

Sam saw a wince of pain as the poison began to bite.

'Why did you have him killed?'

Hoffmann's face contorted and he clutched at his chest. Sam leaned forward.

'Why did you kill Harry Jackman, Günther?'

Hoffmann shook his head, his wide eyes flicking from side to side as if no longer able to see. Indignation wrinkled his brow.

'But I didn't kill him,' he protested hoarsely.

Then the eyes closed and his body sagged into the corner of the seat.

Three minutes. It had been less than two.

Other passengers were entering the far end of the carriage. The Inspektor shouted at them to leave. Suddenly the platform was full of uniforms. The assistance the policeman had called for on the way to the station had finally arrived. From somewhere not far away they heard a siren approaching.

Sam stood up straight, arms hanging limply by his sides, shaken to see the second of the instigators of this heinous plot die before his eyes.

There was a difference between the two men. Hoffmann had been proud of what he'd done to the end, whereas Harry Jackman had sought to distance himself from the crime. The claim of ignorance about the cargo's destination, the clinging to the myth of it being red mercury – the old gun-runner had lied even with his final breath. Had Hoffmann's last words also been a lie – that Harry Jackman's murder had been nothing to do with him? Instinctively Sam felt that at that last moment of his life the German had been speaking the truth. Why deny the charge after accepting responsibility for so many other killings?

Sam backed away as paramedics came pounding pointlessly along the aisle. *Someone* had hired Harry Jackman's killers. And he still wanted to know who they were.

He left the carriage and stepped onto the platform. The machinery of law and order had taken over now. Finding those planning to use the smallpox in Greifswald would be up to the police. Officially, his role was over. He'd delivered.

He stood back from the train watching the men in uniform doing their work and waiting for Inspektor Pfeiffer to tell him whether he could be of further service to him.

He knew that by rights he should be experiencing a sense of satisfaction at this particular moment, but he wasn't. Yes, they'd found their puppetmaster – but not all the puppets. Dr Max Schenk, virologist, had been doing business with Harry Jackman at a time when plans were being laid to create a biological weapons laboratory on Palagra. If it was a coincidence, then for Sam it was a coincidence too far.

Proving it, however, would be another matter.

23

London
Sunday

ON HIS RETURN to London the next morning Sam was driven from
Heathrow airport to a block of mansion flats on the south side of
Hyde Park. Duncan Waddell met him in the entrance lobby and took him
through a security door into the corridor where the lifts were.

'Belongs to the Ministry of Defence,' Waddell explained. 'Top brass
live on the sixth floor, lesser mortals lower down. You're on the first.
The flat happens to be empty for the next month, which conveniently
gives you time to sort yourself out. Don't worry about security here. It's
quite enough to deter your Ukrainian friends. Your stuff's been moved,
by the way. There's nothing left at Brentford or at that flea-pit in Ealing.
Your clothes and personal effects are here. Anything larger has been stored
for you.'

'How thoughtful.'

Waddell's glance said 'don't take the piss'. Keeping him hidden was for
their own sake as much as for his.

The MoD flat was furnished in the damask style that officer families felt at
home with. Sam took a quick look round. One bedroom with twin beds, a
living room, a bathroom and a kitchen. He searched a cupboard above the
sink and found that even his tea and coffee supplies had been installed.

'Fancy a cuppa?'

'Now you're talking,' Waddell rumbled. 'Coffee, please. Milk, no sugar.'

They took their cups to the living room and sat in armchairs. The
windows overlooked a well-maintained private garden. The flat had an
impersonal lavender-waxed smell to it. The walls were hung with Constable
prints and the floor was carpeted in an indefinable green. Sam resolved to
move from the place as soon as the opportunity arose.

His controller was in bustling mode, eager to tie up loose ends and lay
plans for the future.

'You'll be glad to know the German police caught Hoffmann's death squad just outside Greifswald this morning,' Waddell said, 'complete with a pump spray full of smallpox.'

'Excellent. How did that come about?'

'All thanks to some farmhand who'd been working the vines outside Vienna. Seems he'd become curious about a couple renting a little house on the outskirts of his village. Had the impression they were using it as a hideaway. Early on Saturday afternoon he saw their car drive up with a third person in it. A man. They went into the garage, closed the doors and a short while later he heard a yell. Like the chap was having his balls cut off, was the way he described it to the police. Then after another ten minutes, he saw the couple drive the car out again, without any visible sign of their passenger. He thought about it for a while, then rang the constabulary and gave them the car registration number.'

'Brilliant. Hope he's up for a medal. And did they find the passenger?'

'Not yet. They're working on the theory the couple dumped him in a forest somewhere on the route north. Examination of Hoffmann's e-mail suggests the man could well have been Igor Chursin, delivering the smallpox.'

Sam's mind flashed back to Palagra and the terror on the Russian lab assistant's face when Willie Phipps had pulled his mask off. That man knew the lethality of the brew they'd developed.

'How were they going to administer the stuff?' Sam asked.

'They'd got some forged papers identifying them as being from the local health authority. A permit to spray the refugee hostel in Greifswald for insect infestation.'

Sam shook his head. 'Hoffmann was certainly thorough.'

'The Stasi always were.'

'Do we know the full extent of the Lucifer Network yet?'

'Not that large, we think, based on his e-mail contacts. The couple arrested outside Greifswald were former underlings of Hoffmann in the Stasi. And they've been identified by Mrs Klason as the pair who hooked the infected glass splinter into her husband's towel. They seem to have been Hoffmann's hit squad. The rest of his network consisted of people like Rob Petrie in London and the as yet unidentified Swede who bombed the Turkish kebab bar. They're the only ones known to have killed. Other correspondents in France, Spain, Italy and Germany may have been involved in lesser anti-immigrant protests of one sort or another. Hoffmann was the idealist and the money man. Kovalenko supplied him with the scientists and the raw material, and introduced him to our friend in Zambia to arrange the shipping. Kovalenko knew Jackman because he'd sold him guns.'

Waddell was looking smug, which Sam interpreted as meaning that he thought the pieces of the jigsaw were all in place. In his own mind one was still missing, however.

'No e-mails to someone who could have been Max Schenk?'

'No. But he was computer illiterate, remember.'

So he was. Convenient, thought Sam.

'Klason died last night, unfortunately,' Waddell continued. 'The woman victim's hanging on, but unlikely to survive. And you'll be interested to know that a Croat police boat called in at Palagra yesterday. They've asked for outside help to make the place safe and to investigate what was going on there. We're offering a team.'

'Going in with flags flying this time, I suppose. And the human guinea pig who escaped?'

'No sign of him or the girl he took hostage. So we don't yet know if the vaccine worked.'

Sam hooked his hands together and cracked his joints. Waddell could see he was dissatisfied with his round-up of the case.

'You're troubled by something. What've we missed?'

'The fact that Hoffmann in the later stages of his career became more of a manager than a doer. I learned that about him during those long months of trying to make him identify the spy in BAOR.'

Waddell narrowed his eyes. 'Go on.'

'He was a man who, whenever possible, liked to control things at a distance. He was doing it with the Lucifer Network, running everything from the anonymity of an e-mail address.'

'So?'

'So I believe he would have had a medical expert on his team to supervise the handling of the virus samples. The pair who were picked up in Greifswald – were either of them medics?'

'Not that I'm aware of.' Waddell blinked. 'You mean Schenk, don't you?'

'Yes.'

Waddell pursed his lips. 'You're not alone in clinging to the belief that he must've been involved. The Austrians tried to pull him in for further questioning this morning, but he's done a bunk. Not at his home or the clinic. And no one's seen hide nor hair of him since the news of Hoffmann's suicide hit the news bulletins last night.'

'Christ!' How much more proof did they need? 'I thought Collins had someone watching him.'

'He did, but the man was taken off the case after Hoffmann was identified as Peter.'

'So, what's being done?'

'Schenk's description has been circulated to police forces across Europe with a request for an immediate arrest if he turns up anywhere.'

Sam set his jaw, trying to second-guess where Schenk would have gone. Well away from Europe if he had any sense. 'They'd do better trying South America,' he grunted.

'Whatever, it's down to the Austrians now. If he committed a crime, that's where it was carried out. Your part in the Jackman affair is finished.' He said it with a firm finality.

Sam let his eyes wander around the room. They were cutting him out again before the job was finished. He didn't like that. And this place had the feel of an institution. A padded cell. He was in limbo here, as was his whole life now that this case was closing for him.

'What's the verdict, Duncan?'

'About you?'

Sam nodded. Theatrically, his controller picked up a *Times Atlas* which just happened to be on the coffee table. He passed it across to him.

'Exile,' Sam murmured.

'I wouldn't call it that. The firm is keen to retain your services, Sam, but in some place where your face isn't known. Up to a point you can choose your continent.'

Sam put the atlas back on the table, stood up and walked to the window which was coated with a plastic film to prevent splintering in a bomb attack. Death. He'd seen too much of it in the past two weeks.

'As to your father's involvement with the Russians,' Waddell continued, adopting a more formal tone, 'I've been authorised to inform you that it's not an impediment to your continued employment.'

'I should bloody well hope not,' Sam grated.

Beyond the glass a gardener was mowing the lawns. It was an English scene. Something he would miss if he accepted the firm's posting abroad. He was going to have to think about it.

The other matter he needed to give thought to was Julie. The attraction that had begun as raw chemistry and then been soured by her betrayal of him, had returned with a vengeance in Vienna. He'd understood by now that she was there for him if he wanted, but a relationship with her would be a complication at a time when he was about to be shunted overseas. And hovering over it, both in his mind and hers, would be the unresolved issue of her father's death.

Sam turned back into the room, his hands deep in his trouser pockets. Resentment bubbled inside him. Convinced that Hoffmann wasn't lying when he'd denied liability for Jackman's death, he'd churned the alternatives around in his mind until settling on the most disturbing one of all.

'Hoffmann said he didn't kill Harry Jackman.' He watched for Waddell's reaction.

A ripple of discomfort disturbed his controller's expression. Dapper in his crisp blue shirt, he unhooked one grey-trousered leg from the other, then reversed them.

'Did he say that?' The Ulsterman sounded weary. 'And you believed him?'

'He had no reason to lie about it that I could see. He'd already admitted responsibility for Kovalenko's death.'

Waddell pulled a long face. 'In that case, I suppose the motive with Jackman must have been robbery after all.' He sucked in his cheeks.

'Balls, Duncan,' Sam snapped. 'It was *us*. We did it. The firm.'

Waddell pursed his lips and arched his eyebrows. 'To be honest, I don't see that it matters *who* did it. The world's a far, far better place . . .'

'Oddly enough it matters to *me*,' Sam growled. 'You sent me to Africa to negotiate a deal – supposedly. But you weren't interested in one, were you? The real reason I was shipped to Zambia was to set Jackman up for assassination. And to provide the firm with an alibi. *We were negotiating with the man, m'lud. Couldn't possibly have been us that killed him.* You used me, Duncan.'

Waddell contemplated him stonily for a few moments. 'Using people is what the firm does, Sam.' His eyes were devoid of sympathy. 'And look, if you're going to be holier than thou about this, I really can't help you.' He snapped the *Times Atlas* shut, got up and returned it to the bookcase.

Sam glared at his back, reluctantly admitting to himself that Waddell was right. The trade they were engaged in was deception. The only rules were those they wrote themselves. He had no right to complain. He turned and paced back to the window.

'Take a few days off, Sam,' Waddell counselled, walking over to pat him on the shoulder. 'Forget about Harry Jackman. Settle yourself in here and put your feet up for a bit. You've had a hard run. There's a car for you to use out the front. Keys are on a hook in the kitchen. Give me a ring later in the week and we'll do lunch.'

Sam grunted. A few seconds later he heard the front door open and then click shut.

He clasped his hands to the back of his head and flexed his shoulders. Easy for Waddell to say forget about Jackman – he wasn't involved with the man's daughter. Sam had told Julie that SIS wasn't responsible for her father's death. Now he knew different. The issue of the gun-runner's murder had become like a pothole on an unlit road, one it would be sensible to avoid by not going down that road at all.

And yet, what the hell . . . He *would* see her again. He had a craving for her which he needed to satisfy.

He went in search of his mobile phone. It was Sunday, but Steph had said Julie expected to be working all weekend, so he dialled the laboratory. When the number answered, a man's voice told him she'd been given the day off.

'You know where I can contact her?'

'She's got a mobile with her. We loaned her one in case of the need to summon her back in. Who is it?'

'Sam.'

'Ah yes. She said you might ring.'

He gave him the number and Sam called it straight away. When Julie answered, he heard what sounded like geese honking in the background.

'It's Sam,' he told her.

'You're back?' She sounded overjoyed.

'Yes. This morning.'

'That's absolutely wonderful! Um . . .' There was a sudden hesitancy in her voice, like someone who'd plunged into a box of chocolates then remembered it was Lent. 'So, what are you doing . . . ?' she asked timidly. 'Is there a chance we could meet?'

'Every chance. Where are you?'

'I'm in a boat,' she told him, perking up again.

'Where?'

'Guess.'

'The Solent?' he suggested, instantly thinking of the sea and longing for it. He heard her laugh.

'The Serpentine, actually. I'm showing Liam the sights of London. Where are you?'

'Your turn to guess.'

'No. Don't tease.'

'Well . . . I'm about ten minutes' walk away, as it happens.'

'Oh . . .' She waited for him to suggest something.

But the mention of Liam had unnerved him. A getting-to-know-you-better session would be impossible with the boy around.

'We return the boat in twenty-five minutes,' Julie prompted.

'Right.' He told himself to go for it. It would be a damned sight better than spending the day alone. 'I'll be there when you come ashore.'

'Great!'

As he put the phone down, he realised it had done him good to hear her voice. He strode into the bedroom to see what Waddell's staff had done with his clothes. The built-in wardrobe had been neatly filled. Bennett's girl again, he assumed. He chose a fresh pair of casual trousers and a polo shirt, then ran a comb through his hair before making his way to the hall and the front door of the block. It was a warm September afternoon outside.

Traffic crawled through the Alexandra Gate into Hyde Park, much of it looking for non-existent parking spaces. Sam eased his way through the throng of tourists until he reached the bridge over the Serpentine, then stopped and leaned on the parapet, trying to make out the boat that had Julie in it. There were too many of them, clustered together like amoebae.

He began to move again, turning off the road and walking beneath the plane trees towards the lake. There was quite a crowd around the boathouse, some waiting their turn, others rediscovering dry land. He stopped by a tree and held back, leaning against its rough bark to wait.

Out on the lake Julie rowed towards the pier. Several boats were clustered there as their allotted time expired simultaneously. In the bows of the craft, her mother tossed the line to the attendant then scrambled stiffly ashore, turning round to give Liam a hand so he didn't fall in the water. The boy rejected her offer of help, determined to do it on his own. Julie could see he was getting tired and fractious. Her mother had brought him to London on a train early that morning and they'd done the Science Museum before lunch. Julie shipped the oars, then stepped onto dry land, the young male attendant grabbing her arm, more for his own benefit than for hers.

She felt absurdly nervous about meeting Sam. When she'd parted from him at Vienna airport she'd said stupid things about hoping he could arrange for Max to be killed. And she was worried how he'd taken it. The reports on the news that morning about Günther Hoffmann's demise had also been troubling, reminding her how little she knew about Sam. Wherever he went, death seemed to follow. The life he led was so removed from her own she found it impossible to believe anything could come of their relationship. Yet the night in Vienna had confirmed beyond any shadow of doubt that she was in love with him.

She took her son's hand and they pushed through the exit. She didn't have her glasses on and screwed up her eyes, trying to make out Sam's face amongst the blurs around her.

Sam saw her emerge with her boy and felt a quickening of his pulse. When he noticed Julie's mother, his heart sank. Being sucked into an afternoon with the whole family was not what he was after. The women were fussing over the boy, who seemed on the verge of tears. Realising Julie was finding it hard to see him, he stepped forward, waving to catch her attention. When she spotted him she gave her mother a nudge. The older woman looked up quickly, smiled briefly, then led the boy away towards an ice-cream stand.

Julie crossed the grass towards him. She was wearing the same blue shorts and sleeveless slip that he'd seen her in at Woodbridge. He was in love again.

'Hi!'

She smiled self-consciously at him, a lopsided, we've-had-sex-together grin. He was glad to see that the swelling to her lip had gone down.

'Hello.'

They embraced a little awkwardly and he asked how she was.

'All the better for seeing you.'

She glanced back towards the ice-cream vendor. Maeve and Liam were already in the queue. The boy waved. Julie waved back. Sam imagined an elastic thread linking mother and son, stretched drum tight, ready to reel her in whenever she wanted it to.

'Liam's very clingy at the moment,' she volunteered. 'He's aware there've been things going on.'

'If *I* had you as a mum I'd *never* let go of you,' Sam grinned.

Julie pulled a face. 'Are you saying I make him insecure?'

'God, no! I meant . . . oh, you know what I meant.' He hooked an arm round her shoulders. 'Are we allowed to walk a bit, or do we have to stay where Liam can see us?'

'Of course we can walk.' She clicked her tongue at his suggestion. 'Liam's fine with his gran for a while.'

They turned away from the lake, treading the turf without speaking. Sam sensed that Julie was expecting him to say something immediately to clarify the nature of their relationship. Some verbal confirmation that his interest in her was no longer to do with what her father had got up to. But he wasn't ready for such definitions. Beyond his immediate desires he was far from sure what he wanted from her.

Julie too was finding it difficult to know where to begin. Their connection with one another had been a series of dramas. Small talk had never featured. There was so much she still wanted to know about him, most of which she suspected he would never reveal. She decided to begin with the immediate past.

'I heard on the news that that man Hoffmann killed himself,' she ventured. 'Were you . . . were you there?'

'Yes, I was. Thanks to your identification of him I caught him in the act of sending e-mails to his killers. Unfortunately he got away from me. But together with the Austrian police, I tracked him down at a train station.'

'Was it really suicide?' The question had popped out before she'd had time to consider its consequences.

'He had a syringe concealed in a pen,' Sam responded firmly. He didn't blame her for asking, after all that had happened in the past few days.

'And if you want to check up on me, there was an Austrian policeman present too.'

She reddened slightly, then apologised. 'I wasn't really suggesting . . .'

He shrugged to show it didn't matter. They walked on but without touching, as if an invisible screen separated them.

Julie still needed to be clear about things. Ts crossed and Is dotted. 'So the red mercury that my dad wrote about . . .'

'. . . was actually a load of virus samples from a Russian research lab. He shipped them to a remote island where a bunch of cash-hungry Russian scientists turned them into terrorist weapons. Hoffmann's underlings were about to unleash a new strain of smallpox amongst refugee communities in Germany.'

Julie hugged her arms to her chest. 'It's so shaming,' she whispered. 'All so appallingly shaming.'

Sam put his arm round her again. 'We're not responsible for what our fathers do,' he told her pointedly.

'No! We certainly are not.' She bit her lip. There were still details missing. Things he was holding back. 'What about Max? He was involved, or not?'

'We're not sure.' Sam told her about the cut-price medical equipment stolen from African hospitals. 'He claimed that was the only deal he had going with your father, but he went into hiding as soon as Hoffmann's death hit the news media, which suggests he probably *was* involved in the Lucifer Network.'

Julie detached herself from him and clasped both hands to her head. Her brain felt as if it was about to leap from her skull.

'I can't believe I spent all that time with Max and never realised what sort of a man he was.' Then she kicked herself. 'But then, why not? It's been the story of my life as far as men are concerned.' Which was why she was desperate to know what made Sam tick before getting more deeply involved with him.

They walked on. Julie took Sam's hand. She wanted to move them forward. To separate their relationship from the horrors they'd been involved in. But there was one last hangover from the past that she had to clear up.

'What I said to you the other day . . . about wanting Max dead. And sort of suggesting that you might . . .'

'Yes.'

'I didn't mean it. You do realise that, don't you? I was just in a state.'

Sam too wanted to move on. To steer well clear of the subject of death and to engineer a way to part Julie from her mother and son so they could go back to the flat and make love.

'And now?' he asked, caringly. 'You feel okay? Not in a state any more?'

She pulled a tight smile. 'Sort of. I'm pretty well back on the rails.' But she hadn't finished what she needed to say. 'It's just that when I said what I said, I may have given the impression I still thought you were involved in my father's murder . . .'

Sam swallowed and looked away.

'I want to assure you I don't think that,' she persisted. 'I fully accept you had nothing to do with his death.'

There it was, the pothole in the middle of the road.

'Closed subject from now on,' he suggested. 'Okay?'

'Okay.'

She beamed at him. He kissed her tenderly on the end of her nose. Her shiny hair smelled of roses, a scent he wanted to imprint all over that MoD flat.

They reached a footpath and turned right, walking slowly past a Japanese couple bending over a screaming baby in a pushchair.

'And how are *you* after all this, Sam?' she asked, solemnly.

'In need of a bed,' he told her. 'With you in it.'

'Sam . . . I'm serious.' She tugged at his arm. 'I mean, what's going to happen to you?'

'Well . . .' He hugged her to his side. 'I just told you what I'd like to happen.' The need to make love to her had become like a dam, preventing the flow of normal thought and conversation.

Julie resisted him, but gently. She too wanted more of what they'd shared in Vienna.

'I meant what happens about your job, Sam. I blew your cover. You said you faced the sack.'

'Yes, well . . . It's not quite as bad as that.'

She stopped, sensing he was concealing something significant from her. 'You're not saying life goes on as normal?'

'Effectively . . . Yes.'

Sam saw the emotions of hope and expectation pass across her face and realised he was handling this outrageously badly. She was a beautiful woman whose experience of men was of being messed around mercilessly. And here he was stringing her along like the worst of them. The reality was that there was nothing in this for her. Nothing long term, anyway. They inhabited different worlds. Neither could cross to the other's and there was no middle ground. He took in a deep breath.

'I'll be going away.'

Julie let her arms fall to her sides. It was what she'd feared all along. Almost expected. The logical outcome of all that had happened. But it still hurt to hear it. She wasn't ready to lose him, but she didn't know how not to. She looked down, then back towards where she'd last seen her son.

'You'll have to, of course,' she whispered. She shook her head at the irony of it. Because of her stupid loyalty to her father she was going to lose the man who'd exposed his manipulativeness to her. She would never get it right with men. Close by, a solitary old woman scattered chunks of stale white bread to swooping pigeons. Julie imagined herself ending up like that one day. She stuck out her chin, turned back towards the lake and began to walk.

Sam hooked his arm round her shoulders again, slowing her down. He felt great warmth for this damaged woman. He knew what his immediate interest in her was, but the future was another country for him. He could make no commitment to her.

'It's a funny thing, human nature, isn't it?' Julie said, pulling herself together and nestling against him. 'We're attracted most to the things that are bad for us.'

'Should I be reacting to that?'

'Oh, if you like. It *was* a compliment.' They walked on a few more paces. For some reason she couldn't fathom, Julie decided she had nothing to lose by baring her soul. 'I mean I think you'll have got the message by now that I'm strongly attracted to you.' She tried to make it sound matter-of-fact, but failed. 'However, I suppose that if you weren't going away and we ended up in some sort of relationship – it'd probably be a *disaster.*'

Sam stopped walking, bruised by the fact that *she* should have concluded that.

'Why d'you think that?' he challenged.

'You have too many secrets,' Julie continued, looking up at him. 'Too many closed rooms where the light never shines.'

Sam arched his eyebrows, riled at having been written off so easily. Then he looked away and saw Maeve and the boy walking towards them clutching ice-cream cones. Julie followed his gaze. Sam felt the elastic pulling.

'Of course it all depends on what you mean by a *relationship,*' he mumbled defensively.

She swung round to face him again. Of course it damn well did.

'What do *you* mean by it, Sam?'

He looked at her. Saw her need to believe in him and knew there was only one way to achieve that. To give her the blunt, unvarnished truth.

'At this particular point in my life I'm in no position to think much beyond the present, Julie. Therefore a relationship to me is all to do with the here and the now. I'm dead certain of one thing. That I want to make love to you. Now. This very minute.'

Julie knew she would never be able to win with a man, because she wasn't really in control of her own body. It was the pheromones that had the upper hand.

'Well . . . That's nothing if not honest,' she whispered. She turned to look at her approaching child. 'Wait here, will you?'

Sam nodded.

As she began to move towards her son, she turned her head back. 'Don't go away . . .'

He watched as she ran across the grass, then crouched in front of Liam. Half a minute later she was back with him.

'Mum'll take Liam back to Woodbridge,' Julie announced, hooking her arm through his and walking him quickly away before Liam could throw a tantrum. 'It was nearly time anyway.'

They marched through the crowds, brushing elbows with strangers in their haste to get somewhere where they could be alone. It wasn't until they reached the Alexandra gate that Julie thought of asking where he was taking her. Sam pointed to the mansion flats opposite.

'Hey, mister . . . They're pretty grand. I'm impressed.'

'It's just for a few weeks.'

They stopped by the kerb to wait for a break in the traffic, glancing wordlessly at one another, their eyes burning with frustration that something so important to both of them could be delayed by mere machines. Eventually the lights changed and they crossed the road.

At the entrance to the apartments Sam tapped in a security code. Inside the lobby a civilian-suited man with the build of a Royal Marine scrutinised them knowingly, then clicked a button to unlock the inner door. As they passed through and waited by the lift Julie asked what sort of residents merited such security measures.

'Official secret,' Sam mumbled, touching her lips with a finger. The lift doors opened.

'You and your secrets. I said you had too many of them.'

As the doors closed behind them, she was all over him. They kissed like teenagers, their mouths locked. A few seconds later the lift stopped with a jolt.

'Not the penthouse, then,' she grumbled, annoyed the ride had been so short.

Sam led her along the corridor. As they entered the flat she wrinkled her nose at the smell of furniture polish. He clicked the door shut with his heel. She was standing with her back to him, peering into the flat. He slipped an arm round her waist, then with the other hand lifted the hair from the back of her neck, exposing the cirrus cloud wisps at the nape. When he kissed them, she shivered from the pleasure of it.

They shed their clothes on the way into the bedroom. Her breasts were small and round, the nipples already hard. When he kissed them she gave little sniffs of pleasure.

'I want you inside me.' Her voice was as dry as a husk as she sank onto one of the beds. 'Now, Sam.'

He pulled the covers back and they lay down.

'Cos I don't know how much time we've got,' she whispered, as he moved on top of her. 'And I don't want to waste any of it.'

24

THEY SLEPT FOR a couple of hours after making love. It was dusk outside when they awoke, a purple sky visible through the open window. The temperature had dropped quite noticeably. Julie shivered and Sam pulled the covers over them.

'I need your bathroom,' she croaked.

'Next door along.'

He watched her shivering body as she walked from the room. Her skinny stomach and tight little rear gave her a rangy look. By the time she returned from the bathroom he wanted her again.

Julie straddled him and made love to him slowly, trying to prolong the time she had power over him. When he finally reached his shuddering end, she let her upper body fall forward, resting her head in the dip of his shoulder. As his fingers caressed the back of her head, she closed her eyes. Whether this affair lasted a week or a month, feelings this strong came rarely and they were to be savoured.

They lay quietly together, listening to the rumble of London's traffic and the occasional passing jet. Then the noise was echoed by sounds from Julie's stomach. She lifted herself off him and rolled onto her side.

'Any food in this little palace of yours?' she asked. 'We gave Liam a McDonald's for lunch, but all I had was a diet-cola.'

'No idea. I didn't look.'

'Shall I go see?'

'Excellent idea.'

She wrapped one of the bedspreads round herself for warmth and padded into the kitchen. She found the fridge astonishingly well stocked. Eggs, cheese, milk, sausages and a large pepperoni pizza, plus a fresh Romaine lettuce and some tomatoes. On the opposite side of the small space was a built-in oven. She turned it up to 200 degrees.

'Supper in about twenty minutes. Okay?' she shouted.

'Wonderful.'

Thirty minutes later they'd showered and dressed and were seated at the repro dining table, eating. Sam had found a bottle of wine and a CD labelled *Music for Candlelight* which he'd inserted into the hi-fi in the corner.

'Whoever's looking after you must think pretty highly of you,' Julie commented, getting stuck into the food. 'This place is pretty swish for a temporary home.'

Sam shrugged. 'They happened to have it available. If not, they'd have put me in a shoebox at some army camp.'

Julie tried to imagine life for a man always looking over his shoulder, forever on the move. And if he'd had to give up being an intelligence agent, what then? She couldn't imagine him in a normal job.

Imagining was pointless anyway. In a few weeks' time this would be history.

'D'you . . . do you know when you'll be going away?' she asked, breaking her resolve not to raise the subject.

'No.'

They ate on in silence. Her question had made him withdraw into himself and she kicked herself for asking it.

'Coffee?'

Sam shook his head. He was back in Vienna, annoyed with himself for letting Max Schenk slip through his fingers in Stammersdorf three nights ago. Now the man was on the run. Determined to survive. And that made him dangerous.

Julie saw that she'd lost him and decided to bring the day to an end while she was still on a high.

'I'm going to have to go home to Acton,' she told him. 'I've got an early start in the morning. We still have to find an antidote to that rabies variant. The virus exists now, so it'll turn up again. They always do.'

'Mmm.' Sam resolved to ring Waddell shortly to see if the Porton people had found any reference to the mutation on the Russians' laptop. 'I'll drive you home,' he told her.

'That's okay,' she murmured, a little disappointed he'd made no effort to persuade her to stay. 'I can get the Piccadilly Line.'

'I'll drive you,' he insisted.

'Well, okay. Thanks. I'll just clear up a bit.'

'Leave it. You made the supper. I'll clear it up later.'

She shrugged. It was becoming obvious he wanted to be rid of her. She stood up, telling herself not to be upset.

Five minutes later they were in the car driving west. When he stopped at traffic lights Sam gripped her hand. 'It's been great today,' he said gently. 'And I hope Liam doesn't take it out on you when you see him next.'

'He will, but don't worry about it,' Julie answered. 'I give him plenty of attention and he knows I've got a life of my own to lead.' Even if she didn't know where it was heading.

'He's a nice kid,' Sam commented.

'He's lovely – most of the time.' The one part of her life that was constant. The one person whose needs she was certain she could satisfy.

At the Chiswick roundabout, Sam turned north, heading towards Gunnersbury.

'I'll give you a ring tomorrow,' he told her. 'D'you like theatre?'

'I don't often go. Christmas panto was the last time.'

'I'll look in the papers and see what's on.'

'That'd be nice.'

Three minutes later they turned into Julie's street. Sam looked out for the house with the washing machine but couldn't see it.

'Here,' Julie shouted as they drove past her home. Sam stepped on the brake.

'Where's the . . . ?'

'The landlord's moved it,' she answered. 'Having the press snapping pictures of the place shamed him into it. He saw my face in the paper and decided I must be important.'

'You are,' Sam said, kissing her mouth.

'I wonder,' she whispered, hooking her fingers into his shirt. *How* important, was what she wanted to know.

'See you soon, then.'

'Yes please.'

They got out. He draped his arm round her as they walked to the front door. When she turned the key and opened up, the hall of the house smelled of cooking spices and stale cigar smoke.

'Thanks for having me,' she purred, stroking his face.

'Don't suppose you fancy another quick one . . .' he rumbled, nuzzling her ear.

'Get outta here.'

They kissed again and he promised to ring tomorrow. Then he walked back to the car.

Julie smiled to herself as she crossed the hall to the door of her flat. The day had been very special. Whatever happened, it'd be something to hold onto. She inserted her key, opened up and stepped inside her bedsitter, closing the door behind her without turning on the light.

She leaned against the door for a moment, as if unwilling to step further into the emptiness that awaited her here. Preferring darkness to light so she wouldn't see the squalor of the place where she slept. She didn't want to live like a student any more, she realised. She wanted to share some proper, decent living space. To make a home with someone. With Sam.

She filled her lungs with air and let out a long sigh, trying not to let her imagination run away with her. Telling herself it wasn't going to last with him and she simply had to accept it.

Suddenly she froze. She'd heard a noise. The sound of someone swallowing.

Fear gripped her. An icy shiver ran up her spine. The sinister, guttural sound had been very close. Petrified, she reached behind her back for the door handle, knowing that if she didn't get out of this room immediately she was going to die. Because she knew who it was who was in there with her. Knew it from the smell of cigar smoke that clung to him like some vile ectoplasm.

Before she could turn the door handle, a hand clamped over her mouth and another cupped the back of her neck and jerked her forward into the room.

She wanted to scream, but no sound came.

Sam guided the car through the back streets of Acton, heading for the main A4 into central London. By rights he should have been wallowing in the contentment Julie had left him with, but he couldn't get it out of his head that there was a missing link in the puzzle.

Halfway along the Chiswick High Road he pulled into the kerb. Porton had had all day with the laptop which he'd liberated from Palagra. They should know by now whether it contained rabies files.

He rang Waddell's number and was diverted to the duty officer at Vauxhall Cross who patched the call through to his controller's home.

'It's Sam.'

'Heavens. Made up your mind already? About where you want to go?'

'That's not why I'm ringing. I wanted to know what Porton have come up with.'

'Still a mystery. There was no reference to rabies on any of the computer files. There's one simple explanation, of course – whether it's right or not is another matter.'

'What is it?'

'The laptop had only been in use for four months, yet Jackman shipped the virus material to Palagra a year ago. So it's possible the rabies work was done in the first part of the year, with notes written by quill pen for all I know. The records could have gone up in the bonfire.'

It made sense but didn't satisfy Sam's need for certainty. He thanked Waddell and rang off, putting the mobile into the dashboard locker.

He tapped at the steering wheel, then turned on the ignition. He stared at the red light, but didn't start the engine. Unease was fluttering away inside him like a sixth sense. He switched off again and folded his arms. His anxiety was to do with Julie. He should've been more positive. Should have made it clear he was interested in *her*, not just in what she could do for him in bed.

He took the phone from the locker again, not sure what he was going to say, but knowing he had to say something. He felt in his pockets for the piece of paper on which he'd written her number.

Not there. He'd left it in the flat. Too bad. He'd ring when he got back to Prince's Gate.

He started the engine and engaged first gear.

'Damn!'

It was no good. The niggle was getting stronger.

He switched off the ignition once more and snatched up the phone, prodding away at the menu button until he found the call register.

Julie's number was in the memory.

He pressed the redial button and listened to it ringing.

'Come on,' he muttered. No answer. He looked at the display to check he'd got it right. He scratched his head. If she'd turned her phone off, there'd have been a message saying so. Eventually he ended the call.

In his mind he re-ran the parting at her flat a few minutes ago. The 'goodnight' that hadn't said enough. The driving up to the house, the kiss in the car.

He dialled again and let it ring ten times. Still no answer.

'Shit!'

He switched the phone off. But his mind wouldn't let it alone. The walk from the car to the house . . . The front door opening and the smell in the hall . . . Old cigars.

The same damned smell as in that wine tavern bedroom in Stammersdorf . . .

'Fuck!'

He scrambled the ignition, jammed the car into gear and did a U-turn, narrowly missing a bus and a taxi.

Max Schenk snatched the troublesome phone from Julie's handbag and switched it off. She lay on the floor watching his every move. It hadn't been hard for him to overpower her. After dragging her into the room and switching on the light he'd pressed a kitchen knife into her neck so hard it had drawn blood. Then he'd ordered her to kneel on the floor with her hands behind her back while he bound them with tape. Shocked, she'd complied like a lamb. Now there was more tape across her mouth and round her ankles. And he'd switched on a loud CD to confound any ideas she had of trying to make a noise.

She'd thought his intention was rape, initially. The sheets on her bed were half turned down. Then she'd had a vision of him having already done something foul on them, gratifying himself with her pillow or her underwear. Soon, however, she'd realised it was her silence he'd come here for, not her body.

He'd demanded to know why she was here. 'It is the weekend. You should be in Woodbridge. You told me you are always there with your boy on Sunday, until late at night. Later than this.' He'd said it angrily as if she'd cheated on him.

'You came like a spy in Vienna,' he'd hissed, kneeling on her back and twisting a hank of her hair until it hurt. 'With microphones. That was not right.' He'd spoken in gulps, like a child fighting with its emotions. 'You said you saw me with your father last year . . .'

If she could have spoken, Julie would have told him that she'd made that up.

'Then I think that you will start to remember more things, Julie. Things I said to you in restaurants. About politics. About mutated viruses. All of this we have talked about, even if I think you were not always listening. I fear it will come back to you. *Julie knows,* I tell myself. *Julie knows too much.*'

She'd wanted to scream out that she *didn't* know anything and that he should bloody well leave her alone.

'What you know can put me in prison, Julie. You are the only person who can.'

He'd put his hands round her neck, squeezing enough to frighten her. He'd kept sniffing, like a man overcome with emotion. Then he'd goaded her with a description of the death he'd planned for her. Somewhere in that turned-down bed he'd been about to hook a couple of little barbs, coated with a nutrient gel containing the genetically engineered rabies virus. When she'd climbed between the sheets later that night they would have cut her skin and infected her with the very disease she was working to find an antidote to.

Proudly he'd shown her the inside of his briefcase with its vials and syringes and the sealed plastic box containing slivers of razor-sharp glass carved under a microscope in his own laboratory with deep grooves to provide a reservoir for the killer plasma.

And now he was kneeling over her again, fingering her neck once more. Hard, probing movements, as if unsure whether to strangle or caress it. A quivering breath that stank of tobacco. She smelled his sweat, his desire and his readiness to kill. He ran a hand down her back and over her rump, squeezing her cheeks as if testing the tenderness of a steak. He *was* going to rape her, she decided, clenching her teeth. Rape her, then kill her.

Suddenly he stood up. Julie listened for the unzipping of his trousers. Instead she heard him fiddling with the briefcase. Terrified as to what was coming next, she rolled onto her side and watched as he prepared the syringe that would end her life. She knew she had to do something. There was no one else to help her. If only she'd let Sam come into the flat with her. She screamed his name, but from behind the tape it came out as a whimper. And the rock music drowned it.

Schenk knelt over her with the syringe, touching lightly on the plunger so that a small quantity of liquid spurted from the needle. Julie caught the whiff of chloroform.

'It will be quick, Julie,' he mouthed above the blast from the loud-speakers. His razor nose was poised over her like a guillotine.

Julie lashed out, kicking against his shins with all her might. She rolled away from him. Schenk yelped and lunged forward trying to plunge the needle between her breasts, but she rolled again. Over and over, crossing from one side of the room to the other, squealing and coughing, desperate to be heard above the CD's beat.

'*Verdammt . . .*'

Schenk cornered her by the door. He aimed a kick at her head, which she tried to absorb by curling into a ball. Then he put a foot on her neck to hold her down, ripped open her blouse and felt for her sternum.

Suddenly there was a shattering crash. Schenk whipped his head round to see a metal dustbin come hurtling through the curtains into the room, followed half a second later by a man.

'*Scheisse!*'

Sam had cut his head on the broken window pane. Blood trickled into his eyes, but he could see Julie on the floor and Schenk crouched over her.

'Get away from her!' he yelled.

Only when he hurled himself forward to grapple with Schenk did Sam see the syringe. As he lunged at the Austrian's arm, the doctor stabbed forward with the lethal needle. Sam swerved, feeling its spray wet his wrist. Then he kicked, his foot sinking into Schenk's groin. The doctor buckled and Sam cuffed him on the back of the neck with locked hands. As the man stumbled, Sam knocked the syringe from his grip and kicked it away.

He grabbed Schenk by the hair, pulling it sharply backwards so he lost his balance and fell. He jumped hard on his stomach to knock the wind from him, then threw himself across the room to Julie, ripping the tape from her mouth.

She screamed in pain.

'Sorry. There's no easy way to do that,' he apologised.

Schenk was struggling to get up. Sam kicked his face with the side of his foot, then while the man was disorientated, rolled him onto his stomach.

'Where'd that tape come from?' he yelled to Julie above the din.

'On the table!' she screamed. 'God, your head,' she added, panicking. 'You're bleeding.'

'I'll live.' He grabbed hold of the roll and blew the blood trickle from his eye. Quickly he bound Schenk's hands behind his back, then put another strip round his ankles. Once certain that he wasn't going anywhere, he looked around for something with which to cut Julie free. There was a kitchen knife on the small table.

'For God's sake turn that racket off,' he ordered when she had her arms and legs in use again.

The curtain flapped in the wind. When Julie cut the music they heard voices outside, the neighbours taking an interest.

'You okay?' he asked, touching her on the arm. He noticed a spot of blood on her neck.

'No,' she whimpered, slumping against him. He squeezed her gently and stroked her head, withdrawing his hand when she winced from the pain where Schenk had kicked her.

'I need to know what happened here,' Sam told her, keeping an eye on Schenk.

Slowly Julie pulled herself together, found a clean cloth to press against the cut on Sam's forehead and, between gulps of shock and anger, told him about the poisoned barbs in her bed. Then she showed him Schenk's briefcase with its lethal collection of glass fragments.

'Jesus!' He was looking at the tool kit of a serial killer. 'How the hell did he get in here, Julie?'

'He must have had my keys. When I got back from Vienna I found I'd lost them. Assumed they'd fallen out of my bag when he hit me with it in Stammersdorf. I had a spare set at the lab. Had to go there first before I could get in here.'

Sam kneeled beside Schenk. 'Talk to me, Max. Talk to me fast.'

Schenk remained tight-lipped.

'Were you working for Hoffmann or was Hoffmann working for you?'

When there was no response Sam jerked the doctor's arms up behind his back until the joints cracked. Schenk yelled in pain, his face twisting, but he still wouldn't talk.

There was a hammering at the door and an Asian voice demanding to know what was going on.

'I'm all right, Mr Patel,' Julie called back.

'Open the door.'

Sam shook his head.

'I said I'm all right. There was some trouble but it's over now.'

'They break the window,' the voice protested.

'Yes. I'll get it fixed.'

'The police coming. Someone called 999.'

'Okay, Mr Patel. You needn't worry.'

Sam grimaced. When the men in blue arrived, all this would be out of his hands. And Schenk would never spill the beans if handled by the rule book. He had a few minutes at the most. He reached into the briefcase and removed the plastic box of glass splinters, making sure Schenk could see him holding it. The doctor's eyes widened.

Inside the briefcase Sam found tweezers and sealed packets of surgical gloves. He put on a pair, opened the box of splinters and selected one. The glass chip glistened with the gel it had been coated with.

'Now, my friend . . .' He sat astride the doctor to pin him to the floor. 'They tell me just a little nick is enough . . .' He touched the splinter against Schenk's neck.

The man began to cough and splutter.

'Feel it, can you? Wet, is it?'

'Don't do this . . .' Schenk whined. 'I beg you, don't do this.'

'He doesn't have a vaccine,' Julie whispered. 'Look at him. He's scared out of his wits.'

'You'd better talk, Max. It's a nasty way to die,' Sam snapped. 'Tell me about you and Harry Jackman and Hoffmann. Who was running things?'

'Hoffmann,' Schenk whimpered.

'And what was your role?'

'To advise him how the material should be used.'

'Advise? Is that all?'

'Yes. I was not important . . .'

'I don't believe you.' Sam picked the glass splinter up with the tweezers. A tiny blob of gel remained on Schenk's skin.

'Do it, Sam.' Julie was close by his shoulder, her voice a rasp. 'Give him a dose of his own.'

Schenk's eyes swung in their sockets, trying to irradiate Julie with his hate.

'Last chance, Max,' Sam snarled. 'I want the truth this time.' He touched the razor-sharp glass fragment against Schenk's neck again. 'Quick. I haven't got all day.' The man flinched. His eyelids flickered and his lips began to tremble.

'Kill him, Sam,' Julie howled. 'He doesn't deserve to live.'

'All right, all right. I tell you,' Schenk panicked. 'We were partners, Hoffmann and I. We didn't trust the VECTOR scientists. Because they just want money. Like Jackman. They have no principles. I make visits to

Palagra to check what they are doing. At my first visit they have already made the rhabdovirus mutation but don't want to give it to me because there is no protection against it yet. But I insist they bring it to Vienna and I make tests with it. On dogs. When I see how fast it works, I make my own experiments. The glass splinters were my idea,' he added with a touch of pride. 'And I try to make a vaccine.'

'But you failed to develop one,' Julie goaded.

'There was no way to do it.'

'*We'll* find one,' she hissed, fired up by hate. 'But it'll be too damn late for *you.*'

'And Palagra island? Your wife . . . ?'

Schenk nodded. 'She did not know what was being done there . . .' His voice tailed away with the realisation of how much he had lost.

Sam stood up. The last piece of the Harry Jackman puzzle was now in place. He replaced the glass splinter in the box and closed the lid.

Julie's anger had become all-consuming. She couldn't believe Sam was going to let Max live. 'What are you doing?' she gaped.

Sam used a surgical wipe from a pack inside the briefcase to clean off the droplet of lethal gel from the doctor's neck.

'You *can't* just leave it like that, Sam! He has to die. Max has to die!' She stared at him wide-eyed, as if he'd lost his mind.

From outside came the sound of a siren, rising to a crescendo as the police car screamed to a halt in front of the house. Sam closed up Schenk's briefcase and kept hold of it. Then he grabbed Julie's mobile phone from her bag on the floor and dialled Waddell. He spoke briefly and concisely and was told to hold the fort until Special Branch arrived.

There was a hammering at the door.

'Police! Open up!'

Sam saw that Julie had gone as white as a sheet. The shock was getting to her.

'You can open the door now,' he suggested.

Julie's head was spinning. She'd just urged Sam to commit murder, and now the police were here. The authorities. She looked at him in bewilderment. Sam was authority too, she realised, her spastic mind suddenly overtaken by the thought that he might betray her to the police. That she'd be charged with attempted murder. Sam's revenge for her exposing him to the media. The establishment's revenge for her father having revealed what happened in Bodanga.

Sam saw the distress on Julie's face, the panic in her eyes. The look of a woman who'd had one shock too many and was falling apart.

He wrapped his arms round her.

'You'd better brace yourself, Julie.'

'What? What d'you mean?'

'I'm afraid you'll be in the papers again. The lone woman who over-powered Max Schenk and handed him over to the police. They'll make you a hero.'

It was after midnight by the time all the statements had been taken and some minor first aid had been applied to Sam's cut head. Stephanie had arrived twenty minutes after the local force and had worked wonders in twisting arms to ensure Sam's role in the action wouldn't appear in any of the press reports the next day. He and Julie had slipped away without being photographed, the media being kept well clear of the street by a police cordon.

Back at the MoD flat at Prince's Gate, a thorough exploration of the cupboards uncovered a half-full bottle of whisky overlooked by the cleaners. Sam and Julie sat facing each other across the repro table, drinking it.

Julie was still numb with shock. 'You saved my life,' she murmured. 'If you'd come through that window a second later, I'd be dead now.'

'I wouldn't have liked that,' Sam said solemnly.

'Nor would I.' She gripped his hand. Then her brow knitted. 'You know, I really did want you to kill Max, Sam. If it had been me holding that chip of glass to his neck I'd have done it myself.' She shook her head. 'What does that make me?'

'Human, Julie. Human.'

The understanding she saw in his eyes was that of someone who'd been there himself. Many a time.

'What happens next, Sam?' She looked down at her glass.

'He'll be charged in the morning. Attempted murder. The trial will be months away. You'll be a star witness.'

'That's not what I meant,' she rejoined.

'I know it isn't.'

Sam took a deep breath. Nothing had changed, in that he still had no sensible answer for her. But the situation *was* different now. The trial of Max Schenk would probably mean him appearing as a witness in camera. So he would be staying in England for longer than he'd envisaged.

They looked at each other across the table with a softness that neither dared to define.

'I think we should sleep on it,' he answered.

328